Clare Connelly was raised in small-town Australia among a family of avid readers. She spent much of her childhood up a tree, Mills & Boon book in hand. Clare is married to her own real-life hero, and they live in a bungalow near the sea with their two children. She is frequently found staring into space—a surefire sign that she's in the world of her characters. She has a penchant for French food and ice-cold champagne, and Mills & Boon novels continue to be her favourite-ever books. Writing for Mills and Boon's Modern line is a long-held dream. Clare can be contacted via clareconnelly.com or on her Facebook page.

Rebecca Hunter is an award-winning author, reader, traveller, occasional college professor, full-time chocolate lover, and keeper of a very messy desk. Her books have won the National Excellence in Romance Fiction Award (NERFA), the HOLT Medallion and the VIVIAN Award. She writes witty, passionate stories about complex characters and intriguing destinations for Mills & Boon's Modern line. For reading and writing updates, photos and travel plans, join her newsletter on her website: www.rebeccahunterwriter.com.

Also by Clare Connelly

Blackmail to White Veil

Royally Tempted collection

Twins for His Majesty

A Greek Inheritance Game miniseries

Billion-Dollar Dating Deception
Tycoon's Terms of Engagement

Also by Rebecca Hunter

The Carandini Legacy miniseries

Convenient Wife Conditions

Discover more at millsandboon.co.uk.

DIAMONDS OF DESIRE

CLARE CONNELLY

REBECCA HUNTER

MILLS & BOON

All rights reserved including the right of reproduction in whole or in part in any form. This edition is published by arrangement with Harlequin Enterprises ULC.

This is a work of fiction. Names, characters, places, locations and incidents are purely fictional and bear no relationship to any real life individuals, living or dead, or to any actual places, business establishments, locations, events or incidents. Any resemblance is entirely coincidental.

Without limiting the exclusive rights of any author, contributor or the publisher of this publication, any unauthorised use of this publication to train generative artificial intelligence (AI) technologies is expressly prohibited. HarperCollins also exercise their rights under Article 4(3) of the Digital Single Market Directive 2019/790 and expressly reserve this publication from the text and data mining exception.

® and TM are trademarks owned and used by the trademark owner and/or its licensee. Trademarks marked with ® are registered with the United Kingdom Patent Office and/or the Office for Harmonisation in the Internal Market and in other countries.

First published in Great Britain 2026
by Mills & Boon, an imprint of HarperCollins*Publishers* Ltd,
1 London Bridge Street, London, SE1 9GF

www.harpercollins.co.uk

HarperCollins*Publishers*, Macken House, 39/40 Mayor Street Upper, Dublin 1, D01 C9W8, Ireland

Diamonds of Desire © 2026 Harlequin Enterprises ULC

Greek's Ring of Redemption © 2026 Clare Connelly

Heir to Italian Altar © 2026 Rebecca Hunter

ISBN: 978-0-263-41827-9

04/26

Printed and Bound in the UK using 100% Renewable Electricity
at CPI Group (UK) Ltd, Croydon, CR0 4YY

GREEK'S RING OF REDEMPTION

CLARE CONNELLY

MILLS & BOON

This book is a testament to The Love Shack crew: Annie West, Amy Andrews, Michelle Douglas, Jennifer St George, and Ally Blake. You are incredible romance writers, wonderful women, supportive cheerleaders, and friends.
Thank you for the brainstorming, fun, memories, and camaraderie. Nikos and Genevieve were born from our writers' retreat, and I'm so grateful you helped me give them life.

PROLOGUE

Even at the best of times, the island of Therasia Notia, deep in the Aegean Sea, covered in ancient, now-dormant volcanic mountains, was rugged and impenetrable. But when the wind howled and the heavens opened up with lashing rain, and the sky split itself asunder with shocks of light, Nikos Konstantinou could almost convince himself he was the only man remaining on earth.

Just as he liked it.

Just as he knew he deserved to be.

Alone, isolated, and left to suffer, for the sins of his past. Sins for which there was no hope of repenting—no hope of repairing. The mother he hadn't been able to help, who'd turned to prostitution to keep a roof over their heads until she'd died, young and miserable. The wife he'd all but abandoned in his pursuit of success.

The life he'd once forged, through sheer grit, building his private equity business to the point of global domination, was now a distant memory. Though he kept himself apprised of operations, he was no longer hands-on in the way he'd once been—the satisfaction he'd drawn from those long, difficult days was now a poisoned chalice: something he was determined to deny himself. As penance, for what his ambition had done. The pain he'd caused.

He stood in the doorway to the small cabin he'd built,

stone by stone, three years earlier, when he'd bought this island and come to it, not caring if he lived or died. Long, laborious days, finding rocks, carrying them up the steep hill, mortaring them into place until, eventually, walls began to take shape.

It had been a long time since Nikos had needed to work with his hands. Wealth had made him lazy, had risked turning him soft. Not that anyone who encountered him in the business world would ever have dreamt of describing him thus. No, Nikos was famed, not only for his competence, but also his ruthless determination.

It was that same determination that had seen him work twenty-hour days, losing himself to the empire he was intent on creating, at the expense of all else.

Even his marriage.

And his wife's happiness.

At the time, it had seemed like a necessary focus. Not only had he known extreme poverty as a boy, he'd also experienced the galling frustration of being told that ambition was pointless—to give up on wanting more. His father had likely been trying to adjust Nikos's goals to something more 'reasonable', but instead, he'd hammered the point into Nikos so hard that, with each scathing comment, Nikos's determination had formed like steel.

He closed his eyes and took a step further, so the rain now lashed him, his thick, dark hair loose almost to his bare shoulders, the denim shorts he wore covering his body only between the hips and mid-thigh. He spread his arms wide, and surrendered himself to the heavens, the gods, that were said to have created this mountainous island as a prison for one of their erstwhile demi-gods. If they wanted him, they could take him.

For Nikos Konstantinou, one of the most successful billionaires in the entire world, had nothing and no one to live for, and every day, he wondered if it might be his last. His wife had died miserable, because of his neglect; surely he didn't deserve anything other than the same fate?

CHAPTER ONE

GENEVIEVE WILSON COULDN'T claim that setting sail on her own across the Aegean was her stupidest mistake ever—clearly that honour rested on the day she'd said 'yes' to marrying her sadistic bastard of an ex-husband—but it was definitely in the top three.

After all, she hadn't sailed since she was a child. Though she'd sailed then often, and had been very good at it, it turned out sailing was nothing like riding a bike. Some parts were muscle memory, of course. Others common sense. And if the waters had stayed calm, as they'd been when she set off, then most likely she would have been okay—if a little shaken by the experience.

But the storm that whipped up almost out of nowhere, turning the placid Aegean into a turbulent, washing-machine-like high tide, quickly began to rock her small craft from side to side in a way that was instantly terrifying. The rain made it almost impossible to see, and her hands kept slipping on the ropes. Every lesson her father had taught Genevieve, as a girl, seemed to wash out to sea.

Helplessness gripped her. Helplessness and misery. Would anyone even care if the boat capsized and she was lost to the depths of the ocean? Not her now ex-husband. There was no one else. Her father had died when she was little more than a girl, her mother a few years ago, after a series of strokes that had seen her hospitalised for more than a year, before she passed away in her sleep one night. Any friends she'd once been close to had fallen by the wayside as Genevieve had turned herself inside out to become the perfect political wife her senator husband had required, not even missing a step after her mother's death, when her world had been knocked completely off course. Who was there to miss or mourn her?

The frigid and brutal reality of that was, if anything, a talisman to Genevieve. She'd been through too much to give up now. Finally, she had her freedom. At least, in a sense. Courtesy of her mother's eye-watering hospital bills, she was too financially indebted to her ex, who was paying off the instalments, to know exactly how to explore her freedom. At least she was no longer under his complete control—no longer the perfect, submissive trophy wife to be used and humiliated by him depending on his whims and needs. She was setting out on the second phase of her life, a time of rebuilding. She wouldn't die friendless and alone here, where no one would even think to look for her.

There was nothing for it. She needed to bring the boat to shore somewhere. A port in the storm, literally. She cast about, her eyes squinting against the hard-falling rain, until finally, a lightning bolt seemed to burst almost directly overhead, making her scream at the same time she recognised something silhouetted against the storm-darkened sky.

A mountain. And mountains in the middle of the ocean could mean only one thing: an island.

Tacking the boat to the south, she prayed that she could make it there, even as she continued to be rocked violently from side to side, so it was almost impossible to hold her course, let alone stay on board. Enormous waves crashed over the sides, dousing her, and then, finally, she was close enough to shore to jump from the boat. She leaped over the rail, and just in time! As she watched, and tried to work out how to get the boat aground enough to shore, it rocked high on a wave and then capsized, the sail snapping against the seafloor, so she cried out and pressed her hands to her mouth.

It wasn't her most pressing concern, but in the back of her mind she hated to think how much it was going to cost her in damages to the hire company. She had no idea if the insurance policy she'd taken out would cover this sort of act of stupidity. What kind of person rode a sailing boat right into a storm?

That was a bridge she would cross down the track. If she lived to make it that far. For now, she needed shelter. She looked around, helplessly, eyes chasing the rugged coastline of this mountain. She'd become disorientated some time ago, and the map she'd taken from her small, mid-century hotel's lobby, showing the Greek islands, had blown out to sea long ago. She had no idea which island she'd landed on, but she had a sinking suspicion that it might be one of those tiny, uninhabited ones. Which did not bode well for a woman who now had no phone, no handbag and no boat.

She couldn't panic, though.

It had taken grit and determination to extricate herself from her marriage; these were skills she now knew she had in abundance.

Genevieve began to walk. She was so wet that her shorts and long-sleeved shirt were plastered to her body, and her shoes squelched as she moved away from the shallows and began to look around once more. She was in a cove, and there was no sign of habitation. But that didn't mean the whole place was deserted.

Ignoring the dark fears in her mind, that she was indeed

stranded on the unluckiest island in the entire Aegean, she began to traipse along the sand, figuring she could start tracking a perimeter, looking for both signs of life and some kind of shelter. Whichever came first. Dark clouds were rolling over the island, which, combined with the pouring rain, made it impossible to see too far in front of her.

It took a monumental effort to hold onto hope, but more than an hour after crashing onto this island, while the storm continued to rage and her body was exhausted and covered in goosebumps, she finally saw something to give her hope. Even just the tiniest flicker of it. The storm felt like a metaphor for her whole freaking life. One thing after the other, and just when she was at her lowest ebb, bam. Something worse.

Some way in the distance, high up on a hill, was a light. Warm and golden, and not a trick conjured by her desperation. She changed direction immediately, picking her way across the sand and onto the grass behind it. Dense forest followed, which flooded her with terror. Because here, she heard animal noises, and she couldn't help but imagine she'd gone from the frying pan and into the fire. She might have escaped death at sea, but between herself and the golden light stood miles of forest, and it was not implausible to imagine being mauled by whatever animal was making that persistent call.

With the same determination she'd employed in her marriage, to ignore her husband's affairs and the cold brutality with which he treated her, she went on, one step after the other. There was no path to follow, and she slipped, many times, cutting her leg and badly hurting her arm, but eventually she came to a clearing and saw, to her immense and all-consuming relief, that the golden glow was indeed a dwelling. A house! Well, a house of sorts. Four walls and a roof, and it clearly had electricity. She didn't stop to think about who might be inside, but rather rushed gratefully towards it and lifted a hand, banging on the door as though her life depended on it.

Which, come to think of it, it did.

Silence met her thumping. She kept knocking. And minutes later, with the rain still gushing over her and the sky lighting up every few minutes with blades of white, as thunder rolled right into her ear canal, she knew she had little choice but to push open the door. After all, the cabin could well be empty, the light left on by whoever had last occupied it.

Either way, she wasn't going to stay standing out here, getting more and more sodden by the minute, all but inviting lightning to fry her innards.

She pushed the door tentatively at first and then all the way, stepping in with a small grimace at how much water she was dripping onto the rustic timber floor. But there was a fire across the room, glowing warm and golden, so she knew two things immediately: firstly, she wasn't alone. Secondly, she was too cold to care.

Walking quickly across the room, she made it to the hearth and turned her back on it, still dropping huge amounts of water on the ground, as she let the heat wrap around her, comforting and reassuring. She'd been standing there only a moment when another door, on the other wall of the cabin, opened, and a man strode from what her brain quickly suggested must have been a bathroom. Why? Because he was as naked as the day he was born, and every bit as rugged as the forest she'd hiked through to make it to his cabin.

She could only stare as he stopped walking and stared right back. Stare at his height and breadth, at arms that were muscular and a broad, hair-roughened chest that was rippling with abdominal muscles, wide shoulders that almost seemed to suggest he could carry the weight of the world on them. His hips were narrow, compared to his broad chest, but his legs were as muscly and sinewy as his arms, all strength and formidable power in those limbs. He was tall—easily six and a half feet—and handsome in a raw, animalistic sort of way, with features that were chiselled and rough, symmetrical and completely pleasing. His eyes were a dark grey, like the stormy ocean that had tormented her hours earlier, and his hair wasn't cut fashionably short—it might have been, once upon a time, but now it caressed his neck, though it was wet and brushed back from his brow.

As for his very masculine anatomy, her cheeks flushed pink at the way he stood before her, glorious, uncaring, and huge all over.

The thunderous expression on his face should have given her cause for concern, but it was all so shocking and confronting, so confusing, that she could only stand there and drink in the sight of him.

'I—you're—' She tried to speak, to explain, but she was still shivering, and her mouth wouldn't cooperate.

Grimly, he walked towards her, the thunderclouds in his expression growing, if it was possible, even darker.

'We will deal with the pleasantries later. You look as though you are about to pass out. Are you?' His accent was unmistakably Greek, but his English was fluent.

'I—don't—' She closed her eyes then as, indeed, a wave of exhaustion and nausea hit her, combining with the icy chill in her veins. 'I'll be okay,' she said, but slowly, softly, the words lacking conviction.

He grunted and then, to Genevieve's absolute shock, he was lifting her up and cradling her against his naked chest, carrying her across the sparsely furnished cabin, towards the door he'd emerged from a moment earlier. It was almost as large as the other room, though it had only a shower, a basin and a toilet. He placed her down on the tiled floor of the shower and began to run the water. Then, to Genevieve's further shock, his hands curled around the fabric of her shirt and began to lift it.

'D-don't,' she stammered, feeling she must protest. It didn't occur to her to fear the man, despite the notable differences in their size and strength. He was rugged, yes, but there was nothing about him that screamed 'violent'. Her protestation then was all about modesty. Her ex-husband was the only man who'd seen her naked. It was strange to contemplate letting a stranger see all of her bared. And yet, it was also exhilarating. James, for one, would hate it—and that thought was infinitely appealing.

'You need to get out of these clothes.'

'I can manage,' she said, finally finding her voice, and hoping that she wasn't lying.

'Can you? Show me.'

'I'm not going to get undressed in front of you.'

'And I have no intention of leaving you here to pass out on your own. So?'

'I'm not going to—'

'We can argue later, as well,' he said, lips forming a grim line. 'All I care about, right now, is that you do not die on my watch. Whoever you are, and wherever you came from, is not my concern. What you do after leaving here is also of no interest. But for now, I intend that you stay alive. If not least because the inconvenience of having to report your death is the last thing I want.'

She was so shocked that she did reach for her shirt then, but before she lifted it off she turned her back on him so her breasts were shielded from his sight. Her shorts followed, but she kept her briefs on.

The water, in contrast to the rain outside, was scorching and with each moment she stood beneath it, she felt a little strength return. Though her legs felt like jelly after what must have been a ten-mile hike, most of it uphill and over uneven terrain. Fear had made her run much of the way.

He reached past her, his thick, strong arm brushing her side as he flicked off the water and then seconds later wrapped a large, coarse towel around her shoulders. 'Can you walk or do you need to be carried?'

There was no way she was going to admit even a hint of weakness to this man, even though her legs felt as though they were impossibly trembly. 'I can walk.'

'Show me.'

He crossed his arms over his chest, apparently uncaring that he was still naked.

'Do you own clothes?' she muttered, aware that she sounded like a petulant child.

In the living area once more, he lifted a chair towards the fireplace and set it down. 'Sit.'

'I'm not a puppy, you know. You can speak to me like a fellow human being. Or is courtesy in short supply out here, in the middle of nowhere?'

'I didn't ask you to come into my home, and if it weren't for the fact you could not survive out there—' he jerked his thumb towards the single window of this cabin, large and just to the right of the front door '—I would have no compunction in turfing you out. Perhaps once the storm passes…'

'Definitely once the storm passes,' she responded, though she did sit on the chair, careful to keep the towel wrapped around herself, protecting her modesty.

'Good.' He turned away then, disappearing to a rustic-looking piece of furniture near the large bed, and removing—to her relief—a pair of cotton boxer briefs. He dragged them up his body but Genevieve was startled to discover that, clothes or no clothes, the sight of him in all his glorious nudity was burned into her brain.

She looked away quickly, trying to focus on something—anything—other than this man.

'Do you live here?'

'I'll ask the questions.' He turned to face her, gaze narrowed. 'Who are you?'

She opened her mouth to answer that, then faltered. For three long, miserable years, she'd been The Senator's Wife. That was how she'd been defined by her husband, and everyone she'd come to know. Genevieve, as a person in her own right, was nothing and no one.

'Genevieve,' she answered shortly. Why give him the whole tragic story of her life? A first name was enough.

And it appeared to satisfy him, as he nodded once, albeit curtly.

'And you are here, on the island, because…?'

'I crashed,' she muttered. 'The storm came out of nowhere. I was too far out at sea to turn back. Then I saw this island and made my way here…'

'You were in a boat, in this,' he said.

'Well, there was no storm when I set out,' she repeated. 'Or I would never have come so far from the mainland.'

Another grunt, this time the derision was abundantly obvious. 'It is January—you cannot go two weeks without a storm like this.'

'Yeah, well…' She tapered off, hating that he was right. Hating that she felt stupid, and worthless, just as she had almost her whole marriage. The weather had been unseasonably warm, right up until that afternoon. 'I thought it would be fine.'

He crossed the room then with easy athleticism to what she now saw was a rudimentary kitchen. Everything about this cabin was rustic to the extreme. The fact it had electricity and running water were the only saving graces. She watched as he removed a can from a small cabinet, then used an old-fashioned opener to take off the lid. He grabbed a fork from the bench and stalked over to her. 'Eat this.'

She stared at it, frowning, her nose wrinkling at the smell. 'Tuna fish?'

'It's good for you.'

There was something about the statement that drew a small smile to her lips, despite the desperation of her situation. He didn't really seem like someone who'd follow nutritionist accounts on social media or something.

'It will fill you up,' he added.

'It's cold.'

'This isn't a five-star hotel.'

'I hadn't noticed.'

'Hey, if you've got complaints, you're welcome to take your chances out there.' He gestured to the windows again.

'I thought you didn't want my death on your conscience?'

'I don't. So eat something.'

And yet, perhaps in a concession to her, he began to fill a small pot with water and set it on the gas stove—which reminded her a little of the Bunsen burners she'd used in high school science lessons.

She pulled her hair over one shoulder, running her fingers through the ends, squeezing it into the towel, careful not to let the fabric part and reveal her naked body.

There was a small fridge beside the bench and as she watched, he removed coffee from it, and then cream. She dug the fork into the tuna and speared some flakes, lifting them to her lips with a grimace of distaste. She'd never been a huge fan of canned fish, but desperate times…because he was right. She was absolutely ravenous. Now that the shock of the day's events had worn off, she realised she hadn't eaten since that morning, when she'd grabbed an apple on her way out of the door of her hotel. She had intended to spend a few hours sailing around the Aegean, perhaps stopping at a populated island for lunch, if she felt like it, before going back to the mainland. Instead, she'd wound up stranded in a stone cabin in the middle of the woods, God only knew where.

'Who are you?' she asked as he tipped a little coffee into a cafetière and then filled it with the boiling water. His hands were proportionate to the rest of him—which was to say, huge—and as he replaced the lid, she was reminded of a giant, handling a human's possessions.

He pulled a mug from a drawer and began to fill it with coffee, before he added a generous amount of cream.

'You have cream,' she said, blinking at him. 'Is there a shop on the island?'

He arched a single, thick dark brow, cynicism on his face as he strode towards her, mug held out. She took it very carefully, not wanting their fingers to brush. Her side still felt tingly from when his arm had brushed against her in the shower, and she had no need to feel that all over again.

His smirk showed that he'd recognised her gesture and understood her reasoning for it. Well, so what? Why shouldn't she hesitate to touch a strange, enormous man?

'No.'

She frowned, almost having forgotten her question.

'Once a month, supplies are sent over. The cream is long life.'

'Oh.' She nodded slowly, considering that. 'But there must be other homes? Other people?'

'Not unless they have trespassed, like you.'

She closed her eyes against that accusation. 'I was blown here by the storm.'

'So you've said.'

'Do you actually think I'd be stupid enough to wilfully come to this place? It took me hours to get to this cabin, and it's a miracle I didn't fall off a cliff or get eaten by a bear. I mean…truly. This is *not* how I saw my day going.'

He stood in front of her, hands on hips, face giving nothing away. Then, slowly, those dark grey eyes roamed lower. Starting at her eyes, before dropping to her lips, and then lower still, as though he was picturing her naked beneath the towel, before landing on her legs.

By the time he spoke, she was so flooded with heat that she could hardly hear him over the ringing in her ears. And damn it, how she hated that her body was, against common sense and her wishes, responding to him. How on earth could she find his slow, insolent inspection *hot*?

Although, it didn't take a psychology degree to work that out. Her marriage had been ice-like, in the end. Her husband had spent all his time seducing other women, delighting in letting Genevieve find out about his affairs, and lording it over her that it was her fault he'd strayed. Her frigidness. Her lack of responsiveness to him. Her lack of experience and skills. Her failures as a wife that had led him to seek comfort in the arms of other women.

'You're injured.'

She glanced down at her legs and saw the grazes, and, on one of her thighs, a deep cut. She ran her finger over it, wincing as a sharp pain radiated through her body.

'I fell,' she murmured, as much to herself as him. 'A few times.'

'At a later point, we will discuss further how incredibly stupid it was to take this many risks with your life. Stay there.' Her jaw dropped at his rude, insulting comment, even when it was so easy to believe it, courtesy of her husband's conditioning.

He crouched down by the bed and removed a decent-sized box, which, when he opened it, she gathered must have been a medical kit. He removed a small bottle of disinfectant, some gauze and bandages.

She'd been so anxious to avoid touching him, and, despite the way memories of her husband's insults had doused the strange flickering of desire, she still suspected that if he were to reach for her, she'd catch fire.

'I can do it,' she said, holding out a hand for the supplies.

'Drink your coffee,' was all he said, crouching at her feet, and pouring some of the disinfectant onto a gauze pad. His eyes lifted to hers and the whole world seemed to start spinning, faster than she'd ever thought possible.

She opened her mouth to say something, to insist that she do her own treatment, but then he touched her leg, and she closed her eyes on a wave of something joltingly warm. Desire. She wasn't sure she'd ever felt it before—and for a long time, she'd believed she *couldn't* feel it. So despite what she knew she should do, in this situation, she found herself sitting there, breath held, as this beast of a man tended to her wounds with all the gentleness and care of Florence Nightingale.

CHAPTER TWO

It wasn't until his fingers had brushed her naked flesh in the shower that he realised he had barely touched another human being in years. Let alone a naked woman. Not since his wife had died and he'd buried her. On that day, there'd been hands to shake, hugs given. But he'd left mainland Greece afterwards, coming here, not caring if he lived or died.

When he went to Athens occasionally for work, he barely saw anyone from his old life. Not his friends, not her family. No one who might look at him and try to make him 'feel better'. He wasn't interested in that. When Theo came to the island, they shook hands, then set about the business of managing Nikos's extensive financial interests. For all that Nikos had taken himself to the edges of earth, he still oversaw the most critical investments and opportunities, using Theo as a trusted right hand, the manager he relied on as a conduit to his old life. He was the one person Nikos allowed behind the veil, to see him, his life, to understand his headspace.

Besides Theo, he was almost completely isolated, and up until about twenty minutes earlier he would have said, without hesitation, that he wasn't interested in ever seeing or touching another woman again. Certainly not in being intimate with one.

He now knew that to be a lie.

There was no other explanation for the blood that was pounding in his ears, the way his cock was growing hard beneath his shorts, the way fingers that were treating her wounds fairly *ached* to wrap around her calf and hold her there, before tugging gently to part her legs, so he could move his fingers higher, to brush against the sweetness of her sex. Her breasts were right in front of him, though hidden by the towel, and he wanted to take his other hand and pull the fabric away, revealing her to his hungry gaze, before his mouth tasted every single inch of her.

The betrayal of his late wife, Isabella, was like a blade in the gut, but it did nothing to stem his awareness of this woman—Genevieve. Nothing to curtail his desire and the white-hot burst of need overtaking his body, one cell at a time. Besides, desire was simply that: his body's involuntary response and recognition of another. It didn't mean anything, except that he'd been celibate way too long. Solitary and alone, not missing the touch of another, nor the contact and companionship of people. But that wasn't to say he was made of stone, and he would have needed to be not to notice the softness of her skin, the supple, athletic tone of her legs, the light caramel tan to her skin.

Once upon a time, in almost another universe, he would have found her attractive. More than attractive, he'd have said she was beautiful. From her raven-dark hair to wide-set, pale blue eyes, straight nose with a little ski jump at the tip of it, and soft, pouty pink lips that were currently held apart, showing surprise. Awareness.

Yes, he felt it, not as a man might when stirred in a void, but rather, when the same fires of need were burning in his opposition. He felt them spark off each other, rather than simply beneath his own skin.

And then, he did let his fingers trail higher, over her smooth flesh, towards the deep cut in her leg.

'This should have stitches,' he muttered, pleased he still sounded disapproving, despite the torrent of need that was flooding him every bit as quickly as the skies had opened up this afternoon.

Her throat shifted as she swallowed, and he imagined pressing his mouth there and tasting her, sucking until her skin darkened and he left a little mark of his own on that flawless neck. She shivered, perhaps in response to the intensity of his gaze, yet he didn't look away. His finger traced around the cut as he forced his eyes to return to their inspection. Goosebumps lifted over her legs, and his lips shifted in a mocking half-smile.

'Cold?' he asked, though he knew the answer to that. The fire was raging, and they were close enough to be almost too hot. Her goosebumps could be for one reason only.

'What do you think?' was her spirited reply, so he stood and turned his back to conceal something he hadn't felt in a very long time. An actual smile. It was quick. A flash on his lips, before he managed to capture it and smother it away again. After all, what right did Nikos have to feel amusement, particularly at the hands of a beautiful woman?

'I think you would be better off just about anywhere but here,' he muttered as he opened the medical kit again and removed the Steri-Strips. When he turned to face her, she was staring at him not with fear, so much as undisguised curiosity.

'Who are you?' She repeated an earlier question, one he'd instinctively shied away from.

This was his bolt-hole, and it remained that way because very few people knew he lived here. The 'reclusive billionaire' was an apt moniker, in many ways, though it made it sound as though he had a choice in his reclusiveness. When the truth was, he was simply living the life he had earned. The life he deserved. He had caused his wife's death, after subjecting her to years of abject loneliness.

His fate was to share in hers.

He knew the speculation that went on about his life. In business circles, certainly, but even, from time to time, in the society pages. Particularly if he happened to be spotted back in Athens or further afield for any period of time. He had no interest in giving this woman any more information than was necessary.

Then again, she too had stuck to her first name, so he heard himself offer, 'Nikos.'

'Nikos,' she repeated, and something like a shiver ran the length of his spine at the way she turned the two simple syllables into warmed honey. Her American accent disappeared on the Greek word, so he itched to teach her some others. 'And you live here?'

She'd asked him that earlier, too.

He nodded once as he strode back across the room and stood before her, aware that his cock was at her eye height, and that he was growing harder by the minute. So what? Let her see what was happening to him, let her know that she should keep her distance. He was a lit fuse, apparently, and the last thing he wanted was to act on it.

Yet with the slightest invitation from her, he wondered if he'd be helpless to ignore his body's deep, carnal cravings. Though he'd been celibate since Isabella's death, it was less about a sense of betraying Isabella and more about his single-minded determination to deny himself even that pleasure. Never again would he look at another woman in a romantic sense; never again would he allow a woman to care for him, love him, or marry him. He didn't deserve any of that. And up until this moment, he'd never once been tempted.

He heard her sharp intake of breath and knew she'd noticed. Dropping his head to hide whatever expression his features twisted into, he crouched down and lightly touched her injured leg. 'Does it hurt?' His voice was gruff.

'I—'

When he looked up it was to see shock on her face. Confusion, too. Not fear. Not even uncertainty so much as wonder. Slowly, she reached out, her brows quirking closer together as she let her finger hover in the air a little to the right of his cheek and then, with another quick intake of breath, to glance over his jaw. So softly it was feather-light, so he leaned into her hand. He didn't want her tentative touch. If anything were to happen between them, it should be fast and rushed, born purely of need. Not gentle. Not inquisitive. Not a precursor to anything other than wild, animalistic sex, as desperate as the storm raging around the cabin.

'Nikos,' she said, frown deepening, as though his name held some secret, or explanation, to what she was feeling. He unfastened the Steri-Strips and gently pressed them over her wound until it stitched closed. Then he reached for the bandage and began to wrap it around her leg, his fingers brushing the backs of her thighs, then the front, needlessly touching her bare skin, until the gash was covered, and he sealed the end of the bandage to keep it in place.

Her finger stayed on his jaw, her frown in place, as he worked, and when he was finished he looked up at her. He had denied himself every pleasure for a long time, but, God help him, this woman who'd stormed into his cabin was like a vixen, drawing him in, making him want something he'd easily resisted for years.

'If you keep touching me like that, Genevieve, I will want to take you to bed. Is that what you want?'

Her breath exploded from her lips on something like an anguished cry, and her eyes fled to the double bed in the room.

It was a form of madness. What else explained the way he was suggesting sex to a woman who'd blown in with the wild Etesian winds, not an hour earlier?

'I don't even know you,' she said, taking a huge gulp of her coffee. He hadn't realised she was still holding the mug with her other hand. He reached for it, and now she didn't have time to delicately arrange her fingers so they were out of his way. He curved his hand over hers—so much larger, it was the only choice.

'That's not an answer.' And he knelt then, dangerously close to the middle of her legs, so their eyes were almost level. Still, he looked down on her, because of his height, and when she glanced up at him, the towel that had been held in place only through the hand that also held her coffee fell down a little, revealing a hint of her creamy, naked shoulder.

'Genevieve.' His voice was a command, a demanding, insistent plea. He needed her to put an end to it. He was too far gone to listen to common sense, but if she said a single word to dissuade him, if she offered even a hint of opposition, then he would stand and walk away—right out into the storm, if need be.

Growing up as large as he was, Nikos had learned the truth of his strength from a young age. He could easily overpower almost anyone—man or woman—and he had never once used that strength to his advantage. Not in a fight with a man, and never, ever in sex with a woman. The idea repulsed him.

It was always a woman's choice, a woman's pleasure, a woman's needs.

But it was with the greatest willpower in the world that he held himself still, in a kind of sexual purgatory, waiting for her to say something, to give him some indication of what she wanted, even when he knew he should deny himself Genevieve, no matter what.

Except, he *knew* what she wanted. He could see it in the tremble of her body and feel it in the finger that was still tracing the line of his jaw—it was whether or not she was ready to admit that, to either of them.

'I will not touch you unless you ask it of me,' he said, the words dragged from him as he pushed past the final barrier of his internal struggle. 'You do not need to be afraid.'

'I'm not afraid,' she said, but her eyes dropped lower, and her hand pulled away. 'Thank you for taking care of me.'

Her voice was suddenly meek and, despite her words, it seemed almost that she was scared. He stood, and, true to his inner monologue, strode towards the door, pausing only to retrieve a handgun he kept on his bedside table, before making his way out of the house and into the storm. Suddenly, it seemed like the most imperative thing in the world to get Genevieve off his island, to hell with anything else. His helicopter was the beginning and end of that, and, even though he knew he could not take off until the storm cleared, he needed to sight the damned thing, like a talisman. Only then could he take comfort from the certainty that she would be out of his hair just as soon as the storm passed. That he could let her go without succumbing to temptation. Without giving into a pleasure he didn't deserve to ever feel again.

Genevieve's clothes were saturated, so she'd tentatively sifted through his clothing—not that there was much of it—and removed a long-sleeved shirt and pulled it on. She couldn't just sit around half naked: not when her whole body was suddenly a livewire of sexual need. God, but this man was smouldering!

And all this time, she'd thought herself totally asexual. That was an easy thing to believe, when her husband's touch had left her cold. At first, she'd thought pleasure would develop from intimacy, and then she'd at least hoped that some kind of emotional satisfaction would follow sex. But it was never a solution, never anything other than an act she came to loathe. Particularly once she knew he was sleeping with other women. Women who were beautiful and confident, and no doubt vampy in the bedroom, who could be everything he wanted.

She had no idea if she'd always been like this. A slavish dedication to her journalism degree had meant she'd never really dated before meeting James, and then he'd overwhelmed her with his attention, flattered her and seduced her with promises of the life they'd lead, so that the struggle she'd known since her father's death had suddenly seemed like a distant dream.

Throughout their marriage, she'd come to accept that it was just her. She'd even come to pity her husband, to be glad that he'd cheated. At first, he'd kept the affairs private, and she'd pretended to turn the other cheek. But when the headlines had started, and the media had begun to reach out to her for quotes, she'd had to face his infidelity head-on.

Genevieve was midway through making another coffee when the door blew in and, with it, Nikos—whatever his last name was—all wild and wet, just as she'd been when she'd first arrived. His clothes were plastered to his body and her eyes fell to the gun in his hand. She couldn't look away as he stalked across the room, replacing the gun on the bedside table and saying to her, without looking in her direction, 'It is only in case of wild animals.'

Of course it was. And it was a wise precaution, going by the noises she'd heard as she'd climbed through the forest.

Then he turned to face her and, without looking away, without offering an excuse, began to peel his wet shirt from his body, leaving him standing there in just a pair of shorts. Her eyes were as plastered to him as his clothes had been a moment earlier, and her mouth was suddenly bone dry.

'The way off the island has been damaged by the storm.'

Her eyes widened and her pulse quickened. Getting off the island hadn't even really occurred to her. That was to say, it hadn't occurred to her that it wouldn't be as easy as clicking her fingers and calling some kind of water taxi.

'Oh, but there must be a way—'

His eyes narrowed. 'Of course.'

'Okay, good.'

'When the storm clears, I'll arrange it.'

'But can't I call someone now?'

He raised his brows. 'There is no point. No one can reach the island until this clears.' He gestured to the window.

'How long have you been here?' she asked, looking around before her eyes jerked, of their own volition, back to his body.

'Three years.'

She gasped. 'How on earth can you live like this? You must be crazy.'

Yet, he didn't seem crazy, so much as...broken, like some kind of Greek Heathcliff, all tortured and seeking solitude as a result of that torture. She couldn't say why she felt that, only that the image was set in her mind and couldn't be loosened.

He looked around. 'Is there a problem?'

'It's just very sparse.'

'It doesn't bother me.'

'What do you eat?'

He lifted his shoulders. 'There is plenty of food.'

'Tuna?'

He simply held her gaze, without answering, then said, 'I'm going to get undressed, Genevieve. If my nakedness offends you, please look away.'

She *knew* she should look away. Turn her back, give him some privacy, or suggest he use the bathroom. But instead, she stayed right where she was, incapable of doing anything but stare as his big hands pushed into the waistband of his shorts and slowly nudged them lower. She wasn't surprised by his masculinity now—it was burned into her brain—but it overheated her in all the same ways it had before. She just hadn't realised it then—too many feelings were jamming against her waterlogged mind.

His legs were so broad and muscled, as though he ran, every day. She stared at him, completely overwhelmed by the attraction that was flooding her veins.

'Would you like to touch me, Genevieve?' As he asked the question, he took a step towards her, so her eyes lifted to his face, drugged by the silver-grey of his eyes. 'Would you like to feel my body?'

Yes, every cell in her body screamed. She wanted that. She wanted that badly. No, she *needed* it.

She gasped at the realisation that this was so completely out of her control.

'I'll tell you what,' he suggested, voice blanked of emotion, even when she could see the intensity in his features and knew that he was not unfazed by this at all. 'I will stand here for one full minute. You can touch me, or you can walk away. The choice is yours.'

And he came to stand so close their toes brushed, and her body surged with white-hot need at his proximity.

'I don't know you,' she said, tremulously, catching the way his lips pulled in an almost ghoulish smile, revealing his straight white teeth.

'Does that mean you cannot want me?'

She bit into her lip, not sure how to answer that. She'd always presumed romance and connection were prerequisites for good sex, but that had been far from the case in her marriage.

And that was what finally convinced her to act. It was almost as though she'd been handed this opportunity on a silver platter: to explore a side of herself she'd always felt wanting. That she'd been ashamed of, in her marriage, because she couldn't rouse even a hint of sexual interest.

And here was a stranger, offering himself to her, with no strings, and no need for any personal information to be exchanged. God knew her heart was far too battered, her trust too often betrayed, for Genevieve to ever seek out another relationship. The little girl who'd once dreamed of white picket fences and a brood of happy little children at her feet had died a long, slow, tortured death in the face of her husband's cruelty—Genevieve would never want those things again, and certainly never trust another person to deliver them to her.

'What does it mean if I do want you?' she asked, needing him to spell it out though.

'It means nothing,' he answered. Words that were music to her ears.

Slowly, she let her hand shift outwards, to his hip, first, curving around the firm, muscled flesh there, warm despite the fact he was wet from the storm. His breath hissed from beneath his teeth.

'Not like that,' he ground out, and she jumped back, the criticism evoking every single atom of failure that had thrived during her marriage. But he stepped after her, taking her hand, and pressing it more firmly to his side. 'Do not be shy, Genevieve. I am yours to touch and take, as much as you want tonight. For as long as the storm rages, we can indulge this fantasy. After that, we need never see one another again. Yes?'

With her heart pounding in her ears, she nodded, and this time, when her spare hand reached for his other hip, it was like the creaking open of a gate, the pushing open of a door—on the other side, she didn't know what she'd find. Only she knew she couldn't wait to find out...

CHAPTER THREE

IT WASN'T FAIR to make comparisons, but how could she not? He was so different from James. Where James had slid into his late thirties with a definite paunch and softness around his middle, he was also around Genevieve's height, and his skin had that 'Washington tan', all waxy and pale, courtesy of too long spent indoors.

There was nothing virile about him, at all. Nothing that made her feel as though she'd wandered into Tarzan's lair and was ready to be his Jane. Unlike this man, who simply screamed 'man mountain' with every breath he took.

I am yours to touch.

Well, she didn't need to be told twice. Even if she wanted to stop, she wasn't sure she could. Not when he stood so perfectly still, except for the rise and fall of his rugged chest, with each breath, that showed how her exploration was affecting him. As if she needed further proof of that, with his erection huge and hard between their bodies. Her cheeks flamed as she imagined reaching down and grabbing him there, curving her fingers around his length and feeling that warm hardness in the palm of her hands. The intimacy of that! It took her breath away.

Instead, she let her fingers stay where they were, at his hips, for a long time, as she steadied her breath and tried not to pass out from the delirium of being able to do this, and knowing it meant nothing. That it changed nothing!

When the storm cleared and she got off this island, she'd still be herself—divorced, alone, but at least free of her manipulative ex-husband and all men everywhere. This was a slice out of time, a bubble they'd allowed to envelop them, a moment of shared insanity that Genevieve had no intention of resisting.

Her hands moved of their own accord behind his back, fingers splayed wide as one moved higher, and the other lower, to the curve of his muscular buttocks, and lower still, to curve around one cheek. He cursed softly in his native tongue, and her eyes widened at the sheer passion that infiltrated the word. Making her feel as though he'd never known anything quite so perfect as this. Making her feel as though she were the beginning and end of everything he'd ever wanted, even when she knew that wasn't true.

She had no idea what had brought him to this island—nor did she want to know. That wasn't what this was. It didn't matter to Genevieve if he was someone who made a habit of seducing women, or if he did this rarely. She didn't care if he had a string of girlfriends in his past. None of that mattered. He wore no wedding ring, and for this night, he was hers, just as he'd said.

She didn't even need all night, she thought with a flicker of her lips, as she swayed her body forward so her breasts brushed against his chest. Flames exploded through her, starting at her nipples and quickly eradiating her entire body. Her eyes widened in surprise.

'I didn't know…' she said, then quickly tapered off at what she'd been about to admit. That she hadn't known anything, ever, could feel this good.

He caught her chin with one hand, tilting her face up to his, so their eyes locked and his stormy sky gaze searched hers. 'Do you want me to touch you, *koukla*?'

Her skin flushed at his use of the unfamiliar word, but also at the question. She wanted him to touch her, yes. She just didn't have the confidence to say as much. How she hated her ex-husband then, for what he'd taken from her. For how much he'd undermined her, and made her doubt herself as a sexual being.

'I—'

His finger lifted higher, to trace the outline of her full lips. 'It is an easy yes or no question.'

'Easy for you, perhaps,' she whispered.

His eyes roamed her face with lazy indolence, as though he were reading her like an open book. She stood there, incapable of looking away, of shrugging off his gaze. Incapable, too, of hiding her thoughts, she suspected, because a moment later he said, 'Will you tell me "no", if you want me to stop?'

She sucked in an uneven breath and nodded slowly.

'I need to hear you say it,' he said, but his body moved closer, so his erection pressed against her. She swallowed past a strange tightening in her throat.

'Yes,' she said, the word barely a whisper. But it was good enough for the man in front of her, whose eyes flared at the verbal consent. His hands fell to the bottom of the shirt she wore, and he moved quickly to remove it, halfway ripping it over her head to reveal her naked breasts, so she didn't have time to feel self-conscious or embarrassed, to worry about the flaws her ex-husband had been all too ready to point out. Breasts that were too small, for example. She'd been ashamed, for so long, but the way Nikos's eyes fell to and devoured them almost as though they were the answer he'd been seeking all his life…everything inside her flared to life. And it only got hotter when he swore, as if he almost couldn't bear it.

'Christos,' he murmured, dropping his head then, to whisper against the indentation of her jawline. 'Were you sent by the gods to torment me?'

She didn't have enough mental acumen left to ask him what he meant. Besides, in the small part of her brain capable of any kind of thought, she wondered the same thing. Was he a creation of her mind? Had she, in fact, crashed on the shore and fallen into a state of delirium? Surely that made more sense than this...

'Am I tormenting you?' she asked as he dropped his mouth lower, to her décolletage and then to her breast, tracing lines across it with his tongue before drawing one nipple into his mouth and sucking on it hard enough to make her groan as ecstasy overtook her completely. No one, *ever*, had made her feel like this. Stars literally flooded her eyes, making everything in the room sparkle with silver and gold, and her hands went, of necessity, to his shoulders, clinging to him there for dear life.

'You are everything I shouldn't want,' he said, making her wonder why, yet she couldn't ask the question.

His jaw was covered in stubble and it itched her chest as he dragged his mouth to her other nipple now, but in a way that only added to her heightened sense of awareness and arousal. His hand shifted to her waist, digging into the elastic of her underpants—still a little damp from the storm—and pushing them down her legs, until she was able to step out of them.

It all happened so quickly, and he was so close, so again there was no chance to feel self-conscious of her nudity, because a moment later he was lifting her as though she weighed nothing—which she supposed to a man of his stature was true—and carrying her across the rustic cabin towards the solid bed at the centre.

He placed her down on it with a mix of urgency and reverence, and no sooner had her back connected with the surprisingly comfortable mattress than his mouth was chasing hers, kissing her in a way she'd never known she could be kissed. In a way that wasn't inquisitive or tentative, and in a way that wasn't all wet and tongue-ish, as her husband had kissed. This was the exact opposite. It was a kiss that was firm and commanding, a kiss of need that made her whole body feel alive with sensations. It was a kiss that could surely only be a beginning, because she ached for—no, needed—so much more. All of this, all of him, just for as long as the storm lasted. As if to underscore that, lightning burst beyond the window, casting the cabin in a flood of light, before the thunder rumbled right overhead. She was only conscious of it in the back of her mind though—every part of her was absorbed by this. Him. And wild, uncontrollable need.

His knee parted her thighs even as he continued to kiss her, and those hands of his, big and in control, roamed her body as if he was seeing her with his touch. Over the undulations of her small breasts, to the neatness of her waist, lower, to her thighs. Then she squawked a little at the unfamiliarity of that touch, so he lifted up and stared at her, eyes darkened by passion, and said, 'Do you want me to stop?'

She could feel the heat bursting through her face but she shook her head with a wildness that was born purely of the desperate passion he'd invoked. 'Definitely not.'

His smile surprised her, because he seemed very much like a man who didn't smile often—and she enjoyed seeing it.

His hands on her thighs were just as demanding as she'd given him permission to be, separating them so her legs were spread wide, and he stared down at her sex in a way she might have longed to hide from, if this had been anyone and anything else. But somehow knowing him to be just a stranger, who she would never see again, gave this whole encounter a surreal quality that washed away any of her usual self-consciousness and doubt.

Or maybe it was the way a sensual awareness was overtaking every part of her, so she was burning up with the wild, untamed desire he had invoked, and the only solution, in the face of that, was absolute surrender.

When his mouth shifted downward, over her flat stomach, and then lower still, to her most intimate self, and his tongue began to lash against her, she cried out, the sharp sense of pleasure tormenting her, so she arched her back and cried his name, even as the shock of his intimate kiss was pulling her out of the moment.

No one had ever kissed her there. She'd never known this. And it was sublime. Absolutely, achingly sublime.

His tongue was quick and insistent, his hands holding her legs wide when she might otherwise have brought them together, purely because the pleasure he was lavishing on her almost bordered on too intense, but she could only lie there and let him obliterate all sense and reason, as the walls of everything she thought she knew about herself and her sexuality came tumbling down, tipping her over into her very first orgasm. Her very first true sexual pleasure.

It was fast and intense and completely all-consuming, so she pushed up onto her elbows as the waves exploded over her, leaving her throbbing from head to toe with the heady rush of release. 'Oh my God,' she whispered tremulously, fighting back tears at the overwhelming realisation that she was, in fact, capable of sexual pleasure and need after all. It just took this kind of Greek god to stir it to life...

'You taste like heaven,' he muttered, and though the

words were flattering, she heard something in his voice that made her pause. Something that briefly marred the pleasure and euphoria she was surfing. Because he sounded resentful. Angry, even. But why?

Whatever had caused him to speak like that, she couldn't focus on it, because a minute later his fingers were pushing inside her, digging into muscles that were still spasming from the way his mouth had tipped her over the edge.

'See for yourself,' he said, shifting a little to bring his face level with hers and kissing her so she could, yes, taste her own orgasm on his lips. It was so erotic, so raw and animalistic, so absolutely the opposite of the refined, political wife James had groomed her to be. She'd never felt free to surrender to this side of herself, even when it had become clear that James had wanted it, behind closed doors. But not from his wife.

She pushed those thoughts aside, not wanting to think of James, not willing to let him tarnish this moment. How could she think of him, anyway, when Nikos had his fingers buried inside her and was driving her to yet another soul-tingling orgasm? How could she think of anything but this?

'Perfection,' he groaned as she cried out his name, into his mouth, tumbling over into a deep abyss, courtesy of his touch. He made her feel so good, she could almost believe him. She could almost believe she was 'perfection'. At least in that moment, and at least to him. But there was too much evidence to the contrary, and she knew at some point it would consume her anew.

'Don't say that,' she said, arching her back, silently inviting him to take more of her, all of her.

He pushed up, piercing her with his gaze for a long moment. 'Are you on contraceptives?'

The question brought with it a cacophony of sound—it

was so loaded with her past. With arguments with James over conceiving a baby. He'd wanted one, she hadn't. Not yet. At first, because she'd felt too young, as though her life were yet to start. And then, because their marriage had turned toxic so quickly, she couldn't have imagined complicating it by bringing a baby into their home.

'Genevieve.' The way he said her name was laced with urgency, and she nodded.

'Yes, I have an IUD.'

'Thank God. I don't have anything. I'm clean. I presume—'

'Yes.' She blinked her eyes shut. She'd been tested around the time of filing for a divorce, when the extent of her husband's infidelity had become clear. 'I'm clean.'

'And you are okay if we—' He stared down at her, the meaning clear, even without him finishing the sentence.

Her throat felt thick as a familiar sense of panic spread through her.

'I want you,' she said, with a firm nod. But then, biting down on her lip, and focusing on a point over his shoulder, 'But I should warn you…'

'Warn me of what?'

She hesitated, hating her husband so much for the way he'd made her doubt herself. Hating him for the insecurity that was now a part and parcel of who Genevieve was. 'I'm not very good at the sex stuff.'

Nikos's surprise was evident. She saw it on his features when she risked a quick glance at his face. 'I see,' he drawled, and there was something shrewd and insightful in his gaze that made her want to curl up and hide away from him properly. 'How about you let me be the judge of that?'

But what if he judged and found her wanting? What if he made love to her and realised she was just as boring and frigid as James always said?

Ice flooded her veins, turning lava cold. But he was right there, kissing her, as if he knew she needed him to blot out those thoughts—as if he inherently understood their chemistry could do that.

Would it be enough to make the sex okay?

Or would this be yet another big, fat disappointment, for both of them?

And so what? a little voice in the back of her mind shouted. So what if it was a total disaster? They weren't going to see each other again, once she got off the island. Her humiliation would be short-lived.

At least then she'd know, anyway. If sex with this guy fell flat, then she could spend the rest of her life living as a nun, knowing that no man on earth could possibly stir her to the wondrous heat other women talked about.

'Don't say I didn't warn you,' she whispered as his hands moved back to her thighs, parting them, taking care with the bandaged leg not to hurt her. His cock pressed against her sex, parting her gently at first, so she went completely rigid and still, the old, familiar fears reasserting themselves, remembered trauma and disappointment making her brace for what was to follow.

He cursed softly and then, as if he somehow innately understood that the slower he took this, the more time her doubts would have to get a grip, he simply thrust into her in one hard, desperate movement, hitching himself deep, as far as he could, so she cried out at the rush of feeling, the absolute sensation of fullness, such that she'd never known before.

Stars formed behind her eyes and she dug her nails into his shoulder, holding on now as though, if she were to let go, she might fall right off the edge of the earth. Holding on as though he were her sole anchor in this earth.

'Okay?' he asked, scanning her face.

She couldn't talk. She couldn't think. All she knew was that this was so different from—and so much better than—anything she'd ever known.

She managed a jerky nod of her head, and then he was moving his hips, pressing into her until those waves of pleasure built in her body. Her hands traced his entire body, only he caught them, one by one, trapped at the wrists, lifting them over her head and pinning them easily right there, so she was completely his captive, a prisoner of his sexual ministrations, a willing supplicant.

'You feel incredible,' he muttered. '*Christos, koukla*, you have no idea how this feels.'

If she'd been more capable of voicing words, she might have contradicted him, but her whole body was alight with passion and heat, and her mouth couldn't possibly cooperate, so she simply closed her eyes and let the feelings wash over her, again and again, as another orgasm built, and she almost wept at the intensity of the feeling. Pleasure saturated her, and her whole body was singing. She clung onto him as wave after wave of release made her whole body tingle and explode. Then he let out a deep guttural cry in Greek as his own orgasm wrapped around them like an almighty explosion.

Afterwards, only the sound of their heavy breathing filled the cabin, almost completely drowned out by the lashing rain and rumbling thunder. The lights flickered, as though they were tempted to go out, but then stabilised. Genevieve idly traced circles along his arms, blinking up at the man who'd just made wild, abandoned love to her—a man whose last name she didn't even know!

It was so completely out of character, and so absolutely outside the agreement she'd formed with James, an agreement he had the power to hold her to by the sheer amount of debt she was in to him. In exchange for his continuing to pay her mother's medical bills—which were all in Genevieve's name—and not disclosing sensitive information about Genevieve's father that she had foolishly shared early in their marriage, she had sworn she'd stay silent and single, not doing even one interview about his infidelity and *never* being seen in public with another man. At least, not until he'd remarried, and was ready to finally let her go. His damn ego simply wouldn't permit the narrative that she'd moved on first. Despite the knowledge that she'd broken that promise, she couldn't help but smile, like the cat that had got the cream. She couldn't help it. For the first time in her life, she'd felt real sexual pleasure, and she finally understood how life-changing it could be.

Nikos, though, was pulling away from her, his body when he stood a study in tension. 'Excuse me, Genevieve,' he said, without a backwards glance, as he made his way to the bathroom and closed the door. A moment later, the shower started, and Genevieve's heart sank at the obvious, offensive rejection. It shouldn't have been a big deal, but after what they'd just shared, and how he'd made her feel, it hurt, way more than she wanted to admit. She turned her face, tilting it towards the window, and found herself praying for a break in the storm, so that she might have a chance to leave, before she did something really stupid and asked him what she'd done wrong.

CHAPTER FOUR

ALL HE COULD think of was Isabella. From the moment the madness of sexual conquest had faded and sanity had returned, his wife had been there, accusing, angry. Hurt. His failings as a husband had wrapped around him, almost choking him with the cold reminder of how he'd let Isabella down. How often he'd ignored her, how much he'd destroyed her, without realising it.

In the same way he'd denied himself the pleasures of his business, his home, his life, he'd chosen celibacy, after Isabella's death. Why should he experience this sort of pleasure, after what he'd denied her?

He hadn't wanted solace, comfort. He hadn't wanted any hint of happiness. What else explained his existence here, on the edge of the earth, living in the most austere fashion, totally without reward for his hard work? He'd built himself up from nothing, and was now one of the world's richest men, yet he enjoyed no fruits of his labour. Every part of his life was now a question of basic survival, of extreme denial.

But what he'd just done with Genevieve wasn't about survival, even though, at the time, he'd felt as though his life depended on making love to her.

He let the water pour over him, eyes closed as memories sliced through him. He tried his hardest not to think of Genevieve—it seemed like even more of a betrayal of his late wife. But for almost the first time in his adult life, Nikos was out of control. His thoughts wouldn't obey him. They kept throwing Genevieve into his mind, reminding him of her voice as she'd cried his name, of how tentative she'd been at first and then how wild. How good she'd felt. How paradoxically insecure she was.

A thousand questions arose within him, questions he wished he didn't feel. Because if he knew one thing about himself, it was that he didn't like unsolved mysteries. And with the storm trapping them both in the cabin for heaven knew how long, getting to the bottom of this woman's contradictions was tempting beyond compare.

She hadn't even realised she'd fallen asleep until an enormous roll of thunder woke her up. Disorientated at first, she rolled over and gasped at the sight of the man sleeping in the bed beside her, all bare chest and dark hair, parted lips and long, dark lashes. She had no idea what time it was—her phone was somewhere on the bottom of the ocean, and her watch had stopped working courtesy of the waterlogging it received—but there was a hint of light in the cabin, suggesting dawn was upon them.

Her stomach rolled as Nikos shifted and recollections flashed through her mind like some kind of strange film. His touch, his seduction, the way he'd made love to her. The pleasure he'd given her! Pleasures she'd never known possible, much less thought to want for herself. She pushed out of the bed gingerly, her whole body heavy with a sense of what they'd done. It wasn't painful, exactly, so much as different. She felt stretched and aware of herself in ways she hadn't been before. Even her nipples tingled as she walked across to the only window of the cabin, and the fabric of his shirt—which she'd hastily pulled on the night before, as he'd showered, like some kind of protective mechanism—brushed against her.

But those memories were there, too. The way he'd disappeared after they'd finished, pulling away from her and showering, for God's sake, rather than staying and...

And what?

Cuddling?

Well, in that sense, he was just like James. He'd never favoured any kind of tenderness. The only times they'd held hands had been when they'd been attending an event and photographers had been there. One of the youngest senators in history, having taken office just a month after his thirtieth birthday, he was obsessed with cultivating the perfect image, and Genevieve, with her long political pedigree, had been a part of that. In public, he was a doting husband. But it was in such contrast to the way he was behind closed doors, that she had started to bitterly resent the false acts of closeness. It was so performative, so empty.

Nikos was nothing like James. Where her ex-husband was superficial and obsessed with power, Nikos was a man who lived on the land. She had no idea if he'd ever had a job, or if he was a wildling, cast here by the gods, to live out his life alone and desperate. But the thought of him in a suit almost made her laugh out loud, let alone attending one of the society events her husband regularly frequented. Nikos, this caveman, making small talk?

She leaned forward and wiped one of the glass panels, removing the condensation. There had been no abatement in the storm. The sky was a leaden grey and the rain continued to fall as though the heavens had turned the tap on full power. She wasn't sure she'd ever been in a storm of this magnitude.

Quietly, careful not to wake him, she pivoted and looked

around the cabin, seeing it now through fresh eyes. Last night, she'd been in a state of shock, exhausted from her hike to the cabin, and thrown completely off track by the chemistry that hummed between herself and Nikos. Now, after however many hours' sleep, she felt closer to rested. Closer to calm. It enabled her to notice things she hadn't the night before. Like the small table to the edge of the kitchen. There were two chairs, which intrigued her. Why have two chairs, if not to host another person? Did that mean there was someone else on the island? Or someone else who came to the island regularly enough to necessitate a second chair?

A frown tugged at her lips as she continued scanning the room, landing on a shelf with books and files. A curiosity, which she put down to her journalism training, had her pacing softly towards it, with one glance cast over her shoulder to be sure he was still sleeping.

What kind of books did a man like Nikos read? To her disappointment, they were almost all in Greek. With the exception of a John Grisham novel and, to her amusement, a recipe book, the rest might as well have been written in ancient Sanskrit for all they'd offer any entertainment for her. As for the files, she was dying to reach out and flick through them. Surely they'd give her some insight into who he was, and what he was doing here? Maybe he was some kind of scientist, researching the natural eco systems of the island? That would make sense, she supposed. For all they'd barely spoken the night before, she could tell he was an intelligent person. It was in his expression, his turn of phrase, his quickness of reply. Her finger pressed to the spine of one of the binders, but she knew, even as she touched it, that she wouldn't pull it out and invade his privacy by looking through it. Investigating a story was one thing, but this was his life, and these were his secrets.

If he wanted to tell her what he was doing, he would.

If he didn't, well…it would be no worse than or different from the way he'd quickly run away the night before to shower her off him. Colour stained her cheeks as she remembered the pain of that. The insult. What had been such an immersive experience for her had clearly been, on some level, disgusting for him. Or regrettable, at least. It was impossible not to feel James's rejection all over again. The husband who'd never enjoyed sex with her, who'd found her lack of arousal completely disappointing.

So why had Nikos let last night happen? He didn't seem like a man who'd get swept away by passion. To live out here, like this, he must have had incredible willpower and determination. Or have been slightly crazy, she thought with a half-smile, looking around again and startling when her eyes glanced across the bed and she saw that he was now awake, watching her with an expression she couldn't interpret…but which set her pulse alight.

'I was just looking,' she said, dropping her hand away from his files.

He stayed very still, unsettling her with the intensity of his gaze.

'I was curious,' she said, with a small shrug. 'About the kind of man who would choose to live like this.'

But it was all so strange. Last night, something older than time had drawn them together, stripping away any barriers, any constructs of society and conditioning, so they were simply two people, existing in the world for the sake of pleasuring one another. The sense of estrangement now was unbearable.

She stepped away from the bookshelf as though it had bitten her, rubbing her hands in front of herself. 'I'll put another log on the fire,' she murmured. Though the cabin had grown cooler overnight, that wasn't really at the root of her icy feeling. It was the rejection she felt, the sense that he was wishing her gone again.

'I'll do it.'

'No.' Too fast. She had no idea if he was completely naked under the sheet, but she suspected he might be, and she wasn't sure her equilibrium could take another exposure to his glorious, Greek god body. 'I can do it.'

'Do you want coffee?'

Genevieve firmly believed that the first sip of the first coffee of the day was one of life's greatest pleasures, yet she shook her head to demur. 'Let me make it.'

'It is not like you are used to,' he pointed out. 'No flicking a button on a machine.'

'How do you know that's how I make coffee?'

'Am I wrong?'

She hesitated, unable to refute his presumption. 'Well, I saw what you did last night,' she sniffed. 'I'm sure I can manage.'

He simply stared back at her, in that disconcerting way of his, as though he was thinking things he knew better than to say. She prodded the fire back to life first, choosing a large log and placing it into the embers, then using the fire poker to shift the log around until flames began to lick against its sides. Afterwards, she moved to the kitchen, exploring the burner he'd used, the pot for water. It seemed simple enough. Add heat to water, let it boil, add coffee, *et voilà*.

She turned to say as much, only to find Nikos was out of bed and standing right there, in the kitchen, all big, looming, enormous hulk of a human, all gorgeous and, thankfully, wearing a pair of shorts, so at least she was spared from whatever her reaction might have been to seeing his nakedness again.

To remembering the way that nakedness had thrust inside her and turned her world utterly and wholly upside down.

'Allow me,' he said, his eyes probing hers, and now there was something in his face that was softer. Almost gentle, except nothing about this man with his harsh lines was gentle. This was the kind of man who could kill a bear with his hands alone, who could scale mountains and probably even part the sea, she thought with a surprising flicker of amusement.

She'd never known anyone like him.

Hardly surprising, given the circles she'd moved in. A quiet childhood on the outskirts of Boston, an Ivy League college education thanks to a full-ride scholarship, and then marriage to James, which had led to a suffocatingly pretentious Washington life. No chance to use her degree—James hadn't wanted a wife who worked.

'Something amusing?'

Her eyes flicked to his. 'I was just imagining you in my normal life,' she said, honestly. 'I can't imagine you anywhere but here.'

'I don't want to be anywhere but here.'

'I wasn't offering.'

His eyes sparked to hers and the air between them crackled with something that could have been animosity or could have been desire. Her insides tightened with a mix of the two.

'You're just so…rugged. The thought of you in a suit is hard to imagine.'

'Easier to think of me naked?' he asked, the question teasing. Light in tone, in a way she hadn't heard from him before. Her lips quirked but when she glanced at him, he was busying himself making coffee, back turned to her.

There was no comfortable armchair to sit in, and she

didn't fancy the cold hardness of the chairs at the dining table, so she padded back to bed and sat gingerly on her side of it, propping the pillow behind her to create a sort of headrest.

'Do you work?'

He glanced over his shoulder then turned properly to face her as he waited for the water to boil.

'Yes.'

She nodded slowly. 'Are you some kind of botanist?'

At that, he actually burst out laughing. 'No, I'm not a botanist.'

'A naturalist? A scientist of some kind? Some sort of conservationist?'

'No.'

'Then, what?'

'Why would I tell you, when having you guess is more entertainment than I've had in years?'

He turned away again abruptly, reaching for the coffee and adding it to the bottom of the pot. She pleated the bed-sheet with her fingers, contemplating that.

'Since you've been on the island?'

He made a grunting sound that didn't really answer her question.

'Well, if you're not a scientist, I'm at a loss. I can't really fathom why anyone would come and live out here, in the middle of nowhere. I mean, it might be nice for a holiday, I suppose, if you wanted to completely disconnect.'

He poured two mugs of coffee—yet another sign that he did entertain here, occasionally, at least—and carried them to the bed. But rather than handing one to Genevieve, he placed both on his bedside table before sitting beside her, his large frame unsettling the mattress so she was drawn a little into the middle. Towards him. Their shoulders brushed and she startled. Nikos turned towards her, his face so close their eyes sparked, and she could see all the flecks of colour in his eyes—grey, silver, and some a golden amber.

'Are you okay?'

His question caught her unawares, and seemed to tip her world even more to the side. 'I—yes.'

'After last night,' he clarified.

She glanced down at the space between them, only there was no space. Just flesh. His glorious chest was right there, and the sight of it, the memories of him, made her heart pound in a way that was unsettling to the extreme.

She'd spent so much of her marriage lying. Or, rather, faking it. Pretending to be something she wasn't, because she'd thought if she could play the part of the perfect wife, James might come back to her, and be like he had been in the beginning. She'd smothered her own discontent, she'd quietened her upset, in order to keep the peace with him.

But Nikos was a stranger, a man she didn't intend to see again, once she left the island. So why hide the truth from him? What was the downside of honesty, when she didn't actually care what he thought of her?

'Why did you go and shower last night? Afterwards, I mean.'

Even as she asked the question, though, she was surprised by how forthright it was. And proud, too. Why shouldn't she ask? As far as she was concerned, she had every right to wonder. It wasn't exactly the done thing. At least, not according to movies and romance novels.

'Did it offend you?'

She considered that. It had, but perhaps that had more to do with her past than his act. She lifted one shoulder in a half-shrug. She'd signed a non-disclosure agreement as part of her divorce. She wasn't supposed to talk about

James, or he'd stop paying off her mother's medical debts. Worse, he'd do a tell-all interview about her father. While he was long gone, his political legacy lived on; she couldn't be the reason it was tarnished. Despite those threats, was there any harm in talking to *this* man, who had taken himself completely out of civilisation? What was the harm in being honest with him? Did she think he had some kind of hotline to one of the Washington papers? A gossip columnist on speed dial? The thought almost made her laugh out loud. Besides, he didn't know her last name, and had zero idea who James was.

'I'm probably too sensitive around this stuff,' she said, eventually. 'I—was recently divorced.' The words were tinged with bitterness but she supposed, to other ears, it might sound like grief. She flicked a glance at his face, briefly, but his features were set in a mask that gave nothing away. 'Coffee?' she prompted, embarrassed, because she'd revealed something vital and important, and he hadn't reacted.

He turned away from her, took hold of a mug and held it out. Genevieve tried to rearrange herself, to put space between them, but it just wasn't possible in a bed this size, with a man this weight.

She resigned herself to the fact that their shoulders would brush as they sat there.

'And you're upset?'

So he wasn't letting it go, then. She tilted her face to his. 'I'm getting used to my new reality.'

'Was it your idea, or his?'

'Mine.'

He raised his brows. 'You weren't happy?'

She sipped her coffee, closing her eyes as the pleasure of that sip wrapped around her. The last thing she expected was his feather-light touch on her face, a single finger tracing the line of her jaw, before gently angling her chin towards him. 'You were unhappy?' he repeated, eyes tracing her face, so she felt completely exposed to him.

'That's generally the reason people seek divorces, isn't it?'

A frown flickered across his features. 'Not always.'

She sipped her coffee again, purely in an attempt to cut through the connection he was forging by asking her these questions, so close, staring down into her eyes. She didn't want to feel a connection to this man, apart from, she supposed, the physical. She would never be stupid enough to put her happiness in the hands of a man again, even temporarily.

'Well, it was for me,' she said, crisply. 'My marriage was a mistake. I realised within a few months.'

'Yet you stayed.'

'It was complicated.'

'Why?'

She glanced across the room, considering that. 'There were other people in the picture. My mom. His parents. His work. Getting divorced after a few months would have been disastrous for him.'

'And staying wasn't disastrous for you?'

Surprised by his perception, she shot him another glance. There was a haunted look in his face that took her breath away. 'I thought I could fix it,' she said, finally, sipping her coffee, cheeks flaming with regret at that. How silly she'd been. How naïve. 'I thought I could fix him.'

'One person alone cannot fix a broken relationship.' It was too insightful to be anything but personal experience. She opened her mouth to say something along those lines, but he spoke first.

'It's been a long time, since I've been with a woman.

To be honest, I never expected to have sex again.' Her jaw dropped at that. He was far too masculine, too virile, to even contemplate a lifetime of denial. 'I reacted badly, afterwards. I am sorry if that offended you. Believe me when I tell you, my response had nothing to do with you.' He leaned closer, so their faces were almost touching. 'Everything about you was perfect, as I said at the time.'

Her heart leaped into her throat and her pulse went into overdrive. Stars shimmered in her eyes again, all bright and silver, and, of its own accord, one hand lifted to press to his chest. Not to push him away, but to feel his warm skin beneath her palm, to touch him because he was inviting her to. He was opening the door again, to the intimacy they'd shared.

And in that moment, it was all she wanted. To banish all thoughts of James and their marriage from her mind with simple, deeply pleasurable sex with this incredibly gorgeous man.

CHAPTER FIVE

'What do you mean, again?' she asked, and inwardly he smothered a curse. Because he was showing too much. Sharing too much. He was out of practice with people. Aside from his business manager, Theo, and an occasional meeting with some of his executives, Nikos hadn't made conversation with anyone in a long time. And even then, that was business, not small talk. Not the run-of-the-mill, 'getting to know you' conversation. He'd forgotten how to hedge.

And this woman was listening with both ears, taking in everything he said and analysing it. Asking him for more than he wanted to share.

He simply stared at her, not willing to answer her question, even though he'd opened the door to it.

'You said you didn't think you'd ever have sex again. After what?'

'I just mean I'm single. By choice.'

She wrinkled her nose, clearly not sold on the line. And he couldn't blame her. Given the alacrity with which he'd dragged her to bed, he could hardly blame her for perceiving his active libido.

'Why?'

'Does it matter?'

It was like seeing her visibly retract. She shifted a little, blinking away. Another curse flew through his mind. He knew this wasn't about Genevieve. Not really. He'd just met her, after all. It was the sense of failure that dogged him constantly. The awareness that he'd once held something beautiful in his hands, had been entrusted with Isabella's life, her happiness, and he'd destroyed both. He pulled back a little, on the pretence of reaching for his own coffee and taking a long drink.

'So, how does this work?'

His chest twisted. This? Was she referring to 'them'? Hadn't he been clear about that? Sex was one thing, but as soon as the weather cleared, he needed to find a way to get her off the island. There was a radio in the helicopter, and he could call to have one of his staff dispatch a boat to collect her.

'I mean, you don't look like someone who exists on tinned tuna.'

Relief flooded his body. She was talking about his life here, on the island. Her curiosity was natural. When he'd first come here, he hadn't cared if he lived or died. He'd thrown caution to the wind, and somehow, the wind had caught him. Bringing him an abundance of food, of shelter, so, day by day, his new habitat became familiar. Home.

'The island has plenty of food.'

She arched a brow. 'Such as?'

'There's a whole ocean out there,' he pointed out.

'So you go fishing?'

He nodded once, as some of his earliest memories filtered through his mind. The smell of salt water, his father's hands, strong and capable, helping him reel in a catch that might otherwise have dragged him off the jetty, his mother smashing octopus against the rocks, until it was tender enough to char over flames. They'd fished out of desperation, to stave off hunger. On a good day, his father would catch enough to barter for something else, like eggs, or bread.

'Has anyone ever told you having a conversation with you is a little like getting blood out of a stone?'

'I'm out of practice.'

She considered that. 'Do you ever get lonely?'

'No.' Except, that wasn't completely true. He was lonely, a lot of the time. But he relished that feeling, knowing it was the punishment he deserved, because of what he'd put his wife through. His wife who had deserved so much better.

'I'd hate it.'

'Why?'

'I guess I've been lonely enough. My marriage was not happy, obviously, but, because of his job, I found it hard to meet people and really get to know them. I lost contact with a lot of my college friends. I felt alone, a lot. Now that we're divorced, I want to restart my life. I want to find myself again. I know how trite that sounds, it's just…' She tapered off and lifted her shoulders.

'It doesn't sound trite.' His own voice was hoarse. He thought of Isabella with a sense of desperation in his gut. Why hadn't she divorced him? He hadn't deserved her loyalty. Her love and devotion to a man like him had destroyed her. If only she'd done what Genevieve had and walked out. He ground his teeth together, the past too painful to spend much time on. 'What was his job?'

She hesitated for a moment. 'He's a senator,' she said, clearing her throat a little and looking away. 'Very young, very driven, much admired.'

'I see.' The same could have been said for him. He'd been twenty-three, after all, when his private equity firm had become one of the biggest in the world. He'd worked tirelessly ever since, until Isabella's death.

'Everything was about his image,' she murmured, sipping her coffee, keeping her delicate face averted from his. He reached out without intending to, tucking a curtain of dark hair behind her ear, so he could see her better. Heat spread through his body at the simple, innocent touch. 'I guess that's par for the course for a lot of politicians, but I wasn't really prepared for the duality.'

Though they'd only just met, he could understand that. There was something so authentic and real about this woman, he could easily imagine her struggling with the other man's public persona and his private actions.

'So, fishing, huh?' she asked, clunkily changing the subject.

To his surprise, he heard himself say, 'I would go out with my father, early in the mornings, before the sun had come up. He died a long time ago, but I still hear his voice, when I cast in my line,' he admitted, turning away again, this time to put down his coffee cup. They'd been able to coax out an okay living while his father lived, but afterwards, it had been desperate.

'It's the same for me, with sailing,' she murmured. 'My father taught me, before he died. I was twelve, and it felt like the whole world had fallen down around me. My mother was never particularly maternal, but my dad...he always had time for me,' she said, smiling wistfully. 'We would go out on his boat, and he was so patient, explaining everything as many times as he needed to.' Her lips pulled to the side as she lost herself in thought. 'It's why I hired that damned boat,' she muttered. 'It was spur of the moment—a whim. I walked past the marina and saw them there, and just *felt* him, beside me, encouraging me forward. Which is stupid, really, because no way would my dad—or the ghost of him, or whatever—ever put me in that kind of danger.'

Nikos thought about that—the legend of this island, the mythical stories of its creation—and ignored the obvious parallels. He'd never believed in all that nonsense, though someone inclined that way could have said the same thing: that he had been drawn here, by fate, or something like it.

'In truth, he'd have been furious with me for setting out without checking the forecast,' she admitted, on an uneven laugh.

'The hire company should have warned you.'

'They might have. I don't speak Greek.'

He was surprised to feel a smile tugging at his lips. 'You know your phone can translate for you?'

Heat flushed her cheeks. 'I just wanted to get out on the water.' Her gaze was focused on the flickering fire across the room. 'I've felt trapped for so long, the freedom of the sea…' She turned to face him. 'It sounds stupid.'

'No,' he contradicted immediately, hating the vulnerability he sensed in her. Hating the feeling of history repeating itself. His wife had been miserable, yet he'd been too driven to succeed, to never again know the ache of hunger, the fear of poverty, to realise. He had seized every opportunity, flown across the globe, stayed in his office when she'd begged him to come home, because he couldn't imagine neglecting his business.

So he'd neglected his wife—and lived to regret it, with every part of himself.

It was because of Isabella that he was so easily able to spot the signs now, to read the self-doubt. And while he hadn't caused Genevieve's situation, he couldn't help but wonder if meeting her wasn't giving him a second chance. An opportunity to do something good for someone, for once. It would never undo the damage he'd caused Isabella, though. Nothing could, and he would carry that guilt for a lifetime, always atoning for the error of his ways. 'I understand it,' he said. 'The same is true for me, out here. There is a sense of freedom that comes of this life.'

She wrinkled her nose. 'This is a pretty extreme version of freedom, though,' she pointed out, flicking him a small smile.

He dipped his head in acknowledgement. 'It's right for me.'

Her eyes swept his face, thoughtfully. 'When did you last leave the island?'

'About three months ago.'

'Oh!' Her reaction was easy to interpret.

'That surprises you?'

'Yes, honestly. You seem almost to be carved out of the cliff face,' she admitted. 'I don't know if I can picture you anywhere else.'

'I never stay away long.'

Her fingers moved over the sheet, pleating it into neat little folds. 'Where did you go?'

'Athens.'

Her eyes flicked to his.

'Have you been?'

She nodded once. 'I flew into Athens, but I only spent one night. I'd like to go back at some point. Before I head home.' She laughed softly. 'If I ever make it off this damned island.'

'When the storm breaks, you can leave,' he said, as much as a reminder to himself as her.

'But how?'

'We'll work it out.'

'That's not an answer.'

She was right. He was being deliberately cagey, and he realised why. He liked her not knowing who he was. He liked that she didn't know about his money, his business, his empire. He liked that they were sitting here, talking as two people, with shared experiences of grief, though she wasn't aware of his. But why hide the truth from her? He was Nikos Konstantinou, and he had no intention of hiding that from her for ever. He split the difference, in the end, deciding to reveal some details without showing his full biography.

'I have a small, old helicopter in a clearing behind the cabin,' he said, voice neutral. 'I can get the radio working, once the storm stops, get someone to come over for you.'

Her eyes widened. 'A helicopter?'

He reached for his coffee, took a long drink, then glanced towards the window. 'I doubt the weather will clear today, though. You're stuck here a while longer.'

She nodded slowly. 'I can deal with that.' Her cheeks flushed pink, and it was easy to understand why. To know what she was thinking, because his mind was going there, too. They had very limited time together, and he wasn't going to waste it. He'd made his peace with the fact they'd slept together, because it was temporary and meaningless.

Except, maybe it wasn't completely meaningless. Oh, for Nikos it could never be more than a physical connection, but was it possible he could help heal the wounds her terrible excuse of a husband had created? Could he help put her back together, in the way he should have been able to do for Isabella? It would not cure his guilt, but at least it would be something. An offering to the gods of karma, a righting of the scales, in some small, desperate way.

Genevieve stared at the ceiling, cheeks flushed, body covered in a fine film of perspiration, mouth unable to form words. Brain barely able to conceive of them. What had started with coffee in bed had turned into something else entirely, and hours had passed with them exploring each other's bodies. His every touch, his kisses, his fascination with her, until a fever had gripped her and she was spiralling into a whole new dimension, unlikely to ever return to this one again. At least, not as she'd once been. This version of Genevieve was completely different. She was fire and flame, awoken and hungry. It was as if he'd turned on a pleasure tap within her, and now she knew it existed, she had to accept that it was a part of her, and always would be.

How strange to have lived her whole life with no concept that she was a sexual person. With no idea that a single touch could set her skin alight.

Even stranger to see how she'd surrendered herself to this. Because with every minute that passed, every raindrop that fell, the heavens were closer to exhausting their supply of tears, and that meant one thing, and one thing only: she would leave again. She would leave this island, return to the small coastal town she'd rented a little room in, and go on with this holiday. The 'honeymoon', she'd called it, because it was a trip she'd planned to mark a commitment back to herself. It was a way of celebrating her freedom, and the second phase of her life.

Whatever that would look like.

And whatever her 'freedom' meant, because though she'd been able to divorce her husband, he still held the strings. He was her puppet master, and would be until she was able to properly stand on her own two feet. For as long as he held her mother's medical expenses over her, Genevieve had no choice but to be the contrite, good ex-wife, toeing whatever line he asked her to. Even to come away on this holiday, she'd had to barter with him.

Anger rushed through her, catching her totally unawares, because it was something she was usually able to keep under control. Except with Nikos, somehow, he'd uncorked the passion centres of her body, so now everything was heat and flame.

She pushed up onto one elbow, so she could face him. His eyes were closed, his face held tersely, and she frowned, realising that the last time they'd made love, he'd got straight up and gone to shower. Was he thinking about doing that again?

Was he holding back, for her?

'If you need to go wash, you can,' she said, pleased her voice sounded somewhat level.

He turned to face her, eyes landing on hers and causing her heart to thud. 'That wasn't about you.'

'Wasn't it?'

He reached out, brushing a hand over her cheek. 'Where are you staying?'

She frowned, not immediately understanding.

'You said you flew into Athens. Where are you now?'

'Oh. Katanos,' she said, naming a small coastal fishing village somewhere across the Aegean. 'Do you know it?'

His smile was mesmerising. 'I grew up about thirty miles to the south. I spent time there, as a child. It's very beautiful. Why Katanos? It's not really on the tourist track.'

'No,' she agreed. 'But it's where my parents went on their honeymoon. We had a photograph of the harbour, in our lounge room, when I was a girl. I used to look at it and imagine I was a mermaid, diving deep into the ocean, losing myself in that crystal-clear turquoise water. I'm not sure when I consciously decided to come here, but after the divorce, I couldn't think of anywhere else I wanted to be. Strange, right?'

'Are you close to your mother?'

Genevieve's heart twisted. She shook her head once. 'She

passed away a while ago.' She cleared her throat. 'She had a series of strokes,' Genevieve said. 'She was hospitalised for a long time, and then, one night…'

Nikos pushed up onto his elbow, so they were like bookends in bed, facing one another. 'I'm sorry.'

He frowned, eyes roaming her face thoughtfully. 'Did she like your husband?'

'James,' she said, slanting a glance at him, figuring it made sense for him to know her husband's name, seeing as they were speaking of him so often. 'My ex-husband's name is James J. Wilson the third. As you can guess from that mouthful, he's from old money. The prevailing opinion was that I was very lucky to have snagged him.' She rolled her eyes.

Nikos made a sound of disapproval.

'And yes, my mother adored him. Once upon a time, my parents had money, too. My father came from one of those political families, so, on paper, we were a good match. But in reality, I hated that life and lifestyle. It wasn't for me.'

'Your father was a politician?'

She nodded, opening her mouth to speak, then slamming it shut. She'd told James about her father, and he'd held that over her almost from that night, threatening to expose her father, to ruin his legacy. But somehow, she just knew she could trust Nikos. That he'd never, ever do something so unscrupulous. 'He was a politician, yes, with a serious penchant for gambling, which wasn't apparent until after his death. We were left with a heap of debt.' She closed her eyes. 'I can't believe I'm telling you this.'

He made a sound, querying that.

'I never talk about it.' Except for one time, and she'd lived to regret that. But with Nikos, it just felt…different.

He reached out, pressing a finger to her shoulder and shifting it downwards. 'You worship him.'

Her smile was soft. 'I suppose I do, yes. He was a kind man. I wish… His gambling, the fact he hid it all from Mom, was obviously wrong. I know he must have carried a lot of shame, and regret, but I wish he'd been honest with her. Not least because she might have been able to help him,' Genevieve added. 'So when a rich, handsome senator came into my life and started pursuing me as though his life depended on it, Mom was all too keen to buy into the whole thing. A fairy tale, she called it. I think she had a fantasy of James being able to turn us back into what we once were. Instead, it turned into a horror show.'

Nikos moved forward, so their naked bodies were connected, touching leg to leg, chest to chest. His eyes bore into hers with an intensity that took her breath away. 'Did he hurt you, Genevieve?'

'No,' she said, then frowned, because that wasn't strictly true. 'I mean, he never hit me or anything.'

'That is not the only way to hurt someone.'

And there was something about this room, this man, the flickering fire, the heavenly sensations in her body, that made her open herself completely to him. 'He was cold and cruel,' she admitted. 'Nothing I did was ever good enough for him. I was expected to be the perfect political asset and yet I constantly fell short of his expectations. Things between us…' she flushed to the roots of her hair '…in bed, I mean, were…lacklustre, and he made it clear that was my fault.'

The scoffing sound Nikos made should have warmed her, but Genevieve was back in the past, the ice spreading through her veins, so she barely heard him.

'He cheated, and blamed me. If I'd been a better wife, a

better lover, more satisfying, he wouldn't have needed to stray.' She said the words with disdain, showing how little she believed them now. But at the time, when she'd been under his spell, and captive in his home, dependent on him completely, she'd taken each and every sledge to the heart, letting it shape her entire world view.

'Bastard,' Nikos ground out, his indignation bringing a small smile to her face.

'Yes.' How could she argue with that? 'At first, he was careful to keep the affairs secret, and I pretended I didn't know. That I didn't see.' Her skin felt cold and clammy. 'Then one of his mistresses went to the press. The story broke, and that's when things got really bad. Somehow, that was my fault too,' she murmured. 'I tried to leave him then, but he made it obvious he would make my life very, very difficult if I walked out.'

'Difficult how?' There was a darkness to his tone that set her pulse racing. A protectiveness that she'd never known from anyone. It wasn't until that moment that Genevieve realised how long she'd been doing this on her own, fighting all her own battles, bearing her own scars.

'Let's just say he's not someone I want to get on the bad side of.'

Nikos frowned.

'I feel so stupid,' she admitted. 'I really wanted to believe him. To believe that he loved me, that we'd live happily ever after. I bought into the fairy tale, but he was a monster.'

Nikos made another noise, and then his mouth was claiming hers, kissing her until she tasted the salt of her tears.

'You deserved so much better,' he said, with so much darkness she felt it pierce something deep in her soul, conversely letting light in for the first time in years. It didn't occur to her—how could it have?—that he wasn't really speaking to her, so much as a figment of his past. It didn't matter, anyway. The warming effect was the same.

CHAPTER SIX

THE SKY WAS thunderously grey but the rain at least stopped that afternoon, allowing them to leave the cabin. Genevieve's shoes were still damp, but she pulled them on over a big pair of thick socks Nikos had given her. She could have been tempted to stay in bed with him all day, but at the same time the knowledge that her time here on the island was limited had her wanting to see more than just the inside of his cabin—as much as she would always remember every single detail of it.

One glance from the top of the cliff towards the ocean showed the waves coming in thick and fast, the ocean too swollen to make boat travel possible yet, regardless of the storm. She ignored the slight bubble of relief at that, and what it signalled.

So, she liked being here.

She liked—surprisingly—spending time with Nikos.

That didn't *mean* anything.

It would take more than exceptional skills in bed and an interesting conversation or two to weaken the barriers Genevieve had erected around her heart and soul. Never again would she let another man permeate either. She was independent and alone. Even without James's stipulation that she stay single, this was something she intended to do for herself.

There was no hint of her small sailing boat. It had been devoured by the ocean, and a shiver ran down her spine as she imagined herself having suffered the same fate. Had she not been able to make it to this island, she would have undoubtedly been lost at sea.

She ignored the ice-like feeling wrapping around her.

There was no sense thinking about hypotheticals. She'd made it here, and she'd made it to Nikos, which seemed strangely fated, now she thought about it. She dismissed the idea, though, quickly enough. She didn't believe in anything like that. But when his hand reached down and curved around hers, pulling her away from the edge of the cliff face, back towards the cabin and the clearing around it, her whole body began to tingle in a way that definitely seemed other-worldly.

He was silent as they walked, yet a million questions flooded her mind. She realised that for all they'd spent the day alternating between making love and talking, it had been Genevieve who'd shared the most. Genevieve who'd all but bared her soul. Then again, was that really a surprise? She'd had no one to talk to about her failing marriage. No girlfriends she could confide in, and even a psychologist had been out of the question, because of James's privacy concerns.

No, it was this man, this cabin, this island and the storm that conspired to create a perfect slice away from the rest of the world. Only that bubble enabled her to be so open with him.

It helped that he was so far removed from her normal world. They would have no acquaintances in common, having obviously moved in very different circles. She could speak to him without any concerns of it becoming public, and here, well away from humanity and society, there was no risk of their liaison being discovered. It was safe, safe in a way she hadn't really understood she'd needed.

Seeing the cabin now, from the outside, without the fear of the storm bearing down upon her, meant she could regard it properly, taking in more details than she'd been capable of the night before. It was rustic in construction, but obviously very well built. Stones had been placed close together, mortared, to form the walls, and the roof was made of a sort of plaster and wood.

'It's soil and lime plaster,' he said, when she asked. 'Reinforced with sand.'

She nodded.

'I wanted to be able to use it as a second floor. In the summer, I sleep up there, some nights.'

She turned to face him, and the image he created was so incredibly romantic and earthy, so animalistic and pure, that she felt a part of her soul chipping off and coming to rest right here, in this forest, atop a mountain on a Greek volcano. 'Do you mean you built this?' Her voice emerged squeaky, but she couldn't help it. Surprise ran through her veins.

'Builders are in short supply on the island,' he quipped, but, despite having known him fewer than twenty-four hours, she had the sense he was obfuscating, intentionally concealing something from her.

'Still, that must have been quite a challenge.'

'That was what I needed, at the time.'

Why? The question died on her lips; she knew he wouldn't answer. Not yet. She would ask it again, later, when his guard was more fully down. They walked, hand in hand, to the rear of the cabin, and Genevieve let out a small sound of surprise. Here was a vegetable garden as fully developed as any she'd seen. There were fruit trees too, some heavy with citrus.

'This is better than tinned tuna,' she pointed out.

His smile made her heart tremble. 'A little.'

At the back of the house, there was also a large freezer. 'Meat and fish,' he explained. 'Some cheeses that freeze well.'

'You're hardly roughing it, then.'

He laughed.

'Though it's not what I'd call luxurious, either.'

'It's fine for me.'

She nodded, but there was something in his statement that didn't make sense. What kind of humble mountain man had a helicopter casually parked out the back? She glanced through the forest and saw the flash of metal, and knew that was where he had it stored.

'Thinking of escape?' he asked, squeezing her hand.

'I don't think I need to escape,' she replied. 'I'm not your prisoner.'

'No,' he agreed, but his voice was flat.

They didn't walk far. The sky was inclement and, sure enough, after they'd picked their way through the forest for fifteen minutes or so, until they reached a large, verdant tree covered in spiky little orange and red balls, a few drops of rain began to fall.

'It's an Irish Strawberry tree,' he said, reaching for one and picking it.

'I've never seen that before.'

'They're quite common in Greece. There are many on the island.'

'Where exactly are we, Nikos? I lost my bearings in the storm.'

'The island is called Therasia Notia. A few nautical miles south of Psara.'

'I've never heard of it.'

'I'm not surprised.'

'How can it be empty?'

He looked at her, long and hard, then sighed. 'Because I want it to be.'

'That makes no sense.'

Rain began to fall, splishy splashy drops. 'Come on, *koukla*. Come back to the cabin.'

She walked quickly beside him, but her mind was still turning over the statement, his certainty that he could keep the island empty, at a single command.

Rain fell heavier though, and lightning began to spark in the sky once more, so she stayed quiet until they'd reached the cabin and moved to stand in front of the fire.

'Nikos,' she said, eyes lancing him, holding his gaze. She didn't need to say anything else; he understood.

'I own it,' he said, almost defiantly, as though he was challenging her. 'The island is mine, and it's empty because I wish to keep it that way.'

Her jaw dropped. Of course, she knew people who owned things like islands. Some of James's donors had been that kind of filthy, stinking rich. But even in that rarefied upper echelon, it was, in Genevieve's experience, unusual. And to keep a beautiful island like this without capitalising on its possible value?

Suddenly, she felt betrayed. It was stupid, because he hadn't lied to her. But the image she'd had of him as some simple mountain man, existing off the land, was an illusion, disappearing like vapour before her eyes.

'I see,' she murmured, unable to keep the hurt from her tone, and hating herself for that. With James, she'd managed to hide how she was feeling. But years of play-acting had exhausted her, so now only her authentic self was on display.

'I bought it a few years ago, when I was looking to get away.'

She focused all her attention on the fire, ignoring the way he was staring down at her, as if he could read her thoughts if he stared long and hard enough.

'You just bought an island?'

'This bothers you?'

She glanced up at him. It was on the tip of her tongue to deny it but, with Nikos, it didn't feel right to hide herself. 'A little.' She sighed heavily. 'I know I have no right. It's just, you're different from what I thought.'

'Am I? Why?'

She held her hands towards the fire, seeking warmth. 'You're obviously very wealthy, for one thing. All of this—' she gestured around the cabin '—is just pretend.'

'Believe me, it's not.'

'But you could jump in your helicopter at any time and fly somewhere else.' Her eyes narrowed. 'Tell me, Nikos, do you have another home somewhere?'

A muscle jerked low in his jaw. 'This is my home.'

'You know that's not what I'm asking.'

'I have other properties, yes,' he said, eventually.

'I see.'

His brows knitted together. 'I haven't lied to you.'

He hadn't. Not really. Yet his every action had been a lie, of sorts, creating an illusion of something that didn't exist. Beneath the veneer of this rugged, wild beast of a man was someone wealthy and cultivated, civilised, who might be every bit as at home in a suit as her husband had been.

His hands caught her hips then, turning her to face him, and his features held an intensity that took her breath away. 'Who I am, on this island, is the real me. This, here. I chose this life, because it's where I belong. What does it matter that I also have business interests?'

'And money,' she pointed out.

'Yes, and money.'

'I've just known people with money. It's come to be a marker of what I want to avoid.'

'And if we were anything more than this, I might understand why you were annoyed. But true or false, Genevieve—you are leaving this island as soon as you are safely able to do so. What should it matter to you how much money is in my bank account? It changes nothing.'

She opened her mouth to argue that, to dispute it, but he was right. It shouldn't matter.

She looked down at his chest, swallowed past a strangely constricted throat. 'I'm just...wary. After him.'

'That is understandable.' His own voice sounded raw, deep and husky. It set the hairs on her arms on edge with pleasurable anticipation. 'I wasn't born wealthy. If anything, my life was the opposite. I knew abject poverty. I knew what it was like to have to make clothes and shoes last far longer than they should. I was often hungry. I knew longing and need, the struggle of not being able to have things others did, of seeing my mother make unimaginable choices, just so we would have somewhere to live.'

'What kind of choices?' she asked, momentarily thrown off course.

He stared at her, long and hard, and she could practically see his cogs turning. She could feel his internal war as he decided how much of himself he was willing to share.

'The sort of choices I would not wish on anyone,' he said, eventually, the words dragged from him. Then his voice softened. 'So what you see here, on the island, is far closer to who I am, in my heart. All the rest is just…trappings.' He sounded so grim though, so angry.

She lifted her gaze to his face, trying to make sense of it. 'Why does that bother you?'

He shook his head once. 'It doesn't matter.'

But it did to Genevieve. 'Why can't you answer?'

'Because I don't know how,' he said, finally, simply.

She blinked at him, frustration curling inside her. She knew it was partly because of her journalistic training, and partly because of who she was—the latter had made her excellent at the former—but neither looked likely to be satisfied. Nikos was closing up like a drawbridge being raised.

He moved towards the kitchen, removing things from the small fridge, leaving her looking at this man, this contradiction in terms, with the sense that, even if she had all the time in the world, she'd never properly understand him, because he was determined to keep himself under lock and key.

She knew she should have been grateful for that. It was much harder to let herself develop fantasies around a man who kept her at an emotional arm's length. And she was no longer blind to the inherent dangers of remaining on the island. For the longer she stayed, the longer she stayed *with Nikos*, the harder it would be to remember that she never planned to let anyone else in.

Sex was sex, but, with Nikos, it was also the setting fire to her entire universe, and, with Genevieve in the centre of it, she knew that if she wasn't very careful, she was going to get burned beyond recognition.

'Okay,' she said, over-brightly. 'Let's eat. Can I help?'

He hadn't set out to hide so much of himself from her. Perhaps it had been partly because he needed to keep his private life private. His grief was his own to bear, and he had no intention of sharing it with anyone. Let alone someone like Genevieve, who might listen to his heartbreak and try to make him feel better.

He didn't *want* to feel better.

Not better than this, anyway.

But *this* was temporary. This fling, or whatever it could be called, was like quicksand. Not real, not permanent, just a very temporary state of affairs. He wished he didn't know her last name, in a way, because he wanted the insurance policy against reaching out to her again. He wanted to know that when she left the island, that would be the end of it.

Because she made him feel good, and warm. In some brief moments, she even made him feel whole, and he knew he didn't deserve that.

But he hadn't expected her reaction to his statement about owning the island. He hadn't foreseen that she would be angry with him, that she would withdraw.

He'd known Isabella for a long time—years—before they'd begun to date. He'd got a low-level job for her father, organised by a church charity that he'd gone to for food after his mother's death. He and Isabella had been thrown together at certain company functions and events. Them being a couple had grown slowly and dependably. Like building this cabin, he supposed, it had been brick by brick, bit by bit, until suddenly they were engaged and planning a wedding. For Nikos, it had made sense. He hadn't really thought about love. It had seemed an abstract concept—perhaps his childhood and adolescence had made it so.

He had already been committed to his then future father-in-law, indebted to him for the faith the older man had put in Nikos when he was starting out in his career. While it had been Nikos's innate intelligence and skill, grit and determination that had taken his career from strength to strength, it was Isabella's father who'd opened the door, giving him the opportunity to prove himself. In the end, he hadn't been able to lose sight of his goal. Each victory professionally had been the shifting of the goalposts, to work harder, achieve more. His need for success had been insatiable, born out of the flipside of that: poverty and pain.

The freezer on the island was always packed. Constant hunger still bred a sort of food insecurity for Nikos. It was strange that even now, as a grown man worth hundreds of billions of dollars, he liked knowing he had plenty of food available. Then again, on the island, it was a wise precaution.

'Do you eat everything?'

'I mean, not everything,' she said, wrinkling her nose in a way he tried not to find adorable. Sexy, beautiful and alluring were fine. Adorable was a shade of grey he didn't want to approach. 'But most things.'

'Lamb?'

'Love it.'

'Good answer.'

He ignored the warmth in his chest. She was leaving. Asap. This was no big deal.

If anything, having Genevieve here and then letting her go would be an excellent kick in the guts—a refresher course in loneliness. Because, for this short window of time, he was becoming used to company again, to the presence of someone else—a beautiful woman, no less.

While the lamb grilled, he cut up some salad, serving it on the two plates the cabin boasted, and placing it at the small table. He'd built it with Theo and himself in mind— they'd needed space to put two laptops, so they could work, on the days Theo came to the island. It was fine for a couple to share a meal but, he had to admit, he'd never been aware of the intimacy of the space before now.

Everything Genevieve did was dainty, right down to the way she ate. He watched as she delicately sliced into the meat, lifting a piece to her mouth, tasting it thoughtfully before letting out a soft, sensual moan of appreciation that made his cock hard against his pants.

Christo, but she was stunning. A vixen, sent to tempt him. And he'd fallen at the first chance. Guilt slashed him and he let it. He *should* feel guilty, for the rest of his life.

'You're a good cook,' she said, after a few mouthfuls.

'It's easy to make lamb.'

A smile quirked her lips. 'I'm impressed, anyway.'

'Do you cook?'

'I used to. I used to love it. Another thing my father taught me,' she said softly. 'We would make the most elaborate dinners. Mom had little patience for cooking, or anything domestic, so, after Dad died, I took over most of our meals, grocery shopping, that kind of thing.' She hesitated a moment, and he found himself leaning forward a little. 'But when I married James, we had someone who did all that. He…thought it was beneath his wife to cook.'

Disapproval tightened in his gut. 'Even though you enjoyed it?'

Her lips pulled to the side. 'I don't think James really cared what I enjoyed.'

He made a dark sound. How he despised that man. His cruel, thoughtless treatment of Genevieve. But was he any better? He had never wanted to hurt Isabella. He would have given her anything she asked, except his time.

'Do you have a cook?' Genevieve asked, sliding the question into the conversation in a relaxed tone. But he knew what she was doing. Trying to sound him out about his life away from the cabin. She had no idea what a nightmare it had become—how he did almost anything to avoid returning to the home he'd shared with Isabella.

He didn't sell the place, though. Nor did he change it, in any way. Like pressing his finger into a bruise, he forced himself to go back there for certain days of the year. Her birthday, their wedding anniversary. Days when he really felt he deserved to marinate in his failings as a husband— and the consequences of them.

Isabella was everywhere in their home. Her clothes still hung in the wardrobe, her shoes were neatly arranged in the shelves she'd had built to showcase them, like some kind of store. Even her toothbrush was there, in their shared bathroom.

He knew it wasn't healthy, but that was a choice he'd made. To live for ever in a state of purgatory, so that even if he came close to forgetting, to feeling like himself again, he would have physical talismans to remind him of what he'd done wrong. Of how he'd messed up.

'I'm guessing yes, given you own an island.'

He refocused his attention on her. 'Yes,' he agreed, after a beat. 'I had a housekeeper, who also did most of the cooking.'

Isabella had been a terrible cook. The book he'd given her for their first wedding anniversary had been a joke— he still had it. It was one of the few items he'd brought with him to the island—another bruise to be pushed into, to remind himself of what he'd once had, and been too foolish to appreciate. Too selfish to protect.

'What did you study at university?' he asked, turning the questions back on her, seeking temporary relief in the change of subject. With Genevieve here, he found his predilection for sadistic self-torture waning, in favour of enjoying these few days. A slight reprieve, he thought, one that was in and of itself a double-edged sword.

Because he couldn't look at this woman and want her, couldn't look at and admire her beauty, without knowing it was a betrayal of Isabella. The woman who'd deserved so much better than he'd been able to offer.

In hindsight, marrying her had been a mistake. But she'd loved him so much, and her father had desperately wanted the union. Rather than disappointing either of them, Nikos had proposed. But his focus had always been on the business, his passion entirely given over to his professional successes.

In reality, he was no better than Genevieve's husband had been. The thought sickened him, so he blanked it, focusing instead on the woman across from him and the storm raging outside, and the fact it didn't show any signs of dying down. Not that he really wanted it to.

CHAPTER SEVEN

'I COULD WATCH you lose yourself to me all day,' he said, darkly, lifting his head from between her legs to stare up into her eyes. Genevieve felt heat flush her cheeks—now not from the pleasure of what he was doing to her body, but because of the words he gave her.

'I—' The sense of embarrassment had her quickly shutting her mouth, flattening the admission she'd been about to make.

'You?' he asked gruffly, drawing his mouth to her thigh and kissing her there. Her fingers reached down and tangled in his dark hair.

She arched her back as a thousand and one fantasies whispered through her. What the hell? Wasn't honesty her new policy? 'I never knew sex could feel like this.'

He lifted up to stare at her then, bracing himself on his elbows.

In for a penny, in for a pound…

'Until I met you, I'd never actually, um, you know…finished.'

'You mean, come?'

He was teasing her, but there was something dark in the backs of his eyes, a look that spoke of repressed anger. She nodded her head quickly, dropping her gaze. His body moved then, shifting up hers, until his hard cock was at her sex and the weight of him was on top of her, all rough and muscly. 'Your husband—' he spoke darkly, thickly '—is a useless bastard.'

She closed her eyes, a strange sense of loyalty—ingrained rather than deserved—making her want to argue that. But how could she? Objectively, he was right.

'You deserve to feel this often and always. Your husband should have known better.' And he kissed her then as he took her, in the way she desperately wanted: hard, fast, as though they were the last humans on earth and this act alone could save humanity. All thoughts of James fell from her mind as she revelled only in this.

Genevieve woke early the next morning. Her dreams had been a strange mixture of the past. Meeting James, their wedding, her mother's strokes, and death, the hospital, the island, the storm that had brought her here. She tried to turn over and go back to sleep, but her brain was too active, replaying things she would sooner forget. James's affairs. The headlines. The media's calls to her—even from former students of her alma mater, who'd thought that might give them an 'in' with her. The feeling of shame and embarrassment that the whole world must know her own husband didn't even love her.

Eventually, she gave up on sleep, and paced quietly across the cabin, setting a pot of water on to boil, then making her way to the bookshelf. She'd never been much of a crime fan, but she picked up the John Grisham book and read a few pages, before placing it softly back on the shelf and, out of desperation, reaching for the only other English language book available. Even if it was a recipe book.

She lifted it out, fingers flicking through the recipes, until something fell loose from the pages and dropped to the floor. She bent to pick it up at the same time she became conscious of Nikos moving. Standing and quickly stalking towards her. But it was too late; she'd already seen it. Though it made little sense.

For within the pages of the recipe book, a single photo had been stored. Of what looked like Nikos on his wedding day. Her fingers trembled as she picked it up and stared at it, at the beautiful woman in the photo, with bright blonde hair and huge green eyes, and the kind of smile that could light up a whole room. The woman was looking up at Nikos as though he was the centre of her entire universe.

'Give that to me.' His voice was hard, roughened by something—secrecy, pain, anger?

Genevieve's stomach rolled.

'Are you married?'

He took the photo from her fingers, and she offered no resistance, but she quickly stepped back, putting space between them.

His lips formed a grim line; he looked almost unrecognisable. No, he looked as he had that first night. Unapproachable and barely human.

Her whole body felt knotty and strange. If this man was married, if she'd unwittingly become the other woman, a source of pain to another long-suffering wife, as she'd been, she could never forgive herself.

'No.'

Her heart twisted as her eyes lifted to his.

'But you were?'

He reached for the cookbook next, and now when he opened it, she saw an inscription on the front page, where he neatly placed the photo before closing the book and sliding it back on the shelf. He moved towards the kitchen, to make coffee, but his back was ramrod straight, his shoulders squared. Tension emanated from him, no matter how he tried to hide it.

'Damn it, Nikos, don't you think I deserve to know?'

'My marriage is my private business.'

It stung. It stung more than she could ever possibly admit in that moment, and more than she could or would show him.

James had hurt her so many times, with his cruelty and his coldness, and she'd become an expert at hiding that. As soon as she'd realised he was trying to hurt her, she'd refused to give him the satisfaction. It had been a sick, gruelling game, and she'd hated playing it, but at least it meant she was match fit for this encounter.

'Suit yourself,' she muttered, moving towards the window only because it was the furthest point from Nikos she could get. Her eyes swept across the view without her realising at first how far she could see. But then, it dawned on her. The sky was clear. The sun was shining.

'The storm's broken.' And she wasn't even regretful about it. Anger and wariness were taking over everything else. The sense that she'd put herself on the line, sharing everything with this man, even when she'd signed an agreement to prevent her from doing so, and he'd never once told her about his own marriage. His wife.

'Yes. It stopped raining a little after twelve.'

She turned to face him, and just stared. Because they both knew what this meant. They'd promised she would leave as soon as it was safe to do so. Had anything changed? Maybe she'd thought so, at some point over the last two days. But somehow, finding out about his marriage, that he hadn't told her, made Genevieve doubt the sincerity of everything they'd shared. And she'd been burned by falseness once before.

Burned badly enough to never trust again. At least, that was what she'd thought. But she had let Nikos in. She had started to trust and *like* him. To feel…things that were too complicated. It was a salient reminder of why she needed to avoid relationships altogether. Hurt was the inevitable conclusion of caring.

And yet still, there must have been a part of her that hoped he might want her to stay longer, that might suggest another day and night, because it took a huge effort not to react when he said, 'I'll radio Theo to send a boat for you. It shouldn't take more than an hour.' And with that, coffee made, he stalked past Genevieve and out of the front door, presumably to the helicopter's radio.

Her heart sank to her toes, even as she told herself she was glad. This was definitely for the best.

He placed the call to Theo then deliberately stayed away from the cabin, until he saw the boat on the horizon. He knew that if he went back, he'd tell her about Isabella. About his marriage, his regrets, his guilt, and that she might look at him with those soft blue eyes and try to convince him not to be so hard on himself.

He'd heard it often enough from his father-in-law, who'd insisted Isabella had loved Nikos, had understood his drive and commitment. He'd heard it from Theo, who'd known both Isabella and Nikos for years. He didn't want to hear it from anyone else. Couldn't they understand?

He'd neglected his wife to the point of her death. He had been the cause of her misery and finally her loss. But perhaps there was another reason he didn't want Genevieve to know. Because he didn't want her to look at him and see that he too had been an absolute failure of a husband, in so many of the ways that mattered. True, he'd provided financially, more than Isabella could ever want. And their sex life had been decent, when he was home to be with her. But the time she'd craved, the emotional intimacy, he'd withheld—without intending to—because his focus had been so completely on his fast-growing empire.

By the time he returned to the cabin, Genevieve was dressed in the same clothes she'd been wearing that first day, and her hair had been styled into a neat ponytail. She looked so untouchable and sophisticated, so he craved to drop to his knees and remind her of the wildness that ran through her. To make her scream his name, one last time.

But something had shifted between them, with the discovery of the photograph. Her eyes wouldn't quite hold his and her smile, once glorious and glowing, was now brittle like an aged animal bone.

'Is the boat on the way?'

He nodded towards the window. 'It's almost here.'

He didn't look at her to see the reaction.

'Great. I should set off, then.'

'There is another path to the beach,' he said. 'I'll show you.'

'No need.' That same brittle tone permeated her voice. 'If you just point me in the direction, I'll be fine.'

'I don't want your death on my conscience, remember?'

She flinched at that and he made an effort to soften his tone. But he didn't feel soft. He felt the very opposite of it. Anger with his life, his choices, with everything, twisted inside him.

'I will not argue about this,' he said flatly. 'Are you ready?'

Her skin was pale but she held her ground. 'Of course. I can't wait to leave.' She stalked towards the door but then paused, and looked around, as if she wanted to remember it. When her eyes landed on the bookshelf, they narrowed, and her spine straightened with renewed determination. She spun away from him and stepped out into the winter sunshine.

He told himself he was glad to see the back of her.

The whole walk down to the beach—much more easily accomplished through this path, which was wide enough for a car, and had probably been used to bring supplies for the cabin, when it was being built—she fumed. She couldn't believe this was how it was ending between them.

Why hadn't he told her about his wife? And even then, when she'd found the photo, why hadn't he just given her a rundown of what had happened?

It was James all over again. A man she'd given herself to who'd kept the important pieces of himself locked away.

She ground her teeth to stop from crying, but inside, years of grief and pain were folding around this new rejection and hurt, so she felt physically weakened by everything she'd been through. And this was supposed to have been the start of the new phase of her life. Her pleasure. Her redemption arc.

A single tear rolled down one cheek and she was grateful Nikos was walking to her other side, so she could surreptitiously wipe it away as she turned to look at the stunning view. Now she could see other islands in the distance, and possibly even the mainland. So they had not been so isolated, after all.

The ocean was so deceptively calm now. It was hard to imagine the swell that had tipped her boat clean over, snapping the mast in half.

The ground began to level off, and compressed gravel gave way to sand, down the far end of the cove she'd landed in. If she'd kept walking, she would have eventually found this clearing and been able to walk a much easier path to the cabin, she thought derisively. But the weather had been so bad, she had hardly been able to see five feet in front of herself, much less to the end of the beach.

A small rubber dinghy had been brought right onto the sand. She eyed it simply to avoid looking at Nikos.

'Genevieve,' he said, voice deep. She closed her eyes, stomach clenching.

She turned to face him then, waiting, aware that there was a man standing with the rubber dinghy who was also waiting.

'It's fine,' she said, when it really wasn't. But her marriage to James had taught her to hide her pain and process it later. It was her conditioning, and in that moment she was glad for it.

He stared at her, long and hard.

'This was just sex,' she reminded him, pleased her tone sounded light. 'It was great. Fun. But we always knew I'd leave when I could. So...thanks.'

'Thanks,' he repeated, his brows quirking.

She nodded, knowing she needed to leave, but finding her feet strangely recalcitrant. 'Thanks,' she said again. 'And good luck. With the island and everything.' It made no sense. She was babbling. 'Okay. Bye.'

She turned to walk away from him, plastering a smile on her face as she approached the waiting man, who, to her relief, spoke English, so she was saved the further need of involving Nikos. She gave the name of the town she was staying in, and then went to climb into the dinghy. But Nikos was suddenly there, and her heart went into overdrive with an emotion she'd thought she'd learned to suppress: hope.

He was not there to ask her to stay though. Nor to apologise for keeping something so important secret. He simply held out his hand and offered it to her, to steady her as she stepped into the small rubber boat. She thought about not taking it. She thought about ignoring him. But then, the boat rocked a little and the thought of falling into the ocean at his feet had her weakening, and placing her hand in his, to step onto the craft. Sparks exploded beneath her skin as her body, used now to craving him at the slightest touch, burst with anticipation.

She tried to tamp down on those feelings: she'd never know the pleasure of Nikos's possession again. And though the storm had cleared, as the man began to row the dinghy towards the large speedboat, she felt as though a dark cloud had appeared, right over her.

She didn't look back, and he was glad. But for his part, Nikos stayed on the beach, watching the boat, until it had turned into a tiny white dot on the horizon. And the whole time, he told himself he'd done the right thing. He clung to that, until he reached the cabin and saw small signs of her occupancy everywhere. From the neatly made bed—she must have done that while he called Theo then stayed out of the cabin—to the two cups and two plates that were still drying on the edge of the bench from the night before. She was in the Irish strawberries that were in the middle of the table, a pretty arrangement she'd made with the few he'd stuffed into his pockets during the break in the storm. And she was in the bookshelf—the way the cookbook had been placed differently, in haste, by his own hand, made him realise he hadn't pulled it out to look at it in over a year.

He moved to it now and opened it to the page with the photograph, closing his eyes a moment against the swell of pain that predictably enveloped him.

He pressed a finger to Isabella, guilt and grief mixing to push everything else from his mind. 'I'm so sorry,' he said, but he could no longer be sure if he was talking about Isabella or Genevieve.

For the first time in a long time, he dreamed of Isabella. It was a little like a memory, yet it was different from what had actually happened. She looked different. Her hair was short and her eyes were blue. *Why won't you fight with me? Why won't you shout and yell?* He'd never shouted. Why would he? She'd never made him angry, she'd never made him anything other than frustrated, and even then, he'd simply wanted her to be happy. *You keep so much of yourself locked up. I hate it! Don't you think I deserve the respect of honesty, at least? Don't you think I deserve that, Nikos?*

She'd said that often. She'd worried he was cheating, when, of course, he never would. He had simply worked long hours. But to Isabella, honesty had been the hallmark of a good relationship. It had been everything to her. Which was why she'd told him when she'd slept with another man. Only she'd told him in that way of wanting to hurt him, of hoping it might mean he would show something more to her. That it might snap him out of his obsessive work fog. It hadn't. He'd asked if she wanted a divorce, and she'd sobbed, shaken her head, and fallen into his arms. He'd forgiven her easily. It was Isabella; he'd wanted her to be happy.

She deserves the truth, too. Don't be like her husband. Don't hurt when you can heal.

The words were in his dream, but they might as well have been a sledgehammer against his temple, for how they acted to wake him up. He pushed up in the bed and stared at the wall opposite, his mind spinning over that, his breath coming in rushed fits and spurts.

He hadn't wanted to hurt Genevieve. His own pain was something he relished, something he sought at every opportunity. But Genevieve, he'd wanted to help. To heal, just as Isabella, in his dreams, had said.

The thought of Genevieve being back in Katanos, being hurt that he didn't tell her about Isabella, thinking that it was in some way a reflection of her, rather than it being who *he* was, and he knew he couldn't leave things as they were. He'd had three long years to carry his guilt. There was nothing he could do for Isabella now, except suffer because of how he'd treated her. But at least he could explain to Genevieve. It was the very least he owed her.

CHAPTER EIGHT

KATANOS WAS A small coastal town, and though it was very beautiful, it was not really set up to cater for tourists. In summer, she could imagine it might be busier, but now, in winter, the place was quiet, populated sparsely with locals. She'd had her choice of the two hotels, and had opted for the smaller, because it had sweeping views out over the water. Now, however, she couldn't look towards the windows without thinking of Nikos. In the distance, she was sure she could make out the cliff faces of his island, the dense forest that covered them, and any time she happened to glance in that direction, she felt a pounding of blood in her ears.

An anger and hurt, a twisting inside her to know she'd never see him again. It was what they'd agreed to, and she'd known it all along, but, despite her best efforts, he'd got under her skin.

She'd become used to him.

She'd allowed herself to like him. Maybe, in the very back of her mind, even to want *more* from him. How stupid was she? After everything she'd been through with James, she should have been giving all men a seriously wide berth. Not falling into bed with the first willing partner.

Then again, she'd never regret that.

If nothing else, Nikos had given Genevieve the first orgasms of her life. He'd shown her something vital and true about herself, that she'd always doubted—that she was a sexual woman, after all, capable of enjoying that act, of feeling intense pleasure. The problem hadn't been with her. Maybe it hadn't even been with James, so much as their shared chemistry. They just weren't compatible, on so many levels.

Unlike her and Nikos.

She sucked in a sharp breath as the pain of that lanced through her. It was almost impossible to believe she wouldn't see him again.

All night, she'd been disoriented. She'd drifted off to sleep, only to reach for Nikos, looking for the warmth of his huge body, for the pleasure of his touch, only to wake and remember his rejection, his cold acceptance of her leaving the island.

Finally, at dawn, she'd given up on trying to sleep and had slipped out of bed, pulled on a maxi dress and denim jacket, some dark sunglasses, and set off on a long walk, in the hope that, with exertion, she might be able to finally put him from her mind, once and for all.

Katanos was not a large town, and with only two hotels, and the influence of who he was, it took Nikos no time whatsoever to ascertain at which hotel Genevieve was a guest. It took even less time to establish that she'd left that morning, and not yet returned. Unused to waiting, and not enjoying the way locals stared at him in the foyer, he nonetheless settled himself in one of the chairs so he would see when she returned.

Discomfort was his constant companion, though. He was aware of the way people looked at him. His wealth had made him well known, but his reclusiveness made him famous. He'd dealt with this before. Any time he showed his face in Athens, he was treated like some kind of god.

He didn't once consider leaving though. Having decided to speak to Genevieve, he had no intention of failing. Not again. And so, he waited, eyes trained on the door, ignoring the way every man and his dog stopped and stared, unable to believe that they'd seen The Nikos Konstantinou, with their own eyes.

She walked far longer and further than she'd intended, so it was after lunch by the time Genevieve made her way back to the hotel, thinking of the half-eaten sandwich in her small mini bar with a sudden pang of hunger. She had barely eaten since leaving the island, and now felt a little light-headed.

She was distracted as she approached the hotel, so didn't notice the couple standing at the windows, peering inside. Even if she had, she would have presumed they were simply admiring the mid-century décor, or something equally banal.

But when she pushed in the door and her eyes glanced across the lobby, she saw him immediately. How could she not? On the island, there'd been something fitting about his size, his animalistic wildness. But here—even when dressed in dark trousers and a business shirt—he looked like a wolf in sheep's clothing. Quite literally. She stopped walking, almost unable to believe he was here. Unable to believe that she hadn't conjured him up out of thin air. But then, of their own volition, her feet began to move, carrying her towards him, as he stood and started to stride over the orange carpet.

But as they walked towards one another, something was dinging in the back of her mind. A distant alarm. On the island, he'd been so elemental and raw, as if formed from the clay of the cliffs, the wildness of the ocean. Here, in these clothes, there was something almost familiar about him.

She frowned, dispelling the thought. *Of course* he was familiar. They'd spent days becoming intimately acquainted.

'You really do have a death wish,' he muttered.

She startled, staring up at him. The sensible question of 'what are you doing here?' was usurped by, 'What's that supposed to mean?'

'One minute you are gallivanting around on a tiny sailboat in a wild storm, the next you are walking in the middle of the day, without a hat?'

'It's winter.'

'It is warm and your cheeks are flushed. Are you burned?'

She stared at him as though he'd lost his mind. Could he really not work out why her cheeks were pink?

'I'm fine,' she said through gritted teeth, taking a step back, and wobbling a little—from surprise at seeing him again. His hand swooped out immediately, before she'd even registered her reaction, and curled around her back, drawing her against his body. Which really, really didn't help matters at all.

'You look like you are about to pass out,' he muttered, condemnation in the words.

'I'm not,' she denied, though, in truth, she did feel very weak all of a sudden. 'I'm just hungry. I haven't eaten yet.'

He looked as though he wanted to snap at that, and inwardly, she dared him to. She was fed up with this man—blowing hot, cold, and right back into her life when she'd spent the last thirty hours forcing herself to accept the brutal reality of never seeing him again.

'Then let's go and eat.'

She opened her mouth to tell him, witheringly, that she had a sandwich in her room, but as she mentally conjured an image of that small space, with its double bed in the centre, she clamped her lips together. Better to avoid being in a hotel room with this man right now. She might have been annoyed with him, but there was no way she could deny the effect his proximity was having on her pulse.

'Why are you here?' she asked, instead.

'We need to talk.'

She shook her head. 'Not as far as I'm concerned.'

'I owe you an explanation,' he said, still holding her against his body. 'You were right: I should have told you about her.'

Genevieve's eyes swept shut on a wave of surprise. Nikos was clearly different from James in myriad ways, but this was yet another. James *never* admitted to having made a mistake, and he never apologised for anything. He certainly never explained his actions. Nikos's willingness to do so brought a heady rush of power to her brain, and a strangely heartening sense of security. It threatened to undermine all her sense and reason, her rational thoughts. Because regardless of his good points, he was still a man, still someone she needed to treat with caution. Not because of him, but because of herself, her battered heart, her destroyed abilities to trust.

'Yes, you should have,' she said, making a half-hearted effort to push away from him. But he held her up regardless, his arm like a vice around her waist, offering support that, in fact, she did feel she needed.

'Then let me tell you now.'

'Fine. Tell me.' She tilted her face to his defiantly, but his eyes shifted over her shoulder, towards the door. She turned to look in that direction to see a middle-aged couple walking down the street.

'Can we go to your room?'

'No way, buster. Tell me this isn't some kind of inter-island booty call.'

'It's not,' he muttered.

'Tell me here.'

'No.' He looked around, then let out a rough breath. 'Come with me.'

She shook her head. 'Not until you tell me where we're going.'

'For lunch. You need to eat, and I would prefer not to have this conversation in the middle of a hotel foyer.' His eyes bored into hers, as grey as the stormy ocean, and she lost herself for a moment in their depths. She thought she might actually agree to anything he asked of her, if she wasn't careful.

'Fine. I know a place nearby.'

She could see that he didn't like that. Nikos, she suspected, was very used to calling the shots. But Genevieve had been in a relationship like that, and it had nearly been the death of her. She arched a single brow, silently challenging him to argue, but he didn't.

'Fine. I presume it's close?'

'Just next door.'

'Show me.' He kept his arm around her waist as they walked from the hotel, offering her support. She wasn't sure she needed it now the shock of seeing him had passed, but she didn't say as much to him. Not when it felt so good to be held close to his large, strong body. Besides, what was the harm? They were on the other side of the world from Washington—thousands of miles from her ex-husband's sphere of influence. He would never find out about this.

The waiter who'd led them to a table was little more than a child, fourteen or fifteen at most, and he'd shown more interest in his mobile phone than he had in his guests, so for once, Nikos wasn't recognised when he arrived at a restaurant. Thank *Christos*, because the last thing he needed was for this to go out of order.

The more he'd thought about it, the more he'd realised how much of himself he'd kept locked away from Genevieve. Strangely, though, he'd told her many of the most important details of who he was. Away from the glitz and wealth of his success, he'd told her about his father and his upbringing, his values and his life on the island. To say she didn't know him wouldn't be accurate.

Not entirely.

They were seated at a table in the back of the restaurant, and Nikos chose to face the wall, ostensibly to give Genevieve a better view. It had the added advantage of giving him a greater chance of not being recognised.

As they sat down, he ordered pitta bread and dips, and a bottle of local wine, before turning his attention on Genevieve. She was regarding him with an air of mistrust. He couldn't blame her. Not after what she'd been through with her ex-husband, particularly.

'So?' she prompted, toying with the napkin in the same way she had his sheets, reminding him suddenly of bed, with her, and the way their limbs had tangled as they'd made love, each as frantic as the other to be together, as though their lives depended on it.

He looked away quickly, swallowing, trying to control his body's immediate reaction to that thought.

'You were going to tell me about your wife?' Genevieve said, voice slightly rushed.

He jerked his gaze to hers, nodding. 'Yes. Isabella,' he said, clearing his throat afterwards. He hadn't mentioned her name to anyone besides his father-in-law in a long time.

'You're divorced?' Genevieve prompted.

The waiter appeared then, placing the bottle of wine

down, removing the cork, which he shoved into his apron pocket at the same time he removed his phone.

Nikos poured two glasses then sat back in his chair.

'Well?' Genevieve asked impatiently as she reached for her wine and took a sip.

'I'm not divorced, no.'

All the colour drained from her face. 'Nikos.' His name was a plea. At first, he presumed she'd intuited what he was struggling to say, but then he connected the dots and remembered what her loser ex had put her through, with his affairs.

'I can't—' she whispered, taking another huge sip of wine before standing up and looking around desperately, then stepping away from her seat, as if to leave the restaurant.

He reached out quickly, put a hand on her wrist, holding her where she was. Her eyes flooded with tears and, God help him, the sight of her about to cry brought back so many memories of Isabella, he felt the bottom fall out of his world.

'She's dead,' he said, the words catching in his throat. He hated to acknowledge that reality, let alone admit it to someone else. 'My wife died, Genevieve.'

A single tear slid down her cheek as she stared at him, so close her leg brushed his thigh. 'I—she died?'

He dropped her wrist and stared straight ahead. 'A little over three years ago.'

He heard her move seconds before she took the seat opposite him again. But she reached out and covered his hand with hers, all soft compassion in the lines of her eyes. 'And you moved to the island.'

'I didn't move to the island,' he muttered, figuring he might as well give her the whole, ugly truth now. 'I bought it fully intending that it would kill me.'

She gasped.

'I deserved to die, Genevieve. I deserved to know the

same pain and loneliness she had known. You and my late wife have something in common, you see.'

Genevieve was silent, staring across at him.

'You were both married to bastards.'

She shook her head, instantly rejecting his statement. 'Don't say that.'

'I ruined her life,' he said, the words pouring out of him now, so he barely noticed when the waiter appeared, depositing bread and dips. 'I took someone beautiful, something beautiful, and destroyed it. And she told me. She told me again and again how miserable she was, how unhappy. I could have changed; I just chose not to.'

'I don't understand,' Genevieve said, shaking her head. 'You're not cruel, Nikos. How can you blame yourself for this? What did you do to make her miserable?'

'I married her, knowing she loved me with her dying breath. Knowing I was the sun and moon of her existence. I married her knowing that I would probably never feel that about her. And then I ignored her, focusing instead on my work. All I cared about was financial success. Proving myself to the world, her father, my father, may he rest in peace, to the men who took advantage of my mother, to anyone who'd ever doubted me. Isabella was left married to a man who loved her as an abstract concept, an object, rather than through his actions. She deserved so much better.'

Genevieve closed her eyes and he was glad. He couldn't bear the sympathy he'd seen in their depths. It was everything he'd hidden away from, that he knew he didn't deserve.

'Nikos,' she whispered, when she blinked and looked across at him again. 'You cannot carry this burden.'

He stiffened, pulling his hand away from her. 'I didn't tell you because I wanted sympathy. Nor because I wanted you to make me feel better. In fact, that's the opposite of what I want. I intend to spend the rest of my life deep in this regret.'

'Hiding away on your island?' she asked, sipping her wine, her voice neutral and yet still, somehow, scathing.

'You have a problem with that?'

'Well, what good does it do anyone?'

'I'm not seeking to do anyone anything.'

'You're seeking to punish yourself.'

He stared back at her, unable and unwilling to dispute that.

'To what end?'

'I'm sorry?'

She compressed her lips. 'What does it achieve?'

'It is less about what it achieves, and more about what I deserve.'

'Fine. You say Isabella loved you with her whole heart. Do you think *she* would want this for you?'

He felt a muscle tic in his jaw at the sensible question. It wasn't the first time it had been said to him. His father-in-law had implored him not to throw his life away in Isabella's name. But it was what Nikos deserved.

'Honestly, I think you're doing her a huge injustice.'

He made a sound of surprise. 'I beg your pardon?'

'I was in a deeply unhappy marriage. I was young and naïve when I met James, and I let him sweep me up utterly and completely into all that he promised. But it was a terrible mistake. You know what I did?'

Nikos reached for his own wine then, taking a sip, before he replaced it on the table and took a triangle of bread, spreading it generously with taramasalata then putting it on Genevieve's plate.

'Eat,' he said, not even trying to keep the tone of command from his voice.

She glared at him. 'Do you know what I did?'

He looked pointedly at the bread so with a dramatic huff she lifted it to her mouth and took a bite. And despite the tenor of their conversation, his eyes clung to her mouth, her sweet pink lips, as she chewed and swallowed. He looked away abruptly, barely able to focus on what they'd been discussing.

'I left him,' she said, eventually. 'It was hard, and I had to basically sign my life away to get out, but I did it. Because I realised I couldn't live the rest of my days like that. So unless there was something you were holding over Isabella's head, making it impossible for her to leave, unless you were making promises you had no intention of keeping, then I think you can safely assume she stayed because no matter what, she wanted to. Because she loved you.'

'Yes, she loved me,' he spat. 'But I made her miserable. Loving me ruined her life. *I* should have left *her*.'

'You don't think that would have ruined her life, too?'

'Then I should never have married her.'

'Perhaps, but you did. I can only presume you loved her, as well.'

He stopped then, dropping his gaze to his plate as he thought of Isabella as she'd been then. When they'd both been young and carefree. 'Yes,' he said, simply. 'I loved her, but not how she loved me. Not enough. I did want to make her happy. It just turned out that there were other things I wanted more.'

Genevieve's sympathetic expression had his gut turning. 'Please, don't pity me.'

'Why not?'

'Because I don't want it, least of all from you.'

'I feel like there's an insult in there.'

'I don't deserve it from you.'

'Please don't let me become something else you beat yourself up about,' she said, shaking her head. 'You didn't do anything wrong, Nikos. Even not telling me about Isabella was your prerogative. We were clear about the nature of our relationship from the outset. Just because I opened up to you didn't obligate you to do the same to me.'

'You were upset.'

'Yes, I was, but both things can be true at once.'

He quirked a brow.

'I was upset you hadn't told me about Isabella, but at the same time, it wasn't your fault. It's just…one of those things.'

'When you told me about your husband, and how selfish he was, all I could think was that I could give you something special. Something joyous. When you told me he'd never given you pleasure, I ached to offer that to you.'

'And you did,' she said, before her eyes widened and then blinked away. 'Because of her,' Genevieve said. 'It was never really about me, was it?'

He frowned, trying to work back what he'd said.

'You are so torn apart by what you perceive you failed to give your wife that you thought you could make some sort of amends with me. Right?'

He found it hard to draw breath. He thought about denying it, but why? She was right. He had sought penance, in Genevieve. 'Two birds, one stone.'

She let out a low whistle and then glanced over his shoulder.

'Do you know those people?'

He braced himself even as he turned around, to see a group of women by the counter all looking at him. When he turned their way, one of them snapped a photo. He grimaced as he spun back to Genevieve.

'No.'

'They seem to know you.'

He dipped his head in silent acknowledgement.

Genevieve's voice was a little uneven when she spoke next, her eyes widening. He could practically see the penny dropping. Slowly, but dropping nonetheless. 'But you grew up around here, so they must know you, or your parents…'

'They know of me, not me personally.'

Genevieve sat a little straighter, voice strained. 'Why would they know of you?'

'Because I'm Nikos Konstantinou and in Greece, at least, that makes me famous.'

CHAPTER NINE

'Not just in Greece,' she said, voice shaking, looking around with a sinking feeling of absolute desperation. And though Genevieve rarely drank alcohol, she reached for the wine and finished her glass, panic setting her nerves on edge. 'You're famous everywhere. Nikos. Oh my God. You're Nikos Konstantinou. You are...very famous,' she hissed. 'How could you not tell me this?' But how had she not put two and two together? True, he looked very different from any mental image she had of the man—and even then, it wasn't as though she had a clear image. It was his *name* that was synonymous with success and wealth, his *name* that was spoken in all the business circles.

He grimaced. 'Does it matter?'

'Not on the island, no, and not to me. I don't care *who* you are. But those people were taking photos of you. Of *us*. If they end up on the Internet, or on gossip sites—'

'They will,' he muttered, tone frustrated. 'The flipside of living a reclusive life is that when I show my face anywhere, it makes the news.'

'The news,' she exclaimed, looking around urgently. 'I need to get out of here. At least this doesn't look too bad. I can explain having lunch with you,' she rambled, reaching into her handbag and pulling out some money, placing it on the table between them as she stood. 'No one needs to know— Oh, God. But the lobby. You had your arm around me for minutes. Someone probably saw, and took photos there, right?'

He nodded once.

'Oh Nikos,' she groaned, dropping her head into her hands. 'I have to get out of here,' she repeated, looking around. Nikos was standing then, ignoring the cash she'd left on the table. He reached down and took her hand.

'No,' she said, quickly pulling her own away. 'Don't touch me. That's just going to make this so much worse.'

'Let's go to your hotel.'

This time, she didn't argue. At least that was private, and, God knew, sex was the last thing on her mind in that moment. 'Fine,' she said, through gritted teeth. 'Just don't touch me. I need to think.'

She'd never been so grateful in her life than that she'd suggested a restaurant right next door to her hotel. It was easy to pick their way across the cobblestoned footpath towards the lobby. Now, though, that the shock of seeing Nikos had worn off, she was aware of how many people were looking in their direction. Her stomach was in loops as they rode the elevator side by side, for Genevieve's part being careful not to so much as brush her hand against his.

The doors opened into a blessedly deserted corridor, with the same mid-century décor—brown and orange accent colours and yellow light shades. She slid the key into the door, twisted it then stepped inside, holding it open for Nikos to pass. Until he stepped into the room, she hadn't even noticed how narrow the little entrance way was, but it was physically impossible for him to pass by the door when she was standing there without brushing against her. A fact her body rejoiced in even as her mind was trying to calm things down.

He moved beyond her, thank goodness, into the room, allowing her a moment to take in a breath as she shut the door behind them.

'You're Nikos Konstantinou,' she muttered, crossing her arms over her chest as she raked her gaze across the man in front of her.

Not only was the entrance corridor tiny, but the room seemed it now, too. He looked around, as if at a loss for where to stand, and eventually settled for moving towards the window. His gaze shifted to the view, and she wondered if he was doing what she had so often in the last twenty-four hours: looking for the island.

'It's not relevant.'

She compressed her lips.

'Nikos, this is a disaster.'

He angled his face to hers. 'That might be the first time any woman has ever had that reaction.'

She ignored his arrogant response. 'If you're trying to be funny, quit it. This is not amusing.'

His eyes bored into hers. 'Do I look amused?'

'Nikos, I have...an agreement with my ex-husband. I can't be photographed with you. I can't have those photos hit the Internet.' Her skin felt all cold and clammy, and she must have looked awful because a moment later he was sweeping across the room and drawing her to the bed.

'Sit,' he commanded, and then eased her down when she didn't immediately comply. He crouched in front of her, reminding Genevieve of that first evening in the cabin, when he'd patched up her wounds so tenderly. 'Tell me about this agreement.'

Now that she knew who he was, she could see the easy command with which he approached situations. It had been obvious on the island, but she'd put that down to his superior outdoor skills. Now, she saw it for what it was, as she was in possession of all the facts: this man was a born leader. A dynamic, brilliant, world-leading entrepreneur, who was worth more money than she could even contemplate.

If James saw photographs of her and Nikos together, he'd lose it. He'd renege on their agreement, and use her breach as the cause. He'd stop paying the medical bills. He'd go to the press with the truth of her father's gambling, ruining his reputation. She felt herself trembling and clasped her hands together in an attempt to stop it.

'Start at the beginning,' he suggested.

She couldn't really imagine saying 'no' to Nikos. Not when he was in this mode. 'Our divorce was not amicable,' she said slowly. 'He didn't want me to leave, but I threatened to go to the press if he made me stay. It was…a tense negotiation,' she whispered. 'To put it mildly.'

Nikos's face was blanked of emotion, but she knew him too well. Those eyes of his, stormy like the sea, gave away his distaste.

'Our prenuptial agreement was ironclad. I wasn't entitled to anything, besides a very small stipend. My mother's medical bills are insane, and James is paying them. I didn't have a job—James didn't want me to work, and I agreed, at first, because I thought I was in love, and then, because I was so desperate to keep the peace…'

Nikos nodded, silently encouraging her to continue, but Genevieve was in the past, reliving that godawful day when they'd sat across a long table in his lawyers' offices and worked through the details.

And then, the moment he'd had the lawyers leave, to show just how completely he wanted to ruin her life.

She sucked in a deep breath.

'He agreed to pay off the bills, on two conditions. The

first, that I sign a non-disclosure agreement about our marriage. I'm not supposed to have even told you what I did. And if I'd known who you are, and the circles you have access to,' she said, dropping her head forward. 'You and James probably know several of the same people.'

'I have no intention of betraying a word you've told me.'

Even without him saying that, she knew it to be true. She didn't really want to think about the trust she felt for him—it ran counter to every pledge she'd made herself, post-divorce.

'I just thought—'

'That I was a cave dweller,' he supplied, his hand moving to her thigh and rubbing there.

She squeezed her eyes shut. 'I thought you were as far removed from that whole world as anyone.'

'I am.'

She shook her head. 'You're really not.'

'What was his second requirement?'

'I'm not allowed to date anyone. I'm not allowed to "disgrace" or "humiliate" him by moving on before he's ready for me to. His political career is too important to him, and he wants to manage the optics of this,' she said, shaking her head. Hating that, on some level, she understood that. When she glanced at Nikos, she was reminded of the thunderclouds over his island on the day she'd crashed to the shore.

'I see,' he drawled, sounding as though he wanted to punch something.

'I can't…if he sees those photographs, he's going to stop paying those bills, and I can't afford…'

'I'll pay them.'

She blanched, feeling physically ill at the suggestion. 'Absolutely not.' She jackknifed off the bed, somehow managing to sidestep him in her desperation to get away. 'No way.'

'You know I have the money.'

She whirled around to the windows. 'That's not the point.'

'Are you sure?'

'I will *never* make the mistake of being beholden to another man. I will not owe you that.'

'I will pay it as a gift.'

'No!' she shouted, then spun back to face him. 'No.'

'Isn't it better than having him pay the money?'

'He owes me,' she snapped. 'After what he put me through, I have no conscience issues with him paying for my mother's medical expenses. If I'd had a better lawyer before we got married, I would have been entitled to far more in our prenup. But—' She lifted a hand, to silence whatever he'd been about to say. 'I am keeping a tab of everything he's spent, since our divorce, and I intend to pay him back, when I can afford to.'

Nikos's expression grew more thunderous by the second. 'So you would rather let that low-life pay, than me?'

'This isn't about you,' she said, shaking her head. 'I mean, it is. But your money isn't relevant to me. Besides, there's more at stake.'

He crossed his arms over his broad chest, staring her down.

'Early on in our marriage, before I knew what he was like, I told him about my father. His gambling. James has made it abundantly clear that if I don't abide by the terms of our agreement, he'll go to the press with a tell-all story.'

'Who would care?'

'My father,' she whispered.

'Your father is dead.'

'Yes, but his legacy, his family's legacy…it means something. I loved him, Nikos.' She bit back a sob. 'I can't let this be what he's remembered for.'

Nikos's jaw moved as he ground his teeth together.

'This is a disaster,' she said, shaking her head. 'I should never have let this happen. You should never have come here.'

'I had no way of knowing you had entered into this deal with your ex-husband.'

'No, but...' She tapered off, struck by the fairness of his words. She moved back to the edge of the bed and sat down again, dropping her head into her hands. 'He's going to be so angry.'

'Yes,' Nikos said, moving to stand in front of her. 'He sounds like the kind of prick whose tiny ego would be wounded by this.'

She almost smiled at the description but, in truth, her insides were in too much turmoil.

'Nikos,' she groaned. 'You need to leave. If any of the hotel staff saw you come in here and decide to make a quick buck, it's just going to go from bad to worse. I might be able to explain away the lunch...'

'But not the lobby,' he reminded her grimly.

She closed her eyes, remembering the way they'd seemingly embraced for minutes, bodies melded together in an undeniably intimate fashion.

'No,' she whispered.

'Then you can't cross your fingers and hope he won't find out. He'll see the photos.'

She worried her lower lip between her teeth, anxiety spiralling through her.

'The world will see the photos, and your name will be linked to his. It's impossible to avoid, I'm afraid.'

Her gut rolled, because he was right.

'You have two options, Genevieve.'

'Really? I feel like I have zero options.'

He crouched down in front of her. 'Don't do that.'

She blinked at him.

'Don't give up. You survived being capsized during a brutal storm then hiked for miles in the pouring rain, scaling cliff faces in a dark, unfamiliar forest. Not to mention two nights in a cabin with me. You are a fighter. Don't let that piece of shit make you forget it.'

Her heart twisted at that. His words, and his vision of her. It was so warming, so uplifting, she found herself almost forgetting the nightmare of her situation, simply so she could revel in the way he saw her.

'The cabin with you was really no hardship,' she felt compelled to say.

He squeezed her legs. 'Either you face up to him, and suffer the consequences. On your own, if you insist,' he said, before she could argue. 'Or you let me help you.'

Her heart twisted as she shook her head. 'I can't, Nikos. We barely know each other.'

His expression darkened. 'That is not how I would characterise our relationship.'

'That's because you're a hermit,' she muttered. 'And help me how? I don't want your money.'

'I will *loan* you the money,' he said. 'And you can pay me back whenever you're ready. I cannot see it's any worse than owing him.'

She shook her head. How could she make him understand? She didn't want to owe anyone anything. 'Even if you did, he'd still go to the press about Dad. Don't you get it? He's got me over a barrel. He always did.'

A muscle ticced in his jaw. 'Yes,' he said, after a beat. 'Which is why we'll get engaged.'

If she'd been drinking, she would have spat it out. She spluttered her surprise, coughing because then she lost her breath.

'I am *not* marrying you. Or anyone. Ever. No way.'

'I have no intention of getting married either.'

She blinked at him through the tears her shortness of breath had produced. 'I don't understand.'

'Being engaged is not the same thing as getting married. We'll enter into a fake engagement, so your husband knows that if he messes with you, he gets me, too.'

She stared at him with total shock. It was not, in fact, the worst plan she'd heard. Knowing James, the misogynistic jackass, as she did, only the presence of someone bigger, stronger and richer would ever have a chance in hell of cowering him. While she absolutely despised the reality of that, she knew it to be the case. If she took option A, and confronted him alone, she had no doubt James would let all hell break loose. Including humiliating her father's memory, for the sake of it.

But with Nikos apparently in her life and by her side, she doubted James would be stupid enough to do anything.

'I can't ask you to do that,' she said, shaking her head, even as the possibility spread through her.

'You are not asking. I am suggesting it. If I thought it appropriate, I would insist upon it, but it would be better for both of us if you came to the decision yourself.'

She narrowed her eyes at that, ignoring the feeling she might be getting out of the frying pan and into the fire, moving from one dictatorial man to another. Nikos was *not* like James. He was commanding and in control, but he was also respectful and fair.

Hadn't she thought the same thing about James though, at first? Hadn't she believed him to be all that was good and decent?

What if she was wrong about Nikos? She needed an insurance policy, something to protect her. 'This could be a very bad idea.'

'Why?'

'Honestly? Because I'm scared. I'm scared of letting my guard down, especially with someone like you.'

'That makes sense. You don't want to get hurt again.'

She nodded.

'Will it placate you if I promise that, from this point on, I will do everything in my power to ensure that doesn't happen?'

She pulled her lips to the side. 'I don't know.'

'This does not need to last long. A few weeks of being photographed together, and, at some point, the inevitable confrontation with your ex, and then we can quietly go back to our normal lives. If he approaches you, you can contact me through my business manager, Theo, and I will reappear, to make sure he doesn't step out of line.'

It was tempting. Tempting because the idea of having someone like Nikos to throw in James's face made her battered and bruised heart lift with pleasure.

But this was Nikos's life. 'Surely this is your worst nightmare.'

He stood then, looking down at her with a set jaw. 'I could not help my mother. I didn't help my wife. Let me at least help you.'

Her heart then, already ripped to shreds by everything she'd been through, felt newly damaged by Nikos's admission, and how he viewed himself.

'Oh, Nikos,' she murmured, shaking her head. 'I can't use your guilt like that.'

'I will feel it, no matter what. At least this way, I have an option to make amends. Let me help, Genevieve. I'm begging you.'

***

As the words had formed on his lips, and he'd heard them in the room, he'd wanted to suck them right back in again. A fake engagement? And everything that meant? The idea of reappearing on the Athens society circuit, engaged to someone else? So Isabella would be relegated to a figment of his past. Worse, willingly creating the impression that he'd moved on from Isabella?

But the more he looked at Genevieve, and saw her desperate, stressed features, and thought of the man responsible for that, he knew he had to act as a shield for her. To protect her in a way he desperately wished someone had protected Isabella, or his mother.

More than that, he knew Isabella would want him to do this. She would be the first to counsel him to care for someone in need, to give of himself.

So when Genevieve looked up at him and nodded her agreement, albeit with a look of swirling doubt in her eyes, he knew for certain this was the right choice. Which was not the same thing as looking forward to it. All he wanted was to turn tail and run back to his island, to his solitude and cabin, to the life he'd had before Genevieve. And yet, strangely, he wanted to drag Genevieve back there with him, too.

CHAPTER TEN

THE TRANSITION FROM mountain man to billionaire—albeit rugged, enormous billionaire—happened far quicker than Genevieve wanted. When Nikos returned to her hotel room that evening, he'd shaved his island stubble, had his hair trimmed, and he wore a suit. The kind of suit she'd sworn she couldn't imagine him in, because he'd been so at home in casual clothes. Or nothing at all.

Now, though, he wore something that looked custom-made. Well, it would probably have to be, given his proportions. Proportions that fairly engulfed her as they left the hotel and slipped into his waiting car. A man with dark hair was behind the wheel and he said something obviously deferential when they slid into the back seat—going by the tone, rather than the language, which was Greek.

'I don't know if I'll get used to you like this,' Genevieve said, a little breathily, as the car took off from the hotel.

He slid her a look that showed he felt the same, and, with her stomach in knots, they drove the rest of the way in silence. It wasn't far, though. Perhaps ten minutes later, the car slid through a set of open gates then stopped, and when Genevieve looked out, she saw a gleaming black helicopter with a golden 'K' on the tail.

K for Konstantinou.

She fell into step beside him as he opened a hinged door

and then held out his hand to help her up into the helicopter. She glanced at him a little nervously. 'Do I need to lift you?'

'I've only been in a helicopter once. I didn't enjoy it.'

'Do you want to drive instead?'

She looked at him and shook her head, forcing herself to be brave. This was the second phase of her life; she was no longer going to be shaped by fear. And in part, that was because Nikos was helping her grow beyond that. She couldn't run and hide from James for ever; she had to face her demons, to face him.

'No, it's okay,' she said, with renewed determination, as she put one foot on the ledge then swung herself into the supple leather seat. Nikos shut the door firmly then came around to the front pilot side, opening the door and swinging his frame in, before reaching across and threading her arms through the seat belts. Something she definitely could have done if she'd been a little less preoccupied by the whole helicopter thing.

It was when his eyes hooked to hers though, and his hand went between her legs, to retrieve the buckle, that she gasped audibly, gaze falling on him in a way they both understood. No matter what had happened since, no matter how complex this arrangement had the potential to be, this part was simple. He touched her, and her body reacted. And vice versa. She could see it in the way his hand lingered against her sex, the way his lips tightened, as though he couldn't wait to kiss her there again.

'Nikos,' she murmured, without even knowing what else she wanted to say.

But she didn't need to say anything. He took one look at her then crashed his mouth to hers, all dark and desperate, his hands roaming her body, her legs, her sides, her breasts, coming to catch her face and holding her right where she was, so his mouth could ravage hers until she was a whimpering, desperate mess. 'Please,' she whispered into his mouth, heat forming between her legs, breasts tingling with a desperate need for him to take her.

'Soon,' he promised, pulling his head away so he could see her properly. 'I've never known anyone like you,' he said, but with such darkness that she knew, in a way, he wished he hadn't met her. Because she threatened the life of solitude he'd built. She made him want what he wished to refuse himself.

She lifted a hand, curling her fingers over his cheek. 'It doesn't mean anything,' she said, promising them both that, because they each had their reasons for needing to keep that in mind. 'It's just sex. It doesn't change how you loved your wife, or how much you miss her.'

A muscle jerked in his jaw, and then he was pulling away, sitting in his own seat, fastening his seat belt before running through the pre-flight checks and getting the rotors spinning.

Genevieve's sigh was swallowed by the sound of them lifting off.

To her surprise, he landed the helicopter not on a helipad or at an airport, as she might have predicted, but rather, squarely on the top of an enormous yacht, in the midst of what looked to be—going by the size of the boats—an incredibly prestigious marina. The rotor began to slow down, and Nikos flicked buttons and levers before removing his headset and turning to her, his expression now unreadable. 'Ready, *koukla*?'

Her heart gave a little stammer as she contemplated that. It wasn't too late to change her mind. Could she take another day, and try to work out how to explain this to James?

But just remembering the way Nikos had held her—for support—in the lobby set her cheeks aflame. The chemistry between them had instantly flared to life and she had no doubt it would have been captured on camera by some nosy passer-by.

And for all she was determined never to rely on anyone again, there was a part of her that felt relief. Relief at the thought of being able to share her burdens for a while. She'd been alone so long, even within her marriage: aware, constantly, that everything was crumbling down around her and she had no way of fixing it. She'd missed her mother, her father, her old friends, her prospective career, and the man she'd thought her husband to be. Now here was Nikos, with his big broad shoulders, offering to help her. Offering to make her load lighter to carry, to help her manage her ex-husband's response and mitigate his impact in her life.

She would pay him back whatever money was spent, once she was standing on her own two feet. That was a point of pride, and she was determined to do it. But for the rest? Maybe this fake engagement wouldn't just help her. Maybe she could find a way through Nikos's grief, too, and that awful cloak of guilt he carried with him. She was stepping into the second phase of her life; could she encourage him to do the same?

'Yes,' she said, voice unwaveringly clear. 'I'm ready. Let's do this.'

His eyes showed a hint of approval that warmed her chest from the inside out, and a moment later he was stepping out of the helicopter, ducking to avoid the still slowly spinning rotors. Before he could reach her door, though, three men in dark suits, wearing headsets, approached the helicopter. Two moved to Nikos and one to Genevieve, opening the door and saying in accented English, 'Duck your head down.'

She did, glad she'd opted to secure her hair in a low bun as a cool breeze whipped past the marina at that moment.

The suited man gestured towards a set of wide stairs. Genevieve cast a glance over her shoulder, her eyes meeting Nikos's even when he was deep in conversation with the other men. He cut off what he was saying immediately and strode towards her, all confident and strong, still her Greek island mountain man, beneath the contours of that incredibly fine suit.

The helipad was on the aft upper deck, and beyond it was a spa and some sun loungers. Beyond these, there was a set of sliding glass doors, which the man in the suit activated by swiping a card across them.

'Tight security,' Genevieve murmured, with a glance up at Nikos.

He simply nodded once, at the same time he put his hand in the small of her back and a whole kaleidoscope of butterflies fluttered to life inside her stomach.

Once inside, Genevieve almost lost her footing. The luxury of the yacht was beyond compare. From shiny teak surfaces to white leather furniture, enormous windows showing the twinkling lights of the other boats and, beyond them, the city. They walked through the room with Nikos barely reacting, so she knew that, for him, this was normal, and ordinary. The contrast to his cabin on the island was the strongest she could imagine. There, he'd been stripped back to his most basic elements, surviving through his grit, and ability to pluck fish from the ocean. Here, he had every luxury one could want, including, by the looks of it, an army of staff.

Having cut through the room, they reached the top of a sweeping staircase, carpeted in beige, with gold handrails. His hand stayed on her back as they descended, arriving in yet another palatial living area, this one with a grand piano, and more creamy white leather sofas.

'It's beautiful,' she said, frowning a little, because she had never been up close with this kind of wealth. 'Truly, Nikos.'

She glanced up at him to see a muscle jerking in his jaw, as though he was clenching his teeth.

'I mean, it's no stone cabin in the woods,' she joked. 'But it's pretty nice.'

At that, he flicked her a grin, and her heart twisted in her chest cavity. A man in a suit entered and approached a low-set coffee table in the middle of the room. She realised, belatedly, that a bottle of champagne sat in an ice bucket, with two glasses beside it. There was also a small tray of chocolate-dipped strawberries, which reminded Genevieve that she hadn't eaten much in the last two days. Her stomach gave a dip of hunger.

The man in the suit unfoiled the top of the bottle and then turned to Nikos. 'May I, sir?'

Nikos nodded once, staying where he was, at Genevieve's side, as the staff member uncorked the champagne then poured two perfect glasses, before discreetly leaving again.

'You have a small army working on here,' Genevieve remarked as Nikos moved towards the champagne flutes and picked them up.

'It takes a small army to keep it running.'

The yacht was the size of a hotel, and undoubtedly a significant investment. It made sense that he would maintain it properly, to make sure it didn't lose value through neglect.

'Is it always ready for you, like this?'

'Not with champagne,' he said, handing her a glass. Their fingers brushed and a thousand sparks ignited in her bloodstream, reminding her of the way she'd tried so hard, that first night in his cabin, to avoid touching him. Even then, she'd known there was something cataclysmic about his touch.

'To our engagement,' he said, holding his drink towards hers.

Genevieve's heart lurched fully then, almost leaping out of her body. She blamed a combination of factors. The champagne, his suit, the luxurious yacht, the warm, moody lighting, but, for the briefest hint of a moment, when he said the word 'engagement' a part of her forgot that it was fake. And forgot that she never wanted to get married again, that she never wanted to put her heart and life in the hands of another person.

'Fake engagement,' she heard herself correct, with a tight smile that earned an answering flicker of his lips. Her heart twisted back into place.

'Of course. There is nothing fake about this, however,' he said, reaching into the breast pocket of his suit and removing a black velvet box.

Memories of James's proposal slammed into her, and she hated that he had that power. That he would always have that moment in her life, her brain. The way he'd taken her to a celebrity-studded restaurant to make sure the moment would be captured on camera—a wonderful political opportunity for a man who cared so much about his image. Bitterness washed over her, but it did not last long.

Not when she saw the ring. It was clearly an enormous diamond, but it was the lightest blue in colour, shaped like a raindrop. Her eyes lifted to his. Had he chosen it because of the rain that had fallen on that night? The rain and storm that had brought her to him?

Or, more likely, it had simply been what he could find at short notice. The gem itself was surrounded by a circlet of white diamonds, and when he removed it from the box and slid it onto her trembling finger, she fully appreciated the size of the thing, for it almost came up to her knuckle.

'It's...incredible,' she said, staring down at it with a strange feeling that she might cry.

'Your eyes are this exact colour,' he said, putting paid to any idea she might have held that his choice had been random. Her spine tingled with an electrical current as he put the box down on the table and then clinked his glass to hers once more.

But Genevieve felt completely twisted, caught between the illusion of this and reality. Between what she knew had to be her path in life, and what she was glimpsing might just be her fantasy and deepest desire.

For this to be real.

She clenched her champagne glass tighter, a stern voice roaring to life in her mind, warning her off such foolish delusions. She'd already had her heart badly broken by seeing things that weren't there. Nikos had always been honest with her—if not about his wife, about his unavailability. No matter what she might feel and want, he was not interested in anything longer term. She couldn't get swept up in wanting more. No matter how tempting it was.

'I've never thought of that,' she said, sipping her champagne, simply to do something other than speak—lest the words she was thinking tumble out of her mouth.

'It was almost the first thing I noticed about you.'

But he was making it so hard to remember that this was fake. *It's just sex.* She had to cling to that lifeline, to keep it emblazoned in her mind. *It doesn't mean anything.*

'I thought you should have the ring on tonight, as we will undoubtedly be photographed.'

It should have made her feel better, to know that his gift of the ring was linked to their ruse, after all. He saw a weird sort of salvation in getting Genevieve out from under James's shadow, and so he was going to play his part to perfection.

Because Nikos was driven by a torturous guilt, and in fixing this for Genevieve, he thought he could alleviate some of it. Or at least not feel more of it.

'Do you find that strange?'

'The publicity?'

She nodded once.

'I live on my own, in a cabin on an island. What do you think?'

She smiled at that. What she wouldn't give to go back to that cabin... 'Has it always been like this?'

For a moment, his expression darkened, and his jaw grew tight, so she knew she'd hit a sore point. She reached out, putting a hand on his arm. 'You don't have to answer.'

His eyes lanced hers, his features grim. 'It started with my marriage. I had been very successful, professionally, already, and Isabella...she enjoyed the attention that came from being my wife.' He looked past Genevieve's shoulder. 'She courted the media, arranged interviews with high-end, glossy magazines, attended glamorous events and parties. It had the unintended consequence of turning us into tabloid fodder. As my business successes continued, and my wealth became unusual, the press interest likewise increased.' He shifted his gaze back to her face, his eyes stormy once more. 'And when she died, it was as though a pack of vultures had found a fresh carcass. They were everywhere I went. So I went away.'

Genevieve shook her head softly. 'You don't have to answer this, either,' she said, moving closer because it didn't feel right to have this conversation and not be touching him. 'But how did she...?'

'A car accident.'

Genevieve reached up and cupped his stubbled cheek. 'Why do you blame yourself for that, Nikos? An accident is an accident.'

He closed his eyes briefly and she felt his pain as though it were her own. She moved her hand from his cheek to his back, curving it behind his spine and stroking him slowly.

'She had been upset, on the phone, only an hour before she died. She wanted me to come home, but I was working. I was in the midst of negotiating to buy a string of golf resorts across Europe—I had been negotiating the deal for months, and it had come to the final stages. She was furious.'

Genevieve made a clucking sound of sympathy.

'I grew up so poor, Genevieve. After my father's death...' His throat shifted and he shook his head. 'On the island, you asked about the choices my mother had to make. I didn't realise, at first, what she resorted to, in order for us to survive.'

Genevieve blinked up at him, waiting, feeling the way he was opening up to her, sharing himself.

'Selling herself,' he muttered. 'It was her only option.'

Genevieve closed her eyes on a wave of pity.

'I was too young to help, and she died before I turned my life around.'

Genevieve reached out, putting a hand on his forearm. His jaw only tightened.

'Then all of a sudden, I was making money, hand over fist. More money than you can possibly imagine. I didn't care about things like this.' He gestured to the yacht. 'It was about each deal, each metric of success, that made me feel I'd come so far from the boy I'd been. That made me feel safe, like I would never again know that kind of poverty. I can't explain it properly, but growing up like that, it shaped the man I am today. No matter what amount of wealth I have, I have spent years feeling as though that poverty is right there, a shadow waiting to swallow me back into it.'

'I understand,' Genevieve murmured. 'Once my dad died, we struggled, too. It was such a stark contrast to how it had been before. So when I met James and he love-bombed me with expensive gifts and amazing experiences, I got totally caught up in that lifestyle.'

Their eyes held for a long moment of shared understanding. 'But you walked away.'

'That's what I've been trying to tell you. I walked away, because I couldn't possibly stay. I believe, in my heart of hearts, that Isabella would have divorced you, if she'd been as miserable as you believe.'

'The arguments—'

She sighed. 'Arguments are just a way of communicating.'

He shook his head. 'I never listened.'

'You listened. You just didn't agree.'

'She told me what she needed.'

Genevieve compressed her lips, ignoring, for now, the glaring rejoinder: but what about *your* needs?

'I still don't know why you blame yourself,' she said, quietly. Wishing she could fix this for him, with the click of her fingers.

'She was driving to my office,' Nikos said, after such a long silence Genevieve wasn't sure if he'd return to the subject. 'She missed a stop sign. A car was coming through the intersection and to avoid hitting them, she swerved. Her car wrapped around a pole. Isabella died instantly.'

'Oh, Nikos,' she said, tears forming in her eyes.

'There was no investigation. She'd run a stop sign and died.'

Genevieve nodded, knowing he wasn't finished yet.

'When I got home, much later that night, I saw the whisky bottle, on the kitchen counter, with a single glass beside it. Her lipstick on the rim.' His eyes were boring into Genevieve's and, in their depths, she saw the plea he wouldn't voice. *Forgive me.* 'I drove her to drink, and then she was coming to the office, undoubtedly to finish the argument I'd refused to have. She used to hate that I wouldn't fight back. That I wouldn't lose my temper.' His face contorted into a mask of sheer pain. 'You can have no idea how much that has tormented me. How often I have reflected on my choices, the way I treated her.'

Genevieve's tears fell unashamedly now. She shook her head a little, unsure what to say. 'Nothing good can come from hating yourself. You can't change the past.'

'I'm aware of that. And I'm not looking for anything good. In fact, that is the exact opposite of what I want.'

'You want to be miserable and alone.'

'As she was.'

Genevieve sighed heavily. 'It sounds to me as though she loved you a great deal, Nikos. She stayed with you, when she could have left. You need to stop torturing yourself.'

But she could see by his reaction that he had no intention of doing any such thing. 'Let's go to dinner, *agape*. It's time to let the world see you've moved on from your ex-husband.'

She didn't dare ask if he would ever move on from his late wife. Besides, she had the answer, and it sat in her gut like an oversized lead balloon.

CHAPTER ELEVEN

EVERYTHING ABOUT THE night had been scripted to perfection. From the limousine that had whisked them through the streets of Athens to one of the most prestigious restaurants in the city, with striking views of the Parthenon, and the golden glowing city beyond. Whether by request or happenstance, they had been placed on an intimate table on a private balcony, with overhead heating to keep them toasty warm. It hadn't been necessary. Just the way Nikos's legs had brushed hers had lit a fire in Genevieve's soul that only he could extinguish—later, in his own, sweet time.

Though their table had been private, their entry to the restaurant had taken them past a dozen paparazzi, and once inside, she'd been aware of several patrons surreptitiously lifting their phones to snatch photos of the reclusive Greek billionaire and the woman on his arm. Genevieve realised later that the way she'd held his forearm would have displayed her engagement ring—without her intending to— to perfection, leaving no one in any doubt as to what their relationship was. There was also the possessive way Nikos had kept an arm around her waist as they'd left the restaurant, and Genevieve had leaned into his warm side, not caring about the photographers so much as being near him.

The same car had returned them to the marina, to her surprise, where they'd boarded the yacht using the side-facing gangplank. Once they were onboard, it had been retracted, giving them total privacy and security.

'Is this where you stay, when you come to Athens?' she asked as he brewed a pot of dark coffee and came to sit on the sofa beside her. He poured two small cups of the sticky, dark liquid, then sat back in the seat, casually draping his arm along the back so his fingers brushed her shoulder and she tingled.

She hesitated for only the briefest moment before curling her legs up beside her and leaning close to him, her eyes fanning shut as she listened to the solid beating of his heart.

'No. In fact, I've never stayed here before.'

She opened her eyes and glanced up at him. 'Oh. Why not?'

He held her gaze a long moment, then reached for his coffee, taking a sip. He placed the cup on his knee, before returning his eyes to her face. 'I bought the yacht a month before the accident.' His voice had a hoarse quality to it. 'It was intended as a gift, for Isabella.' He closed his eyes then. 'A guilt gift. I knew she wasn't happy, that she liked nice things. I thought—'

Genevieve nodded. She understood. His guilt and grief, the knowledge that he had made the wrong choices then.

'I was trying to keep the peace.'

'And she didn't like it?'

'I didn't get a chance to give it to her. I kept waiting for the right moment—a day in which we didn't argue, a moment when things felt as they once had. Happy and normal, easy. It never came.'

Genevieve placed her hand on his taut, muscular abdomen, inwardly marvelling at the sheer strength of this man.

'So where do you stay?' she asked, rather than pushing him to continue talking about his wife.

She felt him tighten, his belly drawing inwards as though he'd taken a deep breath. 'Our home.'

Her heart wrenched at the pain loaded into those two simple words.

'You lived in Athens?'

He nodded once.

'What's it like?'

'Exactly as it was, before she died,' he admitted. 'I don't go there often. I can't bear to. But there are certain dates in the year when it feels right to remember.'

'To remember your wife, or remember what you perceive you did to her?'

His eyes showed surprise at her perceptiveness. 'Both,' he admitted, after a beat. 'Mainly the latter. It is hard to allow myself to remember her without also recalling the pain I inflicted, by being so careless.'

Genevieve shook her head. 'You know, I wonder if your memory is a little flawed.'

'It's not, believe me.'

'I believe you're remembering things as you think they were, but our memories are fallible, shaped by our present perceptions. I've known you less than a week, yet I know you're not the kind of person who'd willingly, knowingly hurt another.'

A muscle ticced in his jaw. 'She told me how she felt. I refused to listen.'

'Did she listen to how you felt?' Genevieve said, gently, aware that the last thing she wanted to do was criticise his poor, late wife. 'Did your wants change from when you were dating, to married? Or were you always a workaholic?'

He glanced away, towards the windows.

'Because it sounds to me like she knew what she was

getting, and just wanted you to be different, once you were married. People don't change.'

'No,' he agreed, gruffly. 'They don't.' His hand moved to her hair, gently running over it. She shivered at the small, intimate gesture. 'I wish I had, though.'

'She loved you, Nikos. She stayed with you; she fought to be with you. There was enough in your marriage to make her want to stay. Take it from someone who spent almost every day of her marriage planning to leave. Hold onto that, not the arguments, not the blame. Focus on the good memories—I'm convinced that's what she would have wanted.'

He stood then, abruptly, unsettling her as he strode across the room and placed his coffee cup down on a side table, and stared out of the glass windows that showed a view of the distant city. His back moved with each intake of breath. Then, slowly, he turned to face her, his whole body radiating tension.

'I want to help you, Genevieve. I hate what your ex is doing to you. But for the duration of this fake engagement, let us agree that you will not try to make me feel better about my own failings. I do not need it; I do not want it.'

She ran the gamut of emotions. At first, it was easy to feel hurt. She'd been coldly rejected by James so many times that her first instinct was to see the same treatment in Nikos. Except there was nothing cold in Nikos, nor his words. For all he was holding onto his emotions with ruthless self-control, she could sense his feelings thrumming around the cabin. The desperation with which he clung to his guilt, almost as a protective mechanism to save him from fully feeling grief. He was using his wife's death as an excuse, to stop him from moving on with his life, and to protect himself from ever loving—and losing—another person. She could see it so clearly, all of a sudden, and the fact he had his head in the sand about it infuriated her. So much so she stood, and weaved through the furniture, cutting across to him in a scant few seconds, and trying to rally her thoughts.

Trying to calm down, as well, to remember that, in her marriage, she had become expert at holding her temper and her tongue.

Those skills seemed to have deserted her now.

'I don't appreciate being told how I can act,' she said, the words calm enough, though they vibrated slightly. 'James spent our entire marriage sculpting my behaviour and personality, to be the perfect political wife. I will not endure the same from you.'

'You are not my wife,' he pointed out, and now she fully understood what he was doing. Picking a fight with her to push her away. Denying that there was anything real in this relationship because he couldn't bear to face the alternative: that something was happening between them neither wanted nor had expected. Genevieve was terrified of that, too, but at least she was willing to face it head-on.

'No,' she agreed. 'But I'm a grown woman, intelligent and perceptive and I can say whatever I want,' she said. 'You are being so selfish, to wallow in guilt and consign your wife's memory to that alone. Why not talk about how wonderful she was? How clever and loyal, talk about her goals and aspirations? Why dwell only on your guilt? On what you think you did wrong, and the arguments that led you to have?'

'Don't,' he ground out, eyes boring into hers.

But she lifted a hand to his chest, her fingers splayed wide. 'You can't process her loss. You're just treading water, keeping your head in the sand, because you're afraid to move on.'

His nostrils flared. 'What gives you any right to think you know so much about me? We've just met.'

'Am I wrong?' she demanded, lifting up onto her tiptoes and grabbing his face with both hands, holding him still, their eyes locked.

His lips parted on a rush of breath.

'Am I wrong?' she repeated fiercely.

'It doesn't matter,' he said, dropping his head, so their mouths were almost touching. 'Whether you are right or wrong, it is my life, and how I choose to live it is my business. I would ask you again to keep your opinions on this matter to yourself.'

And before she could answer, he was kissing her with all the pent-up passion, frustration, grief, guilt and need that was flooding his system, kissing her as though it could somehow fix everything. And she was kissing him back in the same way, her mouth mashing to his, their tongues meshing, teeth clashing as they let passion control them completely. His hands, so big, broad and strong, curved around her bottom and pushed her against his erection, so she groaned into his mouth.

'Please,' she moaned, moving her hips as those same hands moved to her dress and ruched it in his palms before lifting it, pushing it over her head, leaving her naked except for a lace thong. He cursed against her skin as he moved his mouth to the curve of her neck and kissed her there, as his hands fumbled between them, unfastening his trousers and freeing his cock from the confines of fabric. A moment later, he was lifting her, wrapping her legs around his waist, and moving one step forward, so her back was bracing against the cold glass window as he drove into her in a single motion that had them both crying out on a wave of sheer, giddy relief.

'Nikos,' she cried, digging her fingernails into his shoulders, gripping him hard and tight, the pleasure of his possession unlike anything she'd ever known, even from this man. It was the heightened tension they'd felt in the lead-up, the argument that had been both hyper-emotional but also a form of foreplay. Or maybe that had been the time they'd spent apart, after having each other completely to themselves, on the island. But when he drove into her, it was like the bursting of a bank, and she was incapable of doing anything to stem the tide. She surrendered to it completely; let it catch her and take her out to sea.

'It is bad enough,' he said, dropping his mouth to her breast and flicking her nipple with his tongue, while his hand moved between her legs and brushed her clit, 'that you make me feel like this when we have sex. That in this moment, I feel as though I am a god on earth, that all is right. It is so much more than I deserve, more than I told myself I would ever have.' He moved his mouth to her other nipple and drew it into his mouth sharply, sucking hard enough that she cried out at the agonising form of pleasure. It was almost too much to bear.

'You do deserve—'

'I deserve nothing,' he said, dragging his mouth back to hers and kissing her with the same fevered passion as the tide of pleasure burst around her again, so she cried out at the orgasm he delivered her so swiftly and easily. 'Only the knowledge that this is temporary allows me to give into this. Just for now, not for ever. When you are gone, everything will once more be as it's meant to be.'

He would have had no way of seeing the tears that sprang to her eyes, because she squeezed them shut and sought his mouth with hers, trying to kiss into him the peace she wished he could feel. How could she make him understand?

James was not rocking in a corner in their apartment in Washington, thinking of all the ways in which he'd failed her. He was not bemoaning the poor choices he'd made during their marriage. Because he was the worst kind of man. But Nikos? Nikos was all good. The evidence of that was in his guilt, his grief, and his inability to forgive himself. She wished she could make him understand.

But if there was one thing she'd learned through and through, in her marriage, it was that one person could not change another. Not unless they truly wished to be different. And she had no reason to suspect, let alone hope, that Nikos ever would. He'd chosen his path and, unless he chose to stray from it, she had to leave him to walk it. Alone, as he so clearly wanted.

It wasn't until much later, in the early hours of the morning, when naked with limbs entwined, wrapped in the luxurious million-thread-count sheets of the master bedroom, with the yacht gently bobbing from side to side, and Nikos asleep beside her, that Genevieve realised she hadn't so much as thought of what *she* wanted. And a fear began to curl through her, wrapping around her organs, making it hard to breathe, as she faced the reality of their situation: she hadn't protected herself. Not enough. She'd told herself she would never fall in love with another man, that she would never want what had the potential to hurt her, and yet, in a few short days, she'd fallen utterly and completely under the spell of someone who was determined to be miserable for the rest of his life.

Talk about a glutton for punishment.

It was barely five in the morning when he became aware of the buzzing of his phone, on the bedside table. He reached for it quickly, not wanting to wake Genevieve, who was fast asleep in the crook of his arm. They'd spent hours making love the night before—hard and fast at first, filled with pent-up emotions and frustrations, and then long and slow, with him delighting in delivering the best kind of torture, driving her wild and then bringing her back from the precipice, showing her what her body was capable of, how prolonging release could enhance pleasure exponentially. And then, as proof of how far she'd come since they'd first met, he'd watched as she'd pleasured herself, her cheeks flushed as she'd tipped over the edge, crying his name and reaching for him, even then, wanting—needing—more. Despite that, the buzzing of the phone had woken him, and made him aware that he was already hard and aching for her anew.

He would have silenced the call and turned off his phone, except for the fact that, at the last moment, he saw the call was coming in from Washington, and he had a premonition that made the hairs on the back of his neck stand on end.

He eased himself from the bed, walked as swiftly from the room as he could and then swiped the phone to answer.

'Konstantinou.'

Silence met his pronouncement.

'Yes?' he barked down the line, aware who it was likely to be.

'Senator James Wilson,' came the voice he already hated from the man he loathed and despised. 'We need to talk.'

'Do we?' Nikos drawled, moving deeper into the yacht, further from the bedroom suite. 'About what?'

'You, and my wife.'

'Ex-wife. And I think you mean my fiancée.'

Silence. But a silence that was loaded with animosity; Nikos felt it and understood it. But what grace could he give this man? He'd had Genevieve in his life, his bed, her loyalty and love in his hands to treasure, and he'd treated her like a piece of dirt. For all Nikos had made mistakes in his marriage, it had never been intentional, nor cruel. The effects had been the same—he'd hurt his wife—but that had never been his aim. Far from it.

'Is she there?'

The question was flooded with angry indignation. There was no way Nikos was going to pass the phone to Genevieve. 'She's sleeping.'

A hiss—clear fury. 'You don't know what you're getting into.'

'Do I seem like someone who makes poor decisions?'

'Have Genevieve call me.'

'For what purpose? You're divorced. Whatever you once shared is over.'

'What's the matter, Konstantinou? You jealous?'

He laughed then. A low, soft rumble. 'Of a man who does not even know how to please a woman? Oh, yes. My anxiety is off the charts.'

James cursed. 'Get her to call me.'

'I'll do no such thing. Not when it's clear you can't be trusted to play nice.'

'Oh, Genevieve knows I don't play nice—and she knows what's going to happen now. It's her own fault. And yours too, I suppose.'

'What's going to happen now is that you're going to take yourself off and have a long, clear think about whether or not you want me as an enemy,' Nikos said, letting the words fall. 'You know who I am.'

Silence, but there was no need for an answer, anyway. Not when the other man would have to have been living under a rock not to know who Nikos was. 'You can imagine who my contacts are. With a handful of phone calls, I can make sure your political donations dry up—permanently. And I will delight in doing so, believe me.'

'You—can't—'

'Can't I? Would you like to test me?'

A spluttering sound. 'Fuck you,' he shouted.

'You've said that already, Senator. Surely a man of your intelligence can think of something more creative.'

'She's not worth this,' he threw down the phone line. 'She's a cold, frigid—'

'Setting aside the fact I have much evidence to the contrary, if you ever say anything like that about my fiancée again, if you so much as utter her name in anything but the most complimentary of ways, my threat will come to fruition. This is not an idle promise, Senator. I will ruin you in every way you hold dear if you ever make a single move to hurt her. If you threaten or bully her, if you breathe a single word of anything she told you in confidence, when she was trying to make your pathetic marriage work, I will destroy you. If you ever attempt to contact her, if you see her walking on the street and don't immediately turn and go the other way, you will wish, with every fibre of your being, to be someone else entirely. Do I make myself clear?'

The silence that greeted him made the hairs on the back of his neck stand to attention once more.

'I said, do I make myself clear?'

'Yes.' It was belligerent but also, Nikos was certain, terrified.

'Good boy,' he drawled condescendingly. 'Now get back to your hollow little life, screwing shallow, meaningless women, and think about the fact you had someone very special in your life, for a time, and you ruined it. And then, burn in hell.'

He disconnected the call and threw his phone against the cushions of the sofa, his chest puffing up with outrage at even the sound of the man's voice. And then, in the reflection of the windows, he saw a movement that had him turning around, heart ramming hard against his ribs.

CHAPTER TWELVE

SHE UNDERSTOOD THAT he was talking about himself. That the anger he felt towards himself for having not been able to appreciate Isabella was at the root of his defence, but, at the same time, just hearing him say those things to her ex-husband—for clearly that was who was on the other end of the line—set a fire in her soul. Hearing the way he threatened James, promising to ruin him financially and politically, knowing that was probably the most likely to get through to him, had underscored something very simple to Genevieve. For all she had wanted to stand on her own two feet and walk away from James, he was just the kind of misogynistic horror of a man who would only be affected by this sort of thing.

But it wasn't even about James, and it wasn't about Isabella.

The magic of Nikos's words, his passion, his respect, flooded her veins so she was running across the room and hurling herself at him, fighting floods of tears as she practically scrambled up his body and into his arms, so she could kiss him and hold him and thank him as she wrapped her arms around his neck.

Surprise held him still a moment, but then their predictable, reliable passion flared to life and he was kissing her back, holding her now against him, feet off the ground as he moved them to the sofa and laid her down, before bringing his body weight over hers and nudging her thighs apart with his knee.

'I meant every word, Genevieve,' he said, pushing up to stare into her eyes. 'Even when this is over, and you are back in the States, if he so much as calls you, I expect to know about it. If he ever gives you even a hint of trouble—'

'He won't,' she said, and her smile was enormous because, for the first time in a long time, she truly felt that everything would be okay. Her divorce hadn't given her that freedom. James had made sure of it. He'd found a way to extend his control and manipulation, his cold hurtfulness, well after their legal union had been dissolved. She'd left America, and come to Greece, but his shadow had been over her the whole time.

Until now.

'I can never thank you enough.'

He shook his head, his throat shifting, and she held her breath, waiting for him to say whatever he was obviously thinking, but instead, he offered a smile that didn't reach his eyes. 'Thank me by shouting my name as loud as you can, *koukla*. Shout it so loud he can hear it, all the way in Washington.' And he dragged his mouth down her body, to her sex, and proceeded to make it impossible for her to do anything but what he'd suggested.

Over and over his name tripped from her tongue, a poem she was writing and feeling in her heart, both a joy and a burden. He drove her wild with his mouth, and then his hands, and then his mouth, before finally arranging her on the sofa so he could claim her from behind, his whole body intimately connected with hers as his hands came and clutched her breasts, before one roamed to her sex and made her halfway forget her own damned name. Even as he gave her such pleasure, over and over, she heard the words he'd spoken, and felt them like a blade in her side: *Even when this is over.*

And it just served to clarify for Genevieve the truth of her feelings. The problem wasn't that she'd trusted someone with her heart, it was that she'd trusted the wrong someone. She'd given herself to a man who'd never deserved her. But Nikos was so different. He was her perfect other half, in every way, but it was almost impossible to imagine him recognising that, far less accepting it.

Though she knew she loved him, Genevieve was too proud to stay, if she was truly not wanted. Or perhaps it was that she was seeking breadcrumbs of affection, in the form of his trying to prolong this. Either way, when he said, later that afternoon, that they had reservations at another Athens hotspot, she found herself hesitating before saying, 'Nikos, you've done so much for me. But he knows now, and I'm pretty sure he won't be bothering me again. If you wanted… if you want to go back to the island, I won't keep you here.'

His expression had barely shifted, except for a slight darkening in those stunning grey eyes of his. 'He understands his situation, it's true,' he murmured. 'But wouldn't you like to have the fun of making him suffer now?' he asked, lifting a single brow. 'Every photo of us—of you, living your best life, with me—will be like the twisting of a knife. Don't you think you deserve that?'

Genevieve's agreement had nothing to do with James, though. Whatever Nikos might think, for Genevieve, it was simply a chance to spend more time with Nikos. To lose herself to him, in the hope—albeit a very, very small one—that the more they were together, the more he would see that he deserved this second chance. That the grief he was stubbornly clinging to, the guilt he insisted he must wallow in, were an insult to his late wife, a cruelty to himself, and a deprivation to Genevieve.

'Yes,' she said, simply, and his smile was her reward.

'Then get dressed,' he said, pulling her against his body. 'And let me have the pleasure of watching you.'

Her heart rushed against her ribcage. 'It will be the same dress I wore last night,' she said, with a lift of one shoulder.

'Believe me, I barely notice the clothes you have on—most of my energy is spent imagining how quickly I can remove them.'

Heat flushed her cheeks as he led her to the shared master bedroom, and, rather than watching her get ready, he chose to help her undress, kiss her all over, before slowly, tantalisingly sliding the red slip in place. But as he did so, he removed her lace thong, his eyes clashing with hers.

'For me,' he said, and the heart that was already rushing began to gallop so hard it hurt.

After dinner, when they were back in the limousine, but not yet moving, he pulled her into his lap so her legs straddled him and undid his trousers, eyes hooked to hers as he freed his arousal and said, 'Fuck me, Genevieve.'

'Oh, God,' she groaned, doing exactly that, easing herself over his length and crying out as he filled her so completely and his hands massaged her bottom. His mouth sought her breasts, which were at his mouth's height, but, impatient to taste her, he pulled at the dress she wore, tearing it easily with his enormous hands, so she made a half-laughing sound of surprise.

'I suppose I'll have to go to dinner naked from now on.'

He grinned as he took one of her nipples in his mouth. 'Sounds fine by me.'

* * *

But the next morning, after breakfast, she became aware of the yacht's staff moving to and from the gangplank, and when she went to look, with natural curiosity, she saw they were carrying bags and bags, emblazoned with famous fashion labels, as well as hat boxes and shoe boxes. She whirled around to face him, shaking her head. 'Nikos…'

'I felt bad about the dress,' he said, pulling her sharply against his body, so she could tell instantly that he didn't feel a single bit bad about anything that had happened in the car the night before.

'How bad?' she murmured, eyes raking his.

'Awful.' His grin told a totally different story.

'Care to make it up to me?'

Hours later, naked in his bed, Genevieve pushed up onto her elbow, a feeling growing inside her that she wanted to share, but was almost too nervous to voice. And yet, they'd been so intimate, and he'd taught her so much. Surely there was nothing she couldn't ask of him.

'What is it?' he asked, reaching out and indolently flicking one of her nipples, so she bit her lower lip between her teeth. His eyes fell to the gesture, his eyes darkening as he moved swiftly to claim her mouth with his own, and to drag her lower lip between his teeth.

But she was shy suddenly, too shy to say the words. Instead, she pulled away and moved her body over his, kissing his chest and then moving lower, to his hips, her eyes flicking to his frequently, to see how he was reacting. Anxiety spread through her, until she couldn't bear it. He'd kissed her most intimate places so often—several times a day, when they'd been together—he'd driven her wild with his mouth, and she'd yet to do the same to him.

And she knew why.

James's voice had been in her mind. His criticism of her, his derision when she'd tried, had made her too shy to try again. *You're like a cold fish. This is boring.*

But with Nikos, she wanted, desperately, to take him in her mouth. To feel him there and to see him lose control the way she so often did because of his ministrations.

She reached his hip bone and pressed kisses along the ridge there, her eyes flicking to his again, to see dark colour spreading across his cheeks, his expression so still, and watchful.

'*Koukla,*' he said, with a small shift of his head. She bit into her lip, and his hand moved, cupping her cheek then swiping across her lip, before his thumb pushed between her lips, his eyes following the gesture. 'You don't have to do this.'

'I know.' She moved her mouth away, towards the tip of his cock. 'I want to. It's just… I don't think… I don't know what to do.'

She saw the comprehension in his eyes, the anger that swiftly followed, but he blanked it again, almost immediately. Neither of them wanted James to darken this moment. To be any kind of factor in what they shared.

'Do whatever you want. I'm yours, Genevieve. For right now, here, I'm all completely yours.'

And she took him in her mouth with a heart that was both full and broken. Full because what they shared defied so many hopes she'd held, but also broken, by his subtle, frequent reminders that this was temporary, when she wanted, more than anything, for it to be for keeps.

Everything he'd ever thought he knew about the world split and exploded as she moved her mouth down his length, struggling at first with the size of him and then growing in confidence—and pleasure—at the way it felt to take him like this. She moved her hips with wanton need as she lifted and dropped her head until his whole body was flooded with electricity and heat was flooding his balls, threatening to burst from him.

'Stop,' he said, barely able to speak, the word rasped from his body.

The hurt in her eyes made him want to reach right across the ocean and slam his fist into her vile ex's face. That he could have undermined her sexual confidence so completely was abhorrent. Far from being frigid, Genevieve was sensual and warm, and the more they were together, the more her confidence grew, so he saw now a woman who, not only sought her pleasure, but delighted in it—in taking and giving. In the back of his mind, he knew that was because of him, and that he would always be glad to have given that to her.

'Is it—wrong?'

'*Christo*, no, but I am about to come, and I do not want to do so in your mouth.'

She frowned. 'You don't?'

He grabbed her under the arms and pulled her up his body, shaking his head when their eyes were level. 'For your sake, believe me. For your sake.'

'But I—'

He shook his head once. He didn't want to overwhelm her, not when she was still learning so much about what she liked.

'Let me feel you like this,' he insisted as he held her hips and thrust into her, already spilling a little of his seed, because of how close he'd been. 'You are heaven on earth, do you know that?'

She dropped her head and kissed him, and said something he didn't quite catch into his mouth, something whispered and low, that he didn't ask her to repeat. Perhaps even then, on some level, he'd known things were getting out of hand. But it felt too incredibly good to stop...

She was used to the thundering of her heart, after they'd made love. Used to the way it felt as though it were going to launch clear out of her chest, because no way could her ribs stand up to that kind of punishment. But this time, as she lay in his arms, breath rushing from her lungs, body sated—for now—she knew that her heart was racing for another reason.

I love you so much.

The words had just dropped out of her, whispered from her straight into his mouth, pressed against him without her intention—and without his reaction. The words had been pulled right from the centre of her being, sucked out of her by the truth of her feelings, and they sat in her throat again now, begging to be spoken. To be spoken again and again, shouted, until he understood that this was not just sex, and it wasn't going anywhere.

'Nikos,' she murmured, glancing up at him, to see his face in profile set in firm lines, a slight frown on his face.

As if he'd heard and was processing? Rejecting? Or was he thinking about something else?

If he had been anything like James, she would have stayed quiet. Fear had been her constant companion, and she'd shrunk herself down so completely, hidden who she was from the man who seemed to live to reject her.

But Nikos was not James, and, if nothing else, he deserved to know that she loved him. If he chose to walk away from her, and go back to his isolated island, his life of self-imposed misery, then he would. But at least he'd be going with the knowledge that she loved him—and one day, he might even accept that he was worthy of that love.

He angled his face so their gazes met, and her heart stammered harder. 'I meant what I said,' she murmured, reaching up to cup his cheek.

'And what exactly did you say?'

She swallowed, to see if the words would dislodge, but they refused, so she surrendered to their agency. 'I love you, so much.'

She felt his response. The tightening of his body, the tensing of his muscles. Even before he shook his head, she knew the rejection was coming. 'Genevieve—' His voice sounded disbelieving. 'Why would you say that?'

She scrambled to sitting, pulling the sheet with her, to cover her breasts. 'Because I want you to know it,' she said honestly. 'I'm not asking you to love me back. I'm not asking you to say that. But I need you to know that somewhere along the way, I fell in love with you, and I have absolutely no regrets about that. Because you are good and kind, strong and noble, generous and thoughtful. I love everything about you, Nikos, except for how hard you are on yourself, but even that is a mark of your goodness.'

'Don't,' he groaned, pushing out of the bed and striding across the room, before spinning around to face her. 'Don't say these things. What did I ask of you, when we began this fake engagement?'

She flinched a little at his reckless use of the word 'fake'. As if to echo her rejection of the concept, she began to twirl her engagement ring.

'Am I not allowed to be honest with you?'

He dropped his head forward, staring at the floor. 'Tell me you love me, if you absolutely must, but don't ever imply that I deserve it.' His eyes lifted to hers. 'Don't you understand? The more you offer, the more guilt I feel. After what I did to her, I could *never* deserve you.'

Tears welled in her eyes. 'She stayed with you,' Genevieve said. 'You didn't force her to do that. You didn't make her remain married. She *wanted* your marriage, and she wanted you. You need to accept that.'

'I will not talk about my marriage, or my wife, with you right now.'

She flinched again. 'Because you know I'll make you see the truth, and you can't handle it. You can't handle the fact that the more time you spend with me, the less you hate yourself. Give me another week and you'll never want to go back to the island,' she challenged, eyes meeting his. 'A week after that and you'll be ready to admit that you love me, too.'

He took a step back, a stagger, his face blanching. 'You don't know what you're talking about.'

'I think I do.'

'We've just met.'

'So?'

'So how can you possibly think we are in love, after less than a week?'

'Do you doubt that I love you?'

'I think you're running from trauma, and you ran into my arms. I think I gave you pleasure for the first time in your life, and freedom from your husband. Those are two very seductive, powerful gifts. But gratitude is not tantamount to love. Great sex is not love.'

'You think I don't know that?' She pushed out of the bed then, staring at him with a heart that was weeping. 'You think I'm saying I love you because you can basically give me an orgasm just by looking at me?'

'Perhaps.'

She swore softly, under her breath. She hadn't expected him to return her declaration, but she'd at least expected him to accept it.

'You're wrong,' she said.

'Or maybe it's because you spent three years trying to love a complete jackass that your heart just desperately wants to be put to use now.'

She shook her head. 'Stop.'

His eyes flashed with wildness, and she recognised the cause of it. The panic he was feeling, because she was getting under his skin. Not just with her love, but with the things she kept saying about his marriage, showing him that his wife had loved him, regardless of his long hours and her frustrations there.

'You don't have to tell me you love me. You don't have to give me *anything* you don't want to. But at least let me speak what I feel. I spent my entire marriage squashing myself into a ball, metaphorically speaking, hiding how I felt and what I wanted, pretending to be something I never was. So let me always be honest with you. I love you. From the bottom of my heart, with every single part of me, I absolutely, unfailingly love and adore you. I would spend the rest of my life worshipping you, if you'd let me.' A tear slid down her cheek. 'But I also spent my marriage trying to make a man love me, who never had any intention of doing so. I will not make that mistake again. Either love me freely, or let me go.'

CHAPTER THIRTEEN

'Go,' he said, closing his eyes so he didn't have to see her reaction. Closing his eyes against the bitter, shredding feeling of regret and grief. Of knowing that, once again, he'd taken something beautiful and destroyed it. He doubted he would ever get over the sense of regret.

Cowardice was not his natural bent, however, so Nikos forced himself to open his eyes and look at her, to see the anguish in her face. He looked at her in the way he'd never been brave or aware enough to do with Isabella. Her complaints had fallen on deaf ears. But with Genevieve, her every word, tortured by the fact he would never return her feelings, though whispered, landed with a thud.

'Okay,' she said, nodding slowly, turning her back on him then moving to the wardrobe. He stood his ground, even when his body was desperately trying to propel him forwards. She returned a moment later, wearing the shorts and shirt she'd had on when she'd washed ashore on his island. His gut rolled. 'I don't know how,' she said, lifting one shoulder, looking every bit as vulnerable as she'd been that night. 'I don't have a phone. I can't call a car. Would you—?'

'I'll arrange it, of course,' he said, rocks in his gut rolling together to form a dusty sediment that flooded his whole body. 'Where would you like to go to?'

'I still have the room in Katanos. Can you send me there?'

Can you send me there?

Every single shred of good he'd done her was undermined by the vulnerability in that question. He moved then, crossing the room and putting his hands on her hips. 'Genevieve,' he said, but she shook her head and stepped away from him.

'Just leave it,' she asked breathily. 'I don't think we need to say anything more. We both know how we feel.'

But she didn't know how he felt. She couldn't. Not when those feelings were all so jumbled and tangled, a horrible knotty nightmare of what he wanted and needed, and needed to forbid himself from taking. The pledge he'd made himself on his wife's death he considered to be unbreakable.

Nothing had changed that; nothing ever could.

'Very well. I'll take you back to Katanos.'

'No,' she said, quickly shaking her head again. 'Not you. I think it's better if we say goodbye here. I can take the train. I just need someone to drive me to the station.'

'I'll—'

'No, not you,' she stressed. 'Please, Nikos. Just let me go, okay?'

What could he say to that? She'd given him two options. Love her, or let her go. He'd chosen the latter with barely a moment's hesitation. And he would have a lifetime to live with the consequences.

The trip to the other side of Greece took almost six hours, and from there, she had to take a cab to her hotel, which was another twenty minutes. By the time she arrived, she was exhausted, having not slept more than a few snatched hours on the train over, and even those had been tormented by dreams of Nikos, by her desire for him, her aching for him, her grief for him. Because he deserved so much more, but he would probably never see that.

She would have spent a lifetime trying to make him see it, if he'd let her.

If he'd fought to keep her in his life, in any capacity, she would have stayed. But he was too good and decent for that, too traumatised by his belief that his marriage had, for his wife, been purely bad.

She stared out on Katanos as the taxi approached her hotel, but already, she was mentally pulling herself away from Greece, and the life she'd suddenly built here. It wasn't real. It couldn't be, when the feelings were so one-sided. Besides, she had a life in America she needed to return to. The business of finding a job and finally putting her college education to good use, and, most importantly, the getting on with her own life.

In a way, she supposed she should have been grateful. She'd arrived in Greece feeling emotionally bruised and battered by James, but now she barely thought of the man she'd once been married to. All of her heartache, all of her heart, belonged to Nikos Konstantinou, and always would.

It was the sight of her engagement ring on the edge of the basin that finally got through to him. She'd left, he'd watched her go, but it was seeing that ring—which, for him, had been so meaningfully chosen—discarded as a totem of their time together that really hammered it home to him that she was gone, and because of him.

That he'd hurt her.

Failed her.

That in some ways, he was no better than her husband.

Or wouldn't be, if he didn't at least send her away with more than a panic-driven insistence that she leave.

Not five minutes later, the rotors of the helicopter were turning and he was lifting up, over Athens, his mind already focused on Katanos, and the beautiful woman he knew he'd find there.

Genevieve had been sleeping most of the day. Grief, exhaustion and depression had all caught up with her, and her brain had wrapped her in a protective mechanism, all but sedating her into a deep slumber, so she felt as though she were miles beneath the surface of the earth. So at first, she didn't hear the banging on the door. But then, like a mallet or a ratchet, it burst through her dreams, meaning she woke up disorientated and alert, her pulse thrumming with alarm as her body wondered what was wrong.

'Genevieve?'

Even through the door and across the carpeted floor, she knew instantly that it was Nikos. From the sound of his voice, but also from the ache in her heart. She moved quickly, pushing back the sheet and crossing the small hotel room, with absolutely no idea what time it was. The sun was up, but, as far as she knew, it could have been anywhere from midday to sundown.

She wrenched open the door and stared at him, her insides twisting with love and familiarity, with the recognition that she was looking back at her other half.

'Don't go,' he said, drawing her into his arms and holding her hard against him. Hope flared in her chest, soaring like an eagle, out of control and brilliant. 'Don't go like this,' he said, taking that hope and strangling it into nothing.

'What does that mean?' she asked, pushing back to look up into his face. The expression there almost wrenched her apart.

'I can't let you go,' he ground out. 'I thought I could,

but I need to know that, no matter where you are, you're okay. I need to know you're safe, protected. I need that like I need air.'

Her stomach dropped to her toes. 'What are you saying?'

'I'm saying I can't be with you,' he said, cupping her cheeks and staring down at her with every bit of intensity he possessed. 'You know me better than I know myself; you know why I feel as I do.'

She swept her eyes closed against the assault of his desperation. 'You love me,' she whispered, knowing it was true.

'I can't be with you,' he said, simply.

'That's not an answer.'

'Isn't it?'

Her eyes blinked open to face his and she saw the resolution there, the determination to stick to this viewpoint, no matter how painful it was to both.

'But the thought of you losing your way again, of you ending up with someone like James, someone worse, it would kill me, Genevieve. No matter where you are, you are a part of me. I have to know you're okay.'

'I'll be okay,' she lied, because in that moment she felt as though she never would be again.

'Let me take care of you,' he said, and something tightened inside her, like screws against her ribs.

'Take care of me how?' To her own ears, the coldness was obvious in her tone, but he clearly didn't hear it—or heed it.

'Let me set you up in your own place, take away any financial worries. Let me care for you. And occasionally, God, Genevieve, God help me for my weakness, let me see you and remember that when I'm with you, I genuinely feel as though I am what you say. Let me see myself as you do, from time to time.'

'From time to time,' she murmured, imagining the world

he described with a sense of overwhelming barrenness. The idea of living in that awful state of purgatory, just as he was on the island, one foot between both their worlds.

'I cannot give you what you want, but I can give you so much, if you'll let me.'

She took a step backwards, to put space between them, but he followed, and closed the door behind them, so she startled at the sound of it slamming.

'Please,' he said, and she knew it wasn't a word he used often. It dug right into her heart. She blinked away, turning to look at the view, towards the island, imagining the future she really wanted. Side by side with him, no matter where, no matter how they lived.

'I can't accept that,' she said, swallowing past a lump in her throat. 'It's not enough.'

'It's more than you have now.'

She turned back to him, her lips quivering in an attempt at a weak smile. 'Is it? I have my independence, Nikos, and I fought so hard for it. I would *never* sacrifice that again, except for the deepest kind of mutual love. How have you so fundamentally misunderstood me?'

'Genevieve—'

'No.' She shook her head, holding up a hand. 'There are only two things I want in this world, and I had my whole marriage to recognise that. I deserve to be loved. Wholly, fully, without restraint. Messy, consuming, warts-and-all love.' She tilted her chin, daring him with her defiant expression to contradict her. 'And I deserve to be with someone who knows that I have what it takes to stand on my own two feet.' The last one really hurt. 'With James, I gave up my independence because he said he wanted to look after me, and I ended up with no agency, and no options. If you think I would ever make that mistake again, even with someone

I love as much as I do you, then you really don't get what I've been through.'

He stared at her with obvious frustration and torment. 'Genevieve, *agape*...'

'Don't. Don't stand there and even suggest that you love me,' she begged. 'I thought you did. I really did. But love isn't this. Love isn't measured and it's not conditional, it's not something you can box away. It's not giving someone financial comfort but never giving them yourself.' He flinched, and she knew why, because she truly *understood* him. Perhaps Isabella had said something similar in one of their arguments? Frustration sliced through her. 'If that's all you came to say, you should go. It's just making an impossible situation even worse, to see you again.'

'You know why I can't offer more.'

'Because you were married, and it was unhappy.'

'Because I made her miserable,' he growled.

'Yes.' She nodded once. 'I know that's what you think. But she stayed with you. She loved you. That was *her* choice—at least you let her make it. You're taking mine away from me.'

'I am making the right choice for both of us.'

'How can you possibly say that?' she shouted. 'How does any part of this feel right?'

'It's how it has to be.'

And it was so obvious from the finality in his tone that he would not change his mind, no matter what she said, that a single tear rolled down her cheek, splashing on her arm.

He dragged her towards him, pulling her close, his hands on her back, as though he was trying to speak with his body, to make her understand something he didn't know how to say. She sobbed, though, and it seemed to pull him out of whatever he was thinking. He stepped backwards, staring at her with an expression that was so much more familiar. The mountain man, rugged, determined and completely in control.

'Would you at least keep this?' he asked, reaching into his pocket and removing the engagement ring. She wrapped her arms around her torso, staring at the stunning teardrop diamond.

'I bought it for you. Your eyes, and the rain that fell the day we met. I saw it and immediately knew it had to be yours. Please keep it—unless you ever need to sell it, then do, of course. Let me at least have that small peace of mind, of knowing that, in some way, I have given you something of value.'

She put her hand out and took the ring; he left before she could tell him he'd given her so much more of value than a diamond. He'd given her the determination and sense of self-worth that had enabled her to reject him, the certainty that she could do more and be more than she'd ever really thought. *That* was what he'd given her, and *that* was what she'd carry, close to her heart.

Nonetheless, as he closed the door behind himself and left her for the last time, she slipped the ring on and stared at it, thinking that it wasn't just like raindrops, but also tears, and that seemed somehow very fitting for how things had ended between them.

One of the first things she discovered, upon returning to Washington, was that Nikos had paid off the hospital debt in its entirety. It was the exact opposite of what she'd asked. He'd ignored her, but she knew why.

He couldn't let himself love her, or be with her, but he felt compelled to care for her. To fix things he could fix. To atone for his perceived sins.

And even though it was something she'd fought, out of pride, she knew how much it would have meant to him to be able to liberate her from James. That doing this must have given him some sense of relief. Of pleasure. And so, she let it rest, at least relieved of the burden of owing James anything. Their connections were, finally, severed.

When first Nikos had come to the island, he had seen it as an emotional torture chamber. A place that was cruel and lonely, that would allow him to torment himself with memories of how much he'd once had before him. He'd relished that idea, exposing himself to the elements, to the threat of animal injury, or heaven knew what else.

The very act of surviving had almost been enough to pull him from his grief, and draw him towards life, and light. It had given him a sense of purpose, to find stone for the cabin, to mix mortar and shape the walls. To turn his back on the trappings of his wealthy life and choose the most haunted and isolated of locations. As he'd triumphed over this landscape, he'd felt a renewed connection to himself, to this world. But still, he'd pushed everyone away. Still he'd known he could never deserve another shot at happiness.

He was right to feel that.

Right to stay true to that commitment. Isabella deserved it.

And what of Genevieve? a voice in his head demanded, so he began to hike across the island, forging a path not taken, always listening for animals, gun at his side, but otherwise stalking with confidence towards the crest of the dormant volcano. Stalking away from thoughts of her. Of what he wanted, and could never have.

At the crest of the mountain, he stopped, and finally allowed himself the weakness of looking towards the mainland, his heart throbbing unbearably at the sight in the distance of what would be Katanos. And wondering if Genevieve was still there, achingly close but for ever out of reach for him. Or was she now in America, without his protection, without him?

Far away, geographically, but for ever a part of him, just as he'd promised?

It took every ounce of Genevieve's willpower to drag herself to another job interview. It was her sixth this week, and while she thought the others had gone well, all of them had said they'd take a few days to 'think about it'. In the meantime, she hedged her bets. She was conscious of the settlement she'd received from James, and how desperately she wanted to be able to throw it back in his face.

But finding a newspaper who'd take on a journalism major with an almost-four-year career gap wasn't an easy sell, even with the exceptional letters of recommendation she'd secured from the dean of her alma mater.

It wasn't the incessant interviewing that was exhausting her, though.

It was desolation.

Desperation.

Depression.

Loneliness.

She felt, most mornings, as though she'd been rammed by a truck. Her whole body ached, as if she had the worst flu in the world. She slept poorly, barely ate, and couldn't blink without seeing Nikos, exactly as he'd been that first time her eyes had landed on him, stark naked and so heavenly perfect she'd almost wept.

Every minute of every day, she wondered if she'd made a mistake.

If she'd taken him up on his offer, she could at least have known him to be in her life in some capacity. She could have accepted his terms, and known there was at least a chance of seeing him again, of being held by him, made love to by him... Every single part of her ached for him in a way it was difficult to imagine being able to survive.

She'd never known a pain like it. Not with the death of her father, nor her mother, not with James's cruelty and infidelity, certainly not with their divorce. Every single brick in the path of her life had led her to this moment, but she was still so ill-equipped. Because Nikos had left her by choice. Her father and mother had been taken from her, but with no say in the matter. James had been someone she couldn't wait to see the back of.

But with Nikos, she'd offered him everything she had, everything she was, and he'd responded with only the parts of himself he felt safe to share. Money. Financial security.

Never love.

No matter how she looked at it, she came back to the same conclusion, time and time again. Nikos was a man who reached out for what he wanted with both hands. If he'd loved her *enough*, no amount of grief would have stood in his way, no awful past experience with marriage, either. If he'd loved her *enough*, he'd have given her everything he was, and then some, for the rest of their lives.

But he hadn't, and that, therefore, was her answer. She just needed to find a way to forget she loved him—or, at least, to live with the pain of it.

He lost track of the days. They came, and went, came and went. He told Theo not to visit the island. He ignored work. Whatever remnants remained of his life.

And he hoped. He hoped Genevieve was okay. He hoped

that if she ever needed him, if her ex-husband ever did anything to hurt her, she would reach out via Theo, knowing he would always support her, when she called.

No matter where she was, no matter when it was. No matter if she was single or married, nothing would change the duty he felt to her, the connection he had to her. The compelling need to protect and serve her, to always be a source of strength in her life, even when he himself couldn't be a part of that life.

Weeks came and went, the weather grew warm, the sun stayed high for longer, showing the shift of seasons, and as it did, his bitterness grew. Worse than he'd ever known it. It enveloped him fully, infusing his body, his bones, his cells, his breath. He could not look out upon this island he'd once loved without seeing Genevieve and thus coming to hate it. Because she wasn't here. She wasn't with him. And that had been his choice.

At the time, he'd fully believed it to be the right decision. He believed he'd done what was right for everyone, including Genevieve. How could he trust himself not to break her, as he'd broken Isabella? How could he trust himself not to be someone else she needed to get over? The thought of hurting her after everything she'd been through…

Except he had hurt her. He'd hurt her by offering so little of himself. He'd hurt her by pushing her away even as he told her he loved her. He'd offered her the whisper of a promise, rather than the all-consuming love she rightfully wanted to hold out for.

Knowing that his need not to hurt her was born of love, he'd thought it was noble. Self-sacrifice in the name of what was right. But the truth was, he was not the same man who'd married Isabella. Looking back, he wouldn't have made that mistake now. He had valued her friendship, and been grateful to her father for the opportunities, and he'd wanted, more than anything, to make her happy. But it hadn't been love in the sense he understood it to be now. Or it had been a childlike version of it, easy to ignore, to focus instead on his work. The mistake hadn't just been neglecting her, it had been taking those vows when they'd meant so much less to him than they had her. He'd been wrong to marry Isabella, wrong not to make her a priority in his life, and he would always regret his actions.

But he was not that man any longer.

Those mistakes had shaped him. From the embers of that regret, out of his guilt and grief, something new had formed, someone different, and it was that person Genevieve had seen and drawn out. It was that person she'd fallen in love with.

As the days came and the days went, a certainty grew inside him that he had made perhaps the worst mistake of his life. He had pushed away a woman who saw him, understood him, knew his imperfections and his whole self, and still wanted him. A woman who was prepared to be patient with him, because she believed he was worth it. He had pushed away the love of his life, after everything she had been willing to offer him—her beautiful, bruised heart.

And suddenly, with a clarity that was both desperate and blinding, he saw that more than anything on this earth, certainly more even than his need for self-flagellation, was his need for Genevieve. Imperfect and terrifying, risks and all, if she was willing to be brave after everything she'd been through, then surely, he could be, too.

CHAPTER FOURTEEN

AFTER FOUR MONTHS, she stopped counting his absence in days. Not because she didn't feel each day stretching like a chasm of grief, but because it was a step towards acceptance. And acceptance, surely, was vital.

Accepting that it really was over.

That she'd been strong enough to walk away from a situation that wasn't right for her. Even when so much of it had been perfectly right—sublimely, utterly, indescribably right—it had been missing the one part she considered non-negotiable. Love. Real, freely given, unconditional, no-holds-barred love.

There was no way she could be with another man who didn't love her as she knew she deserved.

But every day—every single day—she felt that ache of regret when she thought of him. It took all of her energy to get through her workday—as a junior reporter for a respected national paper—without giving away to colleagues her deep, abiding heartbreak. In the same way she'd worn a mask during her marriage, holding it together when she felt miserable inside, she was now playing a part. Going through the motions and hoping no one would notice that she'd left her heart and soul in Greece, and knew she'd never be able to retrieve either.

It was exhausting. Draining, demoralising and completely

sapping, so that every day, when she came home to her tiny apartment, she only had enough energy to make a piece of toast, shower and change into pyjamas, before going to bed. She slept fitfully, at best, despite the exhaustion, and woke every morning with a start, as if unable to believe the reality she'd found herself in.

She missed Nikos as a fish would miss water. She missed him with all of herself, and it didn't seem as though it would ever get better. She just had to learn to walk alongside her grief, or it would eat her alive.

The one concession she allowed herself was to continue wearing the engagement ring. Everyone believed her to be engaged to the reclusive billionaire—it would have raised more questions than not, if she'd suddenly stopped wearing it. And having heard the thought he'd put into buying it for her, how could she not? It was a talisman that connected her to him, and she found her eyes drifting to it often as she remembered fractured details of their time together, so her breath would gasp from her on a fresh wave of longing and need.

Of desperate, all-consuming desolation.

It was wrenching. The worst of times.

But she continued to work, knowing that she needed that. She deserved it. Having put her promising career prospects on hold to become the perfect political wife James had wanted, she knew that doing well in her role was a part of reclaiming the person she'd once been. It had mattered deeply to her once, she knew it would again.

Generally, she stayed away from covering political stories. There was too much of a threat of overlap with James, and, despite the true sense of liberation she now felt from that man, she had no interest in stirring up the hornets' nest anew. Her editor had agreed that the potential conflict of interest made it wise for her to stick to other stories.

And yet, on a warm Friday evening, just as she'd walked in the door, her phone started to ring and she saw a colleague's name come up on screen. She contemplated ignoring it, but a phone call out of hours was odd, and Genevieve's curiosity got the better of her.

'Genevieve,' she said, phone tucked under her ear as she hung up her handbag.

'Gen, hey, it's Gary.' Genevieve felt a particular disdain for people who shortened her name when they barely knew her, but she couldn't raise even a hint of that then. She was too tired. Too utterly exhausted. She flopped on the couch. 'I need to call in a favour.'

She arched a brow, wracking her brain for why Gary would think he was owed a favour by her. 'Yeah?'

'This event tonight, I can't cover it. Something's come up. Don't suppose you'd go for me? It's simple. The president will make a speech, a couple of VIPs will talk. You just need to go, get a couple of quotes, an impression of the room, that kind of thing. You up for it?'

No, she wanted to scream. She wasn't up for anything. She wanted to curl up into a ball and cry until she had no tears left. But brittle determination had her nodding. Covering anything presidential was a coup, particularly for a junior journalist. 'Yeah,' she said after a beat. 'I can do that. Text me the details. Will my credentials do?'

'I'll have Tiffany make sure your name is given to the event. You'll be fine.'

'Okay,' she exhaled. 'Good.'

Genevieve had been at events with the president a handful of times, while married to James, so she wasn't as intimidated as she might otherwise have been. She also had the added advantage of knowing how to dress, and do her hair, to look as though she belonged. This, though, was attending in a professional capacity, so, rather than a cocktail dress, she opted for more of a corporate navy trouser suit with a silky oyster camisole underneath. She teamed it with a string of her mother's pearls, and styled her hair in a high ponytail. She hated heels but they were part and parcel of this sort of thing, so she slipped her feet into a pair before regarding herself in the full-length mirror.

Make-up.

She looked like a zombie. Working quickly, she dabbed concealer beneath her eyes, a little bronzer to her cheeks and gloss to her lips, so the next time she checked the mirror, she seemed passably human. Not like someone who'd spent the last four months wishing the world would open up and swallow them whole.

The event was in a five-star hotel on the other side of the city, and, in the interest of living well within her means, she took the bus. Even allowing for public-transport delays, she made it with a couple of minutes to spare.

Something she was not remotely grateful for when the first person she ran into, upon entering the decadent ballroom, was her ex-husband, and his date.

'Well, well,' he drawled, lips flickering with undisguised distaste as he pulled the woman at his side closer. She was very beautiful, in the way all James's mistresses had been, and wore clothes she knew to be to James's taste.

A sense of pity squeezed Genevieve's heart, and she fought an instinct to tell the other woman to run a thousand miles in the opposite direction.

'Senator,' she said, voice clipped, before stepping around him, to leave.

'How's the fiancé?' he asked after her, and her eyes

squeezed shut on a wave of fresh pain. Desperate, aching pain. Nikos. The man she thought of as hers, who never really had been.

She turned around though, and forced a smile. 'Fine. I'm sure he'd want me to say hello. He really did enjoy that little chat you both had,' she added.

James's eyes narrowed and she knew that had it not been for the threat of Nikos hanging over his head, he might have said something horrible. Threatened her in some way. Instead, he stood there silently, face turning a shade of puce.

'Aren't you going to ask me how I am, James?' she prompted, anger stirring inside her at how this man had belittled her, all their marriage.

'I don't particularly care.'

'You never did,' she said, with a shrug of her shoulders. 'And I spent so long wondering what I'd done wrong, to make you so cold, and uncaring. But now I see you for what you are: a psychopath.'

He looked as though he wanted to slap something.

'I truly have no idea what I ever saw in you.' She dragged her gaze over his body, and she couldn't help thinking of all the ways in which he didn't match up to Nikos—and never could.

'Have a nice night,' she aimed at his date, before turning and moving swiftly into the crowd, to the area cordoned off for the press. She recognised a couple of journalists she knew, and settled herself amongst them, already enervated by the need for small talk.

It didn't last long. With the precision of a Swiss clock, the president arrived as scheduled, the crowd falling silent with respect. He began to speak of his hopes for a piece of upcoming legislation around childhood hunger, and then began to speak about the government's charity partners, operations that were working in the field, donors to the cause.

'In particular, I would like to thank, as I welcome to the stage, one of the biggest patrons in this space, a personal friend of mine, Nikos Konstantinou.'

Genevieve dropped her phone to the tiled floor, and felt her journalist colleagues' eyes turn to her. Fortunately, the applause somewhat muted the sound as Nikos's name was mentioned. It was little wonder his appearance had caused such a stir: he was famously reclusive. To have him appearing at an event with the president was a huge coup.

Her pulse exploded. Her heart went crazy. Her eyes stung. She knew her face must be a blotchy mess of pale and pink, she could feel the heat and clamminess growing on her, and it only got worse as Nikos, *her Nikos*, strode on stage, more charismatic than any man had ever been, and stood behind the lectern, though his size dwarfed the thing.

'Here,' someone beside her said, passing the phone to her numb fingers. She stuffed it in her pocket without responding. She couldn't. Every single part of her was focused on Nikos as he began to speak, in his beautiful, accented English, his eyes sweeping the crowd and somehow not landing on her. Not seeing her.

And why would he think to look for her? He didn't know what she was doing for work, nor that she'd be there. Which meant he'd come to Washington and not reached out to her. He'd come to the city he knew she lived in, and made no attempt at contact.

'Oh my God,' she whispered, closing her eyes on a wave of renewed pain.

All this time, she'd been pining for him, craving him, missing him with all her soul, and he'd been getting on with his life. Having paid off her debts, he'd clearly absolved himself of any thoughts of her.

She took a step backwards.

'Hey,' a woman snapped with annoyance.

'Sorry,' Genevieve murmured, holding up a hand. But she needed to get out of there. 'I think I'm going to be sick,' she fibbed, figuring there was no better way to clear a cordoned-off space than that. Sure enough, despite the density of journalists, a path formed for her, so she kept her head down and moved quickly towards the edge, and then along the back wall of the room, head down, towards the doors of the venue.

Her heart was racing as she broke out into the warm evening air, her skin flushed, her insides twisting.

But her feet refused to take her further. Her legs were shaking; her breath was hurting. She looked around, in frantic need of a seat, and instead settled on one of the elegant pillars, to lean against. She pressed her back to the cool stone, and closed her eyes, as she tried to process what the heck had just happened. And how she could ever, ever forgive him for this.

Nikos had seen her the moment he'd walked on stage, and it had taken every single piece of his willpower not to cut through the crowd then and there and pull her into his arms. But though he'd come to the States to see Genevieve, this was a presidential event, and he had no intention of being disrespectful to his friend and the holder of that office.

So he'd begun to speak about the cause, his donations to the charity, keeping his remarks as brief as he possibly could, all the while wondering what she was thinking, how she was, if she was looking at him and missing him as he was her.

He had no way of knowing.

Theo had been able to source minimal information on Genevieve, since her leaving Greece. He knew only where she worked.

Coming here like this had been a gamble, but one he'd had to take. Knowing how he felt about her, he couldn't possibly let another day go by without telling her. Without being brave, as she was brave.

But the sight of her hastily leaving the venue had his whole body on alert. He finished his speech quickly, and slipped off the stage while the crowd was still filling the room with near-deafening applause.

'Genevieve.'

She blinked her eyes open in anguished shock at the voice that had been tormenting her dreams, and her every waking thought, for months on end. She lifted a shaking hand to her mouth, covering the gasp, the sound of shock, of pained betrayal.

It was too much.

She had wanted to see him so badly, but having it take place like this, as a matter of happenstance, because of some charity he was involved with, cut her to the bone.

'Excuse me,' she said, eyes filling with tears as she turned and tried to make her shaking legs cooperate.

But he was right behind her. 'Wait,' he said, and when she didn't stop, his hand reached out and caught hers. 'Please, *agape*. Give me a moment.'

Her heart ached. *Agape*. Love.

'Don't,' she whispered, closing her eyes again as a tear rolled down her cheek. His touch was perfection, but it was also a cruel taunt. She pulled her hand free, and rubbed it against her thigh.

'A moment,' he said, moving to stand in front of her, his eyes raking her face with a look of deep concern. 'I am begging you, Genevieve.'

She tried to swallow, but her throat felt completely constricted, her mouth dry, her brain hardly able to keep up.

'What do you want, Nikos?'

A muscle jerked in his cheek. 'That's difficult to explain.'

Her heart tightened. It shouldn't have been. If it was good news, it would have been the easiest thing in the world to say. *You.*

'Can we speak in private?'

She looked around, for the first time becoming aware that the entrance to the hotel was far from discreet. High-profile guests milled, journalists too.

'I really can't,' she said, shaking her head. 'I mean, I can't talk to you. I can't do this again. It's been four months of torture, of agony, of hoping that each day I would wake up and not feel as though I'd lost a part of myself, and it's not getting better. It's never getting better,' she sobbed, taking a step back from him and twisting her engagement ring out of habit. His eyes dropped to her hand, eyes flaring, and she felt the betraying nature of that gesture, and wanted to curse. 'But seeing you again, it's just going to make it harder. I can't... I can't start all over again. I have to believe I'm making progress, even though it doesn't feel like it. I have to believe that day by day I'm one step closer to getting over you,' she pleaded, as though he could click his fingers and make this all better for her.

Though she'd refused to go somewhere more intimate, Nikos moved his bulky frame to stand between her and the entrance of the hotel, effectively creating privacy for Genevieve by shielding her from view.

'I have to go,' she whispered, shaking her head, staring up at him imploringly. The fact he was here in Washington, and she had no idea for how long, or where he was staying, or any of those vital details, just drove home to her how estranged they now were. Her heart was bursting into a billion pieces.

'Do you think I have not also missed you?' he said, voice dark, as his eyes roamed her face. He was close enough that she could feel his warmth, and her whole body was aching with a need to lean forward and feel his strength, too.

Anger shifted through her chest. 'What?'

'I have been on the island, and you are everywhere there. You are in the trees, the sunlight, the sound of rain on the roof, the fireplace, the bed, you are in my soul, my heart, my very being. I have missed you, Genevieve, in ways I cannot even fathom. I have felt as though I am barely alive, walking this earth, having lost my true north, my reason for being.'

His words were everything she'd wanted to hear, but it was too late. She was so bruised and battered, she couldn't forgive him for putting her through this. She'd given him her heart, and, vitally, her trust, and he'd wanted neither.

'You came to Washington and happened to run into me, and now you're telling me this? What if I hadn't been here tonight? What if I hadn't—?'

'I came here for you,' he contradicted. '*This*—' he gestured to the hotel '—was a guaranteed way of seeing you. I didn't know, otherwise, if you would agree to meet.'

Her jaw dropped. 'But I'm not even meant to be here.'

'I put in a call.'

'You put in a call,' she repeated, dumbfounded.

'I know the owner of your paper.'

She shook her head, her brain not following. 'How do you know where I work?'

A muscle spasmed in his jaw. 'Your stories go online,'

he said, and she nodded, because of course they did, and they ran with her byline. A simple Internet search would have shown her pieces.

'You're very talented.' She ignored the pride in his voice, the warmth she might have felt under different circumstances, and focused on what he was saying.

'So you got me to come to a thing that my ex-husband would be at, just so you wouldn't have to face the possibility of rejection?'

His jaw tightened. 'You saw him?'

'Yes, I saw him.'

'And?'

'And what? I told him what a jackass he is, how lucky I am to be free of him.'

The admiration in his expression was unmistakable. And damn it, her heart thwomped in response, warmth spreading through her that she definitely didn't want to feel. 'But you didn't know that,' she snapped.

'Know that you are capable and brave, and more than a match for that weak-minded fool? Do you think I doubted that, *agape*? Do you think any part of me believes you are not able to handle anything life throws at you?'

Her lips parted. The sweetness of that spread through her and then burst into her belly, like fireworks.

She glanced sideways, needing a second to gather her thoughts, because being face to face with Nikos was making it impossible to think straight. She was unbearably torn between what she wanted and what she needed to do, between heart and head, hope and hurt.

'It's been four months,' she whispered, lifting a hand to tuck an errant wisp of hair behind her ear at the same time he went to do the same, so their fingers brushed and her eyes flew back to his face, her heart leaping into her throat.

'Four months,' she said, imploringly, staring at him, as his fingers curled around hers and then laced through them, lifting them to his lips and pressing a kiss to her knuckles.

'Yes, it's been the worst four months of my life,' he said, eyes hooked to hers. 'Like you, I kept thinking I would get past it, that I would wake up one day and feel like myself again, but I cannot. I will never get used to missing you, my darling, my love.'

She shook her head, willing herself not to believe it.

'I was so afraid of hurting you. After Isabella, how could I trust that I would do what was right by you? Even knowing my heart belonged to you, I could never ask you to trust me with it, to trust me with your life.'

'That's my decision to make.'

'Yes, it always was,' he agreed. 'And you made it. You gave yourself to me, and instead of taking that gift with both hands open, I fled, because even the remotest possibility of hurting you, of making you miserable, of being someone else you had to get over, as you have James… I ran from that, Genevieve.'

She closed her eyes. 'You hurt me, anyway.'

'I hurt us both.'

She bit back a sob at the truth of that.

'I came to Washington because I needed to tell you that I was wrong.'

She kept her eyes closed. His hand squeezed hers.

'I will never forgive myself for how I was with Isabella, but I'm not that man any more, and you are not her. We are different; everything about us is. With my dying breath, I will honour and cherish you, if you will let me. Without me realising it, you have become the most important thing in my life, the only thing I seem to care about, these days.

All I ask is that you consider letting me back in, to prove to you that I deserve what you so freely offered, in Katanos.'

She couldn't bite back this sob. It burst from her as she opened her eyes and stared at him imploringly.

'What does that mean?' she finally whispered.

'That I want to date you,' he said. 'That I want to cherish and adore you, to stand by your side as you make your journalistic mark on the world, supporting your work, your goals, being whatever you need me to be, until you realise that your first instinct about us was right. We are meant to be together, and I will be here, if you'll let me, every single day, until you see that what we share is unique and wonderful—and truly meant to be.'

A tear slid down her cheek. 'And if I *won't* let you?' she whispered, hauntingly.

Grief passed over his features, but he rallied quickly. 'Then I'll still be here, just in case you change your mind. If you need me, or want me, or just need a friend to talk to about your day.' He squeezed her hand again. 'In whatever capacity you'll have me, I'm here. I love you, Genevieve, but I'm not stupid enough to expect this to be easy. I recognise what it took for you to admit your feelings for me, to even *feel* them at all. And I know what my reaction must have done to you. I am for ever sorry for that.'

Another tear slid down her cheek and this time, he lifted his spare hand to dab it away.

'Can we start with you giving me your number?' he asked, and her heart lurched, because it was such a tender, gentle, uncertain request, so utterly nothing compared to what Genevieve wanted, but a part of her felt the need to cling to her protective barriers, just a while longer. Even knowing that he could obtain her number easily, through one of his contacts, she appreciated that he was *asking* her. Respecting her autonomy.

'Yes,' she said, nodding slowly. 'I'll give you my number.'

He expelled a slow breath of relief. 'And I'll be sure to use it.'

CHAPTER FIFTEEN

It wasn't even half an hour later when his text came through.

Are you free for dinner tomorrow?

Her heart stampeded through her body, fairly trampling her other organs, and she couldn't stop smiling as she wrote her reply:

Depends. Where would we go?

He named a renowned Greek restaurant, and she closed her eyes on a wave of memories of dinners in Athens as she tapped out a reply.

Well, a girl does have to eat.

His reply was instant.

I'll pick you up at eight.

Eight o'clock! How on earth was she meant to wait that long? Particularly given she'd been falling asleep well before that, these past few months.

But there was something about having seen Nikos again, and having the prospect of a date with him on the horizon, that made her whole body hum and buzz with energy all day.

By six o'clock, she was tempted to text him and ask him to come over earlier. She didn't, though. She stuck to their original plan, and she took her time getting ready. A long soak in the tub, shaved legs, body moisturised all over, make-up carefully applied to be dewy and minimalistic, hair loose and brushed until it shone, and an outfit chosen with care.

She was determined to keep him at arm's length, but that didn't mean she didn't want to also drive him a little crazy. She was pretty sure he knew what he'd been missing, and would do anything to go back in time and change the way things had gone, on the yacht. Nonetheless, a little reminder would do him the world of good.

She chose a silky slip dress, emerald green in colour, and teamed it with a strappy pair of heels and a matching clutch. The dress was cut on the bias and fell to a couple of inches above the knees, showing her tanned legs and just enough of a hint of cleavage.

When he rang her doorbell, she took a moment to apply a deep red lipstick before pulling the door inwards.

His deep-throated curse was enough to make her body sing.

'Ready?' she asked, blinking sweetly, all too aware of the effect she was having on him.

To be fair, though he'd probably spent considerably less time on his appearance, she was no less breathless and hot under the proverbial collar at the sight of him in a suit, custom shoes, with his hair brushed back from his brow. The thing with Nikos was that no matter what he wore, that ruthless, powerful animalism was just beneath the surface, waiting to burst out. From nowhere, she imagined him pushing her into the apartment and taking her against the wall, hard and fast, until she was crying his name, and warm heat pooled between her legs.

'My car is downstairs,' he said, and her eyes widened as she remembered the time they'd made love in his car.

Suddenly, the idea of keeping him at any kind of distance seemed ridiculous. She believed that he loved her. She knew he did. And she also knew he was sorry. Whatever evidence she'd been hoping to attain to allow her to trust him again seemed completely unnecessary. When she looked back on her time with this man, she saw a thousand ways he'd shown himself to be trustworthy and decent, honourable and kind.

'Let's go to dinner,' she said, against every single wish and instinct she possessed.

As she closed the door to her apartment behind herself, he put a hand in the small of her back, holding her against his side.

To her surprise, he'd booked out the entire restaurant, and their table was in an alcove away from the windows, meaning there was no intrusion into their privacy. She didn't want to think about what it would have cost to secure a venue like this at the last minute. All she could think about was what it meant. No part of this was to do with their original plan, to put James in his place, and get him off her back.

This was about Nikos and Genevieve, and the love they shared.

'Do you think it's weird,' she asked, after dinner, when they were back in his car, on the way to her apartment, 'that I still wear your ring?'

His eyes held hers and then he reached for her hand and touched the diamond. 'On the contrary, it is right, and perfect. My deepest wish is that you will continue to wear it, all the way until such time I can add another ring to be its pair.'

Her heart turned over in her chest and her lips parted.

He swore softly then. 'I don't mean to rush you. I don't mean—it is obviously my wish, but there is plenty of time, my darling, for the rest of our lives.'

She turned away from him rather than answering, because her smile made it impossible to speak.

At her door, he kissed her goodnight on the cheek and then turned to leave. He couldn't push this too hard. He knew it would take time for Genevieve to feel safe trusting him again, to know that he was worthy of all the love and faith she'd put in him before. But hell, he'd wanted to go inside with her more than he could say. Not just because his body was yearning for hers in a way he could hardly live with, but also because he couldn't get enough of her.

Listening to her talk about her work, and how proud she was, how obviously good she was. Listening to her talk about anything, hearing her laugh and knowing he'd caused it. He just wanted to breathe the same air as her, for as long as he could.

For now, though, just the whisper of hope she'd given him had to be enough.

Dinner tonight? The text came through the following morning, and her heart lurched in response.

She had barely slept, but this time, her wakefulness had been caused by the most delirious happiness. Genevieve had lain awake in bed and replayed every moment, every touch, every look, until her heart was humming and her insides were twisting.

She tapped out a reply: Why don't I cook?

I don't want to put you to the trouble.

Nonsense. You cooked for me on the island. It seems only fair.

There was a lengthy pause before he responded: What can I bring?

He arrived with a bottle of wine and the biggest bunch of flowers she'd ever seen. Genevieve buried her face in the blooms to stop from launching into his arms and kissing him with all her passion and love. She arranged them in a vase while he uncorked the wine and poured two glasses.

She had thought she might feel ashamed of her apartment. She knew it was small, in a rough neighbourhood, and pretty cheaply furnished, but instead, when he looked around and had that same proud expression on his face, she just felt alive. Adored. Appreciated, for how hard she was working to achieve her financial freedom. Because she knew he saw that, he would never think she wasn't someone who wanted to stand on her own two feet.

His money was so irrelevant to what they were. It barely even entered her mind to consider the disparity between them, despite his generosity with the hospital bills.

Genevieve had learned to cook from a young age, and she was very good at it. She made creamy garlic prawns for entrée, and then lamb for main course, as he had served them in Greece, and he ate it appreciatively, marvelling at how skilled she was in the kitchen, until she laughed and told him he really needed to stop.

His eyes lifted to hers, and the smile in the creases of his face shifted, sobering. 'I can't stop,' he said, shaking his head. 'I told myself I wouldn't rush this, but being here with you, in your apartment, there is a part of me that wants, more than anything, to press fast forward and start the rest of our lives now.' He closed his eyes then. 'I know it's selfish of me. It's just…for a brief time, I got to call you my fiancée, to know that you were, at least to the rest of the world, truly mine. I cannot wait for a time I can do that again.'

Her heart turned over in her chest and every single piece of her seemed to click in together. She felt the sting of tears in the back of her throat as she took a quick gulp of wine.

'Well,' she said, a little unevenly. 'We never technically announced that our engagement was at an end.'

He stared at her without reacting, but because she knew him, she understood what that took for him to do.

'I suppose it wouldn't hurt for you to still refer to me as your fiancée.'

He nodded slowly. 'Because of James?'

She blanched, and stood then, coming around to the other side of the table and manoeuvring herself into his lap. 'No, not at all. This would be just for you and me.'

'Are you saying—would this be real?'

Her eyes sparkled with unshed tears as she nodded. 'I think that's a great idea.'

She couldn't say who kissed whom first, but their lips connected and it was as though every star in the heavens went supernova simultaneously. Lights flashed in her eyes and her body rejoiced, as did her heart, at the certainty that she was with the man she was destined to find.

And the more she thought about it, the more she truly felt that destiny had had a hand in their meeting. The storm that had blown up out of nowhere, her hiring a sailboat just to feel close to her father—she could never shake the sense that perhaps it had been her parents, and Isabella, who'd somehow created the magic that had brought Genevieve to Nikos in the most unlikely of circumstances.

One week after dinner in Genevieve's apartment, they were at Nikos's luxurious Washington home, and without her realising at first what he was doing, Nikos was down on one knee, holding out another black velvet box.

Her heart stammered in her chest as she shook her head.

'I never got a chance to propose properly,' he said, clasping her hands. 'And I want to.'

'It was proper enough,' she said, because that night remained in her memory as one of the happiest of her life.

'Not for you, my darling. For you I would do anything, go anywhere. I kneel before you as a man who has fallen completely in love, with all of my being. You are the beginning and end of my days, the entirety of my hopes. A thousand lifetimes with you could never be enough. Please, say you'll marry me, because you know that I love you and will always honour you, because you understand that, from this day on, my life will be spent in the service of you and yours.'

She nodded, tears streaming. 'Of course, Nikos, of course. But my ring—'

He cracked open the box to reveal teardrop diamond earrings, the same glorious shade of blue.

'I had them made, to match,' he said. 'I could not get you out of my head, and I knew you should have them. Even if you chose to sell them.'

She gasped. 'I would never.'

'Good.' He stood, inspecting her ears before removing one from the box and beginning to insert it. 'Will you wear them, Genevieve, my darling, and know that they are the beginning of the expression of my love for you, a love that will guide me for all time?'

She could barely cope with the sincerity and extremeness of his sentiment; yet she understood it, because she felt the same.

She waited until he had both earrings in place before she

answered, by pressing a hand to his chest to put a little distance between them.

'How about,' she said, reaching behind her back and feeling for her zip, 'I wear them—' she began to ease it down '—and absolutely nothing else, for the rest of the night?'

She saw his Adam's apple move as he stared across at her.

'And your ring?'

She stripped out of her underwear, until she wore only a pair of heels, her earrings and diamond ring.

His eyes fell to it and she smiled. 'Oh, I'm never, ever taking that off.'

EPILOGUE

LITTLE BY LITTLE, with Genevieve's help, Nikos began to fully let go of his demons. While he'd already come to understand how changed he was, by life and circumstances, he also finally accepted that he had been blaming himself too harshly for his marriage. Isabella had hated his work hours, but she *had* been happy. He finally let himself hear that, from her father, her friends. People that had once been in his life, he'd spent years pushing away, he now got to know again. And in hearing them speak of Isabella, he realised that Genevieve had been right about that, too. His late wife deserved better than to have become a pain point in his life.

Working with Isabella's father, Nikos and Genevieve set up a charity in Isabella's name. Far from ever expressing even a hint of jealousy, Genevieve supported Nikos tirelessly in this work, because she understood how far he'd come. How healthy it was for him to honour Isabella, as a mark of his progress. He no longer had his head in the sand, and that was because of Genevieve.

As Genevieve built her career, he supported her, understanding her drive to succeed, the way she'd been held back by James. No doubt the egotistical man had been jealous of her obvious talent.

Nikos was not completely true to his word, however. He couldn't resist stymying the other man's career. A few well-placed calls ensured he received a challenge at the next election; he lost his senatorial seat, and left Washington, to live a life of quiet, yet wealthy, obscurity.

Genevieve didn't care, though. James had long ago lost any power to hurt her. He was just a speed bump in her life, a brief chapter that had served one wonderful purpose: to bring her to Nikos.

They waited to have children. While they both knew they wanted a family, Genevieve's career was going from strength to strength, and Nikos knew the timing decision had to be hers.

They were blessed with three girls, and each of them was raised to be strong and independent, to know their worth and use their voice powerfully. Isabella, and her father, were a part of their lives, always. They spoke of Isabella as someone Nikos loved, and they included her father in all family events, so that he became a grandfather to their children, a valued member of their family.

* * * * *

Did Greek's Ring of Redemption *leave you wanting more? Then you're certain to love these other steamy stories from Clare Connelly!*

Billion-Dollar Secret Between Them
Twins for His Majesty
Billion-Dollar Dating Deception
Tycoon's Terms of Engagement
Blackmail to White Veil

Available now!

HEIR TO ITALIAN ALTAR

REBECCA HUNTER

MILLS & BOON

To the fantastic Jerry Thompson
for making a home for romance books
and our romance community at Books Inc.

CHAPTER ONE

"He just walked in."

"Is he with the countess?"

The whispers swirled around Ann-Sophie Svensson, and she turned, despite her best intentions. From across the crowded ballroom, Alessandro Carandini shone like a god, even among princes, CEOs and others who likely thought of themselves in such terms. Tall and built, he should have looked just like his twin brother, Massimo, and yet, to Ann-Sophie, he was so very different. His silky black hair curled up at the ends in a hint of unruliness, quite the opposite of Massimo's close-cropped cut, and his bronze skin gleamed a little brighter in the glittering lights of the chandeliers. The cut of his crisp, white shirt hinted at the taut muscles underneath, and his tailored trousers tapered at the waist. Wearing his suit coat at meeting after meeting, he had looked every bit the bold, smooth-talking businessman he was. Now, without it, rumors of the trail of heartbreak he left seemed grossly underestimated. Alessandro towered over the woman he was escorting into the room, a lovely brunette whose hair was held back with jewel-studded clips that sparkled in the lights. Definitely real diamonds, Ann-Sophie thought as she watched them from her corner of the room.

She tucked a stray strand of hair behind one ear, trying

not to compare herself. She was of hardy Nordic commoner stock, raised by a single mother in a comfortable apartment at the end of the subway line south of Stockholm. Though her blond hair and blue eyes held some cachet in the world, she was more pretty-adjacent than pretty, let alone beautiful. Usually, Ann-Sophie was grateful for that. Being a beautiful woman had its downside when said woman wanted, for example, to be acknowledged for her skills. Or travel seamlessly through the world. But today, as she watched the bejeweled woman who was doubtlessly minor royalty place a graceful and strategic hand on Alessandro's arm, then look up at him and laugh, Ann-Sophie wanted to be a little less...well, regular.

Alessandro Carandini was the opposite of regular. He was excess incarnate. A glow seemed to emanate from him that went beyond his astonishing good looks. He had a charisma, a magnetism that animated everything around him.

"You're staring." Ann-Sophie's fellow interpreter, Monique, gave her a gentle tug at the elbow. "Not that I blame you."

Ann-Sophie flashed her friend an innocent smile. "Nothing wrong with dreaming."

Still, Monique gave her a skeptical glance. Swedish Connection Interpreting Services often paired Monique and Ann-Sophie for larger diplomatic events like these, as Ann-Sophie's specialties in Italian, French and Spanish complemented Monique's expertise in a few Slavic and Germanic languages. They had both been with the agency long enough to have earned the trust of their most prestigious clients.

"I thought you had no desire to live in this world," said Monique, gesturing across the dazzlingly ornate ballroom, lit by the glow of countless candles. Ann-Sophie squirmed under her friend's scrutiny, reminding herself that Monique could not see the exquisitely intimate scenes that played through Ann-Sophie's mind. Her friend would never suspect that these longing looks came from a source much deeper than fleeting fantasies. But whatever the theories that played through Monique's mind, her friend did not voice them.

"I don't. I have enough." *Enough.* It was the word her mother had used so many years ago, a word that had put her life into an entirely new light.

"You do have enough," Monique agreed. "But a bit of excess could be fun, too, especially in the form of Alessandro Carandini. Despite his…"

Her friend did not need to complete this sentence. Ann-Sophie was very well acquainted with this man's reputation for a particular kind of excess.

"Excess is overrated," she said. "The newspapers are filled with stories of miserable, wealthy people behaving badly."

Ann-Sophie had always shied away from anything indulgent. She came from a country that valued *lagom*, a Swedish word that lacked a good translation, particularly here, in the glitter of the Côte d'Azur. *Just right* was the best equivalent, "like in the Goldilocks story," she told English speakers. At a young age, before she had understood just how much her mother had given up for her unexpected baby, Ann-Sophie had leaned in the direction of indulgence. She had embarrassing memories of demanding toys, visits to Gröna Lund for a day of roller coasters and candy, more toys and, finally, the ultimate request: a visit with her elusive father.

"I *need* to meet him," she had insisted.

"You will not meet your father," her mother had said, so gently that Ann-Sophie at last heard the finality in her voice. "You must learn to tell the difference between wants and needs, *älskling*. You have enough."

Something had shifted inside her after that conversation. Somehow, those words had done what years of refusals had not. Ann-Sophie finally understood that no amount of wanting would make their father appear. In the space of this devastating realization, she had seen how her want had become a trap, a never-ending thirst. Because she had allowed it to be.

Alessandro Carandini was currently a thirst-inducing want, ill-advised, and yet, she still found herself gazing longingly after the man tabloids called Italy's hottest playboy.

"You don't have to worry. He seems very taken by the countess he's talking to," Ann-Sophie said breezily, as if the sting of watching Alessandro with a woman of his own social class was just a fact of life.

Monique laughed. "I'm not actually worried."

Ann-Sophie laughed, too, and pretended it wasn't another twist of a knife in her gut. A knife that she herself had placed there.

Every attendee, from prime ministers to princesses, administrative assistants to interpreters, had been invited to this last night of celebrations. Those attending the weeklong negotiations between the biggest powers in Europe were government leaders, ambassadors, large international businesses and NGOs. She spent the days side by side with Swedish diplomats and business representatives, clarifying trade strategies that would bring the maximum benefits to all countries involved.

Ostensibly, tonight was different. She, Monique and the other interpreters were like any other guests, free to drink champagne and eat fois gras canapés alongside the royals and company presidents they worked for. However, even at these after-hours parties the interpreters tended to keep to themselves, enjoying a few sips of France's signature beverages from the edges of the ballroom. Ann-Sophie always felt a bit like she was looking in on a world she regularly visited but never truly belonged. And she was fine with this. She didn't have to feel at home here, even if it was technically her workplace, because there were so many other reasons she liked her job.

Even if she did feel more at home here in this ballroom, it would be her job to suppress anything that might make her stand out. Interpreters were supposed to fade into the background, not attract attention. This was yet another reason she hadn't said a word to Monique about Alessandro, not even yesterday morning as the two women wandered down the streets of Nice, with its brightly painted buildings and carefully laid stone streets. They had walked until they'd arrived at the cerulean blue of the Mediterranean, dotted with yachts and jutting white rocks.

"I've barely seen you this week," Monique had commented offhandedly. "Are you having a secret liaison?"

Her friend had laughed away her own comment and didn't seem to notice the heat that had likely turned Ann-Sophie's cheeks pink. They both knew how out of character a secret liaison would be.

But tonight, in this ballroom with its gilded sconces and

exquisitely restored frescos, she was doing a terrible job at deflection. Tonight, her own feelings were on display for Monique and, likely, this entire ballroom of kings and princes and prime ministers. She couldn't take her eyes off Alessandro Carandini, even as she was well aware that it was both uncomfortable and unwise to reveal the ache of want that flowed through her. Want, not need, she reminded herself. The wisest course of action would be to leave, but her feet seemed to be anchored to the floor. Because tonight was the last night. When she got on the plane tomorrow, she would likely never see him again.

So Ann-Sophie turned away from Alessandro to the huddle of interpreters that had gathered in this corner of the room. She flashed Monique a smile and focused on the conversation as it wandered from local restaurant recommendations to beaches. When the string ensemble began to play, she forced herself not to look at the dance floor. The last thing that she wanted to see was Alessandro Carandini gracefully dancing—because, of course, he had mastered dancing the way he had mastered everything else—with another woman in his arms. Ann-Sophie smiled and laughed like everyone else, and as the conversation drifted from one language to another, she pretended that this ache inside her didn't matter. When a colleague asked her to dance, she turned him down, telling him—and herself—that she was both ungraceful and not in the mood.

But as her thoughts drifted, she had clearly tuned out the people around her because, suddenly, she became aware that no one was speaking. Instead, everyone was looking just over her left shoulder. Startled out of her thoughts, she turned and immediately saw what had caught the groups' attention. Alessandro Carandini was walking toward their corner of the room, and he was looking straight at her, as if he had been searching for her all night. Ann-Sophie's body stilled as her heart took off in her chest. She swallowed, trying to break the spell, telling herself it was just a glance as he made his way around the room, entertaining dignitaries. Even though she could have sworn there was a flash of something more complicated in it. Even though he wasn't looking away.

The closer he came, the more hope bubbled inside her, despite her best efforts to quash it. Alessandro did not seem to be headed for any of the other clusters of dignitaries nearby. He was making his way toward her. Whispers rustled from behind her, but as he came to a stop, so tantalizingly close, the whispers died. The whole scene should have felt silly, Ann-Sophie told herself, straight out of some teenage drama made for television, but it didn't. It felt breathtakingly real.

Then Alessandro smiled, letting his eyes graze over the others before settling on her again. "Good evening."

Just his voice, low and seductive, made her shiver. A murmur of greetings rippled behind her, but Alessandro's gaze stayed on Ann-Sophie. "Would you care to dance?"

She should say no. Though no rules prohibited their dancing, it felt so brazen. So excessive. But her body didn't care. It reacted with a jolt of giddy desire that scorched her brain of all rational thought and left her with a jumbled rush of sensations. Her silk dress brushed against her skin, making her aware of all the places she wanted his hands. On her hips. On her breasts. Between her legs. The heat from his dark eyes washed over her body, drenching her in desire.

Out of the corner of her eye, Monique's gaze bore into

her, a mix of confusion and accusation. But Ann-Sophie ignored the twinge of guilt, telling herself it didn't matter right now, not when that familiar rush of joy ran through her limbs.

"I'm not much of a dancer," she said, repeating the excuse she had given a more appropriate partner not ten minutes ago.

Alessandro's smile was hot and intimate, despite the fact that they were very much not alone. "Thankfully, the dance police have gone home."

If he hadn't made her laugh, maybe she would have ignored the heat that washed over her when the Carandini twin famous for his short-lived flings had sidled up to her at the empty bar on her first night in Nice. But his laughably outrageous flirting had included questions about her flawless Italian, and somehow she had found herself trading anecdotes about language blunders, hers mostly, from adventures with her mother, and his, compliments of a Swiss boarding school and a Saudi girlfriend.

Her first night with Alessandro had unfolded so naturally that when the conversation had meandered into more intimate topics, the intensity of her desire surprised her. After a few high-profile affairs, he had a reputation as a satisfying partner, and she had assumed this reputation to be backed by some reality, but she hadn't expected this to feel so…easy. Fun.

This one night of indulgence had proven addictive. When Alessandro let his gaze fall on her, it felt as if he was the sun, and she opened beneath his rays. There had been moments when he had opened for her, or at least it seemed that way. Afterward, she found herself dismissing them, telling herself that the magnetism he exuded was simply an aspect of his famous diplomatic skills, honed for his family's manufacturing empire. She was just getting a very personalized introduction to the skills he used to negotiate deals, to keep onshore factories from closing. His reputation was legendary, particularly the way he had managed to convince CEOs to choose higher-cost options, gambling that the Made in Italy campaign would ultimately pay off in higher earnings. Still, their nights together had felt more singular than that. More private.

Now, as he stood close enough to touch, she was once again drawn in by the way Alessandro could bridge the distance that spanned between them. A distance of life experiences and social position that was far too wide to forget. And yet, his eyes sparkled with amusement, tempting her to forget.

"This feels like a bad idea," she said, as the curious gazes prodded her from every direction.

Alessandro lifted a hand to his heart theatrically. "You wound me with your rejection."

They both knew that these words were just for show. Alessandro never doubted that she would dance with him.

Still, she arched an eyebrow at him. "I should dance with you to save your tender ego?"

He shrugged with an arrogance that was just as real as it was self-mocking. "Is there a better reason?"

"What a charming offer," she said with a little laugh.

But when she reached out to accept the hand he offered, another burst of giddy joy ran through her. She was almost sure she floated onto the dance floor instead of walked, as if the warmth of his large hand was the only thing that tethered her to the ground. Her face was flushed with heat, and she forced herself to keep her eyes on the floor in front of her, away from the prying eyes that certainly watched them from across the room.

"Just follow my lead, *cara*," he said in her ear. The endearment sent a hot lick of desire through her. "I'll take care of the rest."

It was strange that even these words called to her, so unlike what she usually wanted. Guided by her mother, Ann-Sophie had thrived on making her own way in the world. And yet somehow, as she and Alessandro had shifted from flirting to…whatever this was, she had gotten used to him taking charge a bit more. It was a strange feeling she didn't want to think about too much. So she didn't.

Instead, she turned to face him. She placed her free hand on his muscular shoulder, and the heat of his skin through his shirt seemed to feed the heat that was building inside her. Someone had opened the French doors onto the patio, and the evening air wafted in, redolent with flowers. He slipped his hand around her waist and coaxed her close enough to see hints of circles under his eyes, even in the dim evening light.

"Our sleepless nights are starting to show," she said, brushing her fingers over his sharp cheekbone. This gave her a little thrill, that she might have the power to influence this godlike man.

He flashed her a wicked smile. "Do I need to take you to bed and teach you some manners?"

She laughed, and a surge of happiness coursed through her, one she knew she should suppress. They were still here, in the ballroom.

"I thought we only did this under the cover of darkness," she said. It was better for both of them not to give the impression of distraction at these high-stakes meetings. Now that the meetings were over, it mattered much less, though there would still be speculation.

He pulled back a little and eyed her with amusement. "You were looking at me across the room as though you were making late-night plans for us. I just had to hear what they were."

She noted that he did not ask if she wanted to spend this last night together. He assumed. This may have rubbed her the wrong way if their future was more certain, but tonight, she only felt a surge of anticipation.

"I'm still not sure this is wise," she said as they began to spin their way around past the crown prince and princess of Norway.

The ever-present humor lit up his face. "No one would accuse me of being guided by wisdom, Ann-Sophie."

"Nor I, it seems," she said. "At least not this week."

He leaned forward, so his lips brushed against the sensitive rim of her ear. "I wager that these people around us see an incorrigible playboy who found an intriguing woman to dance with. That's all."

It was difficult to concentrate on his words as memories exploded inside her mind. The sound of his whisper in her ear triggered an image of Alessandro, naked in the bed over her as he whispered the sweetest, softest endearments in her ear, driving her crazy, until she shattered.

"No one knows about our nights together, *cara*," he whispered, the caress of his low voice sending another hot lick of desire through her. "They might wonder, but no one will ever know."

The words were supposed to be a comfort, but Ann-Sophie could not ignore their bitter aftertaste. They reminded her of the truth. No one would know because what they had was not real. After tonight, their affair was over. She had entered the entanglement with no illusions of a future, and yet, as she felt his hard, thick muscles more under her hands, so overtly masculine under his tailored shirt, she knew she had been lying to herself. She wasn't ready to let this end.

Alessandro had not planned to cross this room in front of business colleagues and gossipmongers to ask Ann-Sophie to dance. He had planned to wait until the festivities were winding down before he made his way up to her room for one last night of indulgence. But there had been something in the way the man standing a few meters away from her had looked at her. It had rubbed him the wrong way. He had watched the man approach Ann-Sophie, watched his frown when he turned away, and watched the man's frown as he continued to look at her again.

Alessandro was aware that he could be constructing a narrative out of nothing, and yet he felt obligated to act on it. So he had crossed the room for her sake, he told himself, to make clear that this man was out of her league. Yes, there was an arrogance behind this string of thoughts, but that didn't make them false. Alessandro knew his value and his position in life as well as anyone. And right now, he was enjoying every privilege this position allowed him. He was holding Ann-Sophie, and the brush of her soft curves against his body tempted him to forget this last night of diplomatic alliances and enjoy the startlingly explosive chemistry between them.

"I seem to be having my Cinderella moment," she said, and her tone suggested that she wasn't sure how she felt about it.

"Cinderella returned to her old life at midnight, if I remember correctly," he said, checking his nonexistent watch. "You left me with no choice. I needed a place on your dance card before this lovely dress turns to rags."

He used this as an excuse to move his hand over the soft curves of her hip. Under his fingers, her red dress washed over her body in a ripple of whisper-thin silk. It was as if he was almost touching her skin, but almost was never enough. He told himself that this craving he felt was just chemistry. Really, really good chemistry.

There were many things Alessandro had learned to close himself off to over the years, but he had found that he did not need to deny the bottomless ache inside him, as long as he dressed it with humor. In every other part of his life, he exercised control. But he allowed the pull of attraction to feed the hunger inside him. Though there were times that this lack of restraint may have suggested an intimacy that hinted at something more, his reputation spoke for itself. Alessandro never thought about the future when he was in the middle of one of these flings because there was no future. Ever.

"I threw away my dance card when the interpreter from Poland invited me onto the floor," she said, and he could sense her smile, even with his eyes closed, his lips so close to her skin. "He is likely judging me at this very moment for my slight."

She said all of this lightly, in that playful tone they communicated in, signaling that she understood that nothing between them should be taken too seriously, but the words still triggered something inside him that he might have called jealousy. That couldn't be right. Still, there had been moments over this week that had felt…different. He could ignore these strange stirrings, he told himself, because tomorrow she would be his past. The affair with Ann-Sophie would end no differently than the others, even if he didn't feel ready to let her go in the same way as he usually did.

"Show me who my competition is, and I will call him out, tomorrow at dawn."

"On the cruel, dusty streets of Nice?" Ann-Sophie's laugh soothed some of the tension inside. "You aristocrats have a reputation for letting others do their dirty work."

She said the word *aristocrats* in a tone that could have been reverence or mockery. Probably a bit of both. He didn't point out that he was not, in fact, an actual aristocrat, though his family had more money than most aristocrats these days. Instead, he said, "I make an exception when it comes to a woman's honor."

"How principled of you." This time, her tone definitely leaned toward mockery. "It's unfortunate that I will be at the airport when all the excitement takes place. I hate to miss it."

There it was, that little waver in her voice. He had heard it the past night, too, when she had made a passing comment about tonight's event, when she had uttered the words *last day*. And one of those moments that felt so *different* had stretched out between them, like a strange, sweet hunger that had gnawed at him.

He had, of course, dismissed it. There were plenty of reasons their connection felt a bit…intense at times. For example, the circumstances were somewhat different this time. For the duration of these affairs, Alessandro had always eased his conscience with the knowledge that the women came to him, not the other way around. They willingly entered into an arrangement with him, knowing the reputation he had clearly established for attachments that were sizzling, satisfying and short-lived. As a rule, he was never to seek out a woman. Alessandro had broken this rule with Ann-Sophie. Even that first night, when he crossed the empty bar and sat next to her, a sense of foreboding had warned him away. He didn't want to think too carefully about why he hadn't ignored it.

There was something so artless and unselfconscious about her, so much the opposite from the way he kept himself strictly under control. As if she didn't feel the weight of expectations on her shoulders. On that first night he had entered the quiet bar around the corner from the hotel to get away from the wariness he couldn't seem to shake when he spent too much time around Massimo and his new wife. But the moment he had sat on the barstool in the corner, next to Ann-Sophie, he wanted her. Craved her enough to set aside the warning signals and pursue her.

Inexplicably, that feeling had grown over the week, not fizzled out. Right now, in the flickering candlelight of the ballroom, he wanted to touch her in a way that might have rattled him if the end of this affair wasn't so clearly in sight. He wanted to run his fingers over her soft skin right here, in front of every business associate that mattered. Dancing with any other woman tonight seemed impossible, and the idea of seeing her dance with indolent royalty and ruthless businessmen, let alone a colleague who might know parts of her that Alessandro hadn't yet learned… It was a vision he put out of his head. Tomorrow he would let Ann-Sophie go, but tonight she was still his.

She shifted under his touch. "You are confident you will win this duel?"

"Of course, I will," he answered smoothly. "If for no other reason, in addition to defending your honor, my demise would mean my brother would single-handedly control our family's fortune. You must have heard talk of the competitive nature of our relationship."

She laughed at this misleading truth. Leaving his brother alone was the last thing he wanted to do, but it had nothing to do with competition. At fifteen, he had been on a path to destruction at the latest boarding school his parents had shipped them off to. Reading and dyslexia weren't a good match, even for someone willing to put in the hard work of that uphill battle. That wasn't Alessandro. Instead, he turned to other distractions, and when his reckless fights had gotten them both kicked out, Massimo stood by his side. They never talked about the period of their lives, when Alessandro's emotions had gotten so out of hand. Massimo, too, had watched their parents' all-consuming relationship, but while his brother had turned inward, Alessandro had shifted into all-out rebellion. He had let his anger and frustration with the things he could not change control him, and that had almost taken down both him, and his brother with him. The poisonous feelings had controlled him until he had turned off that part of himself. It had been the only way to stop the destruction. He would never, ever make Massimo pay for his own sins again.

If Ann-Sophie detected any of the intensity of the responses he was having, she didn't let on. He was grateful for that, he told himself.

"Of course, you will win the duel, as men like you always do," she said lightly, though the humor in her voice had a bite to it. "And then you will return to Milan and bask in the riches of your newfound deals this week."

It was only the vaguest reference to the future, but this comment brushed up against his rule to never speak about the past or the future. His affairs were suspended in a present of mutually satisfying indulgence. When it ended, he left all of it behind. And yet, this week, he had found his conversations with Ann-Sophie drifting outside these boundaries.

He knew he had to cut off this topic, so he indulged Ann-Sophie's question with an answer that diverted her attention. "I will do my celebrating at my flat in Milan, while my brother and his wife will leave for a remote fjord in Norway, which I have been told has many appeals."

"You have never been there?"

Alessandro shook his head. "I prefer more predictable weather."

In truth, Catarina and Massimo had been so caught up in their arranged-marriage-turned-love-match that he had spent very little time with them, beyond cursory meetings and formal gatherings. Alessandro was pleased that his uncompromising brother appeared to be happily married, but it baffled him to see how the relationship had changed his brother, who let so few people inside of the hard exterior he had forged early in life.

In a twist of irony, it was Alessandro himself who had made the winning arguments for his brother's marriage, an idea that Massimo only reluctantly accepted. At the time, a marriage of convenience had seemed to be the wisest course of action, as, unlike Alessandro, his brother had never struggled with keeping his emotions under control and would therefore withstand any weakness that marriage could trigger. However, seeing the way Massimo visibly softened around Catarina had shaken

Alessandro, awakening echoes of feelings that were better to remained buried.

So Alessandro had stayed away. At first, his brother had not noted the rift, too caught up in his newly discovered romance. But after months of Alessandro's excuses about why he could not meet for dinner or an evening in their flat, Massimo had confronted him.

"You are avoiding me," his brother had said with his usual stark directness that bordered on harshness. "Explain."

"It seems that falling in love truly does make a person detached from reality. I wouldn't have believed it would happen to you, but…" He ended this with a shrug. He was so good at deflecting emotional traps that even Massimo believed him. At times, a part of him wished these deceptions didn't work as well.

But his brother's features had softened, and he gave a nod, as if Massimo himself had agreed with Alessandro's assessment that love detached him from reality. "I just don't want Catarina to think that this is about her."

Alessandro had looked his brother in the eye and told him it wasn't, because that was the truth. It wasn't her. The problem was the way he was watching his brother change before his eyes. It stirred up a reluctant admiration but also an inexplicable discomfort he didn't want to think about. His parents' relationship may not have warped Massimo, but the anger it triggered in Alessandro was a poison inside him that should never be allowed to rise up again.

Though his brother had found himself carried away by his marriage, Alessandro could never let himself fall into that same trap. He reminded himself that he was under control, despite moments of unsettling intimacy the nights with Ann-Sophie had triggered. There was no tomorrow for them. There was only this dance and the heat of her skin under his hands and her soft, lush body pressed against his. There was tonight, and he would spend it in her now-familiar hotel room, surrounded with wine and decadent desserts, with the moon sparkling on the ocean below. They would talk and eat and lie naked, her body against his, and he would get his fill of satisfying Ann-Sophie, over and over.

When she spoke again, her voice was airy. As if none of this weighed on her. "Surely you must have visited the Nordic countries before?"

"Occasionally. But our company has only started to expand to the region, and my brother prefers to be the one who travels there these days," he said, and then, before he could think to resist, he disturbed his careful boundary between now and their lives outside of this hotel. "And you will return to your apartment and recover from the demands of all of us self-important clients?"

"I am the mediator of ideas. I'd rather like it that way," she said, maybe too brightly.

Alessandro found this comment frustratingly guarded. "Surely you must want to use your own voice. I, for example, have been enjoying it immensely this week."

Ann-Sophie laughed. "They pay me a premium to keep my own thoughts—as well as theirs—to myself."

The idea didn't sit well with him, but her hair brushed against his cheek, and he let that sensation distract him. They danced in silence, and he told himself everything was right, the way it should be.

"I will travel to Milan now and then in the coming

months," she said after a moment. There was a hesitation in her voice, an uncertain catch in her breath, and Alessandro knew without a doubt that she was about to tread into forbidden territory. She was opening the topic of the future. He had, of course, encountered this problem before, but instead of shifting the conversation, the way he always did, he was overwhelmed by a vision of her in his own bed. Maybe this vision would have been less disturbing if it had been of her soft cries as he pleasured her, the hard thrusts as he took them both to ecstasy. Then he could have simply written it off as lust. But the image in his mind was of Ann-Sophie sitting on his bed, cross-legged, with the morning light shining in her hair like a halo. She was drinking a cappuccino and laughing. It was startlingly, horrifyingly domestic.

But the time to be to take control and redirect the conversation had passed because she was speaking again.

"I was thinking it might be fun to meet up again. You know, have dinner or just..." She shrugged in that carefree way she had. "Do whatever we feel like doing."

A jumbled mess of emotions bombarded him, so ominous that the only thing Alessandro could think to do was shut them down. Shut *her* down.

"We have no future, Ann-Sophie." He told himself he had kept his voice under remarkable control, considering the torrent of stirrings that were seeping through the cracks of his hard-earned equanimity. He could not let them through. He had buried all these emotions long ago. The alternative was to let them erupt, the way they had all those years ago. The way his parents still spread their poison.

Ann-Sophie's eyes widened, and her forehead creased

in a vulnerable sort of confusion that unsettled him further. He was making this worse. The smile that slid from her face told him his voice had not been nearly as moderated as he had planned.

The music was still playing, but she had stopped swaying, and Alessandro was keenly aware of the way they were standing in the middle of the ballroom. He watched the hurt slash across her face and had the nagging feeling that this was taking a distinctively bad turn. He had the baffling urge to walk back on his declaration, a reaction that released another jumble of emotions, this one more disturbing than the last.

He had to get the situation under control. This was not the first time he had divested someone of their impression that a future between them was possible, and it would not be the last. He had no choice but to go forward. But as Ann-Sophie blinked up at him, he inexplicably found himself wondering whether there was another path. Then anger washed over her face, and the thought was gone.

"My mistake," she said, her voice cool.

She stepped back and he fisted his hands, keeping himself still. Ann-Sophie's eyes were filled with accusations, but she gave him an exaggerated curtsy and a smile that could only be called mocking.

"I would say it was a pleasure to meet you, but I'm currently reassessing that," she said, her voice now hard as stone. "I'd say I hope to see you again, but that would definitely be a lie."

Then she lifted her chin and turned away, leaving him in the middle of the dance floor.

CHAPTER TWO

Seven months later

"THE GOOD NEWS is that your baby is doing well."

Dr. Azzizi's smile was supposed to be comforting, but Ann-Sophie felt far from reassured. Whenever someone started a conversation with "the good news," nothing good came after that.

Ann-Sophie tried to block that thought out and simply focus on the message. Her baby was fine. The cramping that had convinced her to take a cab directly from the airport to her doctor's office was not an emergency. She was not suffering from a miscarriage, nor was she experiencing signs of early delivery. A little pocket of relief formed amid the billowing clouds of worry in her brain. At least that was one worry to cross off the endless list of pregnancy concerns. Ann-Sophie pasted on a smile for the doctor and tried to adjust the blue gown that curved around her growing belly. Then she took a deep breath and braced herself for the next step of this discussion. "What's the bad news?"

"Your blood pressure is still too high." Dr. Azzizi's eyes were sympathetic, but Ann-Sophie was almost sure her blood pressure had just spiked higher. After the first high reading two months ago, she had taken a monitor home with her and discovered that, in the comfort of her apartment, her blood pressure was in the normal range. However, the moment she left for a work trip, the numbers went up and stayed up. This wasn't exactly a surprise. She had always thrived on the excitement of travel and high-pressure meetings. Unfortunately, the baby didn't, so she had limited herself to shorter trips, and in another month, she would have to stop altogether. Which was stressful, too.

"There's just been so much to do," she said. "And my life is going to change so much after the baby…"

She was still trying to get her head around taking care of a newborn *by herself*, let alone imagining how she would work once maternity leave was over. Currently, during a busy month, she spent more weeks traveling than at home. But she couldn't just…leave a baby for days. Would she have to leave her job instead? And who would employ an interpreter who didn't travel?

Ann-Sophie took a deep breath. Those had all been tomorrow's problems. Today's problem was how to handle the stress of travel. She had tried everything to bring down her blood pressure, starting with more frequent walks and cutting out salt, then working her way up to strict bedtimes…all of which were hard to stick to while traveling. Today, for example, she had woken up in Milan before sunrise after the unexpected extension of the previous day's meeting, instead of catching up on the sleep she had lost this week, as she had planned. This was the kind of schedule crunch that meant that, despite increased interventions, her blood pressure at work kept ticking up. This increasing stress was probably why, when the meeting let out early this morning, she had found herself wandering by the Carandini Corporation's head office before she caught her flight back to Stockholm. Because the visit made no rational sense.

"I've been doing everything you told me to," she told the doctor. "Yoga in the morning, plenty of water…"

"I believe you," said Dr. Azzizi. "But sometimes our bodies don't respond as well as we'd like them to. Your job makes a lot of demands on you. Which is why I'm highly recommending that you go out early on medical leave."

Ann-Sophie blinked at the doctor. "What do you mean?"

"Starting as soon as possible," she said as she typed a note into her computer.

Ann-Sophie gaped at her. "I can't just leave my job."

She was already stressed about fitting in all her commitments before her maternity leave began. This was worse. The thought made her want to curl up on the cold, vinyl exam table and take a nap. Or do something to make this situation go away.

Dr. Azzizi finished typing, and when she looked back up, her smile had faded. "I understand that this will be difficult. You will, of course, be eligible for your full pay because it is medically necessary, but I understand that these situations can be tricky."

Ann-Sophie wondered if her doctor could see the scope of what she was asking. If she did, it didn't change her mind.

"It is my strong recommendation that you do this now, before the situation becomes more serious. Right now, your at-home measurements indicate you can almost certainly reduce your blood pressure with a less stressful lifestyle. But if you wait, both you and your baby can find yourselves in a much different situation."

The words rattled through Ann-Sophie's body ominously, making her shiver.

"But I feel fine," she protested weakly.

The doctor raised her eyebrows.

"Fine-ish?" she amended.

But even that was an exaggeration. First, there had been the bouts of morning sickness, and as her belly grew, her feet tended to be sore and swollen at the end of the day. That was just the beginning of the list. Still, the last thing she needed was lots of free time to worry more often. "It's just that my body doesn't feel like I need rest."

"You should definitely stay active," said the doctor. "Swim, walk, stretch. It's the stress that needs to change, and after two months of modifying everything else, we're down to the last option. You need to stop traveling for work."

"But I love to travel," Ann-Sophie whispered.

Exploring new places was one of her very favorite things about her job, and now, her last month of it was gone. When was the next time she could start her morning at a window seat in a new coffee shop with a pastry and her journal? When the baby turned eighteen? Of course, she knew these sacrifices were coming and was willing to make them. She just didn't think they would come so soon. So suddenly.

The doctor furrowed her brow. "You could take a vacation instead. Maybe a solo retreat or go with a friend?"

Ann-Sophie let out a sigh. On her first visit with the midwife at *Barnavårdscentralen*, she was asked to check one of the two boxes on the form she had filled out: single or partnered? Ann-Sophie hadn't hesitated. She'd checked off *single* quickly and deliberately, as if she, like her mother, had made a conscious decision to have a baby without a partner.

Because who wanted a partner who, surrounded by their colleagues, would clarify that their nights together were essentially meaningless sex? She had made the mistake of believing her week with Alessandro had transcended their differences. But in the middle of that opulent ballroom, he had exposed the truth: He could yank that feeling from under her feet at any time. She had felt silly and small. Less than. And it triggered all her leftover feelings from her nonrelationship with her father, feelings she absolutely would not dwell on now, when she had her own child. Because she would never allow this child to feel less than. Unwanted. Abandoned. Not worth their parent's time.

Apparently, Alessandro had been so committed to the message he delivered in the ballroom scene that he decided a further step was necessary. Adding insult to injury, he *blocked her number*. The fact that this move still hurt to think about was yet another source of frustration. What happened to the woman who had loved her single life, surrounded by friends and free to travel, explore and follow her whims and curiosities?

"I'll ask some friends if they're free," she said, though she knew none of them could pick up and leave for a spontaneous trip now, in early September, right after the summer holidays.

"You will be doing both yourself and your baby a favor," said Dr. Azzizi, but Ann-Sophie barely heard her.

As she walked out the door of the office with the printout of her doctor's orders in one hand and her carry-on suitcase in the other, she reminded herself that this phase would pass. Fall had arrived in Stockholm, and a cold gust of wind blew through the narrow streets as she walked to the main office of Swedish Connection Interpreting Services. Ann-Sophie had no memory of what she said to the head of human resources when she wandered into the office. All she remembered was the sympathetic smile Birgitta had given her when she said, "Don't worry. We'll take care of this. Just get some rest, and we'll message you with any questions."

Don't worry? Ann-Sophie had to bite back a humorless laugh.

And just like that, all her clients were reassigned. She was free. Very free and very alone. And now that the buffer of work and travel was gone, she was suddenly terrified. She was having a baby *alone*. And the reality of this very uncertain future was starting today.

Her heart thumped harder in her chest, and she reminded herself to calm down. No freaking out in the middle of the street. Having a baby on her own had upsides, she told herself. She and the little one would make their own family. Soon, she would have a baby to love and care for. This strange pang of loneliness would go away.

She mused that this rudderless feeling was hormones.

As she walked through the crowds at Odenplan, Ann-Sophie dialed her mother, but the call went straight to voice mail. Which was unsurprising, as her mother's journalism assignments often took her far beyond the reaches of mobile-phone services. Ann-Sophie searched her memory for where her mother was supposed to be, but pregnancy brain seemed to have stolen these details, so she left a message, hoping her mother would call back in the evening, when she had more time. Margarita Svensson had not raised a needy child. Ann-Sophie admired her mother, and any wish for a more conventional upbringing had long ago died. But just this once, she wanted to dial her mother's number and hear her voice. Just that thought triggered a wave a guilt. Her mother had already given up too much for her, including the man she loved. Ann-Sophie would never ask for more.

Instead of dwelling on this, she sent messages to three friends, proposing weekend getaways. Two messaged back immediately.

Linnea: Sorry! Lena has a ballet recital Saturday afternoon. Call you later!

Helena: Working over the weekend. :(Hope you're well!

Ann-Sophie ducked into a bakery for her second treat of the day, then headed toward her flat in Vasastan. It wasn't until she was on the familiar back streets of her neighborhood that her mind wandered back to Alessandro.

Ann-Sophie's face still flushed with humiliation when she remembered that last night in Nice. She had been imagining scenarios for her next visit, and he had unquestionably moved on. She was so careful with men, so conscious of her still-tender wounds about being abandoned, but something about the intimacy of their connection that week had made her think this was different. At the very least, he could have rejected her with a little more grace. But she had clearly been wrong about him.

The humiliation turned to alarm two weeks later when she calculated that she had missed her period. Multiple tests confirmed what her body sensed: She was pregnant. Though she always had wanted a child or two someday, the *someday* she had imagined was much further in the future. And she had taken it for granted that she would do this together with a partner she loved. But her mother's words came through shortly after, words about Ann-Sophie's own unexpected appearance in her mother's life: "It's never the right time for a baby. If you want a child, you make it the right time."

So Ann-Sophie had made the decision. She was having a baby. Despite their less-than-desirable parting, she decided to call Alessandro, just to inform him. Which was how she discovered he had blocked her number. Ann-Sophie remembered the sinking feeling when the words flashed across the screen of her mobile. Still, after a few weeks of wallowing, she had swallowed her pride for the baby's sake and tried again, this time sending a discreet email: I have something important we need to discuss. Please call me.

He, of course, ignored it.

She had contemplated leaving a very detailed message with the receptionist in his office, a kind of revenge that exposed his dirty laundry for those he worked with. But as satisfying as the idea sounded, she couldn't do it. She was carrying this man's child, and no matter how humiliated and frustrated she was, they would have this baby between them for their entire lives. The idea triggered a strange rustle of feelings inside that she refused to contemplate, so she had focused on the baby, leaving the situation with Alessandro for later. She would find a way to tell him before the baby came. She was just... working her way up to it.

With each work trip to Milan, the guilt of not telling him weighed a little heavier. She *and Alessandro* had created a baby. And he still had no idea. Though the Carandini family business had nothing to do with her visit, somehow she had still expected to cross paths with Alessandro. She had expected that the opportunity to tell him would simply present itself. Fate had brought them together seven months ago. Wouldn't it bring them together again?

When fate didn't cooperate, she took matters into her own hands and looked up the address of his office. If a detailed phone message was petty revenge, showing up to his office seven months pregnant was positively wicked. And incredibly tempting. She had stood on the sidewalk outside the sleek, modern building in the center of the city, gathering her nerves as guilt warred with unease. What if she confronted him, and he walked away, just like her father did?

Ann-Sophie could not make herself enter the building. At one point, she had thought she'd seen a glimpse of Alessandro through the glass, but if it was, in fact, him, he had turned back the moment he saw her. In the end, nothing had come of the visit aside from higher blood pressure. Next time, she told herself. Maybe there was a chance he would welcome a baby. Maybe every aspect of her baby's life didn't have to depend on her. In truth, she was overwhelmed, daunted by the task of caring for this tiny, helpless being by herself, and she wanted her baby to be welcomed into the world with love, not stress. For the next two months, she needed to do everything in her power to make sure of it...which meant figuring out how to handle the situation with Alessandro.

But before she could think about that mess, she was starving. Again. So hungry that she was clearly hallucinating because the man standing outside her building looked a lot like...

No. It couldn't be.

Because there, in front of her tall, stone building, stood

Alessandro Carandini. There was a starkness to him she hadn't noticed before. His thick, glossy hair was clipped shorter than it had been seven months ago, and the cut of his suit accentuated his wide shoulders, making him look even taller than she remembered. But his eyes were the same, and they triggered sensations from seven months ago she had buried. Heat swept through her, and her swollen breasts tingled and ached. Her body *knew* him. A hot rush of desire mixed with that uneasy giddiness she had refused to think about before. But as Alessandro came into undeniable focus, heat skittered through her body, and she could no longer push the awareness away. This feeling was hope. And for one, heart-stopping moment, he looked at her as if everything in the world had been made right again.

Before Ann-Sophie had time to think through practical questions, like what was he doing here, in front of her apartment building, his gaze drifted down to her belly. Ann-Sophie's heart thudded in her chest as she caught unmistakable desire glittering in his gaze. But the desire immediately disappeared, and his eyes narrowed. He took a step forward, then another, and with each step, his expression turned harder. By the time he towered over her, he looked far from the charming aristocrat she had spent that one glorious week in Nice with. Instead, he looked stunned. And angry.

Lush. Ripe. The sensations fueled by these words roared through Alessandro's body. He stared at Ann-Sophie, trying to contain the racket of emotions that thundered through him. She was *pregnant*. He felt an overwhelming urge to reach for her, to touch her, to feed the hunger that raged inside him. But he gritted his teeth and focused on the other reactions that vied for his attention. Like shock. And outrage. He clung to them, letting them blossom until they quieted the ever-present desire for her that still dogged him, even seven months later. It was this combination of shock and outrage that had spurred this unexpected trip to Stockholm, from the moment his brother had walked into his office and declared that he was almost sure he had seen Ann-Sophie outside their building.

"And she looked..." Massimo, who never found himself at a loss of words, often to Alessandro's dismay, hesitated.

"What is it?" Alessandro's patience had been chronically short in recent months, and this topic wasn't helping. His brother raised an eyebrow, and Alessandro was forced to remember how he had mocked Massimo not so long ago about his brother's sudden turns of temper when Catarina had fled. But this situation was completely different. He gave Massimo a tight smile. "How did she look?"

Massimo frowned, and warning signals exploded in Alessandro's mind. "Her belly looked a bit rounder."

It was as if Alessandro's entire body went numb. He didn't realize he was walking until he was out the door. He found himself in the elevator, glaring impatiently as the floors ticked down until he finally arrived at street level. But Ann-Sophie was nowhere. His assistant searched every hotel until he found the place were she was staying, just three blocks from his office. Except she had already checked out. Still, the fact that she had been there, so close, suggested Massimo had not been mistaken about whom he had seen, though surely his brother was wrong about... Alessandro didn't even want to think about why she might be "rounder."

It implied the unthinkable.

It implied the thing that should never, ever happen.

For the last seven months, he had been haunted by their week together, but Alessandro had sworn to himself that he would never see Ann-Sophie again. The lingering ache for her was the price he was paying for the way he had let his control slip for one, short moment on the dance floor, he told himself. But if she was... No, he would not let himself think about it until he had confirmation.

Which meant he needed to go directly to her apartment and clear up this situation.

"You could be waiting outside her apartment for days," his brother had said over the phone as Alessandro sped toward the airport. "To think it wasn't so long ago that you were the one telling me that I was not acting rational."

"This is not the same," he growled at his brother.

"Not at all," Massimo had replied all too easily. "Because I was actually engaged to the woman I was pursuing. Whereas you are quite far from that."

Somewhere over Europe, in the privacy of his jet, where he could think more rationally, Alessandro had reassured himself that she couldn't be...rounder. Instead, he found himself planning to see her again. If his brother had been mistaken, and he found himself face-to-face with Ann-Sophie, close enough to touch, he would make an excuse for being in town and apologize for his unfortunate behavior. Naturally, she would forgive him. This would soothe both the unsettling memory of their last night together and, if all went as planned, satisfy the desire that had plagued him, and finally put it to rest.

And if his brother was right? Alessandro had turned to stare out at the clouds, trying not to think about that possibility.

But now, as he stood on this narrow street, under the tempestuous Stockholm sky, the evidence in front of him was irrefutable. Ann-Sophie was standing in front of him with a rolling suitcase in tow, and the word *round* didn't begin to capture her belly. *Lush. Ripe*. Those words continued to echo inside him, over and over, despite the fact that here on the street, he could only see a hint of this new development under her outer layers. Seven months of repressing her voice, her laugh, the way her body seemed to be made especially for him—everything came back so viscerally. The hints of new curves under her shawl made his hands clench with the need to touch her in all the ways he shouldn't. Because the hunger that gnawed inside him was mixed with the jumble of emotions he had spent his adulthood shutting off.

He glared at her belly incredulously, focusing on the fact that she hadn't said a word about this situation to him.

"You are pregnant." The words were an accusation that he flung at her, and for a moment she looked as if he had slapped her. Hurt and betrayal flashed across her face, and he hated the way it wrenched at him. Then her eyes narrowed.

"How very observant of you." She tilted her head a little. "You know, I remember you as significantly more charming. Funnier. At least until those last moments on the dance floor."

And he remembered her as easygoing. The last seven months of being pregnant on her own appeared to have given her teeth. Or maybe just the desire to use them on him.

"Is it my child?"

She rolled her eyes, as if this much was obvious.

"How did this happen?"

"My grade four teacher was pretty clear about the process, but maybe your fancy boarding schools left these details vague?"

He glared at her. "We used condoms."

"Most of the time. I've had seven months to go back over our week. It's definitely possible."

Alessandro's anger and lust flared, intertwining into something far more dangerous as he pictured a few choice moments of carelessness. He had spent the last seven months intentionally *not* going over that week. Now, flashes of their nights came back, feeding the storm clouds gathering in his mind. Building, threatening to unleash their power and envelop everything around him. He narrowed his eyes. "You didn't tell me."

"Did you think that email I sent about 'something important' was a plea for more sex?" She huffed out a sigh. "Never mind. I don't want to know how truly impressive your ego is."

He bit back a snappier response because he had, in fact, thought something quite similar. Instead, he made an attempt to soften his voice. "We need to talk."

She glared at him. He waited. Finally, she broke the silent war with a sigh and a shake of her head.

"Let's go inside," she said, and she didn't wait for his answer.

Alessandro followed her through the front door and into the lobby, with its marble floors and brass letter boxes, as frustrations welled inside him—frustrations he didn't know where to aim. She bypassed the elevator and headed for the stairs, despite the fact that she was pulling a suitcase behind her.

"Why are you walking up?" he demanded. "Shouldn't you be…"

He gestured vaguely to her body as he tried to remember what common wisdom said about what a pregnant woman should do. He was sure it included being careful about, well, everything.

"I'm perfectly capable of walking up stairs." Ann-Sophie gestured to the sign taped next to the brass call button, written in unintelligible Swedish. "Also, the elevator is broken. They're ordering a part, but…"

She shrugged, as if she had long ago accepted this fact and moved on. Again, his frustration bubbled to the surface, pushing aside those dangerous poisons of betrayal and lust.

"I will make sure it is fixed today." At least one problem in this mess had a concrete solution.

The dry humor he remembered flashed across her face. "Of all the problems I have right now, that one doesn't even rank in the top one hundred."

The reference to all her problems raked through him uncomfortably.

"Let me carry your suitcase," he said, just barely holding on to his calm facade. His temper must have shown on his face because her expression softened a little.

"Thank you," she said and handed it to him.

Then she turned around and continued up the stairs as he stewed over this last comment. She said it as if she was *humoring* him. This situation obviously needed some clarifications.

Ann-Sophie climbed the stairs, past the second-floor landing of the spiral staircase, and came to a stop on the landing on the third floor, lit by the overcast sky through the window in the stairwell. She keyed the door, and they stepped into a tiny hallway. The floor was filled with mail and newspapers, and as she bent to pick up everything, her full rear brushed against his thigh. His body stirred again, and Alessandro gritted his teeth. This woman had the power to take over his thoughts and make him act irrationally. It had already happened once, with disastrous consequences, and he could feel how easily it could happen again.

"I'll get the mail," he growled.

Everything he did from this point forward must be strategic, and from the moment he had registered her round belly, partly concealed by the billowy shawl she wore, Alessandro knew immediately what the goal had to be. He would never be a negligent father and treat his child like an inconvenience—or worse—the way his own parents had. And though Alessandro had never envisioned himself as a father, he had very strong ideas about how a child should be raised. He needed a solution that would give him some much-needed control over this... situation. Which required keeping the child and Ann-Sophie close. That's what this strange, possessive urge was about, he told himself. The solution he had in mind did not involve intense emotions. As long as he kept himself under control, he could fix this situation into something that worked. He had succeeded with more delicate negotiations, and he always pursued his interests relentlessly until he was satisfied with the outcome. This would be no different.

He took a moment to evaluate her living conditions, which, on the whole, looked perfectly acceptable, though a little small. The apartment's old wooden floors and high ceilings lined with flourishes marked the building's age, but it had been kept up reasonably well. Alessandro hung his coat on a brass coatrack and followed her into a living room. The walls were white and decorated with a series of paintings that could have been Southeast France or Northwest Italy. The most notable feature was an old-fashioned, floor-to-ceiling stovelike fireplace, freestanding and entirely covered with tile. The rest of the room was decorated in the Scandinavian modern style that one might expect, with a low, white sofa and chairs and an area rug patterned in tan and white. On the whole, the room was tasteful and might have even felt a bit impersonal if not for the books. They were everywhere, in overflowing piles on the bookshelves and scattered on the furniture and the low tables, some bookmarked and others propped open.

Ann-Sophie cleared a book from the armchair and gestured for him to sit. "I'm putting on the kettle for peppermint tea. Would you like a cup?"

He shook his head. The drink he needed right now was significantly stronger.

She disappeared through the doorway, and he wandered through the room, inspecting the books that lay open, faced down, half-read and abandoned. There were a few in Italian and English that he recognized, but most were in what he assumed was Swedish. Ann-Sophie clearly loved to read, and Alessandro filed this information away for future strategic use. She returned moments later with a tray that held a cup of tea and a plate that held some sort of sugary bun, which she set next to a stack of older-looking books.

"Cinnamon roll?" She glanced longingly at the braided bun. "I split it in half in case you're hungry."

"No, thank you," he said, and he was almost sure he saw a flash of relief.

Ann-Sophie reached for the sweet, giving it a reverent glance before taking a bite. She closed her eyes, and a look of sensual pleasure swept across her face. Alessandro's body reacted immediately, memories mixing with seven months of self-denial in a surge of lust that for one, dangerous moment took over his thoughts with pure need, reckless and desperate.

"Where shall we start?" she asked a moment later with a tight smile. "Perhaps with the way you so succinctly made it clear you wanted nothing to do with me after a week together? And just so there was no uncertainty in your message, you felt it necessary to block my number. Yes, let's start there."

The new bite he had noted was back in her voice, sinking its teeth into him. A few days after their parting, he had found himself inexplicably checking his phone to see if she might have contacted him, despite the way he'd ended their liaison. Finally, he put an end to that impulse by blocking her number. But this was definitely not the time to get into these details.

"Or we could start with the current situation." He gestured to her belly, but he was distracted by the way the pillows under her legs were propped in such a way that suggested she regularly sat like this. Did her feet bother her? Alessandro didn't like the way that possibility sat inside him.

"Fine. Let's start with today," she said. "Why were you waiting outside my building?"

The question narrowed his focus. They were entering negotiation, an area where he excelled. Growing up as the disappointing twin, the troublemaker, it had been implied in every way that he would be the one who would surely bring down the family name his grandfather wanted so desperately to redeem. When he had finally shut off his emotions, he had learned to hone in on his useful skills.

All his adult life, he had talked his way through situations where his father had betrayed every last ounce of trust that people had in the family name. He had succeeded, winning back clients. Armed with the facts, plans and financial nuances Massimo had compiled, he had explained, flattered and negotiated, all with the air that in the end, it didn't matter to him. That they had lists of investors clambering for access if this particular investor turned down their proposal. While his brother was good at numbers, forecasts and all the things that had plagued Alessandro at school, Alessandro knew *people*. He knew how to charm and enthrall, and he carried out each charm offensive with steely resolve because he had sworn that never again would their lives be out of control, the way that they had been during their childhood. So he ignored the questions about how she was fairing that brewed inside and started on this new campaign.

"I came to ask you the very same question," he said, his voice a peak of equanimity. "Just this morning, my brother told me that he saw you in front of our office, looking 'rounder.' I believed that a pregnancy was out of the question because the woman I spent a week with seven months ago had a job that entirely depended on her integrity. So she would never, ever fail to reveal something as important as a baby."

Ann-Sophie swallowed visibly, but her reply was cuttingly polite. "May I refer back to the email I mentioned?"

"Surely you could have tried a bit harder," he said, ignoring the fact that she did, indeed, have a point. "After all, you managed to make it to the doorstep of our office."

Her lips twitched down in displeasure.

"I'm sorry. I should have," she finally whispered.

A rush of cool satisfaction ran through him. He had found a weakness. She felt guilty about withholding this information. So he twisted the knife further.

"But, as my brother has earned my *trust*—" Alessandro slowed on that last word "—I felt it was my duty to verify that he had made some sort of mistake, that my trust in your honesty was not misplaced."

Again, her guarded expression faltered, and again he ignored the twinge of discomfort this reaction brought and focused on the surge of satisfaction of having found a path forward. A path where he was in control. Alessandro told himself that even if he hadn't made it easy for her, she still should have found a way to tell him about the baby.

"But now, I find myself here, having verified that my brother was not, in fact, mistaken. It was I who was so deceived into thinking that I could trust someone who has security clearances," he said, finishing. Then, he waited.

Ann-Sophie was quiet for a long time as she looked out the window. Finally, she turned back to him. "So basically, you came here to scold me?"

Frustration flared inside him, but it was easy to tamp it down this time because he had her exactly where he wanted her.

"Oh, no, *cara*," he said, softening his tone. "I didn't come to scold you. I came to marry you."

CHAPTER THREE

ANN-SOPHIE WAS almost sure her blood pressure had just doubled. Marry notorious playboy Alessandro Carandini? This was the same man who had jettisoned her on the dance floor the moment she mentioned a future encounter, but now, he wanted her to agree to spend the rest of her life with him? For the last seven months, she had been bracing herself for the possibility that he would abandon the child with the kind of callous disinterest her father showed her. The idea of marriage felt like the opposite extreme and just as overwhelming. She was already so overwhelmed that, for one brief moment, the idea of simply giving in and letting Alessandro take care of things on a day like today was tempting.

Hormones, she reminded herself. Hormones were making her feel vulnerable, along with today's unforeseen news from the doctor. Alessandro had caught her at a vulnerable moment. Why else would she invite this man into her living room, listen to his demands for marriage and not kick him out. Her yoga teacher's voice echoed in her head in a loop, chanting *deep, calming breaths... deep, calming breaths.*

"You must be joking," she finally said.

"I assure you I am not. Marriage is the obvious solution to this..." He gestured at her body, currently sprawled across the sofa, as if he had no words for her state. "It is the best way for both of us to put this child first."

"I'm glad you want to put the baby first," she said, keeping her voice even, "but there are many ways to do this without marriage. Like co-parenting, for example."

"From different countries?"

"We'd have a lot of details to work out, but marriage is no different."

He looked, in a word, determined. His strong feelings about marriage were a surprise, considering the fact that he was the last person anyone would associate with marriage. Ann-Sophie suspected she wasn't getting the whole story about why. Maybe the best way forward was attempting to understand these motivations so she could work out a compromise that worked for both her and the baby.

But before she could figure out an approach, Alessandro distracted her with a lazy smile. "It could be mutually satisfying."

The most maddening thing was how these words in his smooth, low voice still sent a shiver of desire through her. This was the tone he had used in the bedroom for much more pleasurable reasons. Ann-Sophie had thought these feelings had turned off when the uncompromising pink line of the pregnancy test had stared up at her. But the moment his eyes raked down her body, it was as if her blood began to sing. Her body tingled as if ready and waiting for the promise his smile suggested. She was still so vulnerable to his seduction.

To him.

The ache that reached beyond attraction was even more dangerous. Which was why she absolutely should not think about it. She could never let that influence her decisions, not when she was deciding for two.

"But marriage is between *us*," she said slowly. "Why should I say yes to spending the rest of my life with you?"

Alessandro still wore that lazy, seductive smile, the one he had given her back in Nice, the one that made her forget their very different lives and made her dream. But this time, it felt as if he was toying with her body's reactions, using them against her while he remained totally under control. All the frustration she had seen when he glared at her in the front of her building had dissolved, and in its place, she felt a will of steel behind his indolent smile. Was this hardness new, or had it been there the whole time, carefully hidden when she posed no threat to his world order? She had been an insignificant fling—one of many, forgettable, she reminded herself. Insignificant enough to *block her calls*.

"A marriage would mean that you would have my wealth at your disposal," he said with a wave of his hand, as if he was some sort of king that granted his subject's wishes, according to his whims. "This could allow for an upgrade in your living situation, for example. You will not have to work, nor will our child want for anything. You will be free to travel, which you mentioned you'd love to do more of. In fact, you can spend your whole life traveling."

Maybe another day this offer wouldn't have tempted her, but after the news that her world was suddenly getting a lot smaller, travel without limits sounded heavenly. Her mother's words came back to her. *You must learn to tell the difference between wants and needs,* älskling. Travel was a want. Setting up a life for the baby was a need. She couldn't let her own wants get in the way.

Deep, calming breaths. The steel will she heard underneath his comments suggested that even if she dismissed him from her apartment, this discussion was not going away. He was father of the baby she was carrying, which demanded a degree of negotiation, no matter what their marital status was.

His gaze raked over her body, and that unmistakable heat in his eyes made her breasts feel fuller, heavier. She tried to ignore it. "What if I am not swayed by what your wealth can do for me?"

"Maybe you should experience it before you so quickly reject the benefits," Alessandro answered mildly.

"Like endless vacations?" She gave him a polite smile and pretended he was a client to be humored. "And what would you be doing as I took these trips to spas and exclusive resorts?"

"Aside from upholding my side of mutual satisfaction," he began, and she recognized the familiar raw desire in his gaze, "I would be working, the same way I work now."

"The same way you were working in Nice? With the nights reserved for affairs like the one that you had with me?" His expression darkened, but Ann-Sophie ignored it. "I suppose that would mean I am also free to gallivant around with other men, so long as I keep it—"

"There will be no extramarital affairs." His voice had turned hard and icy. He swallowed, and some of the easygoing veneer returned—because she was beginning to understand that this was a veneer. "Not on either of our parts."

She looked away, not wanting him to see how relieved she was that at least one of her concerns was off the table. She gathered herself again and gave him what she hoped would pass for an amused smile.

"So I will have plenty of time alone?" she asked. "Just a baby and me? What a relief for a new mother."

He narrowed his eyes at the wryness in her voice. "Resorts are rarely empty, and you may hire nannies or invite friends to stay with you. Or relatives, which I assume you have. You will not be alone."

"My mother is a journalist with a heavy travel schedule, and my father wasn't around, so I can't picture either of them at a spa with me." There was a sharpness in her voice, and Ann-Sophie wasn't sure why she had made that comment. She usually avoided mentioning her father altogether. She glanced at Alessandro, wondering if the comment had simply rolled past him, but to her dismay, he looked deep in thought. Suddenly, she didn't want to be in the middle of this conversation.

"Wealth would mean choices. You could indulge the child in whatever you chose," he finally said.

"An indulged child. What a charming offer," she said. She wanted a family for her child. She wanted her child to be surrounded by the warm love she had always missed when her mother had gone away to some far-flung location. Right now, this was too much to process, so she feigned a conciliatory tone. "I'll consider it."

She wiggled her feet, which were feeling better, then swung her legs around to the floor without fully taking into account the awkwardness and level of effort it took to stand up at this point in her pregnancy. It was embarrassing, really. At work and in public, she took care to sit on chairs that were higher so as never to get stuck. She had expected herself to be one of those pregnancy women who trained for marathons, not the type to get stuck on her sofa like a pill bug. Still, one of the many benefits of living alone was that, in her apartment, she didn't have to give much thought to it. If she ended up rolling around a bit to make it to standing, no one was here to judge. But the effort of getting up from a sofa that sunk as low and comfortably as hers was decidedly ungraceful. And now that she had begun, it was too late to do anything but forge ahead.

Her face flushed as she rocked forward and leaned heavily on the arm of the couch to get up, but before she made it any farther, Alessandro was on his feet, next to her, helping her up with a gentleness that sent a strange tightness through her chest. A part of her wanted to simply give in to him. She was tired of being strong, tired of putting on a smile and telling everyone that she was fine. She wanted this baby badly, but she hadn't expected pregnancy to be quite this tough. Now, she was close to Alessandro, close enough that she couldn't ignore how much she had missed the scent of him. Or the way her breath caught in her throat when his hand came to her cheek. She turned, and his eyes were hooded with unmistakable desire.

"Please do consider all the advantages of my offer," he said, and his husky voice sent a shiver of need through her.

Ann-Sophie drew in an unsteady breath and forced herself to look away from his deep brown eyes. "I'm going to make supper."

He let her go, but instead of taking this as a dismissal, Alessandro followed her through the hallway. Her body felt so alive right now. Alessandro's sudden appearance and promise to whisk her away into a life of luxury was a rush of relief and hope that made her feel vulnerable.

After the way he'd left her so abruptly, he was the last person she wanted to see her this way.

She turned into her kitchen, with the table in the breakfast nook on one side and the little balcony that looked out onto the courtyard of her building. She headed for the refrigerator.

"Are you hungry?" she asked. "I haven't been home in a week, so I don't have much to choose from. I was thinking broccoli soup and sandwiches."

"You should be eating—"

Ann-Sophie braced herself for oncoming pearls of wisdom on pregnant women—from the man who was likely the least knowledgeable on this topic in the continent. But he stopped, mid-sentence, and she felt a shift in tension in the room. She turned and found Alessandro looking at the built-in shelves next to the table. Actually, *glaring* was a more accurate description, and she immediately saw what had caught his eye. Her blood-pressure monitor, lying on top of the sheet she used to record the results.

Ann-Sophie crossed the room to snatch the paper away before he could get a closer look at it.

"Is there a problem with your blood pressure?" His tone was even, but she could hear a hint of warning in it.

"Right now?" She tilted her head, as if she had to consider his question. "Yes, in fact. The direction of this conversation is likely shooting up my blood pressure. Thank you for your concern."

She wasn't sure what she expected his response to be. Perhaps an argument or maybe blame, much the way she blamed herself. But he said nothing. He simply stared at her, looking genuinely stunned. Finally, he gestured to the table. "Sit down. I will make supper. Please."

The word *please* rippled through her with a rush of relief in its wake. She tried to muster up a little bit of frustration that he was taking over, but she was tired. The early meeting, the apparently less-than-subtle wander to Alessandro's offices in Milan, the flight, Dr. Azzizi's news and the thought of early maternity leave—it was all just...a lot. She closed her eyes, trying to gather her feelings. Even if she had no interest in marrying a man who had so easily ditched her before, he could make her supper. Especially since the other methods of relaxation he could provide were not a good idea.

So she settled at the table as he watched her, arms crossed, his expression inscrutable. "What are you hungry for?"

She chose to ignore the sexual undertones her exhausted mind was gravitating toward and focused on his actual question. She was always hungry these days, a fickle kind of hunger that demanded everything from bacon-flavored chocolate, to pickles, to wasabi peas. And cinnamon rolls, of course. None of those things could be classified as supper.

"It doesn't matter. Whatever you can make from the ingredients in my bare cupboards," she said.

Alessandro waved off her comment and pulled out his phone, and his side of the conversation suggested the person on the other end of the line was waiting for him nearby. He ordered a list of ingredients that made her mouth water, and she felt more of the tension of the day fall away. It was just a meal, she reminded herself. She hadn't agreed to anything. Definitely not marriage, a demand she still hadn't completely processed.

Why on earth was he interested in getting married?

The last thing she wanted to hear about was some antiquated notion of bloodlines. There had been something almost raw in his voice that suggested his real reasons lay closer to the heart. If this man had a heart. After his cold dismissal of her in Nice, she wasn't so sure.

He ended the call and then turned to her. "While we wait, is there anything else you need to tell me? Twins, perhaps?"

"There is only one baby," she said, "though at this point I look like I'm carrying at least two."

"What is the gender?"

"I'm not going to find out," she said, hoping that he could hear that this was not negotiable.

"We will do a paternity test, of course," he continued in a tone that implied that she should be taking notes or doing something to make sure she carried out his wishes to his liking.

"Will we?" She raised her eyebrows. "No one is backing you into this situation. You can walk away at any point."

He opened his mouth as if to reply, then closed it. Frowned.

Ann-Sophie sighed. "There are no other candidates, Alessandro."

"And I should take you at your word?" He gestured to her belly. "You kept this from me for seven months."

She closed her eyes and sighed. "I'm sorry you found out this way. I was going to tell you before the baby came, but I couldn't figure out how."

He raised his eyebrows doubtfully.

She frowned. "I can't change what I did. If you have so little faith in me, then you should probably leave right now. Remember my stress problem?"

Alessandro looked like he had plenty to say on this subject but refrained. As it turned out, high blood pressure was proving to have at least one upside.

He turned to face the counters, and she watched as he familiarized himself with her kitchen, inspecting her utensils and pans. This suggested that he himself was planning to make the meal, which surprised her, considering the fact that he had an army of staff at his disposal to take care of these things for him. But cooking was apparently one of the things he valued, something he had clearly decided not to fully outsource. That thought was a little depressing, considering how quickly he had talked about outsourcing the care of her and the baby to resorts and nannies.

Alessandro's back was to her, and she watched his muscles move under his crisp, white dress shirt, triggering memories of what those muscles felt like under her hands, what it felt like when his arms were around her as he laughed at her stories and kissed her so tenderly. No, it wasn't what his wealth could buy that was the hard to resist. It was the man himself.

By the time Alessandro tossed the pasta with fresh sausage, garlic-sautéed spinach, pine nuts and Parmesan, he was in control of his emotions again. He had been forced to control them after the bombshell of Ann-Sophie's high blood pressure was followed by her comment that suggested that he was, in fact, a current stress factor.

The urge to pressure her was strong, to get her to follow him to the nearest church immediately and get this situation under his full control. Marriage would bring stability to this situation and to their child's life—something he had never had. Right now, he was in no condition to consider what being a father would require of him; he would figure that out when the baby came. Instead, he focused on the way marriage would soothe the volcano of emotions that had been erupting since Massimo had walked into his office this morning.

Guilt, obligation and subtle exercises of power were some of his well-traveled negotiation routes, but these relied on creating increasing stress on the target, a method that was now out of the question. Alessandro needed to drastically reevaluate his approach.

He set the plates of pasta on the table, and she looked at the food with open desire. She took a deep breath of the mingling spices that wafted from the dishes. As she took her first bite, the tension eased from around her eyes.

"You can cook," she said with a hint of surprise, and he noted that her voice had lost a little of its sharpness.

"Of course, I can," he said, waving away the comment. "Meals give us three opportunities every day for pleasure. Why wouldn't I take advantage of them?"

She gave him an amused smile. "Good point."

Was this a negotiation path to marriage, one guided by pleasures? Foods, comforts, luxuries and physical desires... Some combination of these could sway with her.

"I used to cook more often when I stayed with my grandmother during the summers," she said, a little wistfully. Then she gave a little laugh. "A lot of meatballs and boiled potatoes. Not like this."

"I learned to cook from my grandmother, too," he said. She raised an eyebrow, and he raised his hands in protest. "You don't believe me?"

Ann-Sophie shrugged. "I'm just having a hard time picturing it."

"It was an interesting summer," he said darkly.

She rested her fork on her plate and tilted her head, watching him as if she was waiting for him to continue. It brought him back to moments ago, when, reeling from the high-blood-pressure revelation, and struggling to contain yet another surge of emotions, Alessandro had come close to pleading with her. *Please.* That one word had revealed far too much of the raw fear she had triggered, but it had also gotten through to her. The emotions he kept under tight control were another tool he could use, one that clearly got Ann-Sophie's attention. This path was more dangerous, but he would never let himself get out of hand. Never again.

When he didn't continue, she asked, "When are you planning to return to Milan?"

"This depends on many factors," he said, holding her gaze. "Are you planning to return to Italy soon?"

Her forehead wrinkled, and she shook her head. "As of today, I'm on maternity leave."

Judging from her frown, she was not happy about this. Interesting. "You are free?"

"Apparently." She flashed him a tight smile. "My job is triggering higher blood pressure, so I am under doctor's orders to reduce my stress."

She gave him a pointed look those last words.

He studied her closer. "You have no plans for the next couple months except to take care of yourself and the baby, correct?"

"Correct," she said, then gave him a wary look. "Please don't follow that up with a marriage proposal."

Alessandro ignored the comment and gave her a seductive smile because a more specific plan was forming, one that gave him more time to introduce her to the pleasures he could provide for her. "I have a different proposal. Our family's home sits in the foothills of the Alps, amid a countryside that guidebooks call charming. The temperature is warm and mild this time of year, and you can enjoy a swimming pool, fresh-baked pastries from the local bakery, naps and anything else that you may like."

Her eyes widened with unmistakable interest. Yes, pleasure was the right path. She claimed she didn't want his wealth *per se*, but just as he had thought, she would enjoy the spoils of it.

"And this enormous house just sits empty?" There was a hint of censure in her voice that he couldn't read.

"It's a country retreat. I assure you, it's well kept."

She tilted her head to the side, and her gaze was penetrating. "And you, of course, will be busy working."

Alessandro could hear the edge in her voice. This was a test, and he was not sure she even knew what answer she wanted from him. But he had learned from her comment earlier when he had made the calculation error of letting her know she and the baby would be alone. This was not what she wanted.

For the last seven months he did not seek her out, despite the way his body ached for her, he reminded himself. He could remain under control. So he offered her a compromise. "I will stay there when I can get away, if that is what you want."

"Italy is lovely this time of the year," she said, almost to herself. Ann-Sophie, whose job was to be a neutral medium for others' ideas, looked so far from neutral right now. He let her debate this option as they ate. After a few moments of silence, she set down her fork and straightened in her chair.

"Thank you for the offer," she said carefully, "but I'm fine where I am."

But Alessandro had not brought his family's company and name back from ruin by laying all his cards on the table in the first round of negotiation. He hadn't even begun to use all the tools he could leverage. But for now, he focused on the lowest-hanging fruit: This woman loved books. She loved to read, as was clear from the half-read books scattered across her living room.

So he turned to her and smiled. "I neglected to mention a feature of this house that might be of particular interest. We have an enormous library. Perhaps you would at least like to see it?"

CHAPTER FOUR

Two weeks.

Ann-Sophie had given herself two weeks to negotiate how to handle co-parenting their baby. They had to come to an agreement somehow, and if it happened in a country retreat in the idyllic Italian hills, well, that qualified as the vacation Dr. Azzizi had recommended. As Alessandro steered his sleek sports car along the winding two-lane road, Ann-Sophie reminded herself that there was no reason to feel anxious. Yes, she had agreed to this plan in a moment of weakness—how could she resist a library?—but she was on holiday. And in between enjoying all the extravagant luxuries Alessandro had promised, she planned to uncover why he was so set on marriage.

They had landed on a private airstrip, surrounded by lush trees that still wore their summer greens, but now, as Alessandro's steered them toward the Alps, she spotted glimmers of fall. Golden grains from the fields of the lowlands had now made way for endless ribbons of grapevines that lined the foothills, their leaves flaunting hints of oranges and deep reds at the tips. The warm air that blew through the open windows of the red two-seater caressed her, lulling her into a kind of dreamy state, where questions about the future and Alessandro's role in it didn't weigh quite so heavily on her.

This morning, Alessandro had arrived in a well-cut suit, clean-shaven, his dark, glossy hair combed off his face, as if he was ready for a board meeting. The only word she had for the complicated mess of feelings that stirred at the sight of him was relief. Relief as his intoxicating gaze washed over her, and relief that she might not have to care for the baby entirely on her own. Ann-Sophie knew both those feelings were just that—*feelings*, fickle and fleeting, not more concrete realities.

She couldn't forget that he wanted more than just two weeks in Italy from her. He wanted marriage and would likely pursue this goal relentlessly. Alessandro had the kind of wealth that could make too much of the world fall at his feet. He had been raised to expect that he should be the master of his own destiny, so she knew better than to trust any fantasies about the future. The moment he changed his mind, the moment she was not expedient, he could set her to the side. Along with the baby. And she knew too well how much damage that could bring to a child.

Two weeks, she reminded herself. She could leave it anytime if everything became too much. It wasn't as if she would be some sort of captive in his castle, guarded with impenetrable walls and a crocodile-infested moat...would she?

Ann-Sophie turned to him. "The place you're taking me... This was your family's country escape?"

"Massimo and I lived here for a number of years, until we left for boarding school."

She wrinkled her brow at the wording of his answer. "With you parents, right?"

"Occasionally," he said, and there was a guarded note in his voice, as if she had stumbled into well-guarded territory. "My father had business in Milan, of course, and the two of us were a handful. One of the many perks of wealth is that you can hire staff for anything."

There was a twist of bitterness in his voice, but when she glanced over at him, he gave her one of his distracting smiles. It was unsettling how well it worked on her. Right now, with the warm breeze blowing through his hair and his sleeves rolled up, exposing his forearms as he gripped the steering wheel, Alessandro Carandini was more attractive than any man had the right to be.

But after the past day with him, she could see the way he used charm and distraction as tools to get what he wanted, and currently he wanted something from her. That awareness spread through her again, reminding her of just how vulnerable she was to him. Maybe it was better to address their relationship directly.

"I just wanted to be clear about this..." She gestured between the two of them. He glanced at her, one eyebrow lifted.

"We won't be...?" She hesitated.

"Yes?" There was a hint of amusement that teased at the corners of his lips, but he waited for her to explain what she was almost sure was perfectly obvious. Also, she was completely failing at being direct. Her face felt hot, and her blush was certainly obvious. Everything back in Nice had flowed so easily between them, and right now, when he was purposely making this conversation difficult for her, it was clear how easily he controlled the flow.

She let out a little huff of a breath. "I'm talking about the bedroom."

"Is that a proposition?" He looked in her direction and his eyes raked down her body. "I'm definitely open to it, though I usually like a woman to buy me a meal first."

The humor caught her by enough surprise that it cut through her embarrassment. And for a moment, she forgot the mess of her life and the uncertainty of their future and just laughed. After seven months of worries, it felt so good to let go and laugh. It felt dangerously like stepping back in time, to those nights before he so abruptly shut down any questions of future contact.

"I'll keep that in mind," she said. "But my question is about sleeping arrangements."

"I have alerted Olivia to prepare a room for you, though you are free to stay in my bed as often as you wish."

She flushed at a particularly clear memory of lying next to him in bed. "As long as I take you to supper first, of course."

"Of course," he said. Then his expression shifted into something more businesslike. "I have also arranged for a doctor to visit for checkups. In case you change your mind about the paternity test."

Frustration rose inside, still so close to the surface. "I haven't."

"Why not?" he asked softly.

She swallowed, fighting the urge to turn away. Instead, she forced herself to be direct.

"I know that I would not be sitting here in your car if I weren't carrying your child. But nothing between us—co-parenting, let alone marriage—will work if you can't trust me. And I need to know—" She stopped. Swallowed. She didn't need to reveal any more vulnerabilities at this point. "You're going to have to trust that there has been no one else."

His eyes darkened with a gleam at the words *no one else*, and if she didn't know better, she might have called it jealousy.

"Trust is something to be earned, *cara*. But I will let you decide, of course," he said smoothly, though she was almost sure they were not done with the subject.

Alessandro slowed the car at a fork and turned onto a narrow road, a path through a grove of olive trees that curved until she could make out a village. Huddles of whitewashed houses with terra-cotta roofs climbed the hillside, peeking out from behind one another as if they were watching for her arrival. Above them on the hill was what could only be described as a castle. Stark, sturdy towers rose up above steep stone walls, and she caught glimpses of the roofs of a sprawling set of buildings that this fortress protected.

Ann-Sophie did not need confirmation from Alessandro to understand that they were not headed for one of the quaint, whitewashed houses in town. He was a Carandini. Of course, he was taking her to an actual castle, and, of course, he hadn't thought to mention this. In a twist she should have foreseen, she was, in fact, going to be living inside the walls of a fortress for the next two weeks. The possibility of a moat looked questionable in this sun-dried land, and she hoped the same for crocodiles lurking in its murky waters.

Alessandro raked a hand through his hair as he navigated through the narrow stone streets of the village. Here in this fancy sports car, against the backdrop of charming shops and blooming window boxes, he looked much more like the man she remembered and less like the polished businessman that had shown up on her doorstep. More at ease. They passed cafés, bakeries and a small square that held a church and other stately buildings. The town was built in a mix of stone and peeling coats of whitewash, which gave it a look of rustic elegance.

"Does this village have a hotel?" she asked.

Alessandro glanced at her, lifting a skeptical eyebrow. "Are you contemplating alternate accommodations?"

"Maybe." That sounded better than an escape route.

The line of houses came to an end, and they made their final ascent to his family's property. The entire wall of the fortress looked as if it had been built and rebuilt countless times. It was a mix of rough-hewn rock, bricks and finely chiseled stones—definitely solid. The only sign of a moat was a trickling creek that flowed under the narrow bridge just before the entrance. If crocodiles had ever walked this path, they had left long ago in search of swampier grounds.

An iron gate twisted and curled between the pillars that held it, and it swung open theatrically as they neared. Alessandro drove across the bridge, and they entered a cobblestone courtyard. Sprawled out in front of them in the same patchwork of stone was a rambling, castle-like villa. Stained-glass windows glittered from the majestic towers, and arched passages, covered with flowering vines, stretched across the lower levels. Before Ann-Sophie could take in any more details, Alessandro turned into a long, covered terrace, brought the car to a stop and turned off the engine. She blinked, trying to orient herself in this place. It felt as if she was dreaming, and she hadn't even seen the library yet.

Alessandro came around to her door to help her out, which saved her about five minutes of awkward struggle. When she stood up, her body so close to his, she felt the same thrill of awareness as she had the day before in her living room.

"Welcome to my family's retreat," he said, his voice

low and rough, as if he was feeling the same hot current of desire. "I hope it meets your expectations."

Ann-Sophie drew in a breath, trying to focus on her surroundings and not on the man who stood so temptingly close. Though she had toured impressive castles all over the world, they had felt like museums, tied to an impersonal history. But this place was…alive. Almost magical. Somehow, despite knowing that the Carandini family moved in Italy's most elite circles, she wasn't prepared for a place like this. Maybe it was the word *retreat*, which brought to mind the cabin she and her mother had stayed in for a few summers. It had been smaller than the garage in front of her, and the only bath was a dip in the cold lake a short walk away. This walled estate was so laughably far from that.

She started along the cobblestone path, with Alessandro distractingly close by her side. When they reached the main courtyard, where a fountain gurgled, she realized why her mind had gone so incongruously to that tiny cabin in the Swedish countryside. This place was quiet in the same way, without the sounds of the city. Instead, it was alive with the twitters and squawks of birds and the rustle of leaves in the warm breeze. And though its gracefully sloping roof and arched entryway was so far from a cabin in Sweden, for a moment, she felt…at home. *Don't get comfortable*, she reminded herself. This was just for two weeks.

"How long has this place been in your family?" she asked as they walked along the well-worn stone path.

"My grandfather purchased it when the business grew. He was originally from this area and wanted to make sure our family's roots stayed here."

There was a way Alessandro talked about his family that she didn't understand, a distance, as if it wasn't his own family he was discussing but a general period of history he was recounting.

"Did your grandparents live here with you?" she asked.

"They gave the villa to my parents so they could raise their children," he said, and his tone was even more distant, despite the fact that these "children" included Alessandro. "My grandparents did everything they could to guide my father. This place for us, a position in the company, but in the end, he and my mother weren't interested in any of it. My brother understood this much earlier, but I was the fool who defended them for years."

His voice never wavered or showed any hint of emotion, but his words took Ann-Sophie's breath away. She turned, studying the sharp cut of his jaw, the proud line of his forehead, looking for signs of emotion, but she saw no distress. She had no idea what to make of any of this.

They entered the villa through a heavy wooden door, and Ann-Sophie found herself in an extravagant hallway. The ceilings were lined with dark wood, each plank carved and polished, and the floors were tiled in the same terra-cotta as the roofs, covered with area rugs in lush reds and blues.

"All your needs will be taken care of by the household staff," he said as they walked across the front entryway, toward an elegant staircase.

Household staff. Ann-Sophie resisted an eye roll, though she supposed she wouldn't miss doing her own laundry. "I probably need to talk to someone about a low-salt diet."

"I have given Olivia an overview of your situation and

general precautions, but please let her know any specifics," he said, and she couldn't help but notice that his voice was no longer devoid of emotion. When he mentioned Olivia, she heard the kind of warmth he seemed to reserve for his brother. "She fed and kept track of two rambunctious boys. I guarantee nothing you request will pose anywhere near the challenge we did."

Alessandro led her up the staircase and to another hallway, lined with marble busts and paintings of sprawling landscapes in gilded frames. He stopped in front of a door near the end of the hall.

"You may have your choice of bedrooms, of course," he said in that lazy, sexy voice of his, and the word *bedrooms* sent a rush of awareness through her. "But I asked Olivia to prepare one I think you would particularly like."

He opened the door into a room decorated with the same dark, intricately carved woods as the hallway. Across the room, French doors led to a balcony, muted in the sunlight, and on the far side was a majestic bed covered in a silky red bedspread that looked like temptation incarnate. But all of this was eclipsed by shelf after shelf of books. Was she sleeping in the library?

"This is lovely," she said, her voice breathless.

"I'm pleased you like it, but there is another reason why I chose this one for you."

A smile teased at her lips. "Let me guess. Your bedroom is next door?"

"It is." He flashed his heart-stopping smile, so full of the humor she remembered. Her heart thumped harder. "But I suspect you might like what I'm about to show you even better."

Alessandro led her to a door along the sidewall, under an

intricately carved wooden threshold. He turned the handle and revealed an area far too vast to be called a room, even in this castle-like place. As she walked out onto a stone balcony, she could see she was in one of the villa's towers she had spied from the road. At some point, the balconies that lined each level had likely been used for defense, but now the stone hallways were lined with wooden shelves, stacked with countless rows of books. Her room was just a teaser. This was the place Alessandro had used to lure her here, and it was even more spectacular than she had imagined.

Ann-Sophie walked to the edge of the balcony and rested her hands on the polished stone, gazing down the open center. Lit in the rosy golden light of the stained-glass windows was a spiral staircase in the same dark wood as the shelves, and at the corners of each level were small alcoves, fitted with armchairs and lamps, like tiny reading rooms.

Alessandro rested his hand on the curve of her back, and a new feeling rushed through her, one she refused to call hope. He leaned closer and whispered in her ear, "Welcome to the Carandini family library."

She had given him two weeks, and that was exactly what he needed. He would ease her defenses down and seduce her in every way possible again. Marry her. And the restless feeling she stirred in him? The risk of exposing the raw edge this villa evoked in him, haunted by the ghosts of his own past? Anything could be managed for two weeks. Of course, he would let himself indulge in pleasures. Those alone weren't a risk. It was allowing these pleasures and indulgences to take over his emotions.

Which were absolutely under control now.

The more he had gotten used to the idea of this pregnancy, the more he saw the opportunity it presented. A baby of his own would mean a chance to right the wrongs of his childhood. He would never deceive his child. He could never shower this child with false affection, then cast them away when they became an inconvenience with a sprinkle of half-hearted gaslighting. He would set clear expectations and follow through, not blame a child for things they were too young to understand.

"I can't believe your family owns all of this," said Ann-Sophie softly, as she gestured at the shelves.

"It's an impressive collection," he agreed.

"Just looking at all these books makes me outrageously happy," said Ann-Sophie, shaking her head.

The tension that he had carried in his shoulders since the moment his brother had told him about her *roundness* was finally starting to ease. If she could be coaxed into raising the child here at the estate, with its library and the walls, this would contain the unpredictability of their…situation. So Alessandro took a deep breath and let himself enjoy the soft material of her dress under his hand and the lavender scent of her hair.

"This was my great-aunt's life's work," he said, watching Ann-Sophie's features, studying her reactions. "In another era, from another family, she likely would have been an academic. But she and my grandfather grew up without means, and she could never get her hands on enough books. So when my grandfather's fortune exceeded anyone's dreams, he gave this project to her."

"Am I staying in her room?"

"When she stayed here, yes. Though she chose to live in the home where she and my grandfather grew up, she spent a good amount of time here, building the library of her dreams."

"Interesting," she said, but creases were forming on her forehead. She looked up at him, her eyes wide and unguarded. "All of these books just *sit here* in this house, where no one lives?"

She sounded...displeased by that idea. He frowned. "Not anymore. You are here to read them."

She tilted her head a little, as if to consider his answer. After a moment, she said, "Show me around."

Alessandro gestured to the main floor below, where a series of cases stood at the center. "The oldest books are shelved on the bottom floor, away from direct sunlight, where the room temperature can be more carefully controlled."

She nodded, then began to wander along the balcony, taking in the rows of books that glowed in the red light of the stained glass. Alessandro found himself entranced by the way her hair glittered and moved as she reached for one volume, then another.

"The remaining floors of stacks are for more recent books, arranged by language, I believe. You might find something in Swedish."

Ann-Sophie continued slowly, her gaze fixed on the shelves as they passed. She stopped, stooped down and then rose. "Did you grandparents love to read, too?"

"Like many people with new money, my grandfather likely saw this project more as an opportunity to establish the family's prestige."

She frowned a little, and Alessandro found a strange twinge of...displeasure. As if he had wanted her approval. But that couldn't be right. He focused on the fact that her voice had lost the bite he had heard in Stockholm, and right now, she looked like she had in Nice, so curious, so unselfconscious. Except that she was, indeed, rounder. Gloriously so.

His family was not a topic he volunteered information about, as the conversation could so easily slide into territory better left in the past. But this past would soon be part of his child's history, too. The idea had stirred something inside him, unfamiliar and uncomfortable.

"Where did all of these books come from?" she asked.

"Some were here when my grandparents bought the place, which was how the project started. The rest came from auctions, estate sales, travel...everywhere. My great-aunt developed a bit of a reputation, so libraries came to her with older books in need of costly restoration or books they no longer had room for."

"This place definitely has the space," she said, and he heard a trace of awe in her voice.

"If there is anything you want to add to the collection, please let me know."

She shook her head slowly, as if she couldn't quite believe what was in front of her. She continued to wander until she came to an alcove with a velvet armchair and a small table with a reading lamp. "I think I'd start with more readers."

He blinked at her, then nodded. "I'm sure that can be accommodated."

Ann-Sophie let her hand brush over the soft velvet of the armchair that sat in the rays of the afternoon sun.

"My aunt built these nooks on each floor to make sure she could find natural light for reading, no matter the season or time of day."

Ann-Sophie turned to him. "Do you have a favorite place to read?"

"Not much of a reader. Never have been." The moment he said this, her expression fell. She looked…disappointed in him, and he found himself very displeased by this. Displeased enough to reveal a truth he so rarely spoke of, before he could think better of it. "Dyslexia."

"Oh," she whispered, and the hint of judgment that he had seen on her face shifted to something softer.

Alessandro was well aware that this was exactly the kind of softening he needed to exploit. The plan was to use this…emotional reaction he was having to the unearthing of his past, he reminded himself. His most strategic move was to show her a glimpse of what she wanted to see, then shut it all down again.

"My parents preferred the term *lazy*," he added, forcing himself to reveal his past. "My father was particularly affronted by the idea that there was something 'wrong' with his son—his words."

"I'm so sorry," Ann-Sophie whispered. "That's awful."

Her blue eyes seemed to pierce through all his protective layers, leaving him with the disquieting sense that she was *seeing* him.

Alessandro waved off her sympathy. "By that point, it probably didn't matter. I had already decided that being spectacularly bad was much better than being the kid who always needed extra help."

She furrowed her brow. "But they still should have—"

"We don't need to adjudicate my childhood," he snapped. "I've moved on."

Ann-Sophie blinked at the sharpness in his voice. "I'm sorry for prying."

But her penetrating gaze stayed fixed on him, as if she was seeing even more. He felt…off balance.

Warning bells clanged in his head, reminding him of the last time this happened, when he lashed out at her back in Nice. He would absolutely not lash out at her, but he had to do *something*. So he did the only other thing that he could think of. It was the thing that he had needed to do since the moment she had walked down her own street and back into his life. Slowly, so there was no mistaking what his intentions were, he lowered his mouth so it was almost touching hers. She blinked up at him, her eyes widening in surprise. And then he saw the shift, the look he had not allowed himself to imagine for seven months. Open desire, just for him. But now that she was so inescapably close, right in front of him, he stopped resisting.

He closed the distance and gave in. Her lips were as soft as he remembered, and they tasted of that sweet, forbidden fruit he had kept from himself for far too long. His body reacted to the taste immediately with electric arousal. This was the heaven he had been waiting for. He brushed his mouth against hers again, telling himself that this was part of his plan.

He wanted more, so he opened his lips to hers. Her breath hitched, and a wave of satisfaction ran through him. Yes, she wanted him, and he could have her again. The thought echoed inside him, stronger than he expected, the moment she parted her lips. Her soft mouth was hungry, and he could taste a want that matched his own. The fire that had burned unbearably high every night of that one, glorious week flared higher.

Alessandro cradled her jaw in his hands, aching for more of the eager strokes of her soft tongue. He ran his hands over her shoulders and down her arms, remembering each dip and swell. Then he found her waist, testing the changes that he had seen with his eyes. But the touch was so much better. Slowly, he moved his hands over her new roundness, caressing—

He felt movement under his hand. Their child, so undeniably real. Something strong and painful rip-roared through him, turning the heat that moved through him into ice. It was as if a long-healed wound had been forced open, and he needed to staunch the flow of fear and dread.

Alessandro pulled back and looked down at his hands, frozen on each side of her belly. He glanced up at Ann-Sophie, at the crease that had formed between her eyebrows, her unspoken questions hanging between them. He refused to answer them. Instead, he backed away and removed his hands. His body protested loudly, and he clenched his fists, resisting the urge to reach for her. He took a step away. Her eyes were wide, and her hair tousled. Her cheeks had flushed, and the confusion written across her face was mixed with raw want.

Then her mouth twisted down with what could have been hurt. Alessandro clenched his hands to stop himself from reaching for her again, from touching her, from doing so much more than kissing her, just to soothe that hurt away. But he would not subject himself to the emotions that still tore at him. So he took one more step back, ignoring the twist in his gut as Ann-Sophie's expression grew more guarded.

And when he spoke, his voice was fully under control. "Supper is served out in the garden at seven."

Then he turned and walked away.

CHAPTER FIVE

Ann-Sophie stood, frozen in place, as Alessandro's last footsteps echoed on the stone walkway of the tower. When the door closed behind him, she sank into the lush velvet chair, her mind reeling. Was he just…walking away? After that kiss?

For one, short moment it had felt as though Alessandro had exposed a guarded piece of himself, and then they were kissing with a magic that entwined this enchanting library with the man she had lost herself with seven months ago. Seven months of longing came alive, longing she had tried to repress. His lips had caressed hers with the same aching hunger she remembered too well.

And then, just as unexpectedly as this magical moment had started, Alessandro took it away, leaving her with this sensation that something in her was cracking as he walked away. And she was doing all she could to hold herself together.

Maybe she should have foreseen this possibility…and prepared for it. But Ann-Sophie had spent years telling herself and everyone around her that she couldn't be abandoned by a father who had never been there in the first place. Now, she was suddenly faced with the fact that she was absolutely not Just Fine, Thank You, despite the countless times she had said it. Because the moment she pictured the way Alessandro had stared at her belly as the baby kicked, his expression a mask of horror, she knew where this was going.

He was going to leave them.

This made no sense when she considered his expressed desire to marry her, and yet she had felt his reaction viscerally. It had been a live wire straight to the place where she had buried her grief. He had found that place, and her instinct was to flee, to go back to Stockholm. She told herself she could. But first, they needed to come to some sort of agreement about the child, even if it didn't involve the marriage he demanded.

Ann-Sophie had no idea what to do with all these thoughts. The sun filtered through the windows, casting long rays of light across the tower and lighting up the place. She wanted to disappear in this quiet tower library for a while and try to settle her thoughts. Also, at the moment, she was stuck in the chair and too exhausted to get herself out of it. She was so very tired, and this seemed to be the perfect place to take a nap. Then again, everywhere seemed to be the perfect place to take a nap these days, so Ann-Sophie propped her feet on the matching red velvet footstool and let herself drift off to sleep.

She had no idea how long she slept, but when she opened her eyes again, the light had completely changed in the glow of the evening. Also, her stomach was like an empty, clawing pit of hunger. She hadn't eaten since the plane ride, and she was thirsty enough to drink the moat water. Ann-Sophie wrestled with the chair and managed to get herself to standing. She walked through the quiet halls, tracing her way back to the courtyard, then began to circle the house looking for Alessandro. When she found him, they would have a talk about the way he turned on her so suddenly. A bit of food would hopefully help her get her thoughts in order.

She walked through vine-covered archways and past a pool tiled in blues and whites until she came to a terrace with a table, shaded by a large umbrella. The terrace was covered in tiles in the same terra-cotta with accents painted in bright blues and whites in a pattern along the low walls that surrounded it. Just beyond, the breathtaking countryside spread out in front of her, dotted with orchards and vineyards. The table was covered with a white tablecloth, and on top of it, she spotted a pitcher of water. Relief rushed through her as she crossed the patio, grabbed a large glass and poured it full of water. She drank it in a few short gulps, but as she set it down, she took in what she had missed in her desperate thirst: Only one place on the table was set. She blinked, frowning. Were she and Alessandro eating separately?

A door creaked behind her, then footsteps, and her traitorous heart beat harder. She turned, but it was not Alessandro. It was a woman with brown hair streaked with gray, and she was carrying a tray of food. The woman smiled at her in such a motherly way, but after Alessandro's comments, Ann-Sophie knew that this was not his mother.

"I am Olivia," she said, setting a bowl of soup in front of her on the table, followed by a small cutting board with a loaf of fresh baked bread and olive oil. "Welcome to Villa Carandini."

"I'm Ann-Sophie, Alessandro's…" She had no words in Italian—or in her native Swedish—to neatly describe what they were. Then again, her unwieldy stomach spoke for itself.

Olivia's smile grew. "Alessandro told me about you. Please, be seated. He left me with instructions to make sure you are well fed and cared for."

Her mind immediately focused on the word *left*. "Alessandro is not here?"

Olivia shook her head sympathetically. "He had urgent business in Milan. But I am here to take care of everything you need."

Not quite everything, she thought darkly, but she smiled and thanked Olivia, wondering just how much the woman understood of their situation.

"I'll return with your second course when you are ready," said Olivia and she disappeared inside the villa. Ann-Sophie ate a spoonful of delicate tomato bisque, trying to get her mind around the fact that Alessandro had not only walked away from her, but also felt the need to use his car to put distance between them. With the flimsiest of excuses, no less. Where was the trust he spoke of so pointedly back in Stockholm? Ann-Sophie looked around at the castle-like place that rose up around her and the swimming pool that shimmered in the evening lights. All this beauty did nothing to ease the sinking sensation inside her.

Just as she had thought. Alessandro had abandoned her.

This event should be enough to rule out completely the idea of a marriage. She would never let her child be raised by a father who would leave them. Ann-Sophie cut herself a thick slab of bread and dipped it in the olive oil, so rich and lemony it brought tears to her eyes. Or maybe the tears were about something else. But she would *not* cry over this man. She swallowed and looked out at the last rays of sun that glittered across the valley until she felt a little less emotional. When the warm evening breeze worked its magic, she tried to look at the situation more rationally. Alessandro's abrupt change in mood suggested he'd been rattled by their kiss, and for the first time she wondered if he was just as overwhelmed by their situation as she was.

Olivia appeared moments later with a heaping plate of pasta with roasted vegetables and prosciutto. Before she could walk away, Ann-Sophie asked, "Do you have a moment?"

"Of course," said the woman and sat down in the chair next to her.

She had so many questions about Alessandro, but asking them would show how little she knew about the man whom she was having a child with. Or maybe it was too late to care about that.

"How long have you known Alessandro?"

Olivia smiled. "My sister and I were hired to care for the boys from the moment that Alessandro and Massimo were old enough to walk and get into trouble. And they were definitely trouble."

Ann-Sophie tried to imagine Alessandro and his brother as little boys getting into mischief. How did a playful boy turn into the man who had so coldly walked away from her?

"Their parents must have appreciated your work," she said carefully. Nannies were de rigueur in upper-class households, and yet from Alessandro's comments, she suspected that this arrangement was more complicated.

"Their grandmother hired us," said Olivia, and there

was a protectiveness in her voice. Alessandro had hinted at a carelessness in his parents' relationship with them when they had driven in the car that Olivia's answer seemed to confirm.

Ann-Sophie felt an uncomfortable twist of sympathy in her stomach, despite her frustrations. She herself had had a father who had no interest in her, and despite the fact that she had been surrounded by her mother, her grandparents and so many aunts, both those by blood and those by choice, it didn't take away that sorrow of a parent who did not care. Ann-Sophie looked around at the decadent wealth of Alessandro's childhood. More money and more luxuries would not have fixed any of the weight of her hurt, and she imagined it was the same for him.

"How often does Alessandro visit now?" she asked.

"He and his brother celebrate holidays here."

"Does he bring dates?" She bit her lip, wishing she could take her question back.

Olivia paused, giving her a searching luck. "He could. But he never has. Ever."

Until this unexpected pregnancy.

"I can't imagine owning this whole place and leaving it empty," she said.

"It's hardly empty," said Olivia with a laugh. "My family lives here."

Ann-Sophie's face heated. "Sorry."

Olivia waved off her apology, and her expression turned more serious. "When the twins' grandfather bought this villa, the surrounding wall was crumbling, threatening our town. The old owner didn't have the money to fix it, and the state wasn't going to take on the project. Everyone in the village was grateful the Carandinis did. If the family had not bought that property, half of the village's houses would likely be rubble at this point. One of the winter rains would have certainly swept away the wall, taking with it the whole village. Before they came, some breach of the wall took out a few houses on the hillside below. So in the eyes of the town they are welcome to come and go as they please as long as they continue to maintain the place. And both Massimo and Alessandro have promised that."

How nice that Olivia found Alessandro reliable. Trustworthy. Pretty much the opposite of her experience.

"Ah, it's my brother, who is supposed to be at the villa negotiating a marriage that won't singlehandedly destroy our family's reputation we have worked so hard to fix," said Massimo as he leaned against the door to his office, his hands in his pockets, his intense gaze unrelenting. His tone was deceptively casual, but Alessandro could hear the bite in his brother's subtle rebuke. Alessandro had never cared much about his own reputation, but both his grandfather and Massimo had dedicated their lives to the family name. He had spent his teens making both their lives more difficult, and he had sworn he would not do that again. Now, Massimo was invoking the family name, what all their work was supposed to be for.

"Are you back in the office to announce the date of your nuptials?"

"I will take care of it in the next couple weeks," grumbled Alessandro.

He kept his eyes on the screen in front of him, though he had no illusions that Massimo would believe he was reading. The truth was that he had spent the entire morning staring at the same pages. Going word by word through a document had always taken a great deal of concentration, and today it seemed impossible. In truth, he had never spent much time exploring adaptations that could have helped. Maybe the label of laziness was not so far from the mark. Both his parents treated that label with indifference, which Alessandro found far less painful than the scorn they reserved for a learning disability. Looking back, Alessandro wouldn't have called any of his choices during his teens conscious ones. They had been more intuition, which had been his saving grace for so much of his life. Until now.

"Catarina and I would like to attend your wedding. In addition to my hopes that you will also find a path to love..." His brother paused, as if he was thinking of his own surprising path. "I want to head off any speculation that this marriage is a last-minute decision so the child is not born out of wedlock."

Alessandro met his brother's gaze. "It is a last-minute decision so the child is not born out of wedlock. For the family."

This truth was so much easier to speak than the turmoil of emotions that had exploded inside him the moment he had felt a tiny kick from inside Ann-Sophie's stomach. It was no secret that he and Massimo had both dedicated their adult lives to rebuilding the company *for the family*. Just one generation ago, his parents' volatile, explosive relationship had bankrupted the family business and ruined every ounce of good will that his grandfather had carefully built up for his entire career. His parents' relationship had consumed them, so caught in indulgence and petty jealousies and social one-upmanships that it didn't leave time for anything as mundane as running a business. Let alone raising two boys.

The previous year, when Massimo's and Alessandro's acumen, strategy and dedication to their business had still not been enough to quell the speculation that the brothers would get distracted by the kind of relationship that had sunk the Carandini family's reputation and fortune, Massimo had arranged a marriage for the explicit purpose of extinguishing these worries. The plan had worked, both as a public-relations campaign and also privately, to the unexpected satisfaction of his brother. That was supposed to be the end of it.

Now, Alessandro's unanticipated baby threatened the balance that Massimo had gained for the family. Alessandro had made sure he was held to a different standard, that affairs should be expected and would not affect any other part of his life. But, as his brother had rightly pointed out, people would tolerate that behavior only so far.

When Massimo didn't respond, he added, "This is not the direction I saw for my life."

As the words came out of his mouth, the image of Ann-Sophie on his bed that had come to him in Nice reappeared in his mind. He had, in fact, imagined this life, and that image had filled him with an emotion too volatile to handle. "But I will not allow another generation to be brought up the way we were. I will be there for my child."

"I understand," said his brother, his voice softer. "I also want to show that the family is behind you."

Alessandro gave Massimo a nod of gratitude. His brother would always be behind him, even if they didn't always understand each other.

"Your well-known charm is noticeably absent," added

Massimo, raising an eyebrow. "This is the one time all those years of practice should be used."

Alessandro could have answered with a flippant comment and moved on, but he didn't. Instead, he tried to put into words something he had been stewing on all day.

"Some part of me just shuts down." He frowned and added, "I learned to be charming for a reason."

Even saying those words were painful. They brought him back to a time when his selfish anger had controlled him.

His brother frowned. "You are not the same man you were then."

"I am not the same man because I have kept all these impulses in check. I don't think I'm capable of anything that looks like what a family should." The emotions he had felt when he and Ann-Sophie kissed had been so full of the hurt he had built himself up from all those years ago. "Our parents were not suited to have children, and neither am I."

His brother looked like he had plenty more to say on that subject, but he just shook his head. "Save that problem for after the wedding. Right now, you need to get this woman to the altar before she has a baby out of wedlock."

"For the family," Alessandro added with a humorless smile.

"Go back, and I will cover you for the next two weeks," said his brother. "Keep me updated about the wedding."

He couldn't bring himself to resent Massimo's focus on the wedding *for the family*—a plan that Alessandro himself had come up with back in Stockholm. Maybe it was the universe's idea of payback, since he had pushed his own brother into a marriage to a person he had never met? At least Alessandro had chosen his partner himself. And they were undeniably well-suited in the bedroom. Too well-suited, he thought darkly.

As Alessandro left the city behind and drove into the countryside, the rolling hills of his childhood spreading out on either side, Massimo's advice ran through his head: Focus on the wedding, and deal with the rest later. It was questions concerning the future that provoked the eruption of his long-controlled feelings. Until he had secured her agreement, he would block these thoughts from his mind.

Alessandro turned off the main road, through the olive grove, and entered the little village that had been his home for the first years of his life. It had been a long time since he had spent time here, and he made a mental note to ask Olivia about the best bakeries, the most charming areas to show to Ann-Sophie. Would she agree to raise their child here? By the time he climbed the staircase and walked the long, familiar hall, he felt more like himself than he had in the last two days. Anything that was uncertain, he would put off until after the marriage.

Long ago, he and Massimo had learned the lesson that though people told themselves they made important decisions with logic, it so often wasn't true. They made decisions with their hearts. This was why he had earned the rightful place as the silver-tongued charmer. Because for all the pain his parents' emotional manipulations and nastiness had caused him, they had given him skills that he had sharpened into a tool that was just as useful as Massimo's strategic planning. Alessandro could sway people's emotions. He would lead Ann-Sophie to the inescapable conclusion that marriage was the solution that her heart wanted, and he would enjoy the pleasures that this would entail.

But as he came to a stop in front of her doorway, Alessandro felt a twist in his gut. Was it guilt? It couldn't be, not for showering his future wife with attention. This was nothing like the games his parents played with each other. Any misconceptions she might develop were issues for after marriage, and he was not going to consider them before their wedding. So he pushed away the discomfort, telling himself he would only listen to that feeling the moment he walked out of the church with rings on their fingers.

Then he turned the knob to the door of her room and walked in.

Ann-Sophie sat in an antique armchair next to the open French doors, and the warm, sweet breeze blew through her sun-drenched hair, making it shimmer in the light. She looked out the window as she sipped from an espresso cup, suggesting she hadn't heard him open the door. He took a moment to study her. She wore the pajamas he had asked Olivia to find in town and lay out for her, and the silky material spilled over her lush, round body, giving him tempting hints of her new curves. On the table next to her was a tray of breakfast choices. In addition to the fresh pastries and fruit, he spotted the *filmjölk* and granola she had kept in her kitchen, which he had sent his assistant to gather before they left Stockholm. Despite the late morning hour, she appeared to have awoken not so long before, as her cheeks were still flushed from sleep. Seeing her like this, enjoying a slow, indulgent morning, sent a surge of satisfaction through him.

He wanted to just watch her for a bit, search this peaceful scene for more clues about the woman he found so fascinating. He could admit this fascination to himself because it would act as fuel for the next two weeks of negotiations. But after another moment, he was not satisfied with just looking. He started across the room, and after a few steps, she turned, startled. She must have been expecting Olivia because her expression changed. Her eyes widened with surprise, then flashed with what he could have sworn was happiness before she schooled her features into something more guarded.

"I apologize for my absence," he said, his voice low and graveled. "It was unavoidable, but I returned as quickly as I could."

She wanted to believe that his absence was "unavoidable." She wanted to believe him because everything would be so much easier if he had left because of some sort of emergency, some event that would likely never happen again. Because then she could relax into this life that he was spreading in front of her. She could let herself imagine everything that she wanted it to be.

Right now, Alessandro was looking at her the way he had in Nice, his eyes no longer guarded, the distance she had felt suddenly gone. He was looking at her again like there was no place on earth that he would rather be than right there with her. Ann-Sophie's heart soared in her chest, and, oh, how she wanted all of this to be real. How she wanted to forget the way he had turned on her so quickly after the startling kiss in the library. Maybe she could have even put that aside if he hadn't done the same thing back in Nice, so easily shutting her out of his life.

Now, he reappeared, as if he could slip in and out of her life when the whim struck him?

"How kind of you to return so quickly," she said, letting a sharp bite leak into her voice. Ann-Sophie turned back to her coffee and took a sip, welcoming the familiar, bitter taste.

Alessandro moved closer, and when she didn't look up, he kneeled in front of her. He was so inescapably *there*. She had nowhere else to look except the hard line of his jaw and the shadows under his eyes. Ann-Sophie fought against the memory of the last time he was this close, in the library, when he kissed her with a magic that made her forget everything else.

"It was unavoidable," he repeated, and the word grated on her nerves. Then he flashed her an indulgent smile. Did he think he could use her attraction to wave away her disappearance? The nerve of this man...

"You left yesterday without warning," she snapped. "You said nothing about leaving to me."

Alessandro managed to look a little contrite. "I apologize. It won't happen again."

He raised his eyebrows, as if he was waiting patiently for her to calm down. As if he was *indulging* her. Which only provoked her further.

"My father left, and he didn't come back." The words exploded out of her. "I will not be blindsided by you."

Alessandro blinked, clearly unprepared for this burst of emotion. The last of his smile slid off his face. The room was silent, as if everything that surrounded her—the elegant furniture, the books, the extravagant paintings—was just as stunned that she had spoken these words as Ann-Sophie was.

"I'm sorry," he finally said. "I didn't know that."

"Disappearing is not okay for anyone," she said, biting out the words. "I shouldn't have to drag out my own baggage to make this point."

"You're right." His voice was soft, conciliatory.

He reached for her hand, but she pulled away. If he touched her right now, the frustration bubbling inside might turn into something rawer. But now that she had revealed this piece of her past, she found that she wasn't ready to stop.

"I've never met my father," she said, and her voice trembled a little. "He and my mother were assigned to the same team in Sri Lanka—he, a photographer and she, a journalist—and from then on, they often traveled together. They both loved the nomadic life of being on an international correspondence team and were passionate about making the world a better place through their work. They partnered so closely, so it was no surprise that their professional relationship drifted into something more."

Ann-Sophie had known this story since she was a teenager, and yet she had never spoken aloud. Now, a strange feeling swept through her, as if she was a child again, her mother's warnings of why she should never contact her father ringing in her head. She clung to every thread of anger because she would absolutely never cry over a man who couldn't bother with her.

"My mother told him that she was pregnant and wanted to keep the baby. She had always wanted a child and this was their opportunity. She told my father she loved him and that they could have a family together, working and traveling." Ann-Sophie fought to keep the armor of her anger up as she approached this next part. "He told her that he loved her, too, but he had no interest in a baby. He wanted nothing to do with the work of bringing up a child, nor did he want to drag a child along on assignments or take turns staying back. Basically, he gave her an ultimatum—him or the baby. And she chose me."

Her voice wavered a little at these last words. Her mother had been forced to start over, to find a new team to work with rather than face this painful choice every day. She gave up a man she was in love with because Ann-Sophie came along. This was the sacrifice that Ann-Sophie could never forget.

She already felt so vulnerable with Alessandro, who could so easily brush off sudden disappearances. If he was incapable of understanding her position, then no amount of negotiations would make a marriage viable. Now, with that baby coming so soon between them and the trigger of his leaving such a direct hit, that raw feeling scraped inside her.

"We both have been thrown into this situation, but abandonment is not acceptable for me or for my child. My mother made that decision for me, that an uninterested father was worse for a child than no father at all. She did not want me to have to face that pain as a child, and I am grateful for it. The way you just…" She struggled for the words for what had triggered this earthquake inside her, one she was still feeling the aftershocks of. "The way you shut out whatever this is between us—that can't happen. You can decide on your relationship with the baby, and I can't control that decision. But if you want marriage, you should know that this is a nonstarter for me."

"*Our* baby." He was looking at her with a seriousness that she hadn't seen before. He didn't speak again for a long time, and when he did, his voice was low and grave. "First, I will never abandon a child of mine. Ever. On this, I swear on everything that I love."

And she heard a deep resonance of truth in his voice, something that broke through her anger.

"Your parents weren't there for you," she whispered, almost to herself.

But he heard her, and he didn't look away. He lifted his hand to her cheek and stroked it with a gentleness that took her breath away. "I will not disappear without telling you again."

Despite all the reasons she should be wary of this declaration, something inside her eased. The loosening started in her belly and spread through her body, strong, and unexpected, and the heat that had been anger just moments ago turned into something else.

"I am truly sorry," he said, softly.

She brought her hand to his, tracing his long fingers, his warm hand, the cords of his muscular forearms, until she reached the rolled cuffs of his elegant shirt.

Oh, how she had missed him. Ann-Sophie had spent the last seven months trying so hard not to think about this simple truth, letting anger and indignation fill all the spaces where want might settle. Now, every feeling she had suppressed was crashing through her, so much more complicated than desire.

Or maybe this didn't have to be more complicated than desire. Maybe she could just…give in. Give herself a place for all the tension of the past days. Just a little bit.

His fingers traveled down her cheek, over the tender skin of her neck. He traced her collarbone, his fingers lingering just inside the opening of her silk top. The soft material of her pajamas brushed over her skin, and her breasts felt heavy and full as his gaze swept across her face, dipping down to her lips. When his eyes met hers again, they were lit with something that felt raw. Real. There was so much she didn't know about him, so much they had to work out, but right now, as he looked into her eyes, she felt their connection growing stronger. Attraction sparked and sizzled between them, but there was something else there, a contradiction, both an opening and a closing she didn't understand. *I am having a baby with this man.* The idea settled inside her with a flutter of happiness she wanted so badly to trust.

His lips were close. She knew the brush of those lips, the way it felt to have them on her neck, her breasts, everywhere, and her entire body ached for all of it. Silently, Alessandro offered her his hands. She took them, and when he helped her to standing, she brought her hands to his arms, feeling the hard muscles under his perfectly tailored shirt, remembering them. She continued her exploration, tracing the strength of his broad shoulders. Then she slid her hands into his silken black hair and urged him closer. He let out a low groan, a sound somewhere between desire and relief, and his hard mouth met hers. Finally, they were kissing again. She opened for him, and his tongue teased hers, but he slowed, kissing her with an aching tenderness that left her gasping for breath. She let her hands travel down his chest, memorizing, reminding herself of every inch of him. *This was real.*

His hands brushed over her body, and she tensed. She held her breath, waiting for his reaction, as his hands moved slowly over her stomach, exploring the round fullness. He groaned in that deep, masculine way that left no doubt that he was enjoying every moment of his exploration. She looked up at his eyes, heavy-lidded with pleasure. His thick lashes only partially shielded the heat that radiated from them.

"Many good marriages have been built on less than we have between us," he said, his voice rough.

A shimmer of wariness radiated through the languid haze of their kiss. "I suppose it depends on how one defines a good marriage."

"Marriage is whatever we would like it to be."

Of course, Alessandro Carandini thought about marriage as something that was up to him. Of course, a man of his wealth and power thought that what he wanted out of marriage was stronger than an institution that had survived for millennia. She supposed there was some truth to this idea, that everyone could negotiate their own path to some degree. And yet, if he was so bent on getting married, then there must be something inherent about it that he wanted. Maybe he was withholding that from her, or maybe he was only starting to figure this out. After all, she hadn't been prepared for the force of her own reaction. Either way, she would not simply trust that everything would turn out to her satisfaction simply because he said it would. Because, as he had so rightly pointed out, trust went both ways.

He was watching her in that way he had more than once since he had shown up at her door, as if he was making an assessment. Then he smiled. "I hope breakfast was to your satisfaction."

"Somehow it included my favorites from Sweden." She was still a little befuddled about how Olivia had managed this. But when his smile turned a little smug, she understood that he had been in charge of this feat. Back when he had taken stock of her refrigerator, he must have noted what she liked.

"I want to make sure that you are completely satisfied with your stay here," he said, that lazy smile teasing at his lips.

She had no idea what to do with this stunning, sexy, charming man in front of her, or with the overwhelming reactions she had to him. So she laughed. The Alessandro she had spent a week with was definitely back. And she was going to end up in bed with him very soon if she was standing this close to him much longer. Ann-Sophie had not ruled out that possibility, but she definitely needed to think it through under less…compelling circumstances.

"I would definitely be satisfied with a swim this morning," she said. In the pool, they would be outside within sight of others. Also, a little time without carrying the weight of the baby would be heavenly.

"In the bureau you will find a selection of suits in case that might be helpful." He leaned forward and brushed his lips against her cheek. "I look forward to seeing you there."

Alessandro dove into the pool and took a long, slow breaststroke under the surface, then another, letting the refreshingly cool water ease his body. When he reached the shallow end, he turned and sprinted at a punishing speed back toward the deep end. He continued back and forth across the pool, letting the temperature and the exercise soothe his body and his mind. Their kiss had fully awakened the desire that he had felt in Nice, but it was tangled with something new. He knew not to think too much about whatever that new thing was. His disappearance had almost ruined the plan for marriage—he had seen it in her face when she spoke of her father. Ann-Sophie had mentioned her father in passing during their week together, something about him being out of her life, but Alessandro had not registered the way that this had seemed shaped her until he had stumbled on her breaking point. He would not make that mistake again.

He pushed himself, lap after lap across the pool, until his thoughts dissolved, and there was only the cool water around him, shimmering in the sun. He stopped in the middle and stood, slicking back his hair. His control was restored.

Ann-Sophie was sitting at the edge of the shallow end. Her feet dangled in the water, and she leaned back, resting on her hands. Her lush belly was covered with a red swimsuit, a beacon that both called to him and warned him off.

"You didn't like the swimsuits Olivia provided?" he asked.

Ann-Sophie gave him one of her amused smiles. "I prefer the one I brought. I think the days of string bikinis have long passed for me."

"I beg to disagree." He knew better than to approach her right now. If he did, he wouldn't be able to stop himself from touching all her new curves, which he found himself thinking about more and more. Instead, he dove back under the water, cooling himself again, and came up in the deep end. "Will you join me?"

She shrugged. "I was going to, but all your lap swimming is exhausting just to watch."

"I'll pretend to drown for a few minutes if that helps," he said.

"No thank you. Then I'll feel obligated to save you, and I'm not sure I'm spritely enough to manage that." A gust of wind blew her hair across her face, and she tucked it behind her ear.

He flashed her a smile. "Another option is to splash you a few times."

"Fine. I'm getting in." She let out a sweet little huff, then slipped into the water and swam toward him, smiling. The relief of the cool water was written all over her face. He felt a surge of satisfaction that he had given this to her, a feeling that he refused to look too closely at.

"In the water, I feel a little bit more like my old self," she said.

"I like you the way you are," he said with a smirk.

She raised an eyebrow, as if she was matching these words against his reaction to her in the library.

"I can demonstrate how I feel," he said, and she laughed.

He was telling the truth. The explanation for his reaction was too complicated to get into. That would come later, after their marriage. Then he would deal with the part of him that had simply lost the ability to be the person he should be. But if he was going to make it through these next two weeks, he needed to focus on these moments, right now.

CHAPTER SIX

As ONE DAY drifted into the next, Ann-Sophie was lulled into a cocoon of the luxurious present. She could choose the quiet stillness of her favorite library alcove, bathed in sunlight, or she could chat with Olivia and her niece, Cinzia, as they washed and chopped the vast bounties of the day's harvest from the garden. But most of the time, she and Alessandro were together. They spent days at the pool, or walking through the groves of orange trees that were ripening in the countryside just outside the village. She ate fresh oranges from the trees with peels so soft they fell apart, and the sweet juice ran through her hands. Everything about her life right now could be summed up with the word *decadent*.

But there was one way that she had not yet given in to decadence. Every night, after a long, lingering supper on the terrace, filled with wandering conversation and course after course of freshly prepared foods, Alessandro would walk her to her room and kiss her with a hunger he didn't try to disguise. But since the day she arrived, he had never once mentioned sharing a bedroom, let alone marriage. She understood that he was enticing her, using every one of his persuasive skills to enchant her, but she couldn't bring herself to care because this was the Alessandro she knew from Nice, the man who had charmed her with no end goal. Before he abruptly ended all contact, she reminded herself. She couldn't forget that piece.

She was going along with this for the baby, she told herself. All of this pleasure, and all these leisurely, drawn-out evenings lingering by the table must be doing something to lower her high blood pressure. And then she would return to Stockholm. But the idea of looking out her apartment window into the gray autumn skies as the daylight grew shorter felt so far away, and Alessandro's teasing voice, his soft, sensual caresses, his laughter—it was all so very present. So she tried not to think too hard about the fact that the end was coming closer.

One evening, as the sunset turned the sky bright oranges and reds and made the leaves on row after row of grapevines shimmer, Alessandro pulled the lounge chairs to the edge of the terrace to watch Mother Nature's evening show.

"Tell me about the kind of life you would like when the baby comes," he said softly, seriously.

This life. She almost spoke the thought aloud. But the life she imagined here was with Alessandro, and she was almost sure this life had limits they would run into at any time. So instead, she imagined herself back in Stockholm. "I have paid maternity leave for over a year, so I imagine there will be plenty of diapers and feeding and walks in the park."

Over the last seven months, she had passed countless mothers with prams in Vasaparken, and yet she still couldn't picture herself doing the same. It felt so unreal.

"Is that what you want?" His voice was soft, and there was something guarded in his expression.

She swallowed. "Honestly, I don't think parenting a newborn has much to do with what I want."

The corners of his full mouth quirked up at the wryness in her voice.

"Point taken," he said. Then his smile faded. "I still think you should ask yourself this question."

She tried to ask it that night as she lay in bed, with the sweet caresses of Alessandro's lips still lingering. But after years of separating want from need, it felt wrong. As if just thinking about her wants was asking too much.

After a week, she and Alessandro stood in a spacious examination room in a doctor's office, taking in their surroundings. Alessandro had tempted her into walking to the appointment with a promise of a stop at a café in the main palazzo for her new favorite mid-morning snack, a decaffeinated cappuccino and a fresh pastry from the bakery. The doctor's office was just off the palazzo in a majestic stone building with tall windows and stone gargoyles guarding from the top floor. As they had wandered in, she had expected to find the same sort of evidence of times past that she had seen in all of the town's shops, as if the building was etched with a history of the comings and goings of the little town's residents.

But the inside of the doctor's office was nothing like anything she had seen in town. It looked newly renovated and startlingly well-equipped for a village practice in the rural countryside. When she glanced at Alessandro, he was studying her as if trying to read her.

"The doctor will come to the villa at any time, of course, but she suggested a visit at the office, where she had the ultrasound machine and any other equipment she might need at hand," he said.

Her surprise turned to amusement. "I have been to countless doctor's appointments during my pregnancy, and not once have I considered the possibility of a doctor coming to me. I'm perfectly fine with an office visit." Her gaze drifted to the computers and machines that filled the place. "I just can't believe that a small town would have the same services that were in the hospital in the center of Stockholm. This place seems prepared for anything."

Alessandro gave a little nod. "When Massimo and I were young, my grandmother made a long-term commitment to significantly boost the finances of this place. The equipment, building upkeep, bonuses for the staff, whatever they needed."

She blinked. "That was quite generous of her."

"In a way." His expression turned darker. "My grandmother took over some of my father's business roles so he could focus more on his family. When she understood that Massimo and I would be here without the attention of our parents, she switched tactics and built up the community around us to help."

She looked around her at the fully equipped office. "But this is for everyone. She could have just hired a doctor."

"I think she understood that we were a handful, and the task she needed required more than money. Quite frankly, I think she wanted the town to have an incentive to take care of us."

She tilted her head to the side a little. "Maybe that qualifies as self-interested, but this whole town has a state-of-the-art practice. Good has come from it."

He flashed her a wry smile. "I guess all this money does have its uses."

A knock on the door saved her from coming up with a good response to that. A woman with long, graying hair walked in.

"Dr. Cantabella," said Alessandro, and their embrace was warm and familiar.

The doctor shook Ann-Sophie's hand. "I received your medical charts from Stockholm, and I noted the high-blood-pressure readings. Your doctor reported no other complications."

Out of the corner of her eye, Alessandro seemed to stiffen at the mention of her high blood pressure.

"That's correct," said Ann-Sophie, "if you don't count the problem getting in and out of chairs."

Dr. Cantabella smiled.

"I'm hoping a few weeks in Italy have helped to bring my blood pressure down," she added.

"Let's check." Ann-Sophie could feel herself tense the way she always did these days when thinking about her blood pressure…likely triggering higher blood pressure. The doctor seemed to recognize this problem. "Try closing your eyes and imagining yourself somewhere else, a favorite place."

She loved to travel so her favorite place changed all the time, but right now, the place that came to her was her favorite alcove in the library with two velvet seats. She pictured it in detail, the light filtering through the stained glass, the scents of thousands of books, all waiting to be explored. But she wasn't alone. In this vision, Alessandro was there, so close, leaning over her to kiss her and then…

"Your blood pressure looks good," said the doctor with a note of surprise in her voice. "I'm not sure what you imagined but your heartbeat went up at the end of the reading."

Ann-Sophie flushed, but the doctor smiled at her. "Whatever you're doing, it's working."

She let out an audible sigh. She glanced over Alessandro and saw glimpses of relief and happiness.

"Let's check on the little one," said Dr. Cantabella, then rolled the ultrasound machine from the corner.

Ann-Sophie exposed her growing belly, and she could see the way Alessandro's eyes were drawn to it. His expression stayed neutral, but she could've sworn that she saw a flash of desire in his eyes before it shifted into something more appropriate.

As the doctor moved the wand over her stomach, images took shape on the monitor. A nose. Lips. A foot with tiny toes. Their baby. It was there, moving, its tiny body curled, protected inside her. A burst of joy took over, and she turned to meet Alessandro's gaze, to share this moment with him, but all the lightness of the past few moments had disappeared.

His expression was stark, and the haunted look in his eyes cut a hole in her own happiness. The bubbling joy that had run through her just moments ago was leaking out of her so fast she didn't know what to do with it.

"The baby looks wonderful," gushed Dr. Cantabella, startling Ann-Sophie out of her thoughts. She tried to focus on the monitor, but the feeling this visit had just taken a very bad turn stayed with her. The doctor seemed oblivious. "Please continue with your blood-pressure monitoring and come back in a week, but don't hesitate to call or come in before that with any questions."

Never once had a doctor or midwife been this solicitous, and yet Ann-Sophie barely heard these generous offers. All she could think about was the haunted look in Alessandro's eyes.

They exited the modern insides of the doctor's office and started down the steps to the cobblestone street. As they walked across the palazzo, he asked, "Would you like to walk home, or should I call for a car?"

"Walk," she said. A ride involved a driver, and right now, she wanted to be alone with him.

As they started up the hilly streets, he slipped his hand in hers, but there was no connection. It was as if he had simply turned it off.

Finally, she pulled her hand from his and came to a stop. "What happened in the doctor's office?"

Alessandro was wearing sunglasses, but she was almost sure he wasn't looking at her. "I don't know what you're talking about."

She was sure he did. "When you saw the baby, something happened."

He shook his head and began to walk again. As they continued along the street, Ann-Sophie could feel her frustration growing. They were on the edge of town with a few scattered buildings, and the gate into the villa wasn't far ahead. She stopped again. He looked up at the gate, then back at her.

"Let's continue." His voice was now filled with warning.

"No." The word came out stronger than she had expected. "Something happened and it was about the baby."

He grimaced, as if she had slapped him.

"You need to think about your blood pressure," he said. She could see the way his jaw clenched as he spoke these words in a low voice.

She threw up her hands. "Is this a version of telling me to 'calm down'? Because that doesn't work. You need to think about the child."

The words slipped out of her mouth before she thought about how harsh they sounded. She closed her eyes. *Deep, calming breaths.* When she opened them, Alessandro had removed his sunglasses, and his expression was stark. In his eyes she saw fury and pain. "I'm *always* thinking about the child. I can promise you that."

Her breath caught at the graveness in his voice. It rattled through her, the rebuke a slash inside. She swallowed. "I'm sorry. That came out wrong. I didn't mean it that way."

A little of the hardness in his eyes softened. She searched for more words, but nothing seemed right.

"Explain this to me," she finally whispered. "*Please.*"

With the word *please*, his eyes softened a little more. He didn't speak. He looked out in the countryside and she wondered what he was thinking about right now, what he saw in this place and what he saw in her. The distance between them had suddenly widened, and it felt like she would never understand him. The thought weighed heavily inside her.

When he looked at her again, something had shifted. In his eyes, she found familiar spark of heat, and it sent a distracting jolt of awareness through her. "We'll talk back at the villa."

Something had loosened inside of Alessandro in the doctor's office, and it was not settling back the way it should have. The way he needed it to. Instead, he felt the ominous echoes of his younger years, when everything around him seem to trigger a live wire inside him, jolting him with feelings he couldn't process. He had deadened that live wire long ago, or at least he thought he had, but staring at the image of the baby... The bones of his long-buried emotions had rattled to life again, and they threatened everything that he had spent his adult life building.

But Alessandro knew how to fix this. He knew exactly what would channel all these emotions into something that brought temporary relief and not destruction. He had resisted this path for over a week, focusing on the most strategic way forward to marriage, but ignoring his own needs was clearly taking its toll. Because he was not a man who was accustomed to depriving himself, not in this way. He thrived on sensual indulgence, and the woman in front of him was indulgence incarnate. If this situation was going to demand a pound of flesh from him, he would take from it the pleasures of flesh in return.

Alessandro led Ann-Sophie up the path to the villa and through the silent halls of his childhood, past doors he used to peek through, looking for his absent parents, long before he understood that they were not hiding in one of the countless rooms of this villa, but had fled to someplace or another with half-formed excuses. Over the years, they dropped the pretense of reasons for their disappearances, leaving it to Olivia to deliver the news. *The way you did to Ann-Sophie.* The thought rattled inside him, and he shoved it away.

As they continued past the hall to what had been his childhood room, he felt the urge to pause. It was strange. He had not dwelled on this part of his life since Ann-Sophie had arrived. But she seemed to infuse unexpected joy into the place where shadows always lurked. Now, all these memories were crashing down on him. He needed to staunch his wounds before they bled him dry. But first, he would give her what she wanted, a glimpse into the past that had formed him. And then he would ask for what he wanted in return.

Alessandro led them through the halls and came to a stop in front of the door next to her room.

"You really have been sleeping on the other side of the wall from me this whole time?" she asked.

He tucked a strand of silky hair behind her ear, then whispered, "Every night, I imagined what we would do if you came to find me."

Her cheeks flushed a satisfying pink. The lavender scent of her hair was everywhere, and her plump lips were parted and so temptingly close. Just a little more patience, he told himself. When he opened the door, she looked up at him, then entered.

The room was decorated with rich tapestries and hand-carved furniture, and Alessandro appreciated these more impersonal qualities. It lacked the specific associations that his childhood room had.

She stood before a painting of a bacchanalian scene. "Whose room was this? It couldn't have been yours as a boy."

"It was intended for guests, though it hasn't seen any in quite a few years."

She wandered around the room, and he followed her, like an animal closing in on his prey, his eyes drawn to the curves of her full breasts spilling over the bodice of her sundress. When she had finished peering in the closets and pausing at the bookshelves, he gestured to the baroque love seat.

"Please, sit."

Ann-Sophie settled into the little sofa, and Alessandro found a footrest for her to prop up her feet, then sat next to her. He stared at the spray of freckles that had darkened across her nose over the last week in the sun. This life here in his villa suited her, he thought, clinging to the satisfaction the thought gave him.

But before he could let the heat of their closeness distract him, he would give her what she asked for. Honesty. It was an exchange, one he had to make for the outcome he needed, he reminded himself. Soon, this would all be over.

Her eyes lost a little of their hazy focus. "What happened in the doctor's office? I don't know how to describe it. You looked almost…" Her lips curved down into a frown. "You looked haunted when you saw our child. Whatever this is, we need to discuss it before the baby is born."

The words sent tremors through the control he had clawed back, but he gave her a tight smile. "I have my questions about being the father that I want to be, and seeing the baby reminded me of them."

This was all true. Or at least the most palatable version of the truth.

Her frown deepened. "Is this related to what you said about your parents?"

He knew this wasn't an intentional jab, and yet he felt barbs dig into him. "Are you feeling sorry for this poor little rich boy?"

His voice was smooth and cutting, laced with mockery. It happened so quickly, a reflex that he regretted. He wanted to take this woman to bed and marry her, and yet he found himself snapping at her. And they hadn't even begun to get into the details. It made no sense, but this was the problem, wasn't it? This was why he had built up his walls.

Her eyes widened, but to her credit, she didn't shrink away.

"Don't do that," she said with a steadiness he hadn't expected.

Alessandro gritted his teeth and reined in that out-of-control feeling inside him. He *would not* lash out again. Cruelty was straight out of his mother's playbook, and he would not be like his mother. Not at any price.

"I'm sorry," he said quietly, then forced himself to go on. "When Massimo and I were in our teens, we didn't last long at any of our boarding schools. Our records say we both got kicked out for fighting, but that is not quite the truth. I got into fights, and Massimo backed me up.

"Something small would trigger me, my anger was suddenly overwhelming. I would let it out, and, of course, people would come back at me. Massimo and I had always been athletic, and we were raised feral in a way that our upper-class classmates weren't used to, so taking on a couple of them wasn't a problem. But pride is a powerful motivator at these places, so inevitably there was retaliation, and Massimo took my side. Even my grandparents' money and prestige weren't enough to keep us there."

That part was easier to talk about because everyone he went to school with knew it. The next part was harder.

"When we got kicked out the first time, I expected my parents to pick us up and berate us. As it turned out, they couldn't be bothered. We simply got shipped directly to a new school. But after the third expulsion, we were finally delivered somewhere else—our grandparents' estate.

"That alone should have been enough to change my course, but I was a handful, wild, getting into all sorts of trouble with anyone I could find. Usually, my grandmother's lectures were given at the table, so I was surprised one day when I found my grandmother waiting for me one last night as I sulked in the door. She looked at me and said, 'Your parents are not going to come no matter how much trouble you cause or don't cause. You cannot let this anger control you. You must control it or neither you nor your brother will have a future.'"

The fear those words had triggered still sent a chill through him today, but he was too far into this story to stop here.

"I think she knew if she had told me my own future was doomed, I wouldn't have listened. But my brother, the better twin, a smart, ambitious one—that I could and would destroy him? The idea filled me with a kind of fear I had never experienced before."

Ann-Sophie frowned at him, as if she was missing something. "What do you mean by the better twin?"

"When I was younger, my parents told me this in countless ways. I was too loud, my tantrums were driving them crazy and dyslexia was just a badge of incompetence to them. I was a disappointment and made things hard for them. And if my memory serves correctly, there was some truth to that."

He felt numb as he said these words, but when he caught a glimpse of the devastation in her expression, something twisted inside.

Her brow furrowed. "But most eight-year-olds cause

their parents grief. I caused my mother plenty of heartache."

Something flickered in her gaze and he was drawn back to her story.

"But wanting to know about one's father is a natural thing," he protested. "That's not the same."

She tilted her head to the side a little. "Isn't wanting your parents' attention natural, too?"

"Not in the way that I did it. Massimo, for example, managed to get through this without, for example, throwing a piece of priceless art at the wall, chosen specifically because my mother had just bought it."

Ann-Sophie looked at him as if she wanted to disagree but held herself back. "So you went to your grandparents and had a good conversation and that fixed it?"

He wanted to tell her yes, but she had that skeptical look on her face, and he wanted to get through the conversation as quickly as he could. He wanted this to be finished.

"I found a more acceptable outlet for my emotions," he said evenly.

She raised her eyebrows. "I'm curious to hear a teenage boy's boundaries of acceptable."

He laughed, despite all the heaviness he felt. "Teenage boys are not particularly known for acceptable boundaries, nor for their emotional awareness."

The corners of her mouth lifted.

"It's tempting to make something up just to shock you," he said. "But you will probably be able to guess where I found my solution, considering that it is at the heart of my well-earned reputation."

Her brow furrowed again for a moment, but then understanding seem to hit her. "Sex."

He nodded, and she was quiet, as if this idea was sinking in. He let her put together these pieces of him. Part of him regretted telling her this, as she would likely soon understand her own unwitting role in this portrait. But showing her these parts of himself was part of larger negotiations, he reminded himself. Even if this conversation felt like something completely different.

Finally, she gave him a look that bordered on amusement. "So basically, in Nice I was part of a long-term self-styled therapy project to keep your emotions under control?"

He could smooth over the hint of bleakness in her voice and get her to laugh, and this could lead them to what his body was craving. He could have brushed it off, telling himself he had imagined it, but something wouldn't let him do it. He told himself to follow his business instincts, that he was so close to getting what he wanted, but...

It would hurt her. And he couldn't make himself do that.

So instead, he gave her a self-mocking smile. "It was supposed to be like an alternative to therapy. But it isn't supposed to affect others, and with my well-earned reputation usually comes an understanding that there are limits to a fling with me."

"I'm afraid I didn't follow your exploits closely enough to get that message," she said, the sharpness returning to her voice.

He shook his head impatiently. "That wasn't the problem. Others have asked for more, and I have gently, smoothly, led them back to an appropriate understanding. But with you, I didn't. I *couldn't*. I had a reaction and I have spent the last seven months trying to figure out why."

Ann-Sophie blinked, as if this was the last thing she had expected him to say. Then her eyes narrowed, as if she didn't believe him.

"It was why I blocked your number," he added, his voice rising. "It was why I never answered your message. It would have been so easy to slowly let you down the way I, frankly, have done to other women. But even on that last night, I knew if we had any further contact, it would make giving you up harder. So... I took precautions."

"Because we never had a chance? You never imagined anything more with me?"

He knew the answer she wanted, but he couldn't make himself give it to her. It would be a lie. "I have made sure never to imagine anything more with anyone."

"I see." Her voice was a whisper.

"Until now."

The silence that hung between them felt uneasy, precarious. He had just tipped his hand instead of playing his best card, and she could decide what to do with it. And still, *still*, he felt the pull of her body, the longing that had been building since the moment he had seen her in front of her apartment building. And he wanted her like nothing he had ever wanted in his life. He wanted to soothe the riot of feelings that were threatening to take over, but he held himself still, his fingers tense with the effort of not pressing his lips to hers, losing himself in her, and letting all other thoughts disappear.

She lifted her hand and ran it over his cheek, and when he met her gaze, he could see the understanding was mixed with determination. Did she think she could save him? Change him? Did she think this scenario had a happy ending, where he would get over his past and they would live happily ever after? If so, she was not the first to make the mistake. It had happened enough times that he understood this as a warning sign.

He should back away, but at his core he was a deeply selfish man, and some things just would never change. He knew this would create problems further down the road, but he reminded himself he had tried to do the right thing and it still had led him here. So he gave in. He leaned into the lush temptation of her lips and kissed her.

CHAPTER SEVEN

I HAVE MADE sure never to imagine anything more with anyone. Until now.

Alessandro's words looped through Ann-Sophie's brain as his mouth pressed against her for an achingly slow kiss. Her heart pounded in her chest, and it felt as if her body was floating. His kisses were both too much and somehow not enough, and desperation tinged her hunger for him.

I could spend forever right here, in this moment. The thought was startling, overwhelming, but before she could process it, she was suddenly in his arms and he was lifting her, belly and all.

"Where are you taking me?"

The intensity of his gaze was dizzying. "The place I've wanted you since the day I brought you here."

He set her down in the middle of an imposing bed of thick dark wood, but instead of following, he got on his knees in front of her. Alessandro was *kneeling* before her. Slowly, he removed one shoe, then another.

"Thanks. My shoes are hard to reach these days," she said, trying to lighten the mood and this feeling of enormity of the moment.

Alessandro smiled a little. "I am so happy to be of service, as always."

This was the man who had seduced her in Nice, and

she felt a sudden twist of disappointment as their conversation from just moments ago came together with this moment. For him this was a road to forgetting, not connecting. How did that fit with imagining something more?

She told herself it didn't have to all make sense right now, not when she wanted him like this. She had wanted him so many times this week but was afraid of what would happen if she gave in, but now, she had decided to put her fears aside and have him. That thought disappeared when he began to lift her dress, revealing her body. Fear broke through the haze of desire. He hadn't reacted well to the ultrasound of the baby. What would he do when he saw the full extent of her bare belly? It wasn't easily overlooked.

"Are you sure you want to see…all of me?"

His dark eyes glittered. "Very sure."

Then she remembered the way he had looked at her in the pool, with a kind of hunger that suggested that he desired her as she was, right now. But the fear that he would suddenly turn on her, reject her, abandon her—it still lingered, and she didn't know how to make it go away.

He lifted her sundress again, this time exposing the roundness of her belly, and she stilled as he settled his hands on it. The baby moved, and she saw him flinch, but he didn't pull away. Maybe this was what he needed, she told herself, just a period of getting used to the idea of having a child. After all, she had had seven months to get used to it, and Alessandro had had little over a week. She couldn't expect him to seamlessly blend the idea of a baby into his life so quickly, could she? Of course, there would be these little bumps in the road.

They could move forward. She wanted to move forward when being with him felt this good. Maybe if she gave all of this a real chance, their little family could be everything she wanted it to be. Right now, everything was possible.

The tight coil of desire was building inside her, spreading languid heat through her limbs. Alessandro unfastened the top button of his crisp, white shirt, revealing bronze skin and a hint of dark hair. He unbuttoned another and another, each button revealing more of the flat planes of his chest, then his muscular abs, as Ann-Sophie stood, mesmerized. He shrugged off his shirt, his biceps flexing, a reminder of the power and strength her body remembered. He unbuttoned his pants, and her heart thudded relentlessly in her chest as the last of his clothes slid down his body. Alessandro stood in front of her very naked and very aroused. This man was a god, with burnished muscles and the infinite complexities of light and darkness. *And he could be hers forever.*

"I asked the doctor if this was safe when I made the appointment, and she said as long as you are comfortable, we are free to do what we like." He flashed her a smile. "I intend to aim a bit higher than comfortable."

He propped pillows on the top of his bed, then gestured for her to lie back on them. The mattress dipped as he climbed between her legs.

"You have no idea how sexy I find you," he said, his voice a low groan.

She lifted one eyebrow and gestured to her round belly. "Even like this?"

"Especially like this," he said, and the low rumble of his voice left no doubt in her mind that he was telling the truth. But attraction had always been their connection, not an obstacle that spread the distance between them.

Suddenly, she wanted him with a desperation that took

her breath away. Memories of Nice were a montage of sex and laughter and insatiable want, and they flooded through her mind, finally free.

She propped herself up on her elbows and bit her lip.

"How do we do this now?" she said, gesturing again to her belly.

Alessandro crawled up her body, his torso skimming her belly as he moved, and smug satisfaction was written across his face. "We'll figure it out."

Then he brought his mouth to one breast, and all rational thought left her. Her nipples had become more sensitive as the baby had grown, and the moment he put his mouth on her, she felt a jolt of overwhelming pleasure that was somehow connected to that place between her legs. She cried out and he pulled back.

"Does that not feel good?" he asked, frowning, his gaze focused.

"It does. It's just…a lot." She swallowed, then smiled. "I haven't done this in seven months."

Some of the humor left his face as he looked at her. "Neither have I."

Ann-Sophie blinked, registering words that rattled through her. They were chased with another burst of hope, this one stronger than the last. *Everything was possible.* But then his mouth was on her other breast, this time a slow tease, and she was lost in that delicious building pleasure. She let out a soft gasp, and he moved lower, kissing a trail down her stomach.

He slid off her panties and urged her legs open, and then he kissed a line up one of her legs. Her breath caught in her throat. Alessandro was kissing her inside her knee, up her thigh, on her stomach, and then finally, finally between her legs. The sensation exploded through her. It had been so very long, and she trembled under the slow caresses of his mouth. Her legs fell open, and she whimpered in pleasure, both familiar and new. Alessandro let out a low groan, then continued his slow, exacting assault on her senses. She was gasping for air, crying out at the pleasure until ecstasy exploded inside her, too much to hold back. He caressed her slowly, drawing out her pleasure, as her body sank into bliss.

"I'm so sensitive now," she whispered with a husky laugh.

She opened her eyes and found Alessandro watching her with what looked like primal satisfaction. "I noticed. I knew I would enjoy these changes to your body."

He crawled next to her on the bed and lay down behind her, stroking her arms, her waist. He kissed her neck with a tenderness that made her ache inside. And when he pressed his hips against her, she welcomed his hard, insistent length. Desire surged inside her again, and in that moment, she wondered if she would ever stop wanting this man. But then he slid his long, thick length inside her, and she was lost again.

He let out a long, low groan, and she had the urge to turn around, to see the pleasure on his face, to feel the connection, the intimacy that she hadn't let herself think about. Because she remembered the way it had felt to look into his eyes when he was inside her. Every barrier between them had slipped away. She hadn't let herself think about this in seven months and yet now, she wanted it desperately. But he was behind her, and when she turned a little, he gently pressed his hand on her cheek and kissed her neck again. Maybe it meant nothing, but she couldn't help but wonder if he was turning her away from him.

But even this thought disappeared when he began to move, his long length stroking the most sensitive parts inside her, and she gasped and cried as he taunted her with pleasure and teased her until she was there at the precipice again. As he pushed her over, she heard herself cry out his name. Then with a long, low grown, he came inside of her. The room was filled with the sound of their breaths as they lay there, connected. He kept his arm around her, his chest warm and solid against her back, and in that moment, she was happy. This life Alessandro was showing her was more than most people could ever hope for. It was pleasure and security for the baby. It would mean both parents would be a part of the child's life.

And in exchange, Alessandro wanted marriage.

It was not the marriage she had foreseen for herself. But maybe she should try for the baby.

She shifted, turning on the bed until she was facing him. Alessandro looked lost in less upbeat thoughts, but when she met his gaze, some of the heaviness faded. She leaned forward to kiss him.

"What would it look like if we married?" she asked quietly.

He blinked, as if the question caught him off guard. "What do you want it to look like?"

"I want to raise the child in Stockholm, at least some of the time."

"You're not enjoying the luxuries of this life?" He traced the curve of his arm with his fingers.

"I want us to have a more...typical life."

"The baby is not typical. Nothing about being a Carandini is typical."

She smiled a little. "I've noticed."

"This is a lovely place to raise a child, part-time. The child will have you and Olivia…"

"And you?"

"When I can get away."

"I see."

He was quiet for a moment. "You will have my resources at your disposal, and we will have a life together. I can give you pleasure and company, but I cannot give you love."

Ann-Sophie ignored the sting of this comment. "Of course."

"You're not asking for love?"

She hesitated. Neither of them knew what the future held. A week ago, she hadn't expected this moment. But right now. *Everything was possible.*

"I don't expect love," she said carefully.

He met her gaze again, studying her, and for a moment it felt as if the wall between them fell away. He found her hand and laced his fingers with hers. "Ann-Sophie, will you marry me?"

For once in her life, she allowed herself to *want*.

"Yes," she whispered. "I will marry you."

The next week flew by in a flurry of plans and paperwork. The wedding would take place in two weeks, a little after the baby hit the eight-month mark, giving them a little space before the delivery date. It would be a small affair in the village church, and the only invitees would be Massimo and Catarina, who had insisted on coming, and Ann-Sophie's mother, if she could make it.

Ann-Sophie looked thoughtful when he suggested it. "But I think she's away on assignment."

"I'm sure she'll come back for your wedding."

"But it's such a small thing and the baby is almost here. Maybe I should ask her to come for the birth instead."

Alessandro found that he didn't like the way that she so readily made excuses for why her mother didn't need to be there, but he said nothing.

"If I'm telling my mother, then you should let your parents know, too." She lifted an eyebrow. "Or maybe you don't want to invite your parents?"

"It doesn't matter either way," he said darkly. "They won't come. But I'll have Massimo pass on the message."

There were documents to prepare and a prenup to sign, one that specified dual residences in Stockholm and Italy. It made generous provisions for her and the baby under a single condition.

"'As long as the baby is biologically yours?'" she said, reading aloud. Then she looked up at him with narrowed eyes. "I don't even know where to begin with this line."

This topic was infinitely frustrating, and Alessandro felt the control inside him start to crack. "You would not perform a DNA test. You're leaving me with no choice."

"Interesting definition of 'no choice,'" she said, rolling her eyes.

The fissure lines inside him spread ominously.

"Why are you choosing to dig in your heels about this issue?" he demanded.

Ann-Sophie glanced at the lawyer, standing at the edge of the desk and pretending not to listen, like he was paid to do.

"Because it means you still don't trust me," she said softly.

Alessandro swiped a hand over his face, exasperated.

"You're making this more complicated than it has to be. If the baby is mine, then we have no problem."

"I don't think this is complicated at all. Either you trust the woman that you are about to marry or you do not."

The fissure lines inside threatened to break. He had kept his emotions perfectly under control over the last week. She had moved into his bedroom, and they spent their days together, making love at all hours. Everything about this was exactly as it should be. But she wanted more.

"Trust is not easy for me, even under less pressing circumstances," he said, his jaw tight. "I need this from you."

"Fine," she said, turning away, and her voice was cold and distant. "I'll sign it."

He stared at her, waiting for the familiar satisfaction in this win. He had softened Ann-Sophie by giving her pleasure and the emotional vulnerability that was driving him to the brink of his sanity, and he was now reaping the rewards. His plan was an irrefutable success, and he searched for the familiar rush that success always brought. It didn't come.

All he could think about was the way she wouldn't look at him right now. And the chill of her voice, as if he'd ruined everything. As if he was now the bully that he had never wanted to be.

That evening, she was quiet. The moon cast its watchful eye on them, reflecting off the ripples of the pool, as if to reflect every moment of the strain the afternoon had put on them. As they sipped the last of their evening coffee and ate the last bites of almond cake that Olivia had baked, Ann-Sophie turned to him.

"I realize I gave you a reason not to trust me. It was

wrong of me not to tell you for seven months about the pregnancy. But do you really think I would lie about the baby's paternity?"

He closed his eyes. "I don't. But a baby does not change me as a person. It does not take away thirty-one years of carefully guarding whom I trust." *This is who I am.* It was meant as a warning.

And yet she didn't take it as one because she smiled, so beautifully and inexplicably. "Alessandro Carandini... changing? Impossible."

It was the first time she had smiled at him since the papers were signed, and he found himself reveling in it.

"It does sound quite improbable, doesn't it?" he mused.

She shook her head slowly, but her smile grew, and suddenly everything felt lighter. Alessandro tipped his head back and looked at the stars that glowed in the night sky. What would it be like to hold on to this lightness, to share it with Ann-Sophie? And though he knew he was entering dangerous territory, right now, he wanted for this to be possible. Real.

That was the stuff of dreams. But the two of them were inextricably tied to reality, which he had to focus on.

So he turned to her and gave her his most charming smile. "I would like us to attend an event in a few days in Rome. It will be the official introduction of you as my wife."

She blinked, as if she hadn't considered this angle of being the husband of Alessandro Carandini and the mother of a Carandini heir. "What do I have to do?"

"Just be yourself."

Ann-Sophie gave a charming little snort of laughter. "Why am I getting the feeling it won't be that simple?"

CHAPTER EIGHT

"I'M GETTING MARRIED."

"Married?" Ann-Sophie's mother's voice flickered in and out on the other end of the line. Margarita Svensson was in Ethiopia, reporting on coffee beans that still grew wild in the mountain jungle and the farmers that harvested them. Gorgeous location, thought-provoking discussions, but tenuous mobile service at best.

"Yes. *Married.*" Ann-Sophie emphasized the word.

"To whom?"

"The father of the baby." It was a testament to her state of mind for the first seven months of this pregnancy that her mother needed to ask.

"I thought you hadn't spoken with him because he was an—" The connection broke off, but her mother's message was not lost.

"He was. But things feel different now." This reasoning sounded weaker when she spoke it aloud, but it *did* feel different.

"Are you sure that you want to marry him?"

She stared down at the enormous diamond ring he'd slipped on her finger with a seriousness that she hadn't expected. *From my grandmother*, he had said, his eyes guarded.

This was not a marriage built on love, she had reminded herself.

But still, the answer rang inside of her: She wanted to marry Alessandro. She didn't need it, but she wanted it. The problem was that she couldn't stop hoping the marriage would be anchored in something more, no matter how many times Alessandro implied it would be about creating a family. And having a lot of sex, if the past few days were any indication. She was definitely not going to get into this with her mother, so instead she said, "I think this is the best choice for the baby. I want the baby to grow up around both of us."

"You didn't answer my question." But then her mother gave a laugh. "You've always been such an independent child. Who am I to tell you how to live your life?"

The words warmed her. The last thing Ann-Sophie wanted was for her mother to feel like she had been a burden. When her mother had taught her to differentiate between want and need, it had allowed Ann-Sophie to be the kind of child that left her mother free to have some of the kind of life she had before Ann-Sophie came along. It was the least she could do for her mother.

"When is the wedding?"

"In a week," she said. Then, in the silence, she quickly added, "It will just be a short ceremony. No party. Really, a small thing. You don't need to come."

There was another pause on the line, and then her mother said, "Okay. Well, please send me pictures."

"I will," she said. "I love you."

"I love you more than you can imagine." The words came through like patchwork, and Ann-Sophie clung to them after the line died. She lay back on the bed she now shared with Alessandro, telling herself that her mother shouldn't come all the way from Ethiopia just for a wedding that was for the baby, not a fairy tale about love. Even if Alessandro did resemble a fairy-tale prince with an *actual castle*.

The next morning, they left for Rome.

As they drove to the airport, where Alessandro's jet waited, Ann-Sophie thought about how much had changed since they had driven on this road for the first time weeks ago. She was marrying this sexy, enigmatic man next to her, and they were going to an event of the kind she had only attended for work. This time, she was a guest. Alessandro Carandini's fiancée. She would leave the other attendees with no doubt as to the reasons behind this surprise engagement, she thought wryly as she caressed her stomach. *It's all for you*, she whispered to her baby.

"Is your mother coming to the wedding?" asked Alessandro, as the family's jet skirted the coast of Italy, the jagged shoreline on one side, the glittering sea on the other.

Ann-Sophie shook her head. "She has so much going on."

Alessandro frowned but said nothing.

She raised an eyebrow. "Why? Are your parents coming?"

He gave a humorless laugh. "My mother is cruel, and my father's image is more important than anything else. They are the last people we want at our wedding."

"I see," she said, though she wasn't sure she did.

The flight to Rome was short, and when they landed, they were whisked away in a black limousine and delivered to the Hotel de la Ville in the center of town. The lobby was a cool relief from the hot Roman sun, and its black-and-white marble floors shone in the light of the chandeliers.

"It's wonderful to see you again, Signore Carandini," said the woman checking them in, then she glanced at Ann-Sophie. "I have you in the Roma suite, as usual."

As usual. Ann-Sophie tried not to think about the other guests that had visited him in this suite over the years. Alessandro had talked about his past with women in such an impersonal way that she hadn't thought much of it. At the villa, they had their own world, the one they could make their own. But they were far from the secluded life of the villa. Here, Alessandro had a name for himself, a tabloid reputation that she was stepping into. She wasn't sure how she was going to deal with that.

They rode the elevator to the top floor, and an intricately carved red door waited for them at the end of the hallway. They entered into a living room with sofas, a writing desk and abstract art in muted colors. French doors led out to a balcony that overlooked the tall, elegant city buildings, partly obscured by cypress trees. On the coffee table was a tray of drink options and another filled with meats, cheeses, olives, apricots and different spreads for the small loaf of bread.

"I called ahead to make sure you and the baby don't go hungry, as supper will be served late at this event."

She grabbed a handful of spiced almonds. "First, I need to find a dress."

She had tried on her only maternity dress that came close to being suitable and found that she had already outgrown it. In the last three weeks.

"I took the liberty of ordering a selection of dresses,

shoes and intimate wear." His eyes flared with desire at these last words, and he gestured to the doorway into the bedroom. "If you don't find anything you like, we can send out for a new selection."

Ann-Sophie blinked in surprise. She knew personal shopping services existed, and that people like Alessandro lived the kind of life where things were delivered at their convenience, but she still couldn't quite get used to the fact that *she* was living that life. A life where questions of need versus want were irrelevant because she could have both. Alessandro would give her whatever she wanted. *Except the thing you want the most from him*, said a voice deep inside her.

"Thank you," she said and entered the bedroom. The suite was located on the corner of the building, and light poured into the long tall windows that looked out at the ancient buildings that surrounded them. The shadows of leaves filtered the light in ripples across the white bedspread.

Ann-Sophie crossed the elegant room and opened up the armoire. Inside, it was filled with silky dresses, all floor-length but in different colors with different necklines, and at the bottom were stacks of shoeboxes. She ran her fingers over the selection, touching the soft materials. Of course, nothing so gauche as a price tag was in sight. It was all so unreal. She stared at the rainbow of colors and finally picked a light blue dress made of soft silk, the color of her eyes. She slipped off her cotton sundress, one that had miraculously turned up in her wardrobe shortly after arrival, and let the soft silk slip over her body. It fit perfectly. The low *V* emphasized the extra fullness in her breasts, and the gathered material spilled over her baby bump and hung in shimmering waves. She turned to search for a mirror and found Alessandro standing in the doorway. He was leaning in the threshold, his crisp white shirt rolled at the sleeves and his hands in his pockets. His eyes were heavy with desire. She flushed with awareness as a slow smile curved on his lips.

"That one. Definitely."

She walked into the large bathroom suite and stood in front of the full-length mirror. It was so flashy and it definitely highlighted her belly. For the first time since her body had started its accelerated expansion, she felt... beautiful.

"I love it," she said.

Alessandro came up behind her, and his hands skimmed over her arms as he stared at her image in the mirror.

"We'll need to find more places to wear this, *cara*," he said and brushed a kiss on her neck.

She laughed. "Let's see how this evening goes before we make plans for future appearances."

He met her gaze in the mirror, and his smile turned darker. "You will be by my side in this gown. There's nothing else that I want out of this evening."

The words sent a rush of that dangerous, giddy hope she had felt too often this week. When he said things like this, she couldn't stop herself from hoping this could be about more than just the baby and physical attraction. Maybe they could find their way to the kind of *more* she shouldn't think about. Because the real version of fairy tales with castles and princes didn't have happy endings, she reminded herself. They were much more complicated.

The afternoon was a flurry of hairstylists and makeup artists and lounging on the long, surprisingly comfortable sofa, as Alessandro answered calls and plied her with food from the generous trays. And by the time they sat in the limo on their way to the gala, Ann-Sophie was starting to think maybe she could get used to this life. Even if it did not seem attached to any sort of reality she had known.

When they pulled up to the Borghese Gallery, her breath caught in her throat at the spectacular display in front of them. A long red carpet made a trail down the center of the walkway to the entrance, and it was lit by tall votive candles on both sides. In front of them, stately pillars glittered with lights in the dusky sunset.

And then there was the paparazzi. She had attended events at locations like this, but she and her fellow interpreters were treated like extras in a movie, the backdrop for those who mattered. This time, she would be noticed. Photographed and assessed.

Alessandro helped her out of the limousine and laced his large, warm hand with hers as they started along the red carpet. His bespoke tuxedo emphasized his broad shoulders and solid strength, but the unruly curl of his hair was a reminder of the humor that set him apart from his twin brother. Her heart pounded as she glanced up at this breathtaking man. Cameras flashed and crowds murmured.

"I'm glad you talked me out of wearing high heels," she whispered to him, trying to break the tension that was building inside her.

Alessandro chuckled. "As much as I love to sweep you into my arms, I think we should save that for the bedroom."

At the base of the staircase, they stopped to pose for photographs.

"What's your name?" called a voice from somewhere behind the explosion of flashes.

"This is Ann-Sophie Svensson, my fiancée." Then he bent down and brushed his lips over hers. Before she could recover, he was guiding her up the stairs and into the building, leaving a trail of questions behind them.

In the gallery, signs and ticketing lines had been replaced with flowering plants, red velvet and hundreds of candles. Attendees stood in groups of glittery gowns and black tuxedos. They were entering Alessandro's world, where he was known for relationships that were like fireworks—exciting, explosive and short-lived. Out of the corner of her eye, she saw heads turn once, then again in double takes as they walked in together, the swell of her belly on full display.

Ann-Sophie flashed to that last night in Nice, when she watched Alessandro walk in with a countess. His world had felt so far away, a bridge that was impossible to cross. And now, so improbably, *she* was the woman walking in with him. All she had to do was get pregnant, she thought wryly, and she was sure more than a few people were thinking the same thing. But then Alessandro looked down at her with the kind of indulgent smile that made her forget about all of that. It took her back into their own private world.

"I ruined your Cinderella moment back in Nice," he whispered in her ear. "But I hope tonight makes up for it."

She raised an eyebrow. "To be determined."

But she couldn't stop herself from smiling. As she reached out to stroke his cheek, she hoped that in her own version of the Cinderella tale, midnight would never come.

Alessandro understood his assignment for tonight. He was to introduce Ann-Sophie into his world and give a display of love that projected the image of a happy couple that their family needed. Tonight was about showing the world that this relationship was not a possible catalyst for going off the rails, as his father's had. And it wouldn't be.

But Ann-Sophie was so beautiful and lovely that Alessandro's chest hurt. And as he walked through the wide hall of the museum, surrounded by relics of art from fallen civilizations, in a place where the present mingled with the past, anything seemed possible.

They walked through the candlelit gallery, past servers offering flutes of champagne. Not far ahead, the countess caught his eye and gave him a flirtatious smile. It was nothing out of the ordinary, something that she had done countless times. But he was so clearly with another woman—his *pregnant* fiancée—and yet she had felt that it was still appropriate to flirt. As if she was simply waiting her turn before he danced with her. Then again, Alessandro knew that he had given her every reason to expect this. He had conducted himself this way in the past, and never once had he thought twice about it. But the idea that Ann-Sophie could have seen this flirtatious smile, this reminder of what the world expected from him… The unwelcome idea twisted in his stomach.

How had he enjoyed this life before? The question stunned him. Because up until now, he would have said that he had enjoyed his life immensely for all the pleasures it afforded him. And he had taken full advantage of every one of these pleasures. But now, everything about his previous life felt wrong. Empty. The idea of going back to who he was before that day outside Ann-Sophie's apartment building didn't sit well at all with him. So he pushed the thought away and steered them in another direction, toward the dance floor.

"How are we doing so far, Cinderella?" he asked, focusing on the curve of her back under his hand and her lips, the color of ripe peaches.

"I don't think I'll ever get used to a life like this," she said, gesturing to the orchestra and the line of servers, dressed elegantly in black, waiting to attend to the guests. "But I guess you've been doing this forever."

He considered this comment. "It's a role, one I have always played in the family."

"Quite happily, as I remember," she said with a laugh. "You were always flirting, talking with some someone or another, entertaining."

He frowned. "I suppose that's accurate."

"The baby and I are really cramping your lifestyle." She gave him a wry smile.

He didn't smile back. "I haven't been to a single event since Nice."

He hadn't made the decision consciously. He simply hadn't been in the mood, and intuition had always been his best gauge of what to attend, or whom to dance with or whom to sleep with. This was the one place he had allowed himself to be guided by his feelings. And for the last seven months, he simply didn't *want* to be with anyone. He hadn't thought much of it at the time, as he had always had periods where he was busier with more meetings or other obligations, but looking back now, he hadn't had the urge to go out, let alone to sleep with another woman. Since Ann-Sophie. The thought rattled his calm.

Ann-Sophie gave him a skeptical look. "I know you have a past, Alessandro. You didn't know about the baby, and you didn't know you would ever see me again. I wouldn't be at all surprised if you had gone about your life the way you always had."

The string quartet ended the song and there was a pause, a quiet in the room. He should have seen this break as an opening to change course. The most strategic move was to lie and say that he had moved on because the truth—that he had had no interest in other women since their week in Nice—might suggest that he was offering more in their marriage than he was. But honesty was a sore point with her, and though he couldn't give her everything she wanted, he should give her this.

So he looked at her with a seriousness that didn't belong anywhere near this dance floor, with all of society watching them. "I understand that we are allowed to have our pasts. But there has been no one else since you. I promise you that."

Her eyes widened a little, and her breath caught audibly in her throat. The expression that flashed across her face looked too much like hope. Hope she never should have in him. Some part of him wanted to warn her away, but instead, he brought his mouth to hers. He kissed her slowly, teasing her with his lips and the sensual swipe of his tongue, trying to forget that there was a war inside him that had no winners. Trying to convince her that this kiss, this electric connection, could be enough. But soon his own desire turned on him, and he felt his grip of control shake. He pulled away.

She blinked, as if she wasn't quite sure what had just happened. Then she smiled. "Is that your way of ending a discussion?"

"You can take away whatever message you'd like," he said, smiling back, and he felt a bit steadier.

At dinner, he found himself only half paying attention to his conversation with the dewy-eyed heiress he was sitting next to, distracted by the man Ann-Sophie was deep in conversation with across the table. Ernesto Ruzzo, a businessman based in Venice. He was a bit older, good-looking and smiling at Ann-Sophie in a way that was uncomfortably familiar. Especially when his eyes drifted to her generous breasts, so temptingly highlighted by the cut of her dress. Alessandro felt an unfamiliar stab of... jealousy? In the middle of this confusing thought, Ann-Sophie glanced across the table and smiled at him, as if completely unaware of what he was noticing.

That night, as they entered the dark hotel room, he found himself thinking of the man who had been so... attentive.

"Ernesto Ruzzo seemed very taken with you," he said, keeping his voice even as they walked into the living room, lit by the lights that glowed through the French doors.

She shrugged. "We met back in Nice, too, actually."

"He seemed to especially appreciate your dress. Particularly the cut of the neckline." Alessandro complimented himself silently on the way he kept his voice perfectly even.

Ann-Sophie rolled her eyes. "Or maybe he just enjoyed my sparkling conversation."

"Those possibilities are not mutually exclusive," he said darkly.

Tension in his body rose, and for one short moment, he asked himself why he needed to keep up this control. What would happen if he simply let his emotions rule? But he knew the answer. As a teen the results were destructive but not irrevocable. But he was an adult, and with the power and attention he wielded, he could scorch the earth, wreaking havoc on everyone around him. Massimo. The baby. *Ann-Sophie*.

She was studying him, and she sighed. "Fine. I did notice that he might have been distracted by my breasts a few times, but I thought it was harmless because I am quite visibly pregnant with your child right now."

"Men like that might see your situation as an invitation rather than an obstacle."

"Men like that…?" She stopped, as if she was considering a new possibility. "Are you jealous?"

Alessandro shoved away the swell of emotions building inside him and frowned. "Cautious."

That was the most generous word for what he was feeling right now.

"I don't appreciate my behavior being monitored," she said pointedly, and he braced himself for what was next. "But I suppose we both have our demons to struggle with. If we're going to marry, we need to find a way to work together. Support each other."

She gave him a wicked smile that brought him back to one particularly satisfying night in Nice. And then, right there in the living room, she got down on her knees in front of him with a hot burn of desire in her eyes that told him exactly what she meant by *support each other*.

Alessandro knew he should stop her. He knew mixing jealousy and sex was a dangerous game when his control he kept on such a tight leash seemed to be slipping. Yet, he couldn't bring himself to stop it.

"I want to see your breasts." He gritted out the words. "I also find this dress incredibly distracting."

Her wicked smile grew as she slipped the dress off one shoulder, then the other, exposing her generous breasts. He groaned and leaned back against the wall. She turned her attention to his trousers, unfastening them. Then she pulled out his length and licked him, provoking a euphoric shudder so strong his legs shook. She took him in his mouth, and all his tension and jealousy was turning to fire inside him as he watched her pleasure him. Finally, he was allowed to lose control. But he held on to this feeling as long as he could until it was too much, and he came, trembling, leaving him rattled him to the core. He reached down to caress Ann-Sophie's face as he reined in his harsh breaths. Then he lifted her from the ground, and let her to their bed.

"Sit. Please." The words were tight as the need built so precipitously, impossibly fast. She sat on the edge of the bed, and he kneeled in front of her. He moved her panties to the side and found she was warm and so ready for him. So he teased her, letting her gasps spur him until she was crying with pleasure. Then he got to his feet and entered her. He slid in, relishing in how wet she was, how ready she was. She opened her eyes and met his gaze, and he felt a tightness in his chest so strong he had to look away. Instead, he moved, pleasuring her until she arched her back and let herself be washed away is ecstasy. And only after she whimpered and cried out his name did he allow himself to go over the edge again.

CHAPTER NINE

THE MORNING OF the wedding, Ann-Sophie sat in her favorite chair in her favorite alcove of the library. A book lay open on her lap, but she was staring out the window at the town below and the narrow road that curved through the olive grove and out of sight. Alessandro had left on that road in the blur of the early morning.

"I have something I must do," he had said vaguely, and she had been too tired to do anything but nod. Now, she wished she had pressed him or said…something. Because today was their wedding day.

He had left like this a handful of times over the last month since she had arrived. And while he had kept his promise to always tell her when he left, with each departure, she had felt acutely aware of how much she didn't know about him. How much he still kept closed off from her. Alessandro had hinted that after the wedding, when he returned to the travel schedule he usually kept, his absences would be more frequent. So she knew the ache of his absence would only grow stronger.

But he wouldn't disappear, she reminded herself, and the baby would not grow up with the ache inside that she had felt, searching for a father that would never be there. A want that had sometimes felt like a need.

Her thoughts were interrupted by the creak of a door

and the tap of footsteps on stone. Ann-Sophie's heart took off the way it always seemed to do when she thought of Alessandro. She turned and found not Alessandro, but Massimo's wife walking toward her. Ann-Sophie blinked in surprise. They had not formally met, and yet Massimo and Catarina's relationship had been documented by the paparazzi well enough that Ann-Sophie knew her on sight.

"Ann-Sophie? I'm Catarina." Her voice was enchantingly melodic, and Ann-Sophie was reminded of Catarina's famous mother, the so-called Nordic siren, known for her own captivating voice before her sharp decline into cancer. The loss must weigh heavily on Catarina, Ann-Sophie thought. And suddenly the woman in front of her felt much less like the glamorous and notoriously reclusive heiress that had made a splash in the tabloid not so long ago and more like any other person whose life was subject to the same whims of fate as everyone else.

"I'm glad to finally meet you in person. I'd get up but—" Ann-Sophie gestured to her very present belly. "I'm sorry you arrived when Alessandro isn't here."

"Please don't get up," said Catarina with a laugh and sat in the chair next to her. "I'm here to see you, but I hope I'm not disturbing you."

Ann-Sophie shook her head and set her book on the wooden table next to her. "My mind has been wandering all morning."

Catarina beamed. "Because you're getting married today."

Ann-Sophie pushed aside the last of her uneasiness and let herself get carried away by the excitement in Catarina's voice. Today was her *wedding day*.

"It still feels very unreal. I'm just sitting here in my sundress…" Ann-Sophie gesture to the quiet library.

Catarina gave her a warm smile. "I've brought a few things to make this feel more real."

"I guess I have to get out of this chair someday," she said with a laugh and began to pry herself out of it.

She followed Catarina through the halls and into a room that looked as if it had once functioned as a sitting room. Now it looked more like backstage at an elegant theater. There was a vanity table set up with a mirror, boxes of makeup and all sorts of tools for hairstyling. Across the room hung the dress that she had chosen back in Rome. It was made by the same designer as the dress she had worn to the museum event, made with the same soft silk, but the neckline was more appropriate for a church. Hanging next to it was a selection of wraps in white silk, and below it more neat stacks of shoeboxes and a flat pink box from a famous lingerie designer. Two women sat on elegantly upholstered chairs by the window, sipping coffee from a service that sat on the table between them. They turned, and their eyes lit with pleasure when they caught sight of Ann-Sophie.

"You are breathtaking," gushed one of the women as she stood up. She was tall with dark brown eyes and the longest hair Ann-Sophie had ever seen.

"This is Maria, who would love to do your hair for the wedding," said Catarina, then gestured to the petite woman with a sharp black bob. "And this is Elena. She does makeup."

As the women both crossed the room, Catarina added quickly, "No obligation. I just thought it might be fun."

"Definitely," she said, trying to ignore the sudden pang

of longing. She should have asked her mother to come. Even if this marriage wasn't for love, it was still a wedding, a celebration. But all of these wants were not needs, she reminded herself. She had enough. In fact, she had so much more than enough. So she pushed the maudlin thoughts out of her head and immersed herself in the extravagant preparations.

The team helped her into her dress, then as she sat down in front of the well-lit vanity, Elena brought out a long black cape to cover her dress. Maria started with her hair, showing pictures of everything from a regal, elegant updo, to a tumble of curls, both of which she promised she could get Ann-Sophie's stick-straight hair to hold.

"My mother used to French-braid my hair in a sort of crown on top of my head," said Ann-Sophie a little wistfully. "Can you do that?"

Maria's eyes lit up. "Absolutely."

The result was a stunning, professional version of her mother's efforts. "Shall I add flowers or something decorative?"

Ann-Sophie flashed to a memory of Midsummer at her grandparents' farm, picking wildflowers with her mother and putting them into each other's hair. "Flowers, please. Small ones."

"I'll help you find some," said Catarina to Maria.

Maria nodded and disappeared through the door with Catarina, and Elena took a seat next to her. She studied Ann-Sophie's face. "You have such a lovely spray of freckles across your nose, and I'd hate to cover them up, especially with this hairstyle. I'm thinking something that works with this and the peach tones of your lips..."

The woman seemed to have a vision for her makeup

that Ann-Sophie had never herself had, so she said, "Do what you think will look best."

By the time Maria and Catarina returned, Elena had worked her magic, somehow making Ann-Sophie look like herself, but with a glamorous glow. They drank coffee and ate from a tray of fruit and pastries that Olivia dropped off. Maria wove flowers into her hair and Catarina fussed over her shoes—

"No heels," said Maria and Elena in unison when Ann-Sophie teetered on a particularly high pair—and then, with a flare of drama, Elena pulled off the protective cape, revealing her full look.

Ann-Sophie stood in front of the mirror, gazing at herself in wonder. Catarina came up next to her and held out a large jewelry box, tied with a dark blue ribbon.

"Alessandro wanted to give this to you himself, but I chased him away," she said. Ann-Sophie's heart took off in her chest—Alessandro had returned. "I want him to be surprised by all this."

She gestured to the dress and her hair, and Ann-Sophie felt a surge of warmth toward this woman whom she had just met but had made her wedding day a little more special. Ann-Sophie untied the ribbon and opened the old-fashioned box. On top of it was a note, just three words written on thick creamy paper with the words *For my wife*. Nothing more. How strange that her chest seem to expand with the simple words. She had never seen his handwriting before. How fitting, she thought, as she traced the messy scrawl with her fingers before she remembered that she wasn't alone. Ann-Sophie lifted the note and looked inside. Nestled in the silk was a necklace with sapphires and diamonds hanging from it. The pendant earrings were echoes of the same jeweled pattern.

"Oh," she whispered, not knowing what else to say.

"I'm pretty sure these belong to his grandmother," said Catarina. "Do you want to try them on?"

She nodded, and Catarina reached around and fastened the clasp. Ann-Sophie gazed in the mirror one more time. Was this really her life? It seemed so improbable.

The limo waited outside, and she and Catarina rode through the village streets into the palazzo, where the church loomed like an elegant warning. If the Carandini villa was a monument to the eras that had passed, a mishmash of stone and bricks gathered and replaced overtime, the church was the opposite, preserved firmly in the past, as if it had not needed repairs to combat centuries of decay. As if it was preserved by the will of God alone. Catarina helped her out of the car and together they walked across the cobblestone path and through the heavy wooden door.

It took a moment for Ann-Sophie's eyes to adjust. All she could see was the glow of candles everywhere. But after a moment, Alessandro came into focus. He stood by the altar in a tuxedo that hugged his broad shoulders and emphasized his considerable height. And he was looking at her with an intensity that took her breath away. She and Catarina started down the aisle, and as they walked, the priest and Massimo and the exquisite relics from the past all faded away. There was just Alessandro and the thump of her heart, so full of want and hope. Today, she was marrying him. She told herself that this feeling was enough. Tomorrow, she could worry about everything else.

When she reached the altar, Alessandro's mouth lifted

in a smile so warm and intimate that her heart jumped in her chest. "You look beautiful."

The ceremony was like a dream, with Alessandro's warm, large hand the only thing tethering her to reality. When it was time to recite their vows, she found that promises of love fell from her lips like drops of truth she wondered if he could hear. And when he spoke the words of love, she let herself hope that he meant the kind of love that came with time and closeness, not duty. Just for today she could hope, she told herself, because he was looking at her with brown eyes, so dark and solemn that she wondered if he was thinking the same. And when he kissed her, his lips lingered on hers, and under the ever-present heat, she felt something stir between them, something she could believe in. Just for today.

Alessandro sat at the long table, lit by candles, gazing at his wife. *His wife.* Every time that thought ran through his head, it made the tenuous armor of his control crack, breaking too fast for him to repair. And yet he couldn't stop himself from repeating these words, over and over. *His wife.*

He should return to Milan tonight and get control of himself, the way he had every time in the last month that the intensity of being near her had gotten too strong. They were married. His task had been accomplished. And yet he could not make himself leave. Even this morning, leaving her for a few hours had not sat well, even when it was to drive to his grandmother's house so Ann-Sophie could have pieces of the Carandini family jewelry.

Alessandro had counted on her mother's arrival as a distraction that would ease the sting of his departure. He had arranged for Margarita Svensson to fly on a private jet, timed perfectly for the morning of their wedding, and yet, she had not shown up. It had shaken him, despite the fact that Ann-Sophie knew nothing about this plan. He, too, had not expected his own parents' presence, despite the fact that Masimo had mentioned the wedding to them the week before. Both he and Ann-Sophie had been forged by these parental relationships, and they would serve as guide on what *not* to do, he told himself. He was also counting on this to mean that Ann-Sophie would accept the limits in their own relationship because he would not abandon the child.

But those moments in the church today had not just been about the child. He had felt something stir inside him as he looked into the endless rivers of her eyes and spoke his promises of love. For a few, beautiful moments at the altar, as his end goal played out, he found he was not thinking of goals or next steps or any of the tactics he used to keep himself in safe territory. It was hard to make sense of what had happened there, as he spoke his vows. Everything that drove him seemed to fade, and it was only Ann-Sophie.

Now, as he sat in the formal dining room of the villa, lit by candles, he knew he should take this as a warning sign. He knew he had to leave. And he would.

After the night was over.

Alessandro focused on Ann-Sophie as she talked with Catarina and Massimo, so comfortably, and something about that made the turmoil inside grow stronger.

So he rose to his feet and looked from Catarina to Massimo. "We'll see you in the morning."

Ann-Sophie's cheeks turned a delightful pink, and she

glanced at Alessandro, then back at his brother and his wife. "Please excuse this man's manners. I don't know where he got his reputation for being a smooth talker."

Massimo let out a little bark of laughter. "I couldn't have said it better myself."

Ann-Sophie's amused smile turned hotter as they started through the halls and climbed the ancient stairs. But instead of leading her to the bedroom they had shared, he turned down a different hall and led her to the very end of it. When he opened the door, he felt a surge of satisfaction at the catch of her breath as Ann-Sophie took in their surroundings.

The room was much larger than the one they had stayed in. It was the master suite that his grandparents had occupied for a time before they gave the villa over to his parents, and it was covered with flowers. Olivia and Cinzia had spent the morning gathering tangles of rambling rose in white and every shade of pink, and the room sighed with the heavy scent. The flowering vines hung from the tall windows and twined around the balcony. The French doors were open, letting the warm breeze blow new life into this place, pushing out the ghosts of the past. Bouquets of wildflowers from the hillside sat on the bureaus and tables, and the room was bathed in the glow of the sunset.

Alessandro didn't speak. He simply led her along a path of rose petals to the enormous bed, covered in a billowy cloud-like duvet. A sudden rush of joy overtook him as Ann-Sophie stood in front of him. *His wife.* Her smile was warm and intimate, and he ached with a desire that he didn't fully understand, and a thought ran through his head, one he realized had been building inside him.

Maybe this could work. Maybe he could change. Maybe she and the baby would change him and these emotions that bubbled inside him would no longer lead to anger and destruction. He let the temptation of these thoughts guide each touch.

Slowly, he undressed her, memorizing the way it felt to run his hands up her growing belly as he lifted the dress, tracing the fullness of her breasts and the dip of her collarbone. He kissed every one of these places, closing his eyes and memorizing them with his lips. When he finished, she lifted his hand from his own shirt, silently insisting that she undress him, too. She removed his cuff links, studying his hands, and unfastened each button on his shirt. His muscles tensed as her hands explored. Her blue eyes were focused, as if she was discovering something new. It all felt new, as if she was uncovering the layers he kept between himself and the world. Suddenly he was being exposed, and yet, he didn't stop her. He gritted his teeth against each flash of desire and let her take her time until they both stood naked, facing each other. He traced a line up her arm, over her shoulders and up her slim neck until he was cupping her jaw. And then he kissed her.

His body was on fire and his instincts told him to bring them to the ecstasy they both craved, but he held back, just kissing her with the aching desire mixed with something else he wasn't going to contemplate. Her hands explored his body, a whisper over the planes of his chest and the ridges of his abs, until it was too much. Wordlessly, he pulled back. And they stood there for a moment, gazes matched, until that became a different kind of too much. So he led her to the bed and he fixed the pillows so she was comfortable. And then he kneeled before her and entered her. Her eyes met his as she let out a gasp, and he clenched his teeth against the insatiable need to lose himself in the pleasure, in this one place he allowed himself total abandon.

But tonight she held his gaze, and tonight he couldn't look away. Slowly, he began to move, tilting his hips, finding the angle that made her gasp, then luxuriating in that angle with hard, long thrusts. Still, her gaze was on his, open and vulnerable, and he had no idea what she saw in his, but she didn't look away. The pleasure between them grew until she gasped and moaned and fell over the edge of bliss. As he followed her, he could have sworn that he saw tears well in her eyes before she closed them, and it felt as if something had torn inside of him, something that felt ominously irreparable.

He lay beside her in silence in the aftermath, touching. She stroked his cheek and ran her hand over his biceps, and he flexed his muscles playfully, teasing out a smile from her. They hadn't spoken a word, and yet it felt as if he had somehow bared his soul to her and she had done the same. And neither of them had looked away.

He had no idea when they drifted off to sleep, but sometime in the early morning, Alessandro started awake. He sat up in bed, looking for whatever had startled him. An uneasy feeling washed over him, and yet when he looked next to him, there was Ann-Sophie with a sleepy smile. A flicker of relief cut through the unease, but as he bent down to kiss her, a voice floated through the open window, so sickeningly familiar. It cut through all the hopes that had run through his mind and exposed them for the lie they were. Nothing would change.

CHAPTER TEN

"Olivia. I need you at once. I simply cannot handle all this baggage alone…"

The voice coming through the open French doors sounded irritated, as if the woman speaking was unaware of the exasperated tone she was using at—Ann-Sophie checked the stately clock that ticked on the wall—6:14 a.m.?

"I apologize, *Signora*—"

Before Olivia's voice had reached the end of the last word, the other woman's voice began again. "Travel has been a complete nightmare. The storms ruined the last three days in Seychelles, and then, the pilot had the nerve to tell us that he would not fly in the weather. Can you imagine? So I asked him what we were paying him for. Why were we paying the salary of a pilot who won't fly? I demanded the very moment that the airport would allow that we would leave. Which happened to be late at night. As you can imagine, sleeping on the plane, no matter how comfortable they say the beds are on planes, they just never lit live up to expectations. And then…"

The words were now muffled in the distance, leaving only hints of that distinctive voice. Ann-Sophie rubbed her eyes and tried to get her thoughts in order. She opened her mouth to ask Alessandro what was going on, but when she turned to him, his expression had gone blank. The only hint of emotion was an ominous tightness in his jaw.

His mother. It had to be her. Just her voice had taken every ounce of softness, every hint of raw vulnerability that she had seen in him the night before, and turned it all to stone. She lifted her hand to his face, but he flinched and moved away.

"My parents have arrived, only a day late for the wedding." His voice was hard. "I should introduce you."

He managed to make this sound like a threat. Ann-Sophie told herself that this was painful for him, but the past night he had opened himself to her. They could get through this. So she got dressed and brushed her hair. When they started down the staircase, the hand he offered her felt like the one he had offered on the walk home from the doctor's clinic, out of duty rather than care. Ever the gentleman, she thought darkly.

They walked through the endless halls, following that voice and its endless string of commentary and complaints. Ann-Sophie felt as if they were walking to their execution. The thought was a bit dramatic, but when she glanced at Alessandro and squeezed his hand, searching for their connection, he didn't look at her. Instead, he released her hand and continued into the dining room, where Olivia and Cinzia were bringing platters of food to the table.

"Good morning," said Olivia, giving Alessandro what looked like a worried glance. But Alessandro didn't seem to notice. He was looking at his parents.

His mother was, in the most objective sense, lovely, a combination of nature and money that made the most of her features. She wore a cream silk blouse and matching wool trousers that accentuated her fashionably thin figure, and her hair was twisted in a neat updo that suggested careful preparation rather than a night of hardship. She was talking to Alessandro's father, who was reading the newspaper and murmuring in agreement. Neither of his parents seemed to notice their entry until they stood next to the table.

His mother's gaze lifted to her son with a flicker of disappointment. "Alessandro, where is your brother? We were told he was here. We need to talk to him about our flat in Milan, which was simply not usable when we arrived, after hours of horrendous travel."

Alessandro's jaw tightened. "Mother, Father, I would like you to meet my wife, Ann-Sophie."

His father looked up over his newspaper, and gave Ann-Sophie a brusque once-over, then turned back to his newspaper. His mother's gaze was more assessing, and she furrowed her brow, as if confused. Her eyes traveled down Ann-Sophie's body, stopping at her very prominent belly. Then she looked back at Alessandro and gave him an exasperated smile. "Oh, yes. I do remember Massimo mentioning something about a wedding to someone, but it was too…" She waved her hand as if the excuse was self-explanatory. Then her gaze sharpened as it settled on her belly. "Now, I understand."

Ann-Sophie stared at this woman, who had no memory of her son's wedding and certainly no intention of coming for it. She seemed to exist on an entirely different plane of reality—one where everything centered on her.

His mother still hadn't stopped talking. "Poor girl. You got knocked up by the wrong brother. But I suppose he does come with money, so he has some appeal."

Ann-Sophie froze, so horrified by the casual cruelty this woman—Alessandro's *mother*—was capable of. Alessandro had told her, but she hadn't expected…this.

"Get. Out." Alessandro's voice was low and cold enough to make his father look up from his paper.

"You have no right to tell us to get out of our home," his mother said dismissively. Then she turned back to the coffee in front of her and busied herself with the creamer.

"*Get out of this house.*" This time, Alessandro's voice was louder. Harder. Ann-Sophie found herself trembling, not for herself but for Alessandro. All at once, she felt the surge of anger that he kept so carefully buried. This was the emotion he feared, and she was watching as it began to consume him. She had no idea what to do. There was so much hurt behind this and she felt a helplessness that made her angry, too. No one should have to endure the kind of callousness that Alessandro had come to expect from his mother.

"Son." His father put down the paper, and his voice was filled with warning.

"This is not your house," Alessandro snapped at his father. "It hasn't been since you drove your father's business into the ground."

"That might be true," said his mother coldly, as if she was not watching her son's anguish play out in front of her. "But, since you insist on specifics, we all know it's Massimo who keeps this family's fortunes afloat, not you. We'll leave this decision up to him."

Fury blazed from Alessandro's eyes. Ann-Sophie reached for his hand, but he yanked it away.

"Don't." The words came out as cold and hard as the look he gave her. It was the same one he had given his parents. Something twisted in her stomach. She wrapped her hands around her belly protectively, as if shielding the baby from his glare.

"Please, Alessandro," she whispered, fighting every instinct to leave this place, run far away. "Go upstairs. I will meet you there."

He looked at her, but it was as if he didn't quite see her, his gaze was so full of anger. It was as if he was unraveling right in front of her eyes.

"No. You need to get far away from here," he snapped. "And don't come back."

It was an arrow straight for her heart, and it hit. Ann-Sophie startled at the intensity of his voice. Anger and anguish seemed to ricochet between them. Everything about this hurt.

Alessandro closed his eyes. Ran a hand through his hair.

"*Go*," he said, biting out the word.

Ann-Sophie swallowed, torn between his plea and her instinct not to leave him alone with his parents. He glared at her, or maybe it was a plea. It didn't matter. She took a step back. Another. And another until she was at the threshold of the hallway.

When she rounded the corner, out of sight, Alessandro's voice boomed, "If you don't leave my house, I will physically remove you."

It was as if the entire house went still, and in the silence, Ann-Sophie understood that the threat was not empty. Tension coiled around her, and she stopped in her tracks as her belly seized. *Deep, calming breaths*. She took a shaky approximation of a yoga breath and reminded herself that she had four more weeks before the baby was due. Even the false contractions made it sometimes feel like it would be sooner. Ann-Sophie stood frozen in the hallway, trying to breathe her way out of this mess, until the scrape of a chair on the tile floor released her.

Footsteps.

Ann-Sophie started down the hallway, away from the dining room, but her belly seized again. She headed for an armchair and sank into the red velvet cushion.

Deep, calming breaths.

The footsteps grew louder, and when she looked up, Alessandro's mother was there.

"I'm sure this display was educational," the woman said with a forced lightness, but the high flush in her cheeks suggested she was unsettled. "He's always been like that."

As if Alessandro was a teenager throwing a temper tantrum. As if his mother hadn't noticed any other part of him for more than half of his life. Because this description of Alessandro had absolutely no basis in the man that she knew. It was a portrait of the teenage boy Alessandro had hinted at, one he had worked to leave behind. One that haunted him for very real reasons, she reminded herself.

His father came up behind his mother but kept his gaze fixed on the front door.

"I am carrying your grandchild," said Ann-Sophie quietly. "Nothing is more important to me than protecting my family from the kind of harm you so clearly have given Alessandro for his whole life."

His mother turned away, but Ann-Sophie continued. "You have been trading on the Carandini name for years, as far as I can tell, so let me make this clear. If you ever speak to any of us like this again, I will make sure the press knows exactly why we won't allow you around your grandchild."

His father's gaze landed firmly on her, and she got the sense that he was seeing her for the first time. He paused, his eyes narrowed, before he looked away and continued to the door. As the heavy wooden door shut behind Alessandro's parents, Ann-Sophie promised herself that she would do everything in her power to protect her child, no matter where that took her.

Alessandro paced across the dining room like a caged animal. But no matter how many times he stalked back and forth, the anger inside him would not go away. His mother's careless cruelty hadn't just been aimed at him. It had been aimed straight for Ann-Sophie, too, and that had pushed him over the edge. He had not only brought another innocent person into the mess of his family, but he had also let his anger flare out of control. Enough that he had lashed out at Ann-Sophie.

Alessandro glared at the room around him. The excess of food and elegant dishware, combined with the heady scent of the flowers from their wedding, all seemed to mock him with the naive illusion of the night before, when he let himself wonder if he had finally escaped the wounds of his childhood. How wrong he had been. How quickly their poisoned legacy had found him.

Better now than after the baby was born, he thought darkly.

He didn't hear Ann-Sophie enter. He didn't notice her until she was standing right in front of him. The look of devastation on her face dissolved any control he'd managed to claw back. He was so fucking angry at all of this mess.

"I warned you," he said, gritting out the words through clenched teeth. "All along, I warned you."

"They're awful," she said quietly. "I'm so sorry you—"

"*Don't*," he growled, cutting her off. "You know nothing about me."

But the sharpness of his words was like a punch in his own gut. He stumbled back to a chair and sank down in it, his elbows on his knees, his hands buried in his hair.

"I'm leaving," he added when his voice was a little more under control.

The room was quiet, and then her voice came, quiet but determined. "I'll come with you."

"You are the last thing I need right now," he groaned. The words came before he could think to hold them back, and the cruelty of the statement hit him again in his gut. Ever his mother's son.

But being near Ann-Sophie was simply too much right now. She made him *feel*. Even pleasure, the one place he had allowed himself to follow his instincts, was tainted with every other emotion. She had stripped away the barrier he had built and left him vulnerable at the worst possible moment. It occurred to him that this had been his fear for some time now—that he was hurting Ann-Sophie and he was continuing to hurt her, ruining every ounce of good they had found between them.

Alessandro needed to be far away from her, to close this open wound and get himself under control the way he had all those years ago, after their last expulsion from school. Leaving would hurt Ann-Sophie, but not worse than staying. How could she not see this? Alessandro took a deep breath as grim determination edged out a little of his anger. But when he looked up, Ann-Sophie was clutching her belly, and the anger and sadness had faded from her expression. Instead, he saw pain.

Alessandro shot up from his chair. "What's happening?"

Ann-Sophie met his gaze, and her eyes were filled with fear. "It's the baby. Something's wrong."

CHAPTER ELEVEN

The road to the village was much rougher than Ann-Sophie remembered it. Or maybe it was just that every single bump seemed to trigger another pain in her belly. Still a month before delivery, she told herself, but her worries were growing. Which certainly were not helping her blood pressure. The doctor had warned of so-called false contractions, but Ann-Sophie was pretty sure they weren't supposed to feel like this. Her baby was telling her something, and it couldn't be anything good.

"Tell me what is happening." Alessandro's voice broke through her worries. "Has anything changed?"

His mouth was a grim line of determination as he drove the car along the narrow road that led to the village. In her mind, she flashed to the stark terror on his face when he looked up and saw her in pain. All of his anger and frustration disappeared, and she was almost sure she saw...
Think about that later, she told herself, pushing the memory away.

"Nothing's changed. It's just..." She groaned as the pain hit her again, shooting across her back. She took a couple of deep breaths, then tried again. "It's like my entire belly is seizing up. And that covers quite a lot of me these days."

"Just a few more minutes and we're there," he said. "The doctor will be waiting for us."

"Never have I hated cobblestones so much in my life," she muttered.

The car screeched to a stop in front of the clinic, and Alessandro rushed around to help her out of the car. The doctor and three other staff members came to the door and helped her into the bed that was waiting for her. One attendant wheeled her into the room as another took her vitals, then began to hook her up to a series of monitors. Her heartbeat skittered across the screen, ticking higher as her belly seized again.

Just as the pain was taking hold, Alessandro slipped his hand into hers. "Squeeze my hand and take a deep breath."

Ann-Sophie gave him a bewildered look. Just moments ago, he was walking out the door, and now…

She cried out and squeezed as hard as she could.

"Good job," he said, brushing her hair from her face. "Just keep breathing."

"What if something happens to the baby?" she pleaded, gasping for breath.

"Nothing bad will happen." Alessandro's voice was tight.

"We don't know that." Tears began to well, but she fought against them.

His brown eyes were dark and so intense, and she saw fear leaking into his gaze, a fear that mirrored her own. "We don't."

"It's not supposed to go like this," she whispered.

"I want to make this better for you. For the baby. And I can't." His voice broke, and he swallowed, his Adam's apple bobbing in his throat. "But I will be here for you. We're in this together."

Dr. Cantabella looked up from the fetal heartbeat screen and said, "The baby is coming today."

Ann-Sophie stared at the doctor. "I... I'm not due for another month."

The doctor frowned. "Babies have a mind of their own when it comes to due dates. I suppose it's to get to prepare us for life as parents."

"But it's too early," she protested weakly. This was feeling all too much like the visit to the doctor back in Stockholm, the last time her body demanded something she was not ready for.

The doctor nodded. "It is early, but we will meet whatever needs your baby has."

Before Ann-Sophie had a chance to fully process this news, another contraction—because that was what this pain was—hit her.

She sucked in a sharp breath, and Alessandro tensed.

"Can something be done for all her pain?" he growled. "This can't be right. She's suffering."

"We have pain-mitigation options," said the woman gently. "But some partners find it easier to wait elsewhere while the baby comes."

He frowned and shook his head. "If she has to go through this, I will be here."

Alessandro Carandini was a man of his word. He stayed by her through every minute of it, coaching her breaths and stroking her forehead. In the back of her mind, she was still hurt and frustrated, but those feelings faded because the baby was coming. Quickly, in fact. It was all a blur of pain and brusque voices until, finally, the doctor handed her their baby boy. A beautiful baby with wisps of dark hair and bronze skin so much like his father's. Alessandro kneeled by her side as the tiny baby let out a wail.

"He takes after me," he said with a hint of dark humor, but his eyes were filled with astonishment.

It felt as if her heart was expanding in her chest as she looked from Alessandro to this tiny, beautiful baby. A halo of love was growing around her, pushing out their disastrous start to the morning and filling her with joy.

"Hello, little one," she whispered. "Welcome."

The doctor slipped an oxygen mask over the baby's tiny head and pressed a heart monitor to his chest. "We need to do some testing, but this little guy looks strong, so we will give your family a few moments first."

And then, they were alone. The baby's eyes closed, and she wondered at the fact that this moment she had both worried about and dreamed about for so long was finally here. They had a *baby*, the tiniest, most joyful person she had ever seen.

"We will meet whatever needs you have, my love," she whispered to him, as the truth of Dr. Cantabella's words echoed inside her.

Alessandro hadn't said a word, and his expression was inscrutable.

"Can I hold him?" he asked softly.

Ann-Sophie lifted the baby in his arms and held him close, his big, scarred hands cradling the tiny body, and he whispered in a low voice. Tears welled in her eyes as every strong emotion cascaded at once. This day had been filled with so much grief and so much joy, it seemed impossibly overwhelming.

Alessandro's face was etched with a kind of wonder,

but as he handed the baby back to her, the expression faded, shifting to something she couldn't read. "I will go back to the villa and pick up anything you need. Then, when you are ready, I will leave for Milan."

She blinked. "When I'm ready?"

"I promised I wouldn't leave you, and I will respect that promise. You're with a newborn, our child." His voice wavered with a hint of emotion, but when he spoke again, it was gone. "I will not abandon you or the child. But I think it's clear that this situation is untenable."

"What situation?" she asked slowly, and the halo of warmth and joy that had surrounded her just moments before was shifting into something that felt much more ominous.

"*This*." He gestured to the three of them, this tentative little family she couldn't stop herself from wanting. "This has already gone too far. I let out enough poison to send you into early labor. This could've ended so much worse."

He swiped a hand over his face, and she almost missed the haunted look in his eyes.

She let out an exasperated huff. "I know your power in the world is great, but you do not reign over my body."

Alessandro managed to look both doubtful and smug, and Ann-Sophie felt a flash of something more complicated than desire, adding more fuel to the cauldron of her emotions.

"Your parents are callous and cruel," she continued, "and as far as I can tell, you've been bottling up your very understandable anger for over a decade, pretending that nothing touches you. Or maybe you even started to believe it." She ignored his frown and continued. "Of course, it's going to be messy when it comes out. The real question is what you will choose to do now."

"I'm doing what's best for all three of us," he said, frustration seeping into his voice.

"You're doing what's easiest instead of fighting for what we could have," she snapped. Ann-Sophie regretted her words even before his expression shuttered. Desperation was starting to take hold inside her.

"I love you," she insisted. "Not some public image of you but the man I have spent the past month with. That's why I married you. Not just for the baby. I know I was not supposed to fall in love with you, but I have."

And as she spoke the words, she felt the depth of truth behind them. She had told herself marriage was best for the baby, but she knew better than anyone that it was love, not marriage, that made the biggest difference for a child. Alessandro's parents were a stark reminder.

His expression was hard and cold. "You know I cannot give you what you're asking me for. I was clear from the beginning."

She had not asked him for love, not directly, but he had heard it, anyway. But this was a want, not a need, she told herself. Even if it did not feel that way. Even if it felt like something inside her was breaking.

"That is your final decision?" she asked softly.

"It is not a decision. It is our reality."

Ann-Sophie swallowed and forced herself to do what was right. For all three of them.

"Then I absolve you of your promise. I am not afraid of raising a child on my own. Of being on my own." Her voice was so much stronger than she felt. "I will never keep you away from your son—it will be too hard for us to spend time together if you refuse to let yourself free of the grip that the past has on you. So whatever we had between us has to end. I don't want to see you, at least until this is less painful."

He flinched, as if she had slapped him. "You knew I had to offer. You accepted that."

"It's not enough." The word *enough* felt strange as she spoke it, as if it was growing, taking on new meaning.

Alessandro was watching her, his beauty made harsh with the pain that radiated from him. Slowly, Alessandro lifted his hands, palms open, as if he was offering himself to her. His expression was stark. "Am I not enough?"

Ann-Sophie froze as the word *enough* twisted yet again inside her, its sharpest edge finding its way straight to her own wound, the one that had never gone away. Alessandro's question was so raw, so full of honesty. So full of the same unhealed hurt she had been running from. He wasn't hiding it anymore, and somehow it made the devastation of his decision even worse.

"You *are* enough," she said as desperation spread its tendrils through her. "I saw what happened when your parents provoked you, and I'm not scared. I want to be there for you, the way you were there for me through this birth. But you're pushing me away when we both need more. We can be so much more for each other. You *have* to know that."

He lowered his hands but said nothing. She searched his expression for some sign that her message was getting through to him, but all she found was a haunted emptiness in his eyes. And in that moment, she could feel the future of the path they were on taking shape. They would break each other's hearts, over and over again, if she compromised.

Ann-Sophie swallowed, trying to ignore the lump in

her throat. "I can't do this halfway. If you cannot commit to this—to us—then everything between us is over."

He kissed the baby on the forehead and stroked his cheek with a gentleness that took her breath away, and then he walked out the door.

Alessandro stormed through the front door of the villa, determined not to let his unruly emotions get the better of him for the second time today. He was angry at himself. He was frustrated with Ann-Sophie for stubbornly refusing to understand the reality of their situation. And he was overwhelmed by this tide of fear and intimacy and joy that had flowed at the birth of his son and then seemed to drain from him the moment he had walked away. But he had no other choice.

Alessandro gritted his teeth and reined in that out-of-control feeling inside him. He *would not* lash out again. This was straight out of his mother's playbook, and he would not be like his mother. Not at any price. How could Ann-Sophie be sympathetic after the cruelty that had slipped out of his mouth before he had gotten a chance to think better of it? He didn't deserve sympathy. He had failed himself and he had failed to protect her. And yet, she told him that she loved him.

"Hormones," he muttered to himself as he walked up the stairs.

Yet she had looked at him with a seriousness that he couldn't dismiss so easily. Maybe he should send Catarina to bring her belongings, as she and Ann-Sophie seemed to have bonded at the wedding. Or maybe he should call her mother again. Because if he saw Ann-Sophie and the baby again when he was so wracked with…emotions, he wouldn't be able to leave.

Alessandro reached the top of the familiar staircase and turned toward the master bedroom, where he and Ann-Sophie had spent one magical night together. Until his parents spread their poison through the house. Alessandro frowned. His stomach clenched as he thought of their tiny baby, so helpless. Alessandro had wanted to take that baby and run as far away from his parents as he could get. But that was the heart of the problem, wasn't it? He had been running for his entire adult life, and he still could not escape his parents, not when they were so deeply embedded in him. It was why he had to separate himself from Ann-Sophie and the baby.

But he refused to play that last heartbreaking scene over in his head again, so instead he focused on the tasks in front of him. But as he turned the corner, toward the master bedroom, he came to a stop at an open door. The door to his own childhood bedroom.

He stood at the threshold and peered inside it. Who had been in there? Certainly not his parents. They had rarely entered the room, even when he slept there as a child. He stepped inside, this forgotten relic of his past. On the walls were posters of football greats, now long-retired, and on the bookshelf was a collection of cars of all sizes, hiding the few books, their spines unbroken, given to him before the family had given up on his reading.

He had avoided this room, not wanting to go back to the time when his parents had so much more influence on his life. But as he wandered inside, a different set of memories floated through his mind. They transported him back to a time when he felt a strange kind of peace.

A time before he was always angry at his parents, back when he was glad when they would disappear and leave him and Massimo with Olivia and her sister, Natalia, who were so good at allowing the twins to simply be themselves. They swam and kicked the football and wandered into the town for bakery treats, climbing scraggly olive trees along the way. Alessandro hadn't come back here, not wanting to kick the hornet's nest of childhood memories, but as he looked around, he remembered a kind of freedom. A time when his negligent parents had not steered his life.

The real question is what you will choose to do now. Ann-Sophie's voice came back to him, as if she had been there, next to him all along. Alessandro heard footsteps in the hallway and turned, hoping that somehow she would appear. But it wasn't Ann-Sophie that walked into his bedroom. It was Massimo.

His brother raised his eyebrows. "I saw you and Ann-Sophie leave, and she was clutching her belly. What's going on?"

The question shook him back to the present. "She had the baby. A boy."

Massimo frowned. "Is everything okay?"

Not remotely. But he said, "They are both healthy."

His brother looked at him with a gaze sharp enough to make Alessandro look away.

"Why are you in my old room?"

The corners of Massimo's mouth quirked up. "I was telling Catarina about that time I spent a good six months sleeping in this room."

Alessandro hadn't thought about that in a long, long time. "I forgot about your nightmares."

Massimo had awoken, night after night, crying inconsolably, until Olivia had finally moved a second bed into Alessandro's room to see if it would help. It worked so well that Massimo stayed there for months, until Olivia had found them awake at four in the morning, building an enormous racetrack for their cars on a school night. Massimo had returned to his bedroom, and they had all moved on. His brother was such a stoic, determined man that Alessandro, who didn't make a habit of thinking about the past, had allowed incidents like these to fade away.

"Why aren't you with the baby and Ann-Sophie?" His brother was as irritatingly direct as he was persistent.

"We do not have the kind of relationship that warrants my presence. Now that the baby is here, she will likely go back to Stockholm. I will visit them, to make sure I'm a part of the child's life, of course." He delivered this all in a matter-of-fact tone that only confirmed his decision. His voice was under control, even if it felt as if a knife twisted in his gut each time he thought of them.

His brother's eyes narrowed. "I heard every word between you and our parents this morning. I am pretty sure the entire household did."

"Then you must have heard the way I lashed out at Ann-Sophie, too." That knife twisted again, cutting deeper. "I was angry and the words just came out. At her."

He closed his eyes. Even saying this was painful.

"I had forgotten how awful Mother could be to you," said Massimo softly. "I think I just blocked it out, but when I heard her, it all came back."

"Poor little rich kid," he said, trying to lighten the mood a little.

Massimo didn't bite. "I should not have agreed to tell them about the wedding."

"They didn't come for it," he said, his voice filled with bitterness. "Their appearance was just a happy coincidence."

His brother shook his head. "They shouldn't be in our lives. At all."

"It's okay. I've solved the problem."

Massimo frowned. "What do you mean?"

"Ann-Sophie and I are over. Their poison won't reach her and the baby, and neither will mine."

"What?"

Alessandro glared at his brother, who was making this conversation more painful than it had to be, but Massimo just glared back.

"It's better if I disengage," he said with a finality that marked the end of the topic.

Massimo ignored it. "I heard what she said to our parents. She was fighting for *you*."

"I can't give her what she wants," he said, biting out the words. "It's that simple, so drop it."

His brother, of course, ignored him.

"Has she told you she loves you?" Massimo said it in that voice that suggested already he knew the answer.

"It was the hormones talking," he grumbled.

Massimo let out a huff of laughter. "Even I know not to say that to a woman."

Alessandro scrubbed his face with his hands. "I didn't say it."

"But you wrote off her words just the same." His brother's voice was more serious.

That was true, but why was Massimo being so obtuse

about this? Alessandro took a deep breath and laid out the unvarnished reality. "I know our parents are negligent and our mother says things that should never come out of anyone's mouth, but let's not pretend that her words are not based in the truth. I *was* the problem child. I *did* create havoc in this house and drove them away. We both know I would have failed out of school without a little help from money, and I still got us kicked out three times for fights I dragged you into. The last time I almost took you down with me." Alessandro shook his head slowly. "If we hadn't gotten another chance after that, I would have never forgiven myself. I have devoted my life to getting our family's business back for you because I will not let you down again. But a family life? That's not in the cards for me."

His brother was looking at him with an expression that looked very close to stunned. In fact, Alessandro could not remember a time when he had seen his brother looks so surprised.

"Alessandro, it's true that I am very dedicated to our family business. But do you know why I threw myself into it? It was for us. So we wouldn't get pulled in opposite directions. So we could be on a path together." He frowned. "Why do you think I jumped into all those fights with you back at school? Half the time you deserved to get beaten up. But I don't think you ever thought a step further than that fight. What would happen if you walked down to the headmaster's office alone? Our parents would have split us up in a minute. They wouldn't have thought twice before sending you to another school far away. You are my family, and getting split up from you was my personal idea of hell."

The words shook him. Alessandro never considered the larger possible consequences of his fights. It never occurred to him that they could be split up, though now it seemed so obvious. And life without his brother would have been untenable. Unthinkable.

The same way that leaving Ann-Sophie and the baby felt right now.

He pushed that thought away and shook his head. "The moment I go off the rails, I'm going to bring someone down that I love—"

He cut himself off as the echo of his own words rattled through him. He *loved* them. Not just the tiny, beautiful baby, so fragile he was afraid to hold him. He loved Ann-Sophie. And he was afraid he was going to destroy that love.

His brother raised his eyebrows, as if he could read all of Alessandro's thoughts. Then he ran his hand through his hair.

"If it wasn't your temper, it would have been something else," said Massimo, his voice harder. "Mother needed an excuse. She *couldn't* care about us, and she was always searching for ways to blame us. It might have been my nightmares if Olivia hadn't hidden them from our parents—because she knew it would make me a target." He expression softened. "I'm sorry it was you. If I had understood any of this at the time, I would have defended you."

A strange heaviness washed over Alessandro as Massimo's words sank in. It felt as if his anger was draining out of his body, leaving what had lay underneath it the entire time: The heavy sadness that their parents had found every excuse to blame the boys for the fact that they just didn't care very much. Alessandro had done everything not to see this most obvious truth.

The room was silent. Finally, Alessandro gave a rough laugh. "Have you been googling *traumatic childhood* again?"

Massimo smirked. "Catarina drags this kind of thing out of me. Something about emotional openness."

Alessandro and Massimo scoffed in unison, the way they had so many times when they were younger, but Alessandro could see that Massimo wasn't one bit unhappy about his situation.

"If your temper was incompatible with caring for someone, I would have left you behind at one of those schools long ago," he said pointedly, then raised an eyebrow. "I saw Ann-Sophie's necklace at the wedding. I assume you went to see our grandmother. What did she say to you?"

Alessandro shrugged. "Some nonsense about being so in love that I forgot to invite her to the wedding."

"When I was there for the ring, she said that I had spent my life defying our parents in every area. Why wouldn't I do it for love?"

Alessandro gave him a derisive smile. "What a touching afternoon that was for you."

"Don't be thick about this. It applies to you, too," Massimo said, his voice laced with exasperation. "You messed up, and you need to do something about that. Something more than an internet search. But this woman genuinely seems to care for you. And while I'd argue with her taste, I have no doubt about her sincerity."

Alessandro flashed to their wedding, as she'd walked toward him in the church, with flowers in her hair and a mesmerizing dress that emphasized her full belly. It was love he had felt in that church. It was love that burned inside him, and until his parents came, it hadn't turned bad. It had burned brighter all night long.

His brother put his hand on Alessandro's shoulder. "Stop punishing yourself for your teenage mistakes. Facing the past is hard and painful, but it's more than worth it. Especially when you have so much to gain."

CHAPTER TWELVE

ANN-SOPHIE HELD the baby close as he slept. She couldn't take her eyes off him. Peeking out from under the white knit cap were a few silky tufts of hair, and his eyelids were so thin they were almost translucent. His soft bronze skin, his dark brown eyes... Everything about him reminded her of Alessandro and she didn't know what to do about it.

Footsteps echoed in the hallway, and a nurse peeked in her doorway. "There's someone to see you."

Her heart took off in her chest. Had Alessandro changed his mind? Her stubborn heart thumped in her chest, hoping, despite everything that had happened. He was coming *with her belongings*, she reminded herself. And then he could leave.

"Send him in," she said, schooling her expression into something that came closer to neutral.

"I'll send *her* in," said the nurse before she disappeared out the door.

Before Ann-Sophie could register the comment, her mother walked through the door. *Her mother*, so fierce with a beauty not shaped by her features but rather, who she was. Margarita Svensson wore her years of experience etched on her face, and joy still sparkled through it. She was the polar opposite of Alessandro's mother.

"You're here," Ann-Sophie whispered.

Her mother rushed across the room and gathered Ann-Sophie and the baby in a long hug. Then she pulled back a little and gazed at the tiny new family member.

"Hello, beautiful," she whispered.

"How did you find us?"

"I came with Catarina." Her mother looked up at her. "I'm so sorry I missed the wedding. Alessandro had arranged everything for me to make it, but the storms grounded all flights and I couldn't get out."

Ann-Sophie blinked. "Alessandro did that?"

"He wanted to surprise you. So he made arrangements." Her mother gave her a searching look. "Why did you tell me it wasn't important?"

There was a hint of hurt in her mother's voice, and it twisted something inside her. "I didn't want to bother you. You were on this assignment and I wanted to ask you to come for the birth. I didn't want to ask for too much."

"*Älskling*, you have never asked for too much." Her mother's fingers brushed her cheek. "What's the baby's name?"

"He doesn't have one yet." It felt wrong to name him without Alessandro, but maybe she would have to.

"May I hold him?"

Her mother lifted the baby into her arms, and as they sat there together, the two of them in awe of this tiny new life, Ann-Sophie's heart felt a new and different kind of full, despite the sadness. Maybe, in the future, when some of this pain had eased, she could even be happy—as long as she didn't think about what she was missing. It was like her childhood, she thought with a moment of strange familiarity. As long as she hadn't focused on the loss of her father, she had been fine. And it would be the same for her and her own baby. Even though the pain of Alessandro's decision seemed unbearable right now.

"Where is Alessandro?" Her mother looked around, frowned a little. "I was under the impression that he would be here."

Ann-Sophie shook her head. "He left."

She only said those two simple words, and yet, her mother seemed to hear everything in them.

"He left you two? The day after your wedding, immediately after the birth of your child?"

"To be fair, he said that he would wait until I was strong enough. I had made him promise that he wouldn't abandon us like…"

Ann-Sophie's mother face was solemn. "Like your father."

Ann-Sophie nodded. "But I realized that I didn't want him to stick around simply because he had to. I can make it on my own. And I will. It just…hurts right now."

"Oh, *älskling*…" Her mother's arms came around her so that she was holding Ann-Sophie and the baby, and finally, Ann-Sophie let herself cry. Her tears were wiped and her head was kissed until the sadness dulled a little. When she looked up, her mother's eyes were filled with worry. But she had made it through this same situation, Ann-Sophie reminded herself. And so would she.

"Remember a long time ago, when you told me to learn the difference between need and want? I don't need him. I can do this on my own."

Ann-Sophie's mother frowned. "I'm glad that you know you can do this on your own, but that doesn't mean you shouldn't want. And there's a big difference between wanting something that is impossible and wanting something that is hard and complicated."

Ann-Sophie took a deep breath as her mother's words settled inside. This was at the center of the problem. She wanted something she believed in, something he said was impossible. And she didn't know how to convince him otherwise.

"Did he say why he was leaving?" her mother asked quietly.

"His parents are truly awful, and when they came this morning, he was angry and lashed out at them and then at me when I tried to comfort him. He feels out of control, and he…" Didn't know what to do? Didn't care enough to try? She had run through these possibilities and a dozen others. The tears began again, and she grabbed a tissue to wipe them away. "Are you ever sad that you let my father go?"

Her mother blinked, as if this was the last question she had expected. "Not at all."

"But…" Ann-Sophie sniffed. "But you gave up love for me."

Her mother's face seemed to crumple. "How could you think that?"

Ann-Sophie her head slowly. "You gave up love—"

"I chose love," said her mother said, cutting her off insistently. "*You* are the love of my life. And never for one moment have I thought I made a mistake or wondered if I should have chosen differently."

Tears welled in Ann-Sophie's eyes, and she rested her head on her mother's shoulder.

"I'm glad the baby is sleeping through this," she said with a little laugh.

Her mother stroked her hair. "You were so independent, and I didn't want to smother you, to crush your spirit. But you were at the center of my life, even when you were away."

Ann-Sophie let the balm of her mother's words wash over her. Her mother had always been a solace, even from far away, she realized. "I guess I just wish that you could have had both my father and me."

"I don't," said her mother with a sharpness that surprise her.

"What do you mean?"

Her mother looked at her for a moment, then sighed. "When you left for university, your father came back. He praised my work and told me that he had admired the way I had brought you up. Now, he wanted to work together again to see where this took them us. And I had a moment where I considered it. This was what I had hoped for when you were a baby, that he would see how wonderful having a child could be.

"But then I realized that this was actually the opposite of what I had hoped for. I had hoped that he would regret not having you in his life. Having you had changed me so much for the better, and I wanted him to experience this. But he wanted to skip over this entire part of you and me, of what our family had been, and get back to the life he wanted. And that's his right, but as he said that, I realized it never would've worked out between us. The moment we came home from an assignment and tried actual daily living together, our relationship would have fallen apart. So I told him some version of this, probably a lot less calmly and a lot less articulately, and told him to leave. And he did. I have not regretted that for one moment."

Ann-Sophie wiped a tear that had fallen and smiled, and she wondered how her heart would survive so much joy and sadness.

"Your father would have never even thought to call my mother and arrange to get her there for the wedding," said her mother quietly. "Your father was not interested in what I needed, let alone what you needed. When I spoke to Alessandro on the phone, his voice was… He was doing this for you. He wanted to make you happy. I know that this is a rough time, but I just hope he finds a way to let that happiness win."

Her mother kissed the baby's forehead and stood up, cradling her new grandchild. "Go to sleep, sweetheart. You can rest. I'll be here when you wake up. I promise."

Alessandro stood at the threshold of the room. Ann-Sophie's eyes were closed, and her mother faced her as she swayed gently back and forth. His instincts told him to back away, to leave them in peace, but he resisted. Because he could be a part of this scene if he was willing to work for it. And never in his life had he felt more willing to do anything.

So he stepped into the room, and Ann-Sophie's mother turned to him. Her movement must have startled the baby because he let out a tiny wail. Ann-Sophie's mother smiled and offered him the baby.

Alessandro was taken aback. "I don't know anything about crying babies."

Margarita laughed. "None of us do in the beginning. We all just have to figure that out the hard way."

He felt a mess of emotions bubble up, but when she handed him the baby this time, a strange calm fell over him. The mess wasn't gone, but it felt less…powerful. *Because you let yourself be here.* The baby was still wailing, so he began to hum songs he remembered, songs that Olivia had hummed to him. The baby's cries turned to whimpers and, finally, he went back to sleep. Alessandro felt a burst of pride, and he looked up, but Ann-Sophie's mother wasn't the only one watching him. Ann-Sophie was awake and watching him with guarded eyes.

"You can just put my things in the corner," she said quietly and looked away.

"I'm not here to bring you your belongings."

She turned to him, her eyes a little wider. Then she looked away again. Her mother carefully lifted the baby from Alessandro's arms.

"Why don't I spend some alone time with my grandchild," she said, and before either of them had a chance to protest, she was headed out of the room.

They were alone. Alessandro gazed at Ann-Sophie. He couldn't take his eyes off her. Her cheeks were rosy from sleep, and her mouth was parted. His mind went straight to all the ways he wanted to kiss her, to hold her, to lie with her and communicate in the best way he knew how. She looked so much like she had in his vision from the dance floor all those months ago, the one that had stopped him cold.

The thought surprised him. He was no longer scared of this vision, but that wasn't what struck him the hardest. What Alessandro found, now that the fear had left him, was *longing*. Though it had been there from that first vision, it had been too foreign to understand—because he had not let himself. Because he never believed he could have it. Now, the force of this longing hit him hard enough to send a tremor through him. He longed to see Ann-Sophie laughing on his bed. He longed to have her at the center of his life. He had longed for these things from the beginning.

Slowly, Alessandro approached the bed. Her lower lip trembled, but she tilted her chin defiantly. Alessandro fought back the frustration with himself, that he had let his parents win and she had suffered because of it. But they weren't going to win. He would make sure of that.

He sat down on the edge for bed. She had been crying, and he promised himself that he would do everything in his power to right his own wrongs, which started with an apology. "I'm so, so sorry. You told me you loved me and I walked away from that."

She swallowed, and her lower lip trembled again. "You made that choice right after our son was born."

"I didn't want to hurt either of you." He swiped a hand over his face as another wave of regret swept through him. "I thought I was doing the right thing for all of us."

"And you alone know what's best for all three of us?"

He shook his head. "I don't. Clearly."

The murmur of voices outside the room floated farther away, leaving them on their own. Together. Ann-Sophie looked so beautiful right now, from her messy hair to her flushed cheeks. Never had he been so sure of anything as he was right now. This was right. *She* was right. If she would have him.

"Why did you come back?" she whispered.

"Because it felt like I was ripping myself apart when I walked out of the room," he said quietly, and there was a starkness in his voice that he didn't try to hide.

Ann-Sophie flinched, as if hearing about his pain caused her pain. This was the last thing he wanted.

"My brother may have talked some sense into me, too," he added, trying to smile a little. "Something about my ability to care about people and how our past is not my fault. Which sounded a lot like what you were trying to tell me."

Ann-Sophie gave a wry little huff of a laugh, and Alessandro Carandini, who so rarely found himself at a loss for words, hesitated. How could he put into words how wrong he had been…and how much he wanted to make things right? He had to get this right.

"I love you, Ann-Sophie. Even when every sign pointed to it, I still resisted. That was stubborn and selfish of me, and I regret it. If you're willing to give me another chance, I will show you. And if I'm getting it wrong, I will try again." He ran a hand through his hair. "I will not walk away from this because you are what I want. I want our family so bad it hurts."

Creases had formed between her eyes, and he wondered what emotions warred inside her. The chaos of his own emotions were raining down on him: hurt, joy, sadness and…hope? Was this hope that flickered inside him, despite all the ways he had tried to bury it? But the feeling was there, burning inside him. Maybe it had been there much longer than he had realized.

It occurred to him that he was focusing on himself… again. The way he had far too often, if he was honest with himself. It was time to change that, starting now.

Ann-Sophie opened her mouth to speak. Closed it. Frowned. Then, finally, she said, "My *heart* hurts, Alessandro. And I am scared that you're going to change your mind. I love you, Alessandro, enough to let you go if you can't do this. But if you want to stay, it can't be something you check in and out of when it gets hard. You have to want more than that."

It felt as though she was seeing him. Each wound. Each fear. Each vulnerability. Could she also see the hope that flared higher, stronger, as she spoke of possibilities? He wanted it give her the same. He wanted her to know he *saw* her, so he looked into the endless blue oceans of her eyes, searching for the guarded hopes and fears she had held so closely. *I won't leave you*, he promised her silently. *I will be there for you. For us.*

"Do you want this with everything inside you?" she whispered. Her question was so achingly vulnerable, as if she was baring her soul to him.

"Ann-Sophie—" His voice broke as he spoke her name. But instead of fighting the feelings that were swirling inside him, he wrapped his arms around her and held her close. "I want this with all my heart. And I will spend the rest of our lives proving it to you."

EPILOGUE

ANN-SOPHIE TOOK one last glance at the library, then closed the door. The planning was finished. In a week, the Carandini Family Library would open to the public. She had overseen the enormous process of digitalizing the catalog that Alessandro's aunt had so carefully kept, and a small army of librarians and assistants had been hired. The training had covered everything from caring for historical material, to working with academic institutions. But most importantly, they had spent months interviewing the residents of the area to figure out what the community needed from the library, and then implementing the findings. Ann-Sophie's passion of the last year was finally coming to life.

As she made her way through the now-familiar halls of the villa, flashes from the last year came to her. But she kept going back to the days after the birth of little Emilio—named after Alessandro's grandfather—when her mother had stayed with them. Ann-Sophie had enjoyed the greatest gift she had ever received: time with the three most important people in her life…along with some much-needed support.

Alessandro and Massimo had agreed on a step to what Ann-Sophie considered a long-overdue boundary: They changed the code on the villa's gates, ending the threat of their parents' surprise visits. It had worked. As Ann-Sophie had guessed, there was no evidence that either of his parents would change, but their harm was significantly contained. Alessandro was living proof of it. Since the day their baby was born, he had seemed to fundamentally reorient himself toward their little family.

They had also spent time in her Stockholm apartment. She loved her neighborhood and had insisted she wasn't interested in finding something larger but hadn't turned down Alessandro's suggestion for renovations to make the place easier to handle with the baby. And she definitely didn't mind the clear conversation he had had with the property-management company about a commitment to same-day fixes if, for example, the elevator broke. He was just…like that now. Sometimes, she was still stunned at the way her life had taken shape since that one fateful week in Nice.

Ann-Sophie walked outside, onto the pool deck. Catarina was floating in the water, her round belly suggesting that Emilio's new cousin would arrive shortly. Under the parasol on the far side, Alessandro bounced their little baby on his knee as he and Massimo talked. As soon as Alessandro caught sight of her, his face lit up with a smile that still felt like the sun, all heat and light. She crossed the terrace and kissed him, breathing in his warm woodsy scent, then lifted little Emilio into her arms.

"Did the final updates to the catalog go smoothly?" he asked.

She nodded. "It's all ready for next week's opening."

He stood up and tucked a stray strand of her hair behind her ear before Emilio caught it in his little hand. Then his finger drifted over her bare shoulder and onto her back, sending a shiver of heat through her.

"I'm so proud of you," he said, his voice low and private, and he kissed her again, letting his lips linger on hers. Want and need curled inside her, and she didn't try to untangle them. This feeling was a reminder of the shape the word *enough* had taken over the last year. She had always understood it as an acceptance of her missing father, but the wisdom of her mother's words all those years ago had grown to mean something quite different. *Enough* was the anchor of the deep satisfaction with what she had. *She* was enough. Their love was enough to protect them from the storms of life. This life was what she had been looking for all along.

* * * * *

If you couldn't put down Heir to Italian Altar, *then make sure to check out the previous installment in The Carandini Legacy duet,* Convenient Wife Conditions! *In the meantime, explore these other Harlequin stories by Rebecca Hunter!*

Pure Attraction
Pure Satisfaction

Available now!

MILLS & BOON®

Coming next month

MY FIANCÉE PROMOTION
Emmy Grayson

Sera stares at the newspaper with horror etched onto her face.

'What...who took that?'

'One of the event photographers. Once they realised who I was, they decided to make a quick buck.' I toss the newspaper down on the coffee table on top of a stack of books.

She sighs, her hands coming up to her temples. 'The damage is done. I'll submit my resignation on Monday.'

Knots form in my chest, tighten. 'No.'

No, only something drastic will repair this.

A frown draws her dark golden brows together. 'Then...I don't understand. What can we do?'

Something stirs inside me at her use of the word *we*. I may not know the woman standing in front of me like I thought I did, but her dedication to Hawke Financial is one thing I don't doubt.

The one thing I'm counting on.

'I do have a proposal.'

'Okay.' She nods, blows out a harsh breath. 'Okay. What do we do.'

'We get engaged.'

Continue reading

MY FIANCÉE PROMOTION
Emmy Grayson

Available next month
millsandboon.co.uk

Copyright ©2026 Emmy Grayson

COMING SOON!

We really hope you enjoyed reading this book.
If you're looking for more romance
be sure to head to the shops when
new books are available on

Thursday 21st May

To see which titles are coming soon, please visit
millsandboon.co.uk/nextmonth

MILLS & BOON

FOUR BRAND NEW BOOKS FROM MILLS & BOON MODERN

Indulge in desire, drama, and breathtaking romance – where passion knows no bounds!

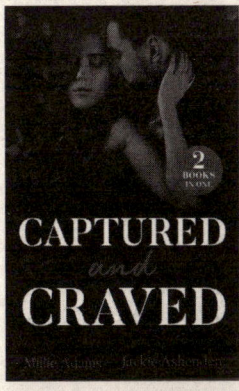

OUT NOW

Eight Modern stories published every month, find them all at:

millsandboon.co.uk

OUT NOW!

Available at
millsandboon.co.uk

MILLS & BOON

TWO BRAND NEW BOOKS FROM
Love Always

Be prepared to be swept away to incredible worldwide destinations along with our strong, relatable heroines and intensely desirable heroes.

OUT NOW

Four Love Always stories published every month, find them all at:

millsandboon.co.uk

OUT NOW!

Available at
millsandboon.co.uk

MILLS & BOON

LET'S TALK
Romance

For exclusive extracts, competitions and special offers, find us online:

- **f** MillsandBoon
- **X** @MillsandBoon
- **◉** @MillsandBoonUK
- **♪** @MillsandBoonUK

Get in touch on 01413 063 232

For all the latest titles coming soon, visit
millsandboon.co.uk/nextmonth